LIGHT UP
IN
WONDER

Praise for
Light Up In Wonder

'This is an exciting story about the birth of the silver screen and all it entailed. From the embryonic beginnings of Universal Films, to the corruption of Hollywood - this story has it all. The romance of the film industry never dies and *Light Up In Wonder* reminds us of a time that electrifies our imaginations to this day!'

Sarah Luddington, international best-selling author of Arthurian Romance

`*Light Up in Wonder* is a novel that makes ingenious use of the early cinema to tell an absorbing tale of a young man's journey from the beginnings of the film industry in Brighton, to the heady days of the movies on America's west coast. Along the way, the author creates a fascinating insight of the pioneers as they strive to perfect their equipment, produce stunning motion pictures, and build successful motion picture companies.'

Dr Frank Gray – Chair, Film Archive UK - Director, Screen Archive South East, University of Brighton - Co-director, CineCity, the Brighton Film Festival

'From Brighton to Hollywood – *Light Up In Wonder* is a passionate exploration of a much neglected period of film history. Superbly revealed by Gooch, his attention to detail and impressive historical accuracy transports the reader into a world of pioneers, piracy and plagiarism; all running parallel to the birth pangs of dramatic on-screen narrative compelling those first audiences to " Light up in Wonder".'

Chris Daniels, Co-Founder of Bristol Silents – Founder and Director of the Annual Slapstick Film Festival

LIGHT UP
IN
WONDER

Patrick Gooch

KNOX ROBINSON
PUBLISHING
London & New York

KNOX ROBINSON
PUBLISHING

34 New House
67-68 Hatton Garden
London, EC1N 8JY
&
244 5th Avenue, Suite 1861
New York, New York 10001

First published in Great Britain and the United States in 2014 by Knox Robinson Publishing

A CIP catalogue record for this book is available from the British Library.

ISBN HC 978-1-908483-77-5
ISBN PB 978-1-908483-78-2

Typeset in Bembo

Printed in the United States of America and the United Kingdom

This is a work of fiction. Names, characters, places and incidents are either the product of the author's imagination or used fictitiously.

www.knoxrobinsonpublishing.com

LIGHT UP IN WONDER

CHAPTER ONE

Brighton, England 1894

`You!...Yes, you!  Come over here!`

I looked up, and wiped my hands on my trousers. The fellow was clearly the leader of the trio I had seen earlier wandering about the gardens. Now he was walking towards me.

There was a feverish sense of purpose about him. His movements, his piercing eyes, set beneath a mop of tousled hair, reminded me briefly of a "whirling dervish", encountered by General Gordon in the Sudan.

In his wake was a colourful individual sporting a brightly-patterned pullover. Over one shoulder, a box on a tripod: on his head a peaked cap. I wondered if he realised he was wearing it back to front. The third, an earnest, mustachioed young man, was holding what appeared to be a timepiece and several sheets of paper.

Hesitantly, I walked towards him. Suddenly, he reached out, grabbed my arm and steered me towards a flower bed. As he did so his companion set down the tripod, tinkered with the box and peered myopically through a wire frame.

Still held fast, I was pushed back and forth, all the while my captor seeking guidance.

`Here?`

`Further back!`

`Here?`

`Move him to your left!`

`OK now?`

`That`s it.`

`Right.` He turned towards me, raising a hand in a theatrical gesture.

`Don`t move a muscle.`

The earnest young man with the papers had retrieved one of my

1

implements. He thrust it into my hand.

`Ready when you are, Mr Smith!`

`Right,` said the arm waver, turning towards me. `Take the spade and dig a hole.`

The fellow with the box started turning a handle.

It was later, in the gardeners` hut, that I learned who he was.

Mr Smith, George Albert Smith, was an illusionist and showman who had acquired the lease on St Ann`s Well Gardens, and was using them for his entertainment shows. I was informed by those around me, they included demonstrations of hot air ballooning, parachute jumping, psychic events and fortune telling. Smith, they said, intended to build a monkey house and even install a hermit in a cave.

Perhaps, I could be forgiven for not recognising my employer. Until a few days earlier I had been working for the Brighton Parks and Gardens Department. Joining as a twelve year old straight from school, I had been working as a gardener for almost ten years. Only in recent times had I judged I had the necessary experience to move on. The other factor that influenced me. I could now walk from my lodgings in Hove to the Gardens instead of cycling into Brighton.

It was a week after the call to dig the hole that Mr Masters, the head gardener, grumpily informed me I was wanted up at the pump house. He was a tall, spare-framed individual, idling his way towards retirement. The impression was of someone forever pushing an empty wheelbarrow, a cigarette attached permanently to his lower lip. He issued instructions, but never lifted a rake, hoe or fork with obvious intention.

`You`d better get your skates on, lad. Mr Smith don`t tolerate dawdlers.`

But I didn`t rush. This time I removed the leather apron, washed my hands, tidied my hair. Mr Masters` eyes followed my every move. Sauntering out the hut, I casually shut the door, then broke into a trot up the hill.

Mr Smith looked up when I was ushered in.

Another person turned in my direction. It was the fellow with the box and tripod. On this occasion he was wearing something in blue and green check, the pattern repeated on the cap overflowing his head. This time it was on the right way round.

`Ah, it`s Lockhart, isn`t it? Here`s our man, Geoffrey. Right...now Lockhart, I want you to look at something.`

Geoffrey walked over to a machine standing on a table. As he did so, I noticed another aspect of his attire: he was wearing plus fours. There were blinds at the window and when Mr Smith turned down the gas lamp the room was pitched into darkness.

There followed a series of spluttering and popping sounds, and Geoffrey was outlined in a halo of white light. The noises continued when he pushed the light source and the wooden box close together.

`Ready.`

`Watch that wall, Lockhart,` my employer commanded.

Geoffrey began turning a handle...and abruptly, in a flickering rectangle of black vertical lines and random blotches, grainy images appeared. It was hard to tell what they were, until an adjustment suddenly brought them into focus.

And there I was...digging a hole in a flower bed. I was spellbound. I had never seen anything like this before. It was a moving picture.

`That`s me!` I cried.

Then it was over...just a bright, stuttering light on the wall.

`So, when Geoffrey says go, don`t look at the camera. Pretend it isn`t there. Just keep your eyes on the shears.`

George Albert Smith, Geoffrey and I were beside a hedge in another part of the Gardens.

`This is a twenty second shot,` said Mr Smith. `Webster,` he called to the earnest young man. `Shout when the time`s up.`

He turned to me. `Lockhart, remember, start clipping when Geoffrey calls out.`

I stood ready, shears poised, staring fixedly at the top of the hedge.

`Go!`

My actions were a little wooden. Nervous, because I was performing in front of a camera and my every move was being recorded. I kept clipping.

`Now the far side of the hedge, Lockhart,` called Mr Smith.

The shears moved forward, keeping up their rhythmic clatter.

`Twenty seconds!` bellowed Webster. Geoffrey stopped turning the handle.

A few minutes later they were arranged the other side of the hedge, against which a bench had been placed. Sitting on the bench was another of the gardeners, a middle-aged man balding at the crown of his head.

Webster gave him a handful of dog`s hair, while Mr Smith issued precise instructions.

`Put your hand to your head, then bring it down slowly and open your hand so the camera can photograph the hair. Look surprised, then furious, stand up and turn towards the gardener, OK?`

He called to Webster. `How long is this sequence?`

`Fifteen seconds, Mr Smith.`

`You,` he said, looking at me, `when he stands up, open you eyes wide and let your jaw drop open.`

When everyone was ready, Geoffrey called: `Go!`

I could not see the expressions on the actor`s face, until he turned towards me. I almost burst out laughing, but managed to follow directions.

`And, fifteen seconds,` shouted Webster.

`Very good,` said Mr Smith contentedly. `All OK with you, Geoffrey?`

`No problem, Gas.`

Gas? . .what did he mean by that I wondered.

`Right, let`s do the final sequence.`

This comprised fifteen seconds of me performing a snaking, twisting run down the path pursued by the irate, fist-waving bench-sitter.

`Excellent,` confirmed my employer. `Now what shall we call it? What`s the title going to be?`

There was a lengthening silence, until I said hesitantly.

`What about "A Hairy Moment"?`

Eyes swivelled in my direction.

`Good...very good,` said Mr Smith. `Let`s use that.`

During the following week, I performed my duties to the indifference of Mr Masters. I was planting out trays of begonias when I heard the sound of urgent footsteps, and Webster appeared by my side. He took a timepiece from his pocket, glanced at it, gathered himself, and said in a breathless rush.

`Mr Smith wants you! You`ve got to come straightaway! `

I wiped my hands on a handkerchief, and lay my apron on the wheelbarrow.

`Right...lead on.`

The same darkened room, spluttering noises issuing from the projector, then the title appeared: `A Hairy Moment` by GAS Films. And there I was... trimming the hedge, and the hair of someone taking their ease on a park bench. Fifty seconds later the film had run its length and the room was flooded by intense light.

The blind was rolled up, the projector extinguished, and Mr Smith said. `So...what do you think?`

I was intrigued. Not so much by what I had witnessed, but by my employer`s manner. He was seeking my opinion.

`I think it`s remarkable, sir. Not only have you got moving images, but an amusing story. If you show that to people, it will certainly capture their imagination.`

`Yes...those were my thoughts. What I want to do is feature the film in my show. In fact, to present my audiences with a number of films, enough for a ten minute performance. So I need to create more motion pictures telling short, amusing stories. Any ideas?`

I walked away from the pump house bemused by what I had seen, and what I had said: surprised at my boldness. I had no idea what prompted me to say, "give me twenty four hours, Mr Smith, and I`ll put together some suggestions".

As I neared the hut I glanced at a tall, silver birch tree that had toppled over in the recent, strong winds. Mr Masters was instructing two of the gardeners to saw it up. Without thinking I walked over, shouting.

`Mr Masters! . .Mr Masters! Mr Smith wants you to leave it as it is for the moment. He told me to pass on the message.`

`Really,` he sniffed. `Why didn`t he come and tell me himself?`

`I guess he`s a busy person.`

`Not too busy to tell you though,` he snapped. `Right you two, leave it for now.`

He picked up the shafts of his barrow, and trundled it up the path.

That`s torn it, I thought, now I have to come up with a story about a fallen tree. That night I sat on the bed in my rented single room and scribbled ideas on bits of paper. I was not aware of the passing time, nor when I fell asleep still clothed and with my boots on.

I awoke suddenly when a stair tread creaked as another of Mrs Earl`s lodgers crept down to the hall, removed his coat from the hat stand, and went on his way with the faintest click of the door catch. It was seven o`clock. I quickly washed, shaved, and changed my shirt. Before leaving for the pleasure gardens I re-read the notes from the previous evening. In the cold light of day they not only lacked humour, the three ideas were far too complicated to convey to an audience in under a minute. Running late, I retrieved my bicycle from the shed and pedalled furiously down Holland Road and up Somerhill Avenue. I waved to the gatekeeper and rode along the path to the gardeners` hut. Dropping the bicycle, I pushed open the door.

`Just in time, Lockhart…just in time,` declared Mr Masters in a sonorous tone. `A minute later, and I would have had to dock your pay. Now, as I`ve allocated all the jobs for the day, you can do weeding.`

On this occasion it was Mr Smith, himself, who stopped by the flower bed.

`I was on my way to the pump house. So…got the suggestions?`

I got up from my knees.

`Yes…though they are not written down.`

`Doesn`t matter. Tell me what you`ve got in mind.`

`OK…but first, I want to show you something.`

We walked several of the paths in silence, until I caught his arm.

`The first involves that tree.` I pointed to the fallen birch. `What I envisage is a series about the "do`s and don`ts of gardening".`

Mr Smith was staring at me intently.

`For example, when cutting down dead wood one should always take a secure position, so no harm can befall. Unfortunately, our hero is sitting on a branch and sawing close to the tree trunk. Everyone assumes the inevitable. Suddenly, the saw cut is through, and he is still sitting there. Instead…` I used my arm to show the action. `The tree has fallen over.`

I pointed to the birch lying on the ground.

`No one realises he is perched on the branch of another tree.`

He grinned. `Any more?`

I nodded. `The next gardening tip would be "don`t over-water your plants". The gardener has a hose pipe and is spraying a flower bed. Up the path comes an attractive young woman. The spraying hose is still falling on the plants, but all the while his attention is on the young woman as she passes by.`

I demonstrated the scene. With my left hand holding an imaginary hose facing the flower bed I slowly pirouette to my right following the imaginary woman`s progress. My face conveying a dreamy, enamoured look completed with a long sigh.

`And?` Mr Smith prompted.

`Well, the next scene, when the gardener turns back, is a view of a lake. Not a flower bed in sight.`

He burst out laughing, and rubbed his hands together.

`Any other suggestions?`

`There are lots more. The next one might be "No litter". The opening shot would be of a grassy area littered with papers, wrappers, and the rubbish left behind after people have been picnicking. The gardener comes along and sweeps it all into a pile. Then he looks round furtively.`

I took a broom from the wheelbarrow and adopted the pose, looking to the left and to the right.

`Then,` I grinned at him. `Then he lifts a turf, and sweeps all the rubbish under the grass ...and taps it down with his foot.`

I was ordered to leave the weeds, the barrow and the implements where they were.

`What`s your full name? I can`t keep calling you Lockhart.`

`Samuel Yardley Lockhart, sir.`

`Right, Sam, go on up to the pump house, and sketch out your ideas, allocating the length of time for each scene. Remember, film comes in seventy five foot lengths, so you`ve only got fifty seconds to play with. Meanwhile, I going to have a word with Mr Masters.`

CHAPTER TWO

GAS Films, the company was known by George Albert Smith`s initials, made thirty one moving pictures during the next twelve months.

I had the ideas and acted in ten of them in the "Handy Hints For Gardeners" series. Not that it was real acting: more facial contortions to convey surprise, alarm or delight. I also did a lot of running. Either to escape someone`s clutches, or to avoid being hurt when things went slightly wrong... which they did with some regularity.

The moving pictures we made during that year conveyed a basic form of humour, little different from that portrayed on the music hall stage or in pantomime. The laughter and applause they evoked was as much for their nonsensical content as the astonishment of seeing moving images appear on a screen. The unsubtle antics and amusing mishaps proclaimed the advent of the medium in the best possible way, appealing to audiences at all levels.

Thanks to the influence of George`s wife, Laura Bayley, almost all the moving pictures we made were comedies, She was an actress who frequently appeared in comic revues: an ideal background.

Laura was attractive, vivacious, and excellent at portraying all the emotions: not only with her expressions, but also her body movements. They added much to the narrative, giving that extra element of humour or pathos. As a result, crowds came flocking to witness the moving pictures in the pleasure gardens, and George`s fame spread rapidly.

I was with Geoffrey in the pump house one morning, discussing improvements to the camera, when George burst into the room, grinning like the Cheshire cat.

`Look at that!` he exclaimed, thrusting a letter into my hand.

At the top of the page was the official heading of the Brighton Town Council. Geoffrey was looking at me intently, as I read its contents aloud.

"Dear Mr Smith,

I have been asked by the Council to submit this request, for the members are desirous of GAS Films presenting their moving picture shows at the Brighton Aquarium.

As you are aware, the Aquarium is fast becoming one of the country`s major attractions. Indeed, it is regularly visited by royalty and people of note.

As a consequence, a moving picture show would add to the Aquarium`s popularity, and doubtless, to your company`s standing in this new medium. I am sure you will agree such an undertaking would be of mutual benefit.

Would you kindly respond to this request within one week of the date shown at the top of this letter.

Yours faithfully,
Robert Escott, Council Secretary."

`So...what do you think of that?` he declared, waving his arms in characteristic fashion.

`That`s terrific news, George,` responded Geoffrey. `It would be the ideal showcase for GAS Films.`

`Exactly.` George looked at me fixedly. `Sam?`

`I`m not so sure we are ready.`

George`s face darkened.

`What do you mean not ready? Of course, we`re ready. It would be our big break. Just think of the audiences the Conservatory at the Aquarium can hold.`

`That`s exactly the problem,` I said firmly. `The size of the audiences. At the moment we project the films onto a white wall in one of the buildings. Performances take place every half-hour throughout the day, and there are always queues. Why? Because the maximum we allow in at any one time, is forty people. The light source is not bright enough to entertain larger numbers.`

`We`ll get a brighter illuminant,` he replied doggedly.

`And what would that be?`

`Limelight, or acetylene. They would do it.`

`George, they wouldn`t be bright enough. You can get more than two hundred people in the Aquarium`s conservatory. No, we`ll have to turn it down.`

`I`m not turning down an offer like this,` he declared vehemently. `It`s a real chance to get the recognition we need. Just think of the sort of people who visit the Aquarium. It`s the largest of its kind in the world. Visitors come from far and wide to see its attractions.

`No, Sam, we are not going to turn it down! I want to show our films in the Aquarium in two months time. When we do, I want them to be seen by a hundred, two hundred people at a time. I want those audiences to see what GAS Films can really produce! So...do something about it!`

With that he stalked out, leaving me, it seemed, with the problem.

We use gaslight as the illuminant in our projector in the Gardens. The trouble is if the gas pressure drops the flame dims, and so does the image.

I experimented with limelight - a block of quick lime heated by an oxygen and hydrogen flame. After that, I tried acetylene gas. But neither produced any greater brilliance.

As I saw it, we would have to use carbon rods. By passing an electric current through two rods set approximately an inch apart, a spark, a steady, bright arc of light is created. However, we would need an electrical supply: something not installed in the pump house.

Of all people, it was Mr Masters who saved the day. It appeared he had a neighbour called, Alfred Darling, who was an engineer.

`He tinkers with film machines and the like,` said the lugubrious head gardener.

I learned he not only frequented the same public house as Masters, significantly, Mr Darling had an electrical supply connected to his workshop.

I joined Masters at a pub called The Signalman one evening, and he introduced me to the gentleman. I bought a round of drinks and we moved to a nearby table. When I explained the problem, Alfred Darling surprised me by mentioning he often carried out equipment repairs for Esmé Collings, another local film maker.

He agreed to help me, but was quick to point out that while the carbon arc produced an intense light, it also generated exceedingly high temperatures. Close to flammable nitrate film, it made for a lethal combination. There was every chance the projector would burst into flames if the heat were not rapidly dispersed.

Several weeks passed while I struggled with the problem.

The answer came from an unexpected quarter. I was walking home one night and called in at a corner shop to buy a copy of the local newspaper, The Evening Argus. While I was waiting for our landlady, Mrs Earl, to serve dinner, I scanned the newspaper and came across an advertisement for electric motors. Mr Gunn, the fellow lodger who left before me each morning, was sitting opposite and noticed the start I gave.

`Everything all right, Mr Lockhart?` he enquired in his broad Yorkshire accent.

`Yes, fine...no problem at all.`

He nodded, and looked up as our landlady came bustling into the room with a tureen of soup.

`Help yourselves, gentlemen. I'll be serving the main course in ten minutes.`

`Tell me, Mr Gunn, what do you know about electric motors?` I ventured, more to break the silence than engage in conversation. Most of the time he was a taciturn individual, given to only the briefest of exchanges.

He looked up, the soup spoon halfway to his mouth.

`A minefield, Mr Lockhart...a veritable minefield.`

I was intrigued. `How do you mean?`

He placed the spoon in the bowl and leaned forward on the table.

`Well, yer need to know the application in terms of loading, the ventilation, and of course, whether its direct or alternatin` current. Then yer should check the insulation. If the wire is `oused in cotton thread, the motor can only handle low temperatures, otherwise `twill burn out.`

`Burn out?`

`Short circuit...cease to work.`

`Oh.`

Mr Gunn retrieved the spoon and took a piece of bread from his side plate.

`Yer see,` he said between mouthfuls, `I know `bout these things. I work for The Brighton Electric Light Company in Gloucester Road. What do you want the electric motor to do, Mr Lockhart?`

`Turn a fan to cool part of a mechanism I'm working on.`

`Is it gonna get `ot?`

I nodded. `Very, Mr Gunn.`

Well, if I were you, I'd buy a motor impregnated with shellac. It improves reliability.`

When the motors arrived - I had bought two, one as a reserve – I hurried round to Alfred Darling's workshop in the shadow of the ferroduct close to London Road Station.

Over the next couple of weeks, Alfred fabricated the case and housing for the carbon rods. We had two small fires before I got the cooling system to work properly. The first was when I switched on the electricity and the motor failed to start. The film buckled, melted, and burst into flame. Fortunately, Alfred was standing beside me with a bucket of sand. He doused the projector and put out the fire. I spent the next two days cleaning the mechanism. When I asked Mr Gunn why the motor had failed to start, he said.

`Did yer give it a nudge like? Ter get it going?`

`No. Should I have done?`

`Don`t wait on chance, Mr Lockhart. Always give `em a nudge.`

Having mastered that technicality, I asked Alfred Darling to create a more substantial mounting for the electric motor between the illuminant and the lens focussing the light onto the film.

When I recounted our success to Mr Gunn, he asked.

`Where does yon light go after it reaches the lens?`

`Well, onto the film. Cranking the handle moves sprockets which mesh with the perforations on the film. Two turns of the handle move one foot of film, approximately sixteen frames. Each frame stops for the merest fraction of a second in front of the camera lens. At that speed the eye is deceived and you get the impression of movement.`

He nodded, then added. `How do yer get the film to stop for that fraction of a second?`

`It`s the same principle as a sewing machine. When fabric is being fed under the needle, the mechanism holds it stationary for a brief moment as each stitch is made. It also moves the material the required distances between stitches. In our case the correct gap between the picture frames.`

`How do yer know yer turning the `andle at the right speed?`

`By what you see on the screen. If you are slow, the action is jerky and the actors` movements unnatural. Turn the handle too fast, and you get the same result, only it`s more amusing.`

`So what `appens when your arm aches?`

`You get someone else to do it. Anyway, the films are only a minute long.`

`Hmm...it`d be much easier if yer `ad an electric motor to turn `andle as well.`

I mentioned this to Alfred.

`It makes sense, Sam. We`ll try that later when we`ve got the cooling system to work properly.`

`Well, we certainly wouldn`t be upsetting anyone if we used an electric motor to drive the projector instead of hand cranking. No one else does to my knowledge .`

I was thinking how to keep our efforts secret. No one was above stealing ideas or suffering at the hands of others. That`s why much of our labours were conducted behind closed workshop doors. Of course, improvements for cameras and projectors were emerging all the time. It was all too easy to devise what one thought was a major advance, to find someone else had beaten you to it, and worse, you were being sued for infringing their patent.

Three weeks before the GAS Films` début at the Aquarium, I brought Smith to the workshop.

`George, this is what we have been working on. OK, Alfred, start it up.`

He set the carbon rods, switched on the current, at the same time nudging the electric motor into action. He began turning the handle. The sheet I had hung at the far end of the workshop was suddenly bathed in bright moving images of one of my gardening films.

For the whole fifty seconds, Smith stood there entranced.

`Briliant Sam! So we are ready to meet the deadline, are we?`

I hesitated.

`There is a problem, George. It doesn`t show up here in the workshop, but it will when we project our moving pictures in a larger auditorium. The film we use currently is frosted. We are going to need film stock with a fully transparent base. We could get away with the initial demonstrations in the Aquarium, but we shall have to use Eastman's film stock in the future.`

`Is it readily available?`

`Yes, supply is not an issue. What is more, it's already perforated with four sprocket holes on either side of each frame.`

`We don't have to perforate it ourselves?` asked Smith.

`No, it's done by the manufacturer.`

`Right, I'll start getting our films copied onto the new stock. Where can we get it?`

`I met a fellow in London recently,` I said reflectively. `When we were chatting he mentioned he had a quantity of Eastman thirty five millimetre film. I've got his card somewhere.`

CHAPTER THREE

`So, `ow`s yer machine comin` along?` enquired my fellow lodger.

`The projector?...very well. We had to overcome a few setbacks, but I`d say we`ve now got it about right. We`ll be ready for the big day.`

I sat back at the dinner table and nodded contentedly.

`So, tell me,` he asked, `did the fan reduce the `eat?`

`Yes, very well indeed. And I`m going to follow up on your suggestion of using an electric motor to drive the projector instead of someone cranking a handle now that I`ve found a way of sticking five films together and putting them on a single reel.`

`Oh, aye.`

A few days later the Eastman film arrived. In the meantime, George had been busy converting part of the pump house into a processing unit. He was anxious to transfer as many of his films as possible onto the new transparent material. Before going to Alfred`s workshop, I called in at the pump house to see how he was getting on.

`It`s going to be a right bugger, Sam,` he said resignedly. `Never mind, we`ll cope somehow.`

I left him to overcome the problem, and took a hansom cab to Ditchling Rise. We had agreed to meet at nine o`clock. Darling must have arrived earlier, as I alighted from the cab he rushed out the gates.

`The projector has gone! Someone has stolen our projector!`

I could not believe what he was saying.

`What do you mean...gone? The gates were locked! The doors to the workshop were well-fastened! You assured me everything would be safe.`

Alfred wrung his hands.

`When I got here the gate had been forced. Wrenched open...and so had the door locks. Two of them.`

I strode through the yard to the workshop. One of the pair of doors was

15

hanging from its hinges. Inside signs of the theft were all too clear. Scattered around the bench and across the floor were the tools, mounts, brackets and jigs we had been using. Torn from the projector for rapid withdrawal. The workshop had been assaulted: all the painstaking labour we had invested now seemingly for nothing. The prize of our labours had gone.

I stood there for several minutes slowly accepting the inevitable. Then I turned to Alfred.

`You`ve still got all the drawings, haven`t you?`

He nodded. His face a picture of misery as he stared at the scene.

`Right…I`ve taken photographs of the various stages of the projector`s construction. I`m going to have copies made of everything we`ve got. We have three weeks, Alfred, three weeks to make another one. We`ve still got the spare electric motor. We`ll use that.`

I started walking out the workshop, calling over my shoulder.

`Less than three weeks, Alfred. I want  that new projector in eighteen days!`

When I told George, he was surprisingly calm. None of his histrionic arm waving.

`Can he do it in time, Sam?`

`I think so. He`ll work night and day…I`ll be by his side to make sure.`

`So, I carry on copying all our material?`

`No, George. Get someone else to do it. Use James Williamson, the pharmacist with the photographic business in Church Road. I think you should spend time preparing our submission to the Patents Office. I`ve got all the drawings and stage photographs, and I`m getting them copied. Whoever stole the projector will have a hard time claiming it for themselves if we get our name in first.`

Before returning to the workshop I took a hansom cab to Brighton police station, housed in the town hall in Bartholomew Square. I gave an account of the break-in and theft at Alfred`s premises, which was carefully pencilled into a journal by a young constable. I had little hope they would apprehend the thieves or secure the lost projector, but if there were ever a legal dispute concerning patent ownership, the fact I had officially reported the loss would weigh in our favour.

I walked the rest of the way back to Ditchling Rise, pondering who might be aware we were constructing the projector, the stage we had reached, the innovations we had introduced.

I considered Alfred Darling. He worked for other film makers and could well have been bribed to disclose our project. He was a prime suspect: yet, he had worked long and tirelessly to perfect some of the ideas. Moreover, I did not think he was that good an actor to portray the abject misery I had witnessed earlier in the day.

There again, everybody knew George Albert Smith had a loose tongue. Given to broadcasting his opinions, and artlessly revealing to all who cared to listen what next he was creating to delight his audiences. If he had mentioned the work in Alfred Darling`s workshop, it would not have taken long for other film makers in the area to learn what we were up to. Brighton was fast becoming the focal point for moving pictures in the country, and the theft could quite easily have been the work of Esmé Collings; James Williamson, our local pharmacist turned film maker; John 'Mad Jack' Benett-Stanford, forever keen to portray the grim realities of war; even the first woman in the industry, Mrs Aubrey Le Blond; or, for that matter, George`s French counterpart, Georges Méliès. Any one of them was more than capable of removing our projector for his, or her, purposes.

When I walked through the gates I was surprised to find the police constable I had spoken to at the station accompanied by a more senior officer. They were checking the workshop doors.

The constable`s superior looked me up and down.

`And who might you be, sir?` he said, squinting at me in the accusing way policemen adopt. The young constable hurriedly explained.

`It`s Mr Lockhart, Sergeant. He`s the one who reported the burglary.`

`I see.`

He continued to eye me suspiciously.

Alfred said. `These gentlemen believe the locks were jemmied to force an entry, Sam.`

The sergeant turned to Darling. `You should have used more robust padlocks, sir. It wouldn`t have taken experienced burglars long to prise these open.`

He hefted one of them in his hand.

`You are probably right, Sergeant.` Then I added. `However, it would have taken at least two people to lift the projector and carry it out to their cart or carriage.`

The police left soon after taking a statement from Alfred. As they went out the gate, I donned my stout leather gardening apron. I had been loath to discard it, and it had served me well working in the engineering shop.

`Before the police came, Sam,` he remarked, `I found all the extra gear wheels we had cut for the projector. So that will save us a lot of time.`

`Well done, Alfred. Let's get started, shall we.`

`Right...I'll start forming the metal casing.`

I looked into his face. A mixture of anxiety and determination. Doubt slipped away. He could not have been party to the theft.

At Mrs Earl's dinner table I recounted what had happened.

`And the thieves got clean away, taking all that Alfred Darling and I had been working on these past weeks.`

`So, what do yer do now, Mr Lockhart?`

`Begin again, Mr Gunn. Though with the show at the Aquarium scheduled to take place in  three weeks time, it will be touch and go whether the new projector is finished in time.`

He looked across the table as we ate our sausages and mash.

`Who do yer thinks taken it, Mr Lockhart?`

`It could be anyone. At least, anyone connected to the film business. There are a half dozen people in and around Brighton who could be the culprits. The trouble is I'm too busy working on another projector to spare the time to check. One thing is certain, though. We shall not only have sturdier padlocks on all the gates and doors, we shall have a guard patrolling the premises at night.`

He used his napkin to wipe the gravy from his mouth.

`Well, I wish you well Mr Lockhart. Let me know `ow you get on when I come back.`

`Are you going away, Mr Gunn?`

`Just fer a week, Mr Lockhart...taking a short holiday...off ter see relatives in Yorkshire.`

`Really? What part?`
`Uddersfield, Mr Lockhart.`

CHAPTER FOUR

`The people from the Aquarium came to see me yesterday, Sam.`

I was with George in the pump house.

`Did you tell them we had been burgled?`

`They already knew. They'd read it in the newspaper. I should imagine the police tipped off the editor. Anyway, they wanted assurances we would be ready for the sixteenth of June.`

`What did you say to them?`

He grinned. `I said they should have no fears on that score. We would be ready in time. In fact, I asked them if we could come in several days earlier to test the set-up.`

`I'm not sure we'll be able to do that, George. It will be a close run thing to get it ready for the sixteenth.`

`I know...but I had to inject a little confidence. I didn't want them thinking it wouldn't happen.`

`It still may not. We're having problems with the feed. I've had to modify the way the film was coming off the reel. You know, to ease the tension on the film. I haven't quite got it right.`

`Well, I've made them a promise, Sam,` he said earnestly. `And I'm not going back on my word. So. . I am relying on you, my friend.`

I nodded, and moved towards the door. `Right, I'd better get back to the workshop.`

I hesitated there for a moment.

`By the way,` I remarked, `did you know the Aquarium has installed several Kinetoscopes?`

`No...do you know, I've never seen one. How do they work?`

`They're similar to those `What The Butler Saw` machines on the piers in Brighton. However, instead of using flip cards to create the impression of movement, the Kinetoscope uses a continuous length of film. You still have to use a peep-hole to view the images.`

'Hmm, that's not a bad thing then. The Kintoscopes will whet people's appetite for the real thing.'

We worked tirelessly from dawn 'till dusk each day, including weekends. We were hampered, briefly, by a fire. Once more, the film burst into flame when, for some inexplicable reason, the electric motor stopped without my realising. Applying a liberal quantity of sand extinguished the blaze, and I worked through the night cleaning all the mechanical parts. There appeared to be little wrong with the motor, but I was not prepared to take any chances. I had bought three new replacements.

Meeting the target date swung wildly between optimism and pessimism. One moment we would reach the pit of despair, another we would go home counting our blessings. As each day passed, it was often one step forward only to be confronted with a resultant step backwards. Alfred and I took to working for much of the time in silence, punctuated only by a ragged cheer when the next hurdle was surmounted.

It was the fourteenth of June when we stood back from the work bench and clasped each other in a manly embrace. Technically, we had produced a new projector from scratch in seventeen days. Aesthetically, our creation was an untidy collection of moving parts. It needed to be cleaned and the grease removed; it needed the rough edges, corners and joints to be filed smooth; it needed to be painted and polished. But it worked: in our minds eye, it was a thing of beauty.

During the days following the theft George had not put a foot in the workshop. When he came, concern was written all over his face.

'What on earth do you call that?' he exclaimed.

'That, my short-sighted friend, is your new projector. Surely you have the vision, a glimmer of understanding of what Alfred and I have achieved? I hope you have submitted a claim to the Patents Office for this fine machine.'

'What I submitted looked nothing like that!'

'Actually, Mr Smith,' grinned Alfred. 'It is the very same...it just doesn't look it at the moment.'

'Hmm.'

'Let us demonstrate its abilities to this uncomprehending heathen, Alfred.'

I was happy to turn the projector handle for all of the five minutes it took to run the films I had glued together into one continuous strip.

When the bright white light died away at the end of the film show, George grinned at me.

`I'll never doubt you again, Sam. Mr Darling you have done a magnificent job. I congratulate you both!`

Then he added. `Just don't let the people at the Aquarium see this contraption.`

`So...all ready for the big day, Mr Lockhart?`

`By the grace of God, Mr Gunn, we are.`

We had finished our meal and were still sitting at the table. Normally, my fellow lodger departs immediately after he has finished eating. This evening he showed no sign of leaving.

`And you've tested your projector have you, in the Aquarium?`

`Yes, it works perfectly. This time we are not taking any chances, there are guards in the building to make sure it does not disappear.`

`Right sensible, Mr Lockhart. Tell me, what time does the film show begin. I might come along.`

`Unfortunately, Mr Gunn, the first evening is by invitation only, and a full audience is expected. But I can probably organise a seat for you another evening.`

`Kind of you, Mr Lockhart. I may take you up on that.`

I had checked the projector yet again, as well as the three reels of film before going home to change into the suit I had rented. Not having worn a dress shirt and bowtie before it felt distinctly uncomfortable. I was all too aware that my part in the proceedings was key to the success of the evening – and the one most liable to turn it into a failure.

When George took to the stage, in front of the large screen we had erected, you could not detect any trace of uncertainty. He was witty, humorous, and at the same time authoritative. He spoke, in glowing terms, on the role of moving pictures, and gave GAS Films a valuable boost. Even when answering impromptu questions, he confidently painted an exciting concept of the years ahead.

Then he was nodding in my direction. My shirt was wet with perspiration.

Hastily, I grabbed a handkerchief from a pocket and wiped my brow and hands. This was it. The moment had arrived.

Suddenly, I was calm and measured. My mind told me to check to make sure the carbon rods were aligned: the gap and angle were correct. To switch on the current, nudge the electric fan, and start turning the handle. Not too fast...slow down a fraction.

I remember taking my time to change the next reel and thread the filmstrip through the gate. Then repeat all the steps to produce another five minutes of moving pictures. I cannot recall doing the second change; as I turned the handle I just watched the faces of the audience light up in wonder.

CHAPTER FIVE

Alfred Darling and I built another projector.

This time, we produced a machine that looked more suited to the Aquarium. It was painted and polished and looked a most handsome piece of engineering. I had tried to incorporate an electric drive, but neither Alfred nor I were satisfied with the result. For some reason there were brief periods when the drive motor would accelerate or slow momentarily.

I brought Mr Gunn to the workshop to examine its installation in the rough-and-ready projector we now used for experiments.

`I think I know yer problem, Mr Lockhart, yer`ve probably suffering from power surges. Now that can be when you`re overloading the circuit with some piece of equipment, or when it`s suddenly switched off. Either way, yer can get a surge, or likely, it could be faulty wiring. What`s yer supply `ere Mr Darling?`

`I`ve got a transformer in the back of the shop which provides a hundred volts alternating current.`

He sniffed. `Aye, well yer won`t `ave much trouble with that. Must be yer wiring.`

He sniffed again. `Yes, it could be yer wiring from yer transformer Mr Darling. P`raps, you should get someone in ter check it proper like.`

But Alfred did not bother, and I continued to crank the handle.

Meanwhile George was busy making films. To overcome the problem of uncertain weather, he built a glass-sided studio: a tall, rather flimsy structure, which I strongly believed would carry to the South Downs in a heavy gust of wind. Surprisingly, it withstood the elements, and though many referred to it as the "glasshouse", we produced a number of moving pictures in this make-shift studio.

Laura was now appearing regularly in her husband`s films: so too was the local music hall comedian, Tom Green. The pairing was one that the audiences at both the Aquarium and the Pleasure Gardens particularly enjoyed. They performed well in, *Let Me Dream Again*, featuring a man dreaming about an attractive young woman and then waking up next to his exceedingly, plain-looking wife.

Another was, *The X-Rays*, a comedy about a courting couple. Occasionally, when a younger man was required, I would act alongside Laura and learned a great deal. She had this facility to project her feelings, to convey her innermost thoughts, even though the films were silent.

For our regular shows at the Aquarium, we hired a pianist to capture the mood. Gerald, a tall, slightly-stooping, young man with a prominent Adam's apple, was a music teacher by day, and our accompanist in the Conservatory at night.

It was not long before our popularity at the Aquarium encouraged the town's corporation to book us for twice daily film shows. At three o'clock in the afternoon and eight o'clock in the evening. George advertised the programme as "The Rage of London. The Photographic Sensation of the Day".

George and I began alternating our presence at the Aquarium. Then we trained Michael Webster, our timekeeper, to make the introduction and work the projector. Gradually our involvement lessened. We still attended notable occasions, when an important guest was expected, but slowly we allowed Michael, and others he trained, to take over the role.

In addition to keeping abreast of the latest developments, and the occasional parts as an actor, I found myself becoming more and more the company salesman. It started when taking orders for GAS Films over the telephone that George had installed. This led to arranging their despatch, then contacting likely buyers and informing them of our latest productions.

Soon, I was writing and creating a printed catalogue for circulation to clients, keeping a watching eye on our finances, and trying generally to bring a sense of order to the workings of the company.

Charles Urban, the general manager of the Warwick Trading Company, was a frequent visitor. He had been the supplier who had first sold us Eastman film. Urban was keen to sell his "Bioscope" projector, which was not dissimilar to the revised version Alfred Darling and I were working on. We had also created a spooling system that collected the film on a reel instead of allowing five hundred feet of film, cemented together with fish glue, to fall into a linen-lined basket.

What surprised me was George's suggestion to Urban that he incorporate our double rotating shutter to overcome the flicker problem in his projector. We had perfected a system of two blades revolving in opposite directions, which lessened the time interval of the gap through which shone the lighted image. This was a major improvement in shutter speed. I could not say much because the patent had been lodged in George's name.

It was successfully engineered into their machine by Cecil Hepworth, Warwick Trading's engineer. It was Hepworth who also came up with the idea of an automated film developing process. However, when I joined Charles and George on one occasion, I was perturbed by Urban's remarks.

`The thing is, George,` he commented, `if you partitioned off more of the pump house, you could do your own processing on site. You might even consider offering the service to others. My automated system wouldn't occupy more than a hundred square feet, so it wouldn't take up too much room. What do you think?`

George glanced at me.

I turned to Urban.

`Surely, Warwick wouldn't want to lose the business this system could bring in?`

Urban grinned.

`Actually, I've registered the patent in my name, so I can do what I like with the process. I'll get rid of Hepworth, and we could work together, George. You've got the ideal premises.`

I frowned. `Are you saying you'd deny Warwick the development invented by one of its own employees?`

`This is business, my young friend.` Urban turned his back on me. `I repeat, what do you think, George?`

George Smith had that guarded look of uncertainty.

`I'll think about it, Charles.`

Some weeks later I became aware of building works being carried out in the pump house. I had been away, doing the rounds of our major customers. It had been a successful trip and I was keen to tell George of the orders for the current batch of films, and for those we were going to make during the next six months.

`So you went along with his proposal, I see.`

George looked up. `It was an offer I couldn`t refuse, Sam. We need to make as much money as we can to finance our film making.`

`Hmm. . .you know what I think? Charles Urban has got you round his little finger. He dangled the bait and you were hooked.`

I walked out and strolled down to the gardeners` hut.

Mr Masters came through the door a few minutes later. We all heard the rhythmic squeaking of the wheelbarrow heralding his arrival.

`Allo, Mr Lockhart, what are you doing here?`

`Hello, Mr Masters, ` I stood to shake his hand. `I thought I`d call in to see how you all were.`

But the atmosphere I had once enjoyed had evaporated. I was no longer one of them: I was an outsider. Worse, a close companion of Mr Smith, the boss, and their future lay in his hands; and as they saw it, conceivably in mine.

CHAPTER SIX

George asked me to accompany him on a trip to France. He had been invited to the home of Georges Méliès, a film maker rapidly gaining recognition for the new techniques he was introducing.

Marie-Georges-Jean Méliès, to give his full name, lived in Montreuil just outside Paris. His studio, in the grounds of his home, had a glass roof and walls to allow filming in even in modest light. Close to the building were dressing rooms and a warehouse for storing his stage sets.

Because we all used orthochromatic film, sensitive only to green and blue, colours would often photograph in unexpected ways: rendering blue skies as perpetually overcast, blond hair as washed-out, blue eyes almost white, and red lips nearly black.

To some degree this could be corrected by makeup, lens filters, and lighting; but it was never completely satisfactorily. As a consequence, when Méliès showed us round, all the sets, costumes and actors' makeup were in varying tones of gray.

What particularly appealed to George, my George, was the manner in which Méliès used "trick photography". His English was not extensive, and I could see George Smith looking increasingly bewildered. I stopped Méliès in his halting explanation by saying in French.

`Perhaps, you would care to speak in your own language, Monsieur Méliès. Then I can translate what you say for George`.

`Thank you. I would prefer that.`

Méliès, I translated for George, came from a theatrical background. He had been an illusionist, and he, too, saw film shows adding to his stage performances. He had seen the early Lumière Brothers efforts, had been inspired and even remade a number of their films.

`Ask him how he started doing the trick photography,` Smith queried eagerly.

Méliès smiled and gave me a lengthy response. I cut much of it out when I explained that it happened initially by accident. His camera jammed in the middle of a sequence. A Madeleine-Bastille horse-drawn bus changed into a hearse and women changed into men. The substitution, called the stop-trick, had been discovered. However, there was little doubt the film effects and unique style of film magic were his own.

We spent the day with Marie-Georges-Jean Méliès, and when invited to stay the night we continued our exchanges over dinner. It was at the dining table that the suggestion was raised by Méliès that there could be a ready market for GAS films on the continent.

`How would we go about that?` George enquired

`Start in France, there's an huge demand for good films.`

I translated Méliès' response.

` I suppose we would need an agent,` mused George.

I translated his response.

`Not with Samuel speaking French so well.`

The following morning, when just the two of us were having breakfast, George remarked.

`I suppose selling our films in countries this side of the Channel would make sound, commercial sense. Could you do it?`

`Well, I would have to improve my German ...but, yes, it certainly would be the way to expand the business.`

`Tell me,` he asked, taking a piece of toast. `Where did you learn to speak the language?`

`My mother is French. She used to work on the French ferries into Newhaven. She was a stewardess on the steamship, Calvados. My father also did the Dieppe run on the paddle steamer, Brittany. They met at the terminal. Six months later they married and bought a cottage in Piddinghoe, a village north of Newhaven.`

I took a roll from the basket. `Could you pass the butter, George?`

`So your mother taught you?`

`We used to speak it all the time at home, though my father's accent was never very good.`

We nodded to Méliès when he came in from the garden.

`After breakfast, my friends,` he said, rubbing his hands, `I have arranged a little picture show for you.`

It was the unedited version of Méliès` popular moving picture, *A Trip To The Moon*. In the film Méliès stars as Professor Barbenfouillis, whose space vehicle is a large artillery shell. The shell is shot from a cannon and hits the "Man in the Moon" in the eye. The space travellers explore the moon's surface before being attacked by moon men.

Méliès smiled. `The moon men are acrobats from the Folies Bergère.`

The moon explorers are chased back to their spaceship, and somehow it falls from the moon back to earth, landing in the ocean.

`I was quite pleased with that scene,` Méliès explained. `I superimposed a fish tank to create the illusion of the deep ocean.`

We were impressed. More so when he told us it ran for fourteen minutes, and cost ten thousand francs, about four hundred pounds.

`Hmm...thirty pounds a minute,` murmured George thoughtfully.

Back in Hove, George was inspired. He now wanted to produce longer moving pictures. He also introduced a more narrative style to his film making, including numerous optical effects such as superimposition to suggest dreams, parallel action, and reverse action - getting the angles right when two people are supposedly talking to one another.

Several months after our visit to France, he appeared in the pump house when Geoffrey and I were chatting about ways of improving the stage lighting.

`Have you seen Hepworth`s film about trains? I think we could use it in one of our productions.`

`Is that the Hepworth Urban fired from Warwick Trading, George?` asked Geoffrey. `If it is, he won`t let you anywhere near it.`

`He doesn`t know about the processing unit in the back of the pump house,` George said. `Anyway, his argument is with Charles, not with me.`

His eyes narrowed. `Still, just in case, it would be better if you spoke with him, Sam. I want you to find out if we could use his moving pictures of the train in one of our productions.`

`Where is he, do you know?`

`I believe he has a company in Surrey.`

`So tell me, what exactly do you want from him?`

`I want to use shots of his train going into a tunnel, and then more footage of it coming out.` He grinned. `In the middle we`ll introduce a scene of two people in a compartment indulging in a little hanky-panky. What do you think?`

`That`s a bit risqué for the Aquarium, George,` Geoffrey remarked.

`No, it would all be done in the best possible taste. It wouldn`t be offensive...just a little titillating. Sam. . ?`

`I like the idea.`

`Good...because I want you to star in it with Laura. If you are in the film you`ll be more able to sell the idea to Hepworth.`

`Wouldn`t Tom Green be better?`

`He`s a good actor, Sam, but he`s too old for the part.`

I had not realised that The Hepworth Manufacturing Company was fast developing a reputation in the business. A number of popular theatre players, such as Chrissie White, Alma Taylor and Henry Edwards, were now in his employ.

From all that he had achieved I expected Cecil Hepworth to be fairly mature. The man I met was no more than thirty, only six or seven years older than myself.

I was shown into a room used as the office by a fellow called Monty Wicks. I later discovered he was Hepworth`s business partner.

`Take a seat, Mr Lockhart. Can we offer you a cup of coffee?` asked Wicks. It was difficult to find an empty chair, all three in the room were covered with cans of film and manuscripts.

`Just put them on the floor, Mr Lockhart, I`ll pick them up later,` commented Hepworth. `As you can see, we`re a bit short of space.`

They operated from a small house in Walton-on-Thames. No wonder, I thought, that many of Hepworth`s films were made on location.

Invariably, when film people get together the discussion turns to news of the latest developments, what pictures were being released, and the latest gossip going the rounds. It was Monty Wicks who eventually brought the conversation round to the purpose of my visit.

`I hear George Smith is doing great things on the south coast, Mr Lockhart. Is that why you have ventured all this way to our humble studio?`

I took his question at the flood. Launching in on an explanation of Smith's dreams, his visions of the future direction film making might go... and the merits of cooperation.

'How do you mean, cooperation?' asked Hepworth in a quiet voice, glancing at his partner.

'For example, gentlemen, you have recently made a film of a train entering a tunnel. Taken from the front of the engine, it's certainly a novel approach. But what is the ending? The train exits the tunnel, and that's it. Very well produced, but it needs something to lift it from the ordinary...to give audiences either a little drama, make them laugh, or portray another aspect no one else has considered.'

'And you have something in mind do you, Mr Lockhart?'

We were walking through the Pleasure Gardens while I recounted the story. George clapped his hands in delight when I got to the point when both Hepworth and Wicks agreed to let us have copies of the negative film, with full permission to incorporate it in our film.

'I even told them the title. It would be called, *A Kiss In The Tunnel*, but done with a certain elegance, . .nothing that would offend. I also said we would feature their company's name at the end, so we would both share the recognition and the income.'

'Excellent, Sam, I'll get the train compartment built while you and Laura rehearse the scene.'

CHAPTER SEVEN

I told Mr Gunn about the film over dinner.

`Fascinating, Mr Lockhart. So after the train goes into the tunnel you have a kiss an` a cuddle with Laura Bayley, an` yer get paid for it? That`s what I call `avin` yer cake an` eating it!`

`Well it`s only pretend, Mr Gunn. I mean, we don`t do anything improper.`

`But yer kiss her, right? What does her `usband say about that?`

That was my worry too. How could I kiss Laura with George standing there watching? The film would only be a minute long, but twenty-five seconds of that would be the activities taking place in the compartment.

At eleven the next morning Laura came into the pump house.

`Hello Sam. Where are we going to rehearse our scene?`

I led her through to George`s office, where two benches had been arranged facing each other.

`I...er...thought we might use this set-up. Is it all right do you think?`

`Fine, I`ll just put on the hat I`ll be wearing. We should practise so it doesn`t get knocked awry when we kiss.`

I sat nervously on one of the benches while she adjusted it in a mirror.

Laura smiled when she joined me on the opposite bench.

`Before we start, Sam, take this top hat and practice putting it on and off. When we are in the compartment you`ve got to be able to remove it with flair, then put it back on straight.`

It is harder than it looks. It took almost half an hour before I had perfected the technique with one hand.

`Good...now do you smoke?` Laura queried.

`No. Do I have to?`

`It`s the establishing mark of a gentleman if he smokes a cigar, Sam.`

That took even longer. After several bouts of coughing, eyes watering, leaving the building twice when things threatened to overwhelm me, I eventually mastered the rudiments of smoking a cigar.

`Sam, the key is not to inhale,` Laura advised. If only she had told me sooner, I might not have felt so wretched.

After lunch we choreographed our movements. I now realised I had never really been an actor, more a mime artist. Laura took me through the routine time and time again, adjusting my actions to hers. We were like two dancers moving between the benches. At the end of the day I felt exhausted. As we left the pump house, Laura`s parting words brought back all my uncertainties.

`See you at the same time tomorrow, Sam. Then we can practise our kisses.`

Once again Laura fussed with her hat while I went through the routines I had learned the previous day.

`Right, let`s take our places,` she called.

We were alone in the compartment. I was supposed to be smoking and reading a newspaper when the train enters the tunnel. As the walls close in I lean forward and caress the woman`s cheek sitting opposite. She gasped in mock horror. Then, rising from the seat, I remove the cigar from my mouth with one hand, and the top hat with the other. I bend forward and kiss her again on the cheek. She appears disconcerted, yet flattered. Emboldened, I again remove the hat and the cigar with a flourish and kiss her full on the mouth.

At least I should have done. But kissing George`s wife in that way suddenly felt dishonourable. Our faces were inches apart, and I couldn`t do it.

Her eyebrows flexed in puzzlement.

`Something wrong, Sam?`

`It...it doesn`t seem right, Laura. You`re George`s wife,` I murmured hesitantly.

Our faces were still close.

`We are only acting, Sam. It doesn`t mean anything,` Laura said fiercely.

She was getting irritated, I screwed up my eyes, leaned slowly forward, and gave her a faint peck.

`What was that?`

`The kiss.`

`I get a better performance from my canary,` she said impatiently. `This is what you've got to do.`

She took hold of my head, pulled me forward and kissed me hard and long.

`Got it? Now let's do it all again.`

Twenty minutes later, after a number of attempts, Laura said breathlessly. `Right, I think we're nearly ready. We'll do the whole scene and time it.`

By this time I was quite dexterous with the hat and the cigar. The two of us went through the well-practised scene and had just reached the moment when I kiss her passionately, when George walked through the door.

I sat back heavily on the bench and flattened the top hat. He was staring hard at me, his face a mix of emotions. Fortunately, Laura, who had interpreted his reaction, said brightly.

`Good...I think we are now ready, George. We've been rehearsing and can do it in the twenty five seconds you wanted.`

Suddenly, understanding spread across his features.

`Oh...right...that's good.` But when he turned back to me I was convinced there was suspicion in his glance.

`We've had a telephone call from our distributor in Paris, Sam. He wants to know more details about our forthcoming film schedule. He speaks English after a fashion, so I was able to give him the gist of what we had in mind. But, I don't want him to change suppliers. It might be worthwhile you paying him a visit.`

I was in George's office the next morning.

`Absolutely, George. When do you want me to go?`

`I suggest you go in the next couple of days, Sam. Before he starts thinking about other film makers.`

`What about the film I'm working on?`

`Don't worry about that. I'll take your place.` He grinned. `I'll even keep in the bit where you sit on the top hat.`

I spent almost a week in Paris. Meeting the distributor on several occasions to agree aspects of the contract. He eventually signed the document confirming our mutual association for the next two years. Between times I visited Georges Méliès in Montreuil.

He talked much about the success of his film, *The Trip To The Moon*, particularly in America

`It's an excellent market, my friend, but you have to be very, very careful. People will steal your material or produce pirate copies of your films if you are not well represented.`

Méliès discovered that film producers such as Thomas Edison and Siegmund Lubin, had pirated copies of his film and made substantial amounts of money. This had prompted Méliès to open his own office in New York City, with his brother, Gaston, in charge.

Georges told me that when he went to New York he discovered the full extent of the piracy in the United States. I was not overly surprised when he told me that the American Mutoscope and Biograph Company had actually paid royalties on Méliès` film to a promoter called Charles Urban..

`I see the future of this industry in America, Sam. You should find yourself a good distributor and get GAS Films established over there.`

CHAPTER EIGHT

I had to admit George did a far better job than I would have done as the amorist in *A Kiss In The Tunnel*. When the picture was shown at the Aquarium it even attracted a half page review in the Brighton Argus. On its first night I took Mr Gunn, my fellow lodger, to see it.

As we walked back to Mrs Earl`s, he said. `Pity you didn`t get to snuggle up close to Laura Bayley, Mr Lockhart. She`s a right lovely piece, and no mistake. So, tell me, how was it done, like?`

I launched into a detailed explanation of using existing film stock of the train, and cutting and editing in the love scene.

`Hmm...that`s interesting, Mr Lockhart. It makes a right, good film.`

I reported to George all was well in France, and then mentioned Méliès` advice about marketing our films in the United States.

`How would we go about that?`

`Well, we`d have to get an agent, a distributor with an honest reputation.`

`From what you`ve just told me, no one can be trusted. And all that way away we wouldn`t know if they were cheating us or not. We could lose more money than we earn.`

`I seriously believe we should consider it.`

`Hmm...I`ll think about it.`

We sat in his office, the silence lengthening, until he remarked.

`By the way, Sam, I`ve been wondering. Why is it our film sales are OK in much of the country, and do well in Scotland, but not in that band across Yorkshire and Lancashire? Is the humour different up there?`

`I`ve noticed that as well. I haven`t done much about it because we`re doing fine elsewhere. Do you want me to look into it?`

`It might be a good thing to understand why.`

A few days later I was in James Williamson`s new store in Western Road.

He was telling me of the latest films he had produced, when Esmé Collings walked in. Although competitors, a friendly rivalry exists, and during the conversation I mentioned that GAS Films were not doing particularly well in the north of the country.

Esmé nodded. `You know why that is, don`t you?`

James said immediately, `R. A. B.`

`That`s right.`

I was puzzled. `What`s R.A.B?`

Collings murmured. `More precisely, James Bamforth.`

`OK,` I said. `Who`s James Bamforth?`

`He runs Bamforths, a family company that started out producing magic lantern slides and seaside picture cards, but has moved into film making,` Collings explained. `They are based in Holmfirth, in West Yorkshire. Not so long ago Bamforths got together with a company in Bradford called Riley Brothers, which sells cameras.`

`This mutual concern is called RAB Films,` added Williamson.

`How do you know of them?` I asked Collings.

`Because Bamforth has copied the storyline of several of my films.` He added. `As he has done with others.`

`How did you stop him?`

`I couldn`t. We haven`t got copyright on storylines.`

I mentioned the conversation to George Smith, who at the time was working on an intricate production called, *The Haunted Castle*. He was employing a form of double-exposure he had perfected to create ghostly apparitions you could see through. With prior agreement, he was doing a re-make of one of Méliès` earlier films. Though shorter, viewing the unedited material, it was evident it would be technically superior to the French version.

`So where`re yer off to this time, Mr Lockhart?`

We were enjoying one of Mrs Earl`s trifles for dessert.

`To your home territory, Mr Gunn. I`m going to Yorkshire.`

`It`s a big place, Mr Lockhart. Where exactly?`

`Well, first I`m taking the train to Blackburn in Lancashire, to visit the Norden Film Company. I want to check out the shows Mitchell and Kenyon put on. Apparently, they last for about two hours, with actors performing both drama and comedy. Though, I'm told the main attraction is the films they make, which are mostly scenes of local life.`

`Aye, I went to one they put on in Halifax once,` commented Gunn. `It were a good evening. We all went in a charabanc. It were a coal cart, and fer the trip the owner installed rows of seats. By the time we arrived we were covered in coal dust.`

`I can imagine. After that I'm off to Bradford to call on a couple of film distributors, to see what we can do to improve sales. I also want to see a company that make cameras. Oh, and I'm going to a town called Holmfirth, which, I'm told isn't too far away. I want to visit a company called Bamforths.`

Mr Gunn rose suddenly from the table.

`I'll bid you goodnight, Mr Lockhart. Things ter do...things ter do.`

An abrupt departure, I thought. He had not even finished his trifle.

I was made welcome by Sagar Mitchell and James Kenyon.

`Most of our business, Mr Lockhart,` said Kenyon, `comes from our films on street life. Up here, we prefer moving pictures to feature real people. They're mostly of street scenes, such as workers streaming out of factory gates, parades, marches, walking out on Sunday, people enjoying themselves in fairgrounds.`

`So there's no interest at all in comedy or drama films?`

Mitchell put his coffee mug on the desk. `There is for slapstick humour, but not much else. The folk up here prefer seeing pictures of themselves, of real life.`

`You see, Mr Lockhart,` interjected Kenyon, `in this part of the country, people are poor. When you don't earn a good wage and you've a family to support, there's little interest in watching someone, even though it's make-believe, who lives and eats well. Better to see others like yourself facing similar hardships.`

`We try to make our films of working class people capture the camaraderie, the spirit of those who have little else to offer,` Mitchell explained.

I nodded thoughtfully.

`Would you like to see what we've been working on recently?` he asked.

`Very much so.`

Mitchell led me through the studio to a small viewing room.

`This was taken in Liverpool a few days ago.`

The street scenes were busy with pedestrians wandering in front of slow moving carts. There were trams, some horse-drawn as well as the new electric vehicles. Mitchell and Kenyon had also added variety by filming from the trams while they were on the move. Bicycles were plentiful; and they showed that rare novelty, a motor car.

At the docks, warships and steamboats were tight on the wharves. Emigrants were shown boarding the *RMS Saxonia*, bound for Boston in America. As the crowds passed by there were a few who came up to stare or wave at the camera.

When it was finished, Mitchell explained. `We even develop the films on the same day so relatives can come along that night and watch the scenes of their departing families.`

`Where do you show your films?` I enquired.

`We are what you might call self-publicising showmen,` grinned Kenyon. `We use fairground tents, local meeting halls, even music halls. Our advertising slogan, which we put outside each venue is, `See yourselves as others see you`.

`In Bradford and Leeds, people are more affluent,` remarked Mitchell. `They`re more impressed watching moving pictures that portray drama and pathos.`

`That`s Yorkshire for you,` muttered Kenyon. `In the big towns they can`t face reality. They prefer films which allow them to escape real life.`

`Or be titillated,` added Mitchell. He turned to me. `They flock to films like this latest one, *A Kiss In The Tunnel*. Have you seen it?`

I was about to say we made it, when Kenyon said. `I don`t know what Bamforth was thinking…making a film like that.`

The train was late. By the time I reached Bradford it was six o`clock. I had reserved a room at the Alexandra Hotel in Great Horton Road. Leaving my case in the room I asked the porter for directions to the People`s Palace.

`Just before Little Horton Lane joins the Manchester Road, go down St John`s Court. You can`t miss it.`

`How far?`

`Now`t but a short walk.`

Though officially known as the Star Music Hall, I had learned from

Mitchell and Kenyon that the People's Palace was the popular name,. What was unique about the building was its two-tier construction. Above the music hall was the Princes' Theatre. Its more elaborate interior was styled for opera and classical drama.

I paid my shilling, and took a seat.

A brass band came onto the stage and played for almost an hour. It was clearly a favourite with the audience, and when they began to interpret tunes of the day, everyone sang along with the music.

The crowd hushed when the films started.

The performance lasted fifteen minutes. Some of the titles I remembered. They included, *The Barber's Shop*; *A Dentist's Operating Room*; *The Blacksmith's Forge*; and *A Kiss In The Tunnel*.

A Kiss In The Tunnel was not nearly as imaginative or well-crafted as the GAS film which had a lively, more balletic quality to it. The players in Bamforth's picture did not know what to do with their hands and were quite wooden after the first embrace. Plus the fact that you watched the train going into the tunnel; ours had the cameraman perched on the front of the train. Audiences were given the impression they were also entering the tunnel.

But that was by the way. Bamforth had copied our film right down to the title. Pure plagiarism. How on earth had they found out so quickly?

The film show was followed by several music hall acts. I left my seat before they had finished and made my way to the projection box. I knocked and turned the door handle at the same time. The projectionist was busily winding back the film from a linen-lined basket.

`Sorry, you're not allowed in here,` he said sharply.

`It's all right, I'm a film maker myself. I'm with GAS Films in Brighton.` I handed him my card.

`Oh, aye. What yer doing up here?` he grinned. `Seeing 'ow it should be done?`

`You could say that. I was interested in that film you've just shown...*A Kiss In The Tunnel*. Where was the tunnel located?`

I wanted to find out if it were cut from Hepworth's film as well.

`I think it were near Keighley. I remember Mr Bamforth telling me that he "ad a camera up there for several days before 'e got right shot".`

I took a closer look at the projector. It was an almost exact copy of the one stolen from Alfred Darling's workshop.

`Who made this?` I asked the projectionist.

`The maker's name is on that plate,` he said off-handedly.

I peered at a brass strip. `Riley Brothers, Bradford.`

`I know for a fact it was built for them by Cecil Wray,` the projectionist declared. `They contracted him to do the work.`

`Where's Cecil Wray's premises?`

`Borough Mills, on the Manchester Road.`

`Thanks for your time.`

As I left the building I thought, first thing tomorrow morning I shall be paying Mr Wray a visit.

`So, how can I help you Mr Lockhart?`

`I was intrigued by the projector I saw at the People's Palace last night, Mr Wray. It carried the Riley's badge of manufacture, but I'm told you were the person who constructed it. An interesting design, using an electric fan to dispel the heat from a carbon arc lighting unit.`

`Frankly, Mr Lockhart, I'm not sure about carbon arc lighting. It's a bit too dangerous. Although we've had electricity in Bradford a few years now, to my mind it's still raises uncertainties. Give me the tried and tested limelight any day.`

`So you don't hold with the carbon arc. Then why did you construct such a machine for the People's Palace?`

He stared at me intently, clearly wondering why I wanted to know.

`The Rileys asked me to build a projector with carbon arc lighting. The strongest illuminant was to be used so all the seats for the film shows in the People's Palace could be sold.`

`So you haven't used arc lighting before?`

`No, I've always thought it too risky.`

`That's true, Mr Wray. So tell me, how did you come up with the construction of the projector if you haven't used carbon arc lighting before?`

He was beginning to show concern. Had he said too much? `Who are you, Mr Lockhart? Why all the questions? I thought you were a possible buyer, but you're not are you? I think you'd better leave.`

`Mr Wray. I work with George Smith in Brighton. The projector in the

People`s Palace is an exact copy of the one stolen from us. We hold the patent on the design you`ve copied, and we shall sue you, Mr Wray, for infringement of our rights. Good day to you, sir.`

As I turned he grabbed my arm. `You can`t do that! I didn`t know! The Rileys were given a projector and told to make an exact model of it. They passed it to me to do the job for them.`

`Who commissioned them to produce a copy of the projector, Mr Wray?`

He stared at the floor and mumbled.

`I can`t say Mr Lockhart.`

`I suggest you do say. Otherwise, you and the Rileys will appear on the summons sheet. Moreover, as the declared manufacturer, Mr Wray, your name will be broadcast in the newspapers and around the town. You`ll be shunned by your fellows. I`ll see to it.`

His face was pale when finally he looked up. He took a deep breath, and said hesitantly.

`James Bamforth.`

`Right. Now show me the projector you copied.`

He led me to a room at the back of his workshop. On a workbench were the carcass and remains of what was once the machine Alfred Darling and I had spent many hours crafting.

Two days later, accompanied by Mr Strong of Wilton, Richards and Strong, we took the short walk to Godwin Street. It was a wasted effort. I was informed the Riley Brothers were away on business.

With a little inducement, surreptitiously slipping a florin into the gatekeeper`s hand, he let it be known they had gone to Holmfirth. That was enough. A hansom cab took us the eighteen miles to James Bamforth`s works in Station Road.

`Sorry, sir. I`m afraid Mr Bamforth cannot be disturbed,` said the young man who appeared when I rang a small bell.

`Oh, I think he will see me. Tell him I am from GAS Films. Mention that before I go to the police, I`ve come to discuss the illegal removal of a projector from our premises in Brighton. You might add that the projector has been deposited with someone well-versed in the laws of patent infringement. Moreover, that gentleman has accompanied me today.`

I had been busy during the past forty-eight hours. I had telephoned George at St Ann's Well Gardens, and a copy of the patent document had been sent by train to Bradford. In the meantime, I had studied the Bamforth catalogue and the activities of the Rileys. I had also engaged the services of a solicitor versed in patent matters. He had prepared two writs, one for issue to Bamforth, the other to the Riley Brothers.

The young man disappeared through the door.

A few minutes later we were ushered into a room where a tall, imposing figure stood behind a desk. He wore a full beard and moustache, and his eyes glared angrily at Strong and myself. Then, leaning forward, laying both hands on the work surface, he imperiously demanded the reason for this intrusion.

`You are Mr James Bamforth, are you not?`

`I am, sir, and you haven't answered my question. What gives you the right to interrupt me when I have important business to conduct? Tell me, confound you!`

`If, as I suspect, the young man relayed my message to you correctly, you know why I am here. Furthermore, why I am accompanied by this gentleman. He is a man of law, an expert in patent infringement, which you have contravened.`

`How dare you! Get out, I say. Leave these premises!`

His voice was loud, and carried beyond the room in which we stood. The next moment two people burst through the door.

`Are you all right, James. It sounded as if you were about to be attacked?`

Bamforth broke his stare at me, and turned to the one who had spoken.

`No, no, William, just two objectionable characters I have asked to leave.`

I stepped towards the two men.

`Do I presume you are the Riley brothers?`

The fellow who had enquired about our presence, looked puzzled, but he nodded.

`My name is William Riley...and you, sir?`

`Samuel Lockhart, of GAS Films in Brighton.`

He nodded. `I've heard of your company. You make some good films. What brings you here?` He glanced at Bamforth. `What's going on, James? These people are in the same line of business as ourselves.`

Before he could answer, I said swiftly. `I am here, Mr Riley, with Mr

Strong, of Wilton, Richards, and Strong, a firm of Bradford solicitors. He is about to do his duty.`

Riley turned to Strong. `I know you, don`t I?`

`We have met at various functions,` responded Strong. `I am, of course, aware of your company and its area of trade. Which, in the circumstances, makes me all the more concerned.`

Arnold Riley interrupted. `What the hell are you talking about, Strong? What duty?`

`To serve a writ, sir, in accordance with the law. You appear to have broken the rights of patent by manufacturing a machine which is an exact copy of that registered to GAS Films.`

`What?` exploded William Riley. `That projector was given to Cecil Wray to manufacture. We didn`t know it was patented.`

He looked round at Bamforth. `You said nothing about it being registered to someone else. What have you got us into? Did Wray know its origins?`

Riley turned back to me.

`You`d better have a word with Cecil Wray. It`s nothing to do with us. We purchased it from him in good faith. We just put our plate on it.`

I studied the two Rileys. `The question is, who gave the projector to Mr Wray to copy?`

Both Rileys stared at Bamforth.

`Err...well I did. But I didn`t know it was stolen.`

`Really?`

`A fellow in the workshop mentioned he had obtained a projector that used carbon arc lighting. I knew the Rileys wanted such a system for the People`s Palace. He got hold of it and I paid him a fee. But I didn`t know its provenance.`

Mr Strong gave that dry cough all solicitors seem to acquire along with their diplomas.

`I`m sure you are aware Mr Bamforth that, in the eyes of the law, ignorance is not a valid excuse.`

`Now look here, Strong,` he blustered loudly. `Don`t you start accusing me of anything underhand. I run an honest business here!`

`I`ve been looking through your catalogue, Mr Bamforth,` I said quietly. `Several of the films you have made are not included. Why is that, I wonder?`

He glanced at me sharply. `What? Oh, they are only for local viewing, not for general distribution.`

`Why? Is it because they are copies of films others have made, and would be frowned upon if they had wide circulation? Such as, *A Kiss In The Tunnel*, by way of an example?

`Damn good film that,` said William Riley.

`Would you be surprised to learn, Mr Riley, that GAS Films in Brighton made a film about a train going into a tunnel and two people kissing before it exits? Would you be even more surprised to know that it was called *A Kiss In The Tunnel* as well? That it was made some time before Mr Bamforth's version. It may not, unfortunately, be unlawful, but at the very least, it is unethical. The reason it has not been widely publicised, sir, is that people might learn the truth. Isn't that right, Mr Bamforth? And you call this an honest business?`

`Is this true, James?` asked Arnold Riley quietly.

`Someone I know, who had been in the south of England saw the film and suggested we do one like it. It was he who nominated the title.`

There was a lengthy, uncomfortable silence.

William Riley broke it. `So, what do you intend to do, Mr Lockhart? Are you going to issue these writs and we answer the charges in court? Or can we settle this some other way?`

`Perhaps we should all sit down,` I ventured.

We formed a rough circle. Strong and I were sitting together, as were the Rileys. Noticeably, they had moved their chairs to distance themselves from Bamforth.

`As I see it, gentlemen, you each have a case to answer.`

Strong nodded, emphasising the point.

`Equally, I am aware that you,` I looked in the direction of the Rileys, `are hoping to give a film presentation to Royalty at Balmoral in the near future. That would be jeopardised if you were hauled before a judge and a case found against you.`

I turned to Bamforth, who sat glowering at me.

`I would have no hesitation in asking Mr Strong to serve this writ on you, Mr Bamforth. I realise you did not mastermind the theft of the projector, but I feel you capitalised on it by failing to enquire after its origin. In law that is a sin of commission.

`Moreover, I am not much concerned about your creativity. Comparing the two versions of *A Kiss In The Tunnel,* I see little need to regard you as a competitor.

`I am not a vindictive man, and nor is George Smith. So these writs will not be served. But you.` I looked in the Rileys` direction, `I would take great care whom you choose as a business partner.`

I rose from my chair, and stood looking at James Bamforth.

`My earnest advice, sir, is to stick to what you do best...saucy seaside postcards. If anything were ever to happen like this again, we would have little hesitation in bringing down upon you the full force of the law. Mr Strong and I bid you good-day.`

CHAPTER NINE

I told George what I had done, along with the invoice from Wilton, Richards, and Strong.

`Time and money well spent, Sam. Well done. Fancy you coming across our projector in Bradford of all places.`

`Thinking about it, George, I believe I know how it got there. I`ll tell you more in the morning.`

I had come straight from the station to the pump house, and started to gather up my belongings.

`Just a minute, before you go, Sam. There`s something I want to say. I`ve been pursuing your idea about selling our films in the United States. I had a long chat with Charles Urban about it. He is suggesting we use a distributor called The American Mutoscope and Biograph Company. What do you think?`

For some illogical reason I resented Urban`s interference. But he was an American, knew the American film market, and had infinitely more knowledge of the companies over there than George or I.

` Sounds a sensible solution, George. Do we contact them, or does he?`

`I thought he should. You know, one American to another.`

`Right.`

`There`s something else I want to tell you.`

He was now looking a little shame-faced. I wondered what was coming next.

`I`ve been thinking. There`s quite a bit to do here. Organising the team, selecting the locations, all the administration. That keeps you pretty busy, and then you`ve been looking after sales as well. Charles suggested, because of your workload, that he may be able to help.`

I turned towards him.

`Oh...in what way?`

`Well, he is proposing that he looks after our distribution.`

`What, the Warwick Trading Company?`

`Err. . no, he is setting up his own.`

`So what you`re saying is that, from now on, I don`t get involved in organising the sales or the distribution? He does it and we pay him to do it?`

`That`s about the size of it.`

`So, what I have been doing...`

`Very successfully,` George added.

`What I`ve been doing, Urban will now take on and charge a hefty fee for the same job?`

`I don`t quite see it like that, Sam.`

`What other way is there?`

`Well, it will free up some of your time.`

`I don`t want to free up some of my time. Unless, of course, you believe I`m not doing a good job?`

`Look, Sam, let`s give it a try. If it doesn`t work out, we`ll go back to you being in charge of sales and distribution. What do you say?`

`I don`t think there is much to say, George. You`ve made up your mind.`

I grabbed my things and walked out the office.

I got back to Mrs Earl`s lodging house that evening. Depositing my case and coat in my room I went downstairs for dinner.

The table was set for one.

When she came into the room with a single bowl of soup, it confirmed I was dining alone.

`Mr Gunn has left us, dearie,` she remarked, as the bowl was placed before me.

`All very sudden. Came home from his place of business on Tuesday, took his post to his room. Shortly afterwards, he came down and told me he was leaving. Paid his rent, didn`t even stop for an evening meal. A half an hour later he was gone. I think he has gone back north, you know, to Huddersfield.`

I nodded grimly. Huddersfield was only six miles from Holmfirth.

CHAPTER TEN

Charles Urban was becoming a fixture at St Ann`s Well Gardens.

Whenever, I went into the pump house, he was invariably at George`s shoulder. I could find little time for him. I thought my feelings were disguised, but Laura was quick to notice my antipathy.

`You don`t like Charles much, do you, Sam?` she said openly one day.

We had met at the gate, and strolled up the path together.

I raised an eyebrow. `Not much, Laura.`

We walked another ten or so paces.

`Is it because he has taken over film distribution?`

`In a way, yes. I can see little point in paying him a fat fee when I did it as part of my job. I would accept that selling that cache of films to Vitagraph and proposing the Mutoscope and Biograph Compay in America to act as our agent was a good suggestion. It`s working well. But taking over first the British, and then continental sales, when he can`t even speak a foreign language defeats me.`

She said nothing for several moments.

`Did you know he put money into the company, Sam? He funded the alterations to the pump house for the processing section, and the studio that was built. That`s why George went along with the idea.`

I opened the door for her.

`I wasn`t aware of that, Laura.`

I was talking with Geoffrey Summer in the room we use as a general office, when Urban walked in.

`Morning, seen George?`

I shook my head.

`I don`t think he is here yet, Charles,` said Geoffrey.

`OK, I`ll wait here if you don`t mind. How are you guys? Putting together some new ideas?`

`Sam was talking about making longer films,` remarked the cameraman. `As he sees it, if no scene is longer than a minute, we could glue them together into a continuous five to six minute picture.`

`Interesting you should say that,` commented the American. `Our outlets on the continent are looking for five to ten minute features. From what I know back home, the people still enjoy the one minute sock-it-to-them comedy movies. String several of those together and you`ve got yourself a film show in the States.`

`So you see them as two separate markets, do you?` I remarked. `Maybe there is a slight difference in taste at the moment, but eventually audiences everywhere will be looking for films like books. They`ll want material with a beginning, a middle and a good ending. The point I was making is perhaps GAS Films should start now, lead the way. Ultimately, everyone will be wanting longer moving pictures than even we are thinking about.`

`You may be right, Sam. It could be we Americans are easily satisfied at the moment. Though there was a real hullabaloo when they filmed the recent Jim Jeffries, Tom Sharkey title fight. Did you hear about it?`

Geoffey and I shook our heads.

Urban grinned.

`It went twenty five rounds. They managed to change the film in the three cameras they were using between the rounds. That is until the twenty-fifth and final round...when they ran out of film. The two boxers had to come back a week later to do the last round for the cameras.`

The door opened on our laughter, and George Smith came in to the room.

`Did I miss something?`

`I was telling them about the Jeffries, Sharkey fight in the States. The Mutoscope and Biograph people filmed the whole lot...except the last round. They ran out of film stock. Would you believe it?`

`They filmed the fight did they? On their seventy millimetre film I suppose. When will they adopt the thirty five mill film, and change the perforations like the rest of us?`

Urban glanced quickly at me.

`Err, George...That`s what I want to talk to you about. Can we have a word?`

Later that morning George put his head round the door. `Got a minute, Sam?`

In the corridor, he took my arm.

`I`ve got a better idea. Let me take you to lunch.`

I did not say anything, but felt strongly that the invitation had been prompted by his conversation with Urban. That became a certainty when he said. `Let`s take a hansom into Brighton, shall we?`

At first we talked generalities. When he ordered a bottle of wine I knew it was something significant. We discussed the film schedule and who should act in each of the pictures. Of the twenty three titles, all were no more than seventy five feet in length.

`George, I want you to do me a favour. I`d like two of them to be longer. I was thinking of *Grandma's Reading Glasses*, and *Letty Limelight In Her Lair.* I want to check on audience reaction. What do you say?`

He stared at me intently over his wine glass.

`Charles mentioned you`ve got this bee in your bonnet about doing longer productions.`

He swirled the wine in the glass, and drank from it.

`OK…we`ll do it. But I want something from you.`

I looked at him questioningly.

`I want you to go to the States and sort out our distribution.`

I gradually got the full story.

There was bad blood between Thomas Edison and the founder of Mutoscope and Biograph, William Dickson, who had worked for Edison five years earlier.

To avoid violating Edison's motion picture patents, Biograph cameras used a seventy millimetre film, and a friction feed rather than Edison's sprocket drive, to guide the film through the aperture. But still the writs mounted up. Edison`s people kept an eagle eye on what their rival was up to.

Now they had issued an injunction on Biograph to halt its distribution of imported thirty five millimetre films. While the legalities were being pored over Dickson had decided to hold back on foreign films.

`We need that market, Sam. Charles can`t go to the United States at the moment, so it`s down to you. What do you say?`

One half of me wanted to say no. He had shrugged off my sales efforts in favour of this American upstart, now it had come back to bite him. However, my other half was more amenable.

`OK, George. As I see it, it`s for the good of the company. When do you want me to go?`

`Immediately.`

CHAPTER ELEVEN

The next few days were a whirlwind of activity. I travelled up to London to acquire a passport; buy my passage at the White Star Line offices near Trafalgar Square; and buy clothes together with a good size suitcase.

I paid Mrs Earl, thinking at the time I should really rent or buy a property of my own, rather than confine myself to a single room in a lodging house. However, I had not realised how attached I had become to the dwelling or to my landlady. I kissed her goodbye when the hansom cab came to take me to the station, and she sniffed her farewell through tears.

`Make sure you eat properly, Mr Lockhart, and be careful of all that foreign food. You`re far too thin as it is.`

The following Wednesday I joined hordes of others making their way to the Liverpool Docks. I had not appreciated that the ship, the *Oceanic*, was an emigrant vessel, taking a steady stream of Europeans to resettle in the United States.

I was travelling steerage, such was the budget we could afford, which meant sharing a small cabin fitted with bunk beds with three other men. It was cramped, and though I tried to speak with them in French, they only understood my halting German.

The dining arrangements were a free-for-all. We took our meals in a low-ceilinged section between decks, sitting on swivel chairs bolted to the floor. The only way one could dine was to sidle into position and then swing round to the table. At mealtimes the body odour, the sweet smell of sea-sickness, the press of humanity filling these quarters, seemed to taint the very food we ate.

There were several hundred first and second class passengers, and over a thousand in steerage. My three cabin-mates and I often went to the dining section together. Although we found it difficult to converse, an unspoken camaraderie developed. I gradually discovered that they were Jews escaping The Pale of Settlement, a prescribed territory to which Jews were restricted by Imperial Russia. It extended from the eastern *pale*, the demarcation line, to the the Kingdom of Prussia and the Austro-Hungary Empire.

Their company was something of an insurance. In steerage there were often scuffles and fights when tempers flared. In these over-crowded conditions it was small wonder that some were given to exercise force. Moving around as a quartet, we were rarely called out, and generally given a wide berth. As one might imagine, the novelty of ocean travel soon wore off during the eight day voyage.

Outside New York Harbour, the ship awaited clearance by the medical authorities. Thereafter, the immigrants were shepherded onto barges and removed to Ellis Island, where they were subjected to physical examination and questioned about their future.

I had promised to wait for my companions, although I learned it could take up to five hours before immigrants were released ashore. They had suggested we find suitable accommodation together, which, in an unknown city, seemed the safer option. It was agreed we would meet at the ferry terminal in Battery Park.

It was a depressing day, grey, windy, with intermittent squally showers dampening one`s clothes and spirits. What struck me was the number of well-dressed men waiting around the terminal. At first, I presumed they were there to meet incoming relatives; but I noticed they would flock towards any pretty young woman that came out the terminal without a male escort.

A fellow standing nearby, recognisable as an emigré by his style of dress, murmured. `They never stop recruiting, do they?`

`Sorry?`

Those people...trying to entice pretty girls into their trade with the offers of jobs.`

`What trade is that?`

He looked at me uncertainly.

`Prostitution, of course. They are pimps. They try to hook women before they know what life is all about here. It`s a big racket, mister, and getting bigger all the time. Something should be done about it.`

When eventually the trio arrived at the terminal, my low spirits were in absolute contrast to their exuberance.

`Come, my friend, be happy for us,` declared one in German. `We are to begin a new life. My name was Szczepan Krotkiewicz, now it is Steven Kruger.`

He gave a wide grin, and pointed to the other two. `He was Piotr Walczak, he is now Peter Walsh. and Tomasz Tomaszewski is Thomas Thomas. We are new people!`

` We must go to my aunt`s house,` said Peter, taking from a pocket a much-folded slip of paper. `I wonder how we find where it is?`

I went over to what appeared to be a taxi rank. There was a line of peculiar looking vehicles, nothing like the hansom cabs back home. For one thing there were no horses, and they certainly were not motor cars.

`Is this a taxi service?` I enquired.

`Sure is, my friend. Where do you want to go?`

Peter had given me the slip of paper.

`Yonah Shimmel's Knish Bakery on Houston Street.`

`No problem, everyone knows Yonah Shimmel. How many of you?`

We hired two of these machines called Electrobats. They accommodated two passengers in a front facing chair, with the driver standing behind the canopy above a battery-powered electric motor.

We travelled sedately in convoy through the district I learned was the Lower East Side, eventually coming to a halt on the junction of Houston Street and Lafayette Street.

`That`s it, gents. Can`t get any closer. Yonah Shimmel's is four hundred yards down on the right.`

Everywhere was jammed with barrows, stalls, and a multitude of shoppers, heaving, pushing, all talking at once. We gathered our various belongings and began walking east on Houston Street. As we neared the bakery I asked Peter what a knish was.

He grinned at me. `Sam, it`s a sort of dough mixture filled with anything you like, from mashed potato, ground meat, sauerkraut, onions, or cheese. Then it`s baked, grilled, or deep fried. It`s a Jewish snack...very, very popular.`

Walking through the crowds I picked out the American English spoken with a slight nasally overtone, German, and another language I could not place. I asked Peter.

`That`s Yiddish. It`s spoken by the Ashkenazi Jews from central Europe.

It`s a mix of Hebrew and German.`

As we neared Yonah Shimmel's, there was a small gathering massing around the entrance. One of them looked up, and saw us approaching. She said something to the others, and suddenly half a dozen women came rushing towards us.

I stopped abruptly, while Peter and the others quickened their step. They met in the middle of the road surrounded by a sea of people: laughing and crying they embraced and kissed. I`ve never witnessed such a public display. Although I soon came to appreciate that was how they behaved: their hearts on their sleeves. Then I too was pulled into the middle of the heaving group. My hair was rubbed and subjected to hearty kissing.

We were led to Eldridge Street, a road lined with tenements above rows of shops. We climbed stairs to a fifth floor apartment, everyone still talking excitedly in Yiddish. In a large room, dotted with an assortment of chairs, bottles of beer were passed round and we drank, from what I could make out, to our safe arrival.

That night, after a heavy meal, I staggered across the hallway to another apartment and shared a room with Peter. I had drunk too much beer. The following morning, I did not awaken until my shoulder was rocked by a small boy. As I came to, this juvenile face was studying me intently.

`Are you awake?` said a piping voice.

`I think so,` I croaked. `What time is it?`

`It is ten o`clock, sir. Do you like my bed? Do you want to get up?`

I staggered from the bed apologetically.

`I always give up my bed when people stay. I sleep with my cousin downstairs.`

I re-crossed the hall ten minutes later and knocked on the door. One of Peter`s aunts clapped her hands.

`Now you must have some breakfast.`

I was embarrassed.

`Have you been waiting for me? I`m sorry, I should have got up sooner.`

`Poof! It is nothing. The others have already eaten and gone to Fulton Market. They`ve gone to buy fish for tonight`s meal. We always have it Friday evenings.`

I sat down at the table and ate some toast while she poured the coffee.

`So, if you are not an immigrant, Mr Lockhart, what brings you to New York?` asked Peter`s aunt, a short, round woman with a big smile and a mass of greying hair beneath a scarf tied under her chin.

`I have a meeting with a company. They`ve got offices on Broadway. Is that near here?`

`That depends which Broadway you want. There`s East Broadway, which is six or seven blocks south of here, or there`s the main Broadway running north. Which is it?`

`I`m told it`s near Union Square.`

`Then that`s the one running north. What number?`

`Eight four one.`

She stared reflectively at her cup of coffee. `Yes...that would be near Union Square. When`s your appointment?`

`Monday or possibly Tuesday morning.`

`I`ll get Alice to take you before she goes to work at the hat makers in Clinton Street.`

`I don`t want to put you out. You`ve been kind enough already. I can easily get a room somewhere, and find my way there on Monday.`

`I wouldn`t dream of it Mr Lockhart...`

`Please...call me Sam.`

`As I was saying, Sam, I wouldn`t dream of it. You and Peter can have my sister`s boy`s room as long as you wish.`

An awkward situation. GAS had provided the money for me to stay in an hotel: nothing lavish, a comfortable room with meals. Here I was staying in an apartment where the people were clearly not well off, having to work hard for every penny they earned. Yet they had befriended me. They were willing to share their food and give me a bed. It was not that I felt obliged to remain. Far from it. I enjoyed the family life around me. I welcomed the laughter, the shouting, the warmth of their companionship. Infinitely preferable to a solitary stay in a dispassionate lodging house.

`That`s very kind, er...`

`My name is Eszter, Sam.`

That night, before we ate, candles were lit and blessings recited over the wine, food and the children. Peter whispered. `It`s Shabat, Sam.`

I must have looked slightly puzzled for one of his many relatives said. `The beginning of the Jewish holy day. It lasts until sunset tomorrow evening.`

At the table I sat next to Eszter, who mentioned during the meal.

`By the way, Sam, you`ve been invited to a Bar Mitzvah on Sunday. It`s to celebrate Simon`s, my cousin Rachel`s thirteen year old, coming of age. I`ll tell you more about it later.`

After we had eaten, and everyone helped wash up and clear everything away, Eszter took me to one side.

`You won`t be able to attend the service at the synagogue, but Rachel said you are most welcome to the meal at her place afterwards. We`ll be back there at about one o`clock. So, if you come to their apartment at about half past one, everything will be ready.`

`I`d love to come, Eszter, thank you. Tell me, does one give presents?`

`There`s no need, Sam. We do, as family, but outsiders are not expected to.`

`Perhaps, but I`d like to. What is the custom at such events?`

She looked a little uncertain.

`Well, we shall give Simon a kiddush cup. His parents will most likely give him a tallis or tefillin. These are ritual shawls and small leather boxes. As I say, these are gifts from parents, grandparents and those close to the family. Others usually give money.`

She hesitated. `Unfortunately, it is most often donated in multiples of eighteen, which represents both good luck and the Jewish symbol, Chai, which means "life". But they wouldn`t expect you to observe such a tradition. Just give what you can spare, Sam.`

The next morning I went for a stroll around the Lower East Side.

I had started out present hunting, but more and more I realised that money would be the most welcome gift. But I could not give the boy eighteen dollars. That would have been equivalent to three weeks of his father`s salary. Walking east on Grand Street I came to the waterfront along the East River. Turning upstream I had to dodge the carts and porters unloading in front of the riverside warehouses, Teamsters pulling wagons piled high with cotton, lumber, coffee, tea, molasses and spices; carpenters hammering together barrels almost as fast as they could be filled. Ahead of me were the huge building works around a new bridge being erected. To avoid them I struck off once more into the hinterland of the Lower East Side.

I had not appreciated the extent that human beings can congregate together in less than ideal conditions. I gazed upon tall, heavily populated tenement buildings with iron fire escapes zig-zagging down their fronts; washing strung haphazardly on lines outside windows; the ill-smelling shops; foreign houses of worship; and dingy coffee houses where men of all ages sat playing cards or dominoes.

The streets were black with purchasers, and bright with the glare of hundreds of torches from the pushcarts. There was a constant cacophony coming from the voices of peddlers crying their wares. Fish carts abounded. The cries of the would-be purchasers filling the air with many strange tongues; and, of course, the ever-present Yiddish of the elders mixing with the English of the younger people.

It all made for a strange medley of sounds. Not unpleasant: for in their plight of living cheek by jowl, having little money and many mouths to feed, there was an underlying sense of kinship. Of suffering in concert.

I stopped to watch children playing a game. A piece of wood was laid on the ground, and the batsman touched the end lightly with his stick. It rose into the air two or three feet, when it did so he struck it sharply. Sometimes it was sent half a block, and the batsman ran round a circuit before one of the fielders returned it to the home base.

Eszter had warned me that the Lower East Side could be frightening, dangerous, and noisy. Yet I suppose to the many migrant Jews it was a place of relative safety compared with the oppressive anti-Semitic Russian Empire. However chaotic and cramped it might be, the Lower East Side of New York now housed the greatest concentration of Jewish life in nearly two thousand years.

When I got back to the apartment, Eszter and Peter expressed their concern.

`We thought something might have happened to you, Sam,` she exclaimed.

`No, I was fine, just doing a little shopping.`

I hefted a large bag of groceries onto the kitchen table.

`I hope this makes a small contribution to my stay here.`

She had refused money. This seemed the only way to repay her kindness. As she unpacked, her eyes gleamed at the quantity and variety of what I had bought.

`To make sure I didn`t offend anyone, I bought it all in a Jewish store in Orchard Street.`

`Rozanski`s?`

`Yes, I think that was the name.`

When it was stowed away in the cupboards, Eszter took my hand in hers.

`Thank you, Sam.`

A simple show of gratitude; but it meant a lot to me.

`By the way, I saw some boys playing a game in the streets. They were hitting a piece of wood into the air. `

Eszter nodded. `And once they`d hit it, did they run round jackets lying on the ground?`

`Yes, they did.`

`That will be `One o' Cat`. It`s a favourite with the boys of Hebrew families. The trouble is people want to stop it on account of the accidents to shop windows and passers-by. It is dangerous, I must admit, to be hit by a flying piece of wood. But at the same time it would be sad to deny them the chance to play.`

The following day everyone made their way to the synagogue further down Eldridge Street. Looking out the window, it was quieter than on a weekday. The shouting, the noise of push-cart vendors, the buzz of conversation were now predominantly from the gentile inhabitants of the neighbourhood. With time to spare I began penning a letter to George Smith telling him of my safe arrival. I left out my living arrangements. I would make use of the money saved on hotel accommodation in much better ways.

In the afternoon I went for another walk, this time heading west. Eventually I reached the far shoreline at West Street, and headed south to Battery Park. It was a warm, pleasant afternoon, so I ventured onto a ferry to the Statue of Liberty on Bedloe`s Island. Though I did overhear an official mention they were thinking of calling it Liberty Island, which seemed more appropriate.

I climbed to the crown of the statue to the observation windows up a narrow staircase; stopping halfway for a breather. In all there were three hundred and fifty four steps rising at every turn among crossbeams, girders and bracing struts. But the view at the top was spectacular. I could see the Brooklyn Bridge spanning the East River; up the North River as far as Forty Second Street, where the liners moored; and across the skyline of Manhattan.

It was early evening when I got back to Eldridge Street.

On Sunday, after they had gone again to the synagogue, I retrieved my suit from the case, brushed and hung it to allow the creases to fall out. The shirt I had saved for my appointment with the American Mutoscope and Biograph Company was also draped next to the suit. I would have to be careful not to spill anything on it before tomorrow's meeting.

I was to join the celebrations of the Bar Mitzvah at an apartment off Stanton Street. I shaved carefully, and cleaned my shoes. After the sound of pattering feet and the high and low pitched chatter within the apartment of recent days, it was now surprisingly tranquil. I walked into the kitchen, part of the main living area, and sat quietly reading the newspaper I had bought the previous day.

It washed over me. I neither understood American politics, social injustices nor the country's economics. Though one item caught my eye. It was a large picture of a woman called Mary Harris Jones, leading child workers in a demand for a fifty five hour working week. In Britain the law only allowed children to work an eight hour day, six days a week. The United States still had a way to go.

As I was reading the paper, the thought came that there were few who would leave a complete stranger alone in their household. It certainly would not have happened at home. They obviously trusted me; something I found heartwarming.

I made a cup of coffee and turned to the sports pages. This was even more puzzling. Not only could I not comprehend American games, the terms and descriptions were completely beyond me.

An hour before I should be there I started to get ready: leisurely and with care. I tied my tie three times until it sat neatly under the collar; I rebrushed my shoes; slicked down my hair; and staring into *The Mirror* wondered if

I should grow a moustache. At last I was ready. I also donned a hat I had purchased. At home, in Brighton, I had never bothered. But in New York everyone wore one. When in Rome I guess...

Sauntering up Eldridge Street I turned on to East Houston, and stopped for a coffee in Katz Delicatessen. I had plenty of time. When I reached the corner of Stanton and Pitt Street, it appeared to be more residential. Fewer shops lined the foot of each housing block.

I climbed the stairs to the fourth floor and knocked on the door. I could hear laughter and loud conversation. I was beginning to wonder if anyone had heard me, when suddenly it was yanked open and a short, stocky man, holding a glass and a cigar, welcomed me in, saying.

`Hi, I`m Carl, you must be the Englishman Eszter`s been talking about.`

I was quickly made welcome, given a glass of wine and offered anchovies, black olives and some chopped liver paste. None of which I had ever tasted before.

Twenty six of us sat down for a meal which entailed friends and relatives bringing their own tables, chairs, plates, glasses and cutlery. The many dishes had also been prepared in several of the neighbours` kitchens. Fortunately, the apartment was quite large and the sitting area "L" shaped, which meant half the guests were round the corner; but everyone was seated

It was a joyous gathering. The Bar Mitzvah boy, Simon, gave us a reading from the Torah in Hebrew, and a brief homily in English. Then we were addressed briefly by the Rabbi. When it came to giving Simon gifts, I stood next to Eszter as we came up to the young man. I handed him an envelope containing money. Then we returned to the table for cake. Jewish women, I discovered that day, excel at making cakes. They come in all shapes and sizes, and are remarkable for their design and content.

After the main meal there was no formality in the seating, and I took a place between Eszter and Carl, the fellow who had opened the door to me.

`I told you there was no need to give a present, Sam,` murmured Eszter. `But it was a nice gesture.`

Her curiosity got the better of her.

`By the way what did you give him?`

`Well, you told me eighteen was a lucky multiple, so I gave him eighteen twenty five cent coins.`

She glanced at Carl.

`That`s four dollars fifty. That`s a lot, Sam.`

`That was generous, Sam. May I call you Sam?` remarked Carl.

`Of course.` I half-turned and shook his hand.

He studied me for a moment.

`By the way, what brings you to New York? You`re not an immigrant are you?`

`No, I met Eszter`s nephews on the ship, they brought me along, and she invited me to stay for a few days. I`m here for a meeting with a company, then back to England.`

Eszter commented. `He`s here to see the American Mutoscope and Biograph Company in Lower Broadway. Alice is taking him there on Monday.`

`Really, what`s that about?`

`Until recently the company was distributing our films. We produce films in England and sell them over here. At least, we did. The Mutoscope and Biograph people are now reviewing whether the arrangement should continue. I`m here to find out the reason, and to persuade them to carry on.`

Again Carl nodded. `That`s a difficult one, Sam. You probably don`t know the problems Biograph, we just refer to them as Biograph, are facing with Edison.`

`Well I heard something about patent infringement. But that is a fact of life in the film business.`

`I am only too well aware, my friend.`

I was intrigued. `Do you know about the moving picture industry?`

`Yes...I do. You see that guy over there? That`s Isadore Bernstein, my brother-in-law. He`s the one who got me an invite to the party. We`re in business together, and about to set up a film distribution company called "The Laemmle Film Service". It`s a pity we can`t help each other. Perhaps in another couple of years.`

This was useful. Someone involved in the American film business.

`So what chances have I got continuing with Biograph, do you think?`

`I don`t want to spoil your day, Sam...but hardly any if they are on thirty five millimetre format. What they might earn from selling your films would be lost in the costs of litigation. Thomas Edison is tightening his grip on the film stock patents he owns, and now he`s trying to extend it to imported motion pictures. Biograph is already up to its eyes in lawsuits, so I don`t think you`ve got a cat in hell`s chance.`

`Well I shan`t give up trying. I`m not prepared to go home without some arrangement in place.`

`Good for you. Look, if it doesn`t work out, come and see me. I can`t help you personally, but I may know some people who might.`

CHAPTER TWELVE

Alice and I walked along Broome Street to the junction with Lower Broadway. She was sixteen, slim, and I thought a little naïve for her age. That is until she said, `we take the streetcar from here, Sam. Stay with me when I walk out into the road.`

A few minutes later an omnibus without horses appeared. It made a curious high-pitched whining noise as it clanked to a standstill.

`Come on! We board it at this door.`

It droned into motion, rocking on narrow wheels as it ran along rails recessed into the cobbles.

`It works by electricity, Sam.`

`We`ve got a similar system at home, an electric railway. It operates along the seafront at Brighton, where I live. But I`ve never seen one on the roadway before.`

We alighted just before Union Square.

Alice grabbed my arm and pulled me back as a cart lumbered by. We eventually made it to the pavement without further upset.

`Looking at the numbers, Sam, eight four one must be up there, on the left. I`ll leave you now, I`m off to work. Hope all goes well.`

With that she skipped across the road and jumped on a streetcar going south.

I walked on towards Union Square, crossed the road, and there was the entrance to the building sandwiched between a restaurant and an optician. Pushing through the glass doors, I checked the board and found the company I wanted was on the third floor. Mounting the wide staircase I climbed the six flights and came to a frosted-glass panel set in a heavy mahogany door. Painted in large black letters on the panel was American Mutoscope and Biograph Company Incorporated.

I knocked, turned the handle, and walked in.

I was in a reception area. In front of me was an unoccupied desk on which stood a diary and a telephone, which started ringing. A blond young woman came through another door, glanced at me and picked up the telephone.

`AMBC, Can I help you? Hello, Mr Drew...he is busy right now in the studio. Can I ask him to telephone you later, when he`s free?`

She replaced the receiver on its cradle.

`Good morning, can I help you?`

`My name is Lockhart, Sam Lockhart of GAS Films in England. I have an appointment with Mr William Dickson.`

Her eyebrows lifted a fraction. `I`m afraid he`s in Fort Lee today, Mr Lockhart.`

She opened the diary.

`He wasn`t sure when you`d be coming, Monday or Tuesday. The Fort Lee visit was urgent, he had to organise some exterior scenes. So, if it`s all right with you, can you make it tomorrow at the same time?`

I sat at the table drinking coffee with Eszter. Everyone was out; including Peter, Steven and Thomas, who were looking for employment.

`So now I know where it is, I can make my own way there tomorrow. Actually, it`s not that far. I walked back along Fourth Avenue, past Cooper`s Square and down the Bowery, which seemed to be full of German beer gardens and theatres.`

`Do you want me to wash that shirt for you?`

`No, that`s OK, Eszter. If I take it off now it will be fine for tomorrow.`

I went next door to the other apartment, and changed both my suit and shirt, donning more casual clothes.

When I rejoined Eszter, someone else was there.

`Hello, Sam. I thought I`d call in to see how you got on with Biograph.`

It was Carl Laemmle.

`I was telling Carl, Sam, your appointment has been put back until tomorrow,` said Eszter.

`Yes. Understandable in a way. It was made for either today or tomorrow. Travelling such distances, it`s hard to be precise on the timing.`

`Especially, when you`re crossing an ocean,` added Eszter.

The three of us sat at the table.

`I`ve been thinking since our chat yesterday, Sam,` Carl remarked. `I`ve seen several of your films...they`re good. They deserve to be shown in film parlours over here. If it doesn`t work out with Biograph, I might be able to help.`

`Really? How?`

`As I mentioned, my distribution company is not yet up and running. But I know of an organisation that just might be in a position to help you. But there`s a snag.`

`What`s that?`

`It`s based in Chicago...a thousand miles away.`

`Sorry I missed you yesterday, Mr Lockhart. I didn`t know which day you might be coming, and so I made the decision to go to Fort Lee.`

`I understand, Mr Dickson.`

We were standing on the roof of the Hackett-Carhart Building on the leeward side of a large chimney stack. The wind was tugging at my jacket and the principal of The American Mutoscope and Biograph Company was also feeling the effects of the chilling breeze.

`I don`t think we are going to get much done up here today. Even in the screened area the actors won`t be too happy working in this weather. Let`s go downstairs to my office.`

As we made our way to the rooftop door, I said. `Am I right in thinking you do close-up work here, and long shots and out-door scenes in New Jersey?`

I had found out from Laemmle that Fort Lee was fast becoming the centre of the American film industry, with a good many companies having offices in Manhattan.

`We produce quite a few of our movies here on this roof,` explained Dickson. `It saves having to travel upriver. But eventually, I suppose, we shall have to relocate all our production facilities there.`

In his office the young woman I had seen the previous day offered us coffee. As soon as she had served us, Dickson started the ball rolling.

`No doubt you are wondering why we may not be able to continue distributing GAS films. No final decision has been taken yet, but I would say, Mr Lockhart, that our association is likely to come to an end. Perhaps, only for a short while, how long is uncertain. It probably needs a fuller explanation than the letter I sent to your agent, Charles Urban. The point is we are under enormous pressure from the Edison Company to pay royalties on their patent for thirty five millimetre film stock. Now, I know the patent doesn`t extend to Britain, and you can take advantage of the situation. But Edison has the court`s ear, and is seeking payments on imported stock. We, at Biograph, are going to fight it. But I need to make our case as strong as possible, to sway the court in our favour. So, if we stop importing motion pictures on thirty five mill, and we can demonstrate it unnecessarily penalises moviegoers because domestic film maker cannot meet the demand, we might win the day.`

I nodded, not in agreement, but more in understanding the explanation.

`Tell me, Mr Dickson, just how far does Edison take possible infringement of this patent? I mean, does he sue companies throughout the United States? If he does, he must be busier attending legal tribunals than patenting new inventions.`

Dickson stroked his chin. `No...I don`t suppose he does. But then there aren`t many film producers in other parts of the country. The majority are here, on the east coast. At least the ones that matter.`

`Well, I`m not going to take up any more of your time, Mr Dickson. When I leave this office, do I presume that the understanding we have no longer applies, and that I am free to seek another distributor? Because, sir, there are companies out there ready to do business with us, even if you are not.`

`Well, that`s for you to judge, Mr Lockhart. Do you wait to see if we can win the court case against us, and we continue to do business, or do you take it elsewhere?` He looked at me shrewdly. `Personally, I don`t think you will find anyone willing to take you on at the moment. As I said, they are all waiting to see which way things will go.`

He was pushing the decision in my direction.

`Tell me, Mr Dickson, when is the hearing scheduled?`

`Perhaps in nine to twelve months time, I honestly can`t say. Though, I can`t imagine there would be a final decision in under a year.`

`I can`t wait that long, Mr Dickson. So if you are expecting me to make a decision, I`ll do it.`

I stood up. `Thank you for your time and for explaining your problems.

No hard feelings, but the agreement between our two companies is now cancelled. I'll confirm that in writing when I return to England.`

CHAPTER THIRTEEN

We took the ferry from the terminal at the foot of Barclay Street across the North River to Jersey City. That was as close as the trains could get to New York City.

It had been an interesting few days.

I had finished and posted the letter to George Smith. It told of my visit to the American Mutoscope and Biograph Company, and that it had been in both our interests to terminate the current agreement. I was now seeking a fresh distributor, and would contact him as soon as I had more information. I did not mention that there were few other companies prepared to take us on, and that I was en route to Chicago in the hope of encouraging someone else to act on our behalf.

When I returned to the apartment in Eldridge Street, Eszter had quickly seen through my flimsy air of unconcern. After taking a few minutes to give her the briefest of explanations, I had disappeared into the room I shared with Peter.

I lay on the bed not knowing which way to turn. We badly needed an outlet in America, and I had been unable to hang on to the one we had. I wondered if Charles Urban had known all along, and had encouraged George to let me walk into it, presuming I would return with my tail between my legs.

I felt quite low; and the thought of meeting everyone later, and being asked how the meeting had gone, made the situation worse. There would be sympathy, and overflowing commiseration. The others would try to diminish my setback, attempt to make light of it, to cheer me up. But in my mind I had failed.

I turned over and faced the wall and shut my eyes to block out recurring images of a confrontation with George at St Ann`s Well. I must have fallen asleep: with a start I awoke to tapping on the door.

`Sam...Sam, are you in there?`

It was Eszter. How long had I slept? It was dark outside.

`Yes...I won`t be a minute.`

Scrambling off the bed, I brushed my hair and smoothed down the suit I was still wearing. I went across the hall. In the kitchen Eszter had poured three cups of tea. For her and me, and for a visitor, Carl Laemmle.

`Sit down, Sam, Carl wants to have a word with you.`

I eased onto a chair.

`Am I right in thinking, Sam, that your meeting with Biograph this morning did not go as you had hoped?` he enquired.

I glanced at Eszter.

`How did you get him to come here? Or was he just passing and called in?`

I heard the acerbic tone in my voice.

`Don`t take on so, Sam,` exclaimed Laemmle. `Eszter sent me a message because she was worried for you.`

Suddenly, I felt contrite. This was what belonging meant: looking out for each other. I had never experienced this with my own family. Being an only child, I had kept my own counsel, my personal secrets, my own disappointments. I had never learned to share life`s ups-and-downs.

I put out my hand, covered hers, and squeezed it in apology.

`Biograph wants to discontinue the distribution agreement until their court case with Edison is resolved. I told William Dickson I couldn`t agree to that, and if he didn`t carry on as we are now, I`d tear up the contract.`

`And?`

`He said he couldn`t, so I said that`s it...you are no longer our distributor.`

`A big decision, my boy. What are you going to do about it?`

`Hopefully, find another company.`

He nodded. `You won`t find anyone on the east coast who`ll take you on.`

`I now realise that.`

`So...let me see if I can help. Do you remember I mentioned a company the other day which might agree to distributing your films?`

`Yes...you said they were in Chicago.`

`Right, so do you want to come to Chicago with me?`

We boarded the `Pennsylvania Special`, and occupied two Pullman seats. When at the booking office I had asked for a third class ticket. Carl had pushed me firmly to one side, countermanded my request, and bought two first class return tickets. I was concerned. I did not have a great deal of money with me, how was I going to repay him?

`We don`t travel for twenty hours in the third class section. I did it once... never again. And don`t worry, pay me when you can. I have a feeling you`ll be able to in the near future.`

I stared intently out the window at the passing countryside as we steamed southwards. I am not a good traveller, not being able to sit in one place too long, After an hour or so, I said to Carl. ` I`m just going for a stroll.`

I had thought just up and down the carriage, but surprisingly, I opened a door at the end, through another door, and entered the next carriage. I walked the length of the train, and felt the better for it.

`Did you know you can walk right through the train.`

Carl nodded, and grinned.

After covering a hundred miles, just before the train pulled into Philadelphia, Carl said. `Let`s go and have something to eat.`

We went the opposite way to my tour of the train and found ourselves in a restaurant car.

`Do they serve meals on trains?` I murmured.

`They do now. Not so many years ago, trains would stop at railside restaurants. But they do it on the move these days.`

We were shown to a table, and I studied the menu. Another surprise, their offering was a substantial cut above the fare on the rail services at home. Over lunch I encouraged Carl to talk about his involvement in the moving picture business.

`Well, as you`ve gathered, I`m an immigrant too. My roots are in Germany. I followed my brother, Joseph, to America when I was seventeen. I wasn`t forced to come, not like many braving the sea journey and the anxieties of Ellis Island today. At first I worked in the clothing trade in a town called Oshkosh, in the state of Wisconsin, two hundred miles north of Chicago. In fact, that`s where I met my wife.`

He called the waiter for some water.

`I couldn`t see myself working there forever. I had saved a few thousand dollars, enough to buy my own outlet in Chicago. But on one occasion, when I happened to be in the city looking for property, I came across a nickleodean.`

He saw the puzzled look on my face.

`Do you know what a nickleodean is, Sam?`

I shook my head.

`When moving pictures changed from being a novelty to a form of mass entertainment, Kinetoscope parlours, lecture halls, even stores, took to moving pictures and became somewhere you could go for a cheap evening out. The admission charge was usually a nickel...five cents. Hence the name `nickelodeon`. They usually remain open from early morning to midnight, and people often sit there and watch repeats of the programmes. I was hooked. Instead of buying a shop, I bought a nickelodean. In fact, I bought two.`

He grinned, and resumed eating.

`Where do you buy your films?`

`From many sources, Sam. When you have two picture houses you`ve got to keep them supplied. However, to do that effectively, I now realise I`ve got to start making and distributing my own films. I`m at that point now. I`ve opened an office in New York, and I`m about to invest in a studio in Fort Lee. I need production facilities before buying more nickelodeans.`

By the time we got back to our seats I had discovered much about this dapper, diminutive, Jewish gentleman. I suppose common with all immigrants is the desire to make good. To provide their loved ones with a far, far better life than they would have had in their mother country. In the process, many would become ruthless in their pursuit of riches. Not Carl Laemmle. I got the strong impression he was a hard-headed but fair business man; and more, one who cared deeply for the welfare of family and friends.

`Tell me, Carl, is your name spelt L.E.M.L.E.E?`

No, it`s L.A.E.M.M.L.E, an old Bavarian name. I come from Laupheim in southern Germany. What about you? I know you live in a town in England called Brighton, and that you work for George Smith. Anything else? For instance, how old are you? Have you always been in this business?`

I spent the next hour telling him how I had left school at twelve, and worked for ten years as a gardener. I then recounted the tale of being filmed in the gardens, and the changes in my life stemming from the `Handy Hints for Gardeners` series.

`I`ve seen some of those. So you wrote and performed in them. I thought your face looked familiar.`

`Actually, I was never a very good actor. Laura Bayley, George Smith`s wife, proved that to me. So I moved on to looking after sales, and camera and projector development.`

Carl was a good listener.

I got on to the subject of patent infringement, and it was not long before telling him of the situation I had faced in Yorkshire, and how I had resolved it.

`Hmm...I could use someone like you, Sam,` he mused.

`So, the company we are going to see is called what?` I enquired.

`Not us, Sam...you. I`m not doing business with them, though GAS Films might. The company is The Kleine Optical Company, and you have an appointment with the owner, George Kleine, on Friday morning.`

And so the rest of the day passed. Carl dozed, I went on periodic walkabouts. We adjourned, once more, to the dining car for an evening meal. It was while we were dining that the train came to a halt at a station called Altoona.

`Why have we stopped here, I wonder?`

Carl looked out the window, and said. `The trains going west stop here for additional engine power. Two engines are attached to push us up and round Horse Shoe Curve. It`s a steep slope, and our single engine wouldn`t make the gradient.`

There was a shuddering thump as the buffers withstood the shock of their arrival. Minutes later the train jerked forward. We were on the move again.

In the dusk of evening the train wound round the hillside. I could see both the front and the two rear steam engines. As we laboured up the steep, curving incline, smoke belched from the stacks, footplates were aglow in bright, orange light as the firemen relentlessly heaved coal into the roaring fireboxes.

Back in our seats we were provided with blankets; and several hours later we came to a hissing standstill in Pittsburgh. I could hear the faint sounds of the locomotive being fed coal and water. As I drowsily fell asleep, the Pennsylvania Special thundered through the night heading for Cleveland and Chicago,

CHAPTER FOURTEEN

The train pulled into Chicago's Union Station at ten the next morning.

'We're going to check into the rest house I normally use, then we'll discuss tactics over lunch,' announced Carl, as we walked across the concourse.

Outside he waved down a horse-drawn cab, and said to the driver. 'Three, one, one, one, South Aberdeen Street.'

'Right...it's the monastery you want, is it?'

'Monastery?' I queried. 'I thought you said we were going to a rest house?'

'We are. You'll see,' grinned Carl.

Fifteen minutes later the cab drew into the kerb and we alighted in front of a genuine monastery. Carl knocked at the door, and a few minutes later it was opened by a Benedictine monk.

'Carl, my friend, come in...come in!'

He shuffled to one side and we entered a wide, tiled area with stairs leading to floors above. I sniffed. There was a pervading smell of floor wax, incense and cinnamon.

The brother looked at me keenly. 'You can smell it, can't you? Brother Brendan always bakes cinnamon rolls on a Thursday.'

He turned to Carl. 'Your rooms are ready, We had a telephone call to say you were on your way.'

The cleric picked up Carl's small case and led the way up the stairs. I followed disbelievingly. How could an out-and-out Jew, who spent every Saturday praying in the synagogue, persuade a Catholic institution, The Brothers of The Holy Cross, to give him food and shelter?

I was shown into a modestly furnished room and sat on the bed shaking my head in disbelief. What was an ex-gardener, cum film salesman, doing in a religious house in middle America?

There was a tap on the door, and Carl came in.

`No one will believe me,` I said slowly, `when I tell them that an Ashkenazic Jew has just persuaded a deeply religious, Benedictine monk to give us bed and breakfast. How on earth is this happening?`

`A few years ago I met one of the brothers in the local market. During the course of our conversation he mentioned times were hard for them. I came along and began advising them on a number of money-making schemes. Their kitchens now have regular orders for the bread, rolls and pastries; and at the moment I am setting out a plan for them to take in travellers and tourists, providing overnight accommodation and breakfast. As their helpmate, they allow me to stay here whenever I`m in Chicago.`

After lunch in a nearby restaurant, we strolled the banks of the south branch of the Chicago River. It was a pleasant afternoon, and as we walked side-by-side, Carl told me about George Kleine.

`His father was an optician and sold optical equipment as a sideline. George followed him into the business. Seeing the potential in moving pictures, he started selling cameras, projectors and distributing films to outlets in the Midwest. It has grown into quite an organisation. However, at the moment he does not deal in imported movies. So here`s your chance to sell him on the idea.`

He picked up a stick and threw it into the river. Then a stone, which skimmed across the surface.

`How about that! Five bounces!`

I had to have a go; but could only manage four.

Carl continued. `There are not enough films being made for him to expand his business. If you play your cards right, I have a feeling he will jump at the chance.`

The next morning I took a hansom cab to State Street, the headquarters of the Kleine Optical Company. As I entered the main door, a bald, mature fellow sporting a moustache appeared.

`Mr Lockhart?` he enquired.

I removed my hat. `Yes, good morning. I have an appointment to see Mr Kleine.`

`Indeed, you have, sir...indeed you have. Come this way.`

He led me down a wide corridor to an imposing door. He pushed it open and stood to one side to let me pass. As I did so I saw that the room was well furnished, but empty.

`Is Mr Kleine not in the office?`

`He is now, Mr Lockhart.` The fellow took the seat behind a large, imposing desk.

`Would you care for some refreshment?`

`Err...no thank you.`

He nodded, and leaning forward on the desk, said. `Now, how may I help you, sir?`

I cleared my throat.

`I represent a film production company in Great Britain, Mr Kleine, and we send our moving pictures to the United States. Or rather, we did until there was a difference of opinion with our distributor over here.`

`You mean, of course, the American Mutoscope and Biograph Company. I'm well aware of the type of films you produce, Mr Lockhart, I've seen a number of them. I also had a word with William Dickson once I knew you were coming. He told me of the situation both he and your goodself are facing. Biograph wants to drop GAS Films not only to halt the number of court summonses they are receiving, but also to reduce the number of films available to the American public. If there is widespread indignation at being starved of entertainment, this could weigh in Biograph's favour when their court case is heard.`

`Right. As a consequence, I am looking for a distributor who can do a good job from which we would both benefit.`

He nodded, and picking up a silver letter opener, started turning it end-over-end on the blotter before him.

`Do I presume you want my advice on whom you should choose? What company would be of the calibre you are seeking?`

An interesting tactic. I decided to play along.

`Exactly, Mr Kleine. I don't know the type of films people prefer in the Midwest, so your help would be invaluable.`

Kleine smiled thoughtfully.

`Well, first of all Mr Lockhart the folk here in Illinois go for westerns. You know, cowboys and indians, lots of shooting, horse riding and arrows flying.

79

Do you make that kind of thing?`

I too smiled, but ruefully.

`We prefer comedy pictures, Mr Kleine. What we`ve done is analyse people`s reactions to the films we show when they leave the theatre. If they go out with a smile on their faces we have not only entertained them, they are contented with what they`ve seen, and they`ll come back the following week. To us, that`s important...continuity in audiences.

`We vary the comedy style, of course. No two films are ever the same. It`s all too easy to get into a rut, don`t you agree? Giving filmgoers what they think they want all the time, and suddenly they`re bored. The result...they don`t come for a while, and you lose money.`

He changed tack.

`Right now, Chicago is really taking off as a film making centre. I think it will soon overtake Fort Lee in New Jersey as the movie capital. There are any number of companies springing up.` He rubbed his hands. `And Kleine Optical is in just the right place to provide their equipment. I should imagine that will become the mainstay of our business in the future.`

`Which will mean more picture houses in the Midwest exhibiting films. More than enough business for everyone. If, as you say, the output will be mainly westerns, it would be a wise supplier who offered a mix of those and light-hearted comedy films. So if you have some names of up-and-coming distributors, companies that can seize the main chance, I`d be obliged of your help.`

He nodded thoughtfully, walked across the room, opened the door and called a name. A slight young man appeared, and Kleine mumbled something I did not catch. A few moments later he reappeared with a tray on which there was coffee and a sheet of paper.

`I took the liberty, Mr Lockhart of requesting coffee for you. Will you join me?`

`Thank you Mr Kleine, that would be welcome.`

He passed the cup and saucer across the desk.

`Tell me, Mr Lockhart, what would you be offering a distributor? So I can refine the list of names, you understand.`

`GAS Films are about to start producing one reelers, Mr Kleine. Moving pictures that will run for fifteen, twenty minutes. They will still be mainly comedies, but quite a number will be feature films. Portraying a solid story with a good ending. We shall, of course, continue with the one minute, humorous pictures. We find they are much liked by audiences when shown between the more serious motion pictures. In the round, I would say our yearly output will be between forty five and fifty films.`

`And what would your prices be for the various films? Bearing in mind they would have to be shipped half way across America.`

I grinned. `Now that would be a matter for discussion between the company we work with and ourselves. It`s not the sort of information I would openly discuss, Mr Kleine.`

His lips pursed.

`Anything else you`d like to offer your sales agency?`

`I`ve been thinking, Mr Kleine, what I would really want to do is change the way the distribution business operates these days. But again that`s a matter for consideration between the two parties, GAS Films and its new agent.`

I could see he was intrigued by that comment.

`Well, Mr Lockhart, let me pass over the list of distributors who might work with you.`

He pushed the sheet of paper in my direction.

There was only one name on it. "Kleine Optical Company".

`Now let`s get down to it. Tell me your pricing structure, and what is this idea you have about different working methods, Mr Lockhart?`

At dinner with Carl Laemmle that evening, I recounted what had taken place in George Kleine`s office. Carl had spent the day with the managers of his nickelodeans, and attended several other business meetings.

`I told you he is a wily character, Sam. But you obviously matched him. Well done. So what happens now?`

`I had an outline agreement with me, which we both signed, and we are now in business together. When I get back to Brighton I`ll send him the formal contract.`

`So, you`ll be spending more time over here in the future?`

`I hope so, Carl.`

He picked up his wine glass and saluted me, tipping it at an angle in my direction.

`However, I have to acknowledge what really sold him on the arrangement was your concept of the film rental system we talked about on the train ride,` I said deferentially. `That`s a winner, Carl`

`Well, I have been thinking about it and shaping it in my mind for quite some time,` Carl remarked. `It`s the sort of operation I`m going to introduce back east shortly, when the Laemmle Film Service is up and running. So tell me, what did he say when you explained the idea?`

`First of all I told him the scheme I have in mind would ultimately make more income than selling the films to nickelodeans, movie parlours, and other exhibition owners. It`s a simple plan, summed up in one word – rental!

`As the demand by moviegoers increases, there still remains a curb on the frequency of film shows, because exhibitors need to make a good return on the purchase price of a film. Moreover, it`s a big initial outlay for a distributor, say, to buy a hundred copies. But, if he bought half that number and rented them out for a week or a fortnight, when they`re returned he can hire them out again. Over a month, four weekly rentals would probably equate to the purchase price he would have paid; and not only can he keep on renting it out, the film continues to be the property of the distributor. Moreover, if a film is changed every week, patrons will get into the habit of coming to see a movie every week. Everyone wins!

`Kleine had sat there stroking his chin. But I knew he would go for the idea. A few minutes later he said, "OK, let`s do it". I took the draft from my case which proposed the main elements of a working agreement and, as I said, he signed and, thanks to you, we are now business partners.`

That night I finished the letter to George Smith. It was a fulsome account of what had transpired at American Mutoscope and Biograph Company, and a blow-by-blow résumé of setting up in business with the Kleine Optical Company. The following day, Saturday, Carl and I started back for New York.

When we were on the ferry from the train terminal to Manhattan, Carl asked. `When are you intending to return to England?`

`I thought I`d spend a few days in New York, and try for a mid-week passage, why?`

He leaned on the rail and stared at the city skyline.

`I`ve got to go up to Fort Lee tomorrow. Perhaps, you might like to join me. You might be interested in seeing some of the companies working up there.`

`I`d love to, Carl. Thank you, and for all the help you`ve given me let me take you out to dinner this evening.`

`Can we make that lunch tomorrow, do you think? I`d like to spend tonight with the family. Better still, come home with me and taste what an old fashioned, Jewish meal is really like.`

We took an electrobat cab to his apartment on West End Avenue, where I was introduced to Carl`s wife, Recha, and his two children, Rosabelle and Carl Junior. The meal was preceded by a brief prayer - *Blessed are You, Hashem, our God, King of the Universe, by whose word everything comes to be.*

`Now you must eat everything, Sam, You`re too thin for your height,` said Recha, as she filled my plate with a variety of starters. What was excellent was the main course, which I learned was beef brisket in a burgundy–orange sauce. It was outstanding. When I complimented her, Recha smiled and said. `Really, it`s the wine I add. I put in twice what`s recommended in the recipe.`

I staggered out their apartment block just after ten, and managed to halt a passing horse-drawn cab which took me across town to Eldridge Street. It had been an eventful five days.

CHAPTER FIFTEEN

I met Carl at the ferry terminal.

`We`ll take the boat up the North River to Edgewater. It`s about a thirty minute run.`

It was a sunny morning, and standing on deck as the ferry steamed between the Manhattan and New Jersey shores was an invigorating start to the day.

`Carl, I thought this was the Hudson River. Why does everyone call it as the North River?`

`One of those things. Yes it is the Hudson, but New Yorkers have always referred to the southern stretch as the North River. It reverts to the Hudson River northwards of the Palisades. He was one of yours, Sam. An Englishman working for the Dutch East India Company when he sailed up here in the early seventeenth century.`

From the Edgewater quay we took a horse-drawn cab the mile and a half to Fort Lee. As the carriage jogged along, Carl said. `We could have come by railroad, on the West Shore Line, but it`s not so bracing as the ferry boat, and we would still have had to cross the river.`

I was intrigued. The main street in Fort Lee was not unlike Western Road in Brighton. There were the usual food and hardware stores, but also a number providing photographic equipment, processing facilities and film copying. A hint of nostalgia briefly welled up.

We drew to a halt outside a tavern. I paid the driver, and we went in to slake out thirst before Carl set forth to look at possible sites for what he called, "his movie studio".

As we entered the tavern I sensed him stiffen. Sitting at a nearby table were four men. One caught my eye. A mature gentleman in his mid-fifties, with piercing eyes and a shock of reddish-coloured hair turning white. As we approached the bar, he stood up and came towards us. He was as tall as I was.

`Mr Laemmle,` he opened in a quiet voice, `I have heard word you are thinking of making films up here. You are aware, sir, that using any of my equipment means you would have to pay a licence fee ...that`s if I granted it in the first place.`

`I`m glad I`ve seen you Mr Edison,` Carl declared, looking up at the man. `I can tell you now, to your face, I shall do no such thing. I cannot believe you can force anyone to pay you for using cameras, projectors and thirty five millimetre film stock which are now commonplace.`

Thomas Edison towered over him assuming a threatening attitude. His voice was low, and carried only to the two of us.

`You will pay, Laemmle...you will pay,` he hissed.

Although almost a foot shorter, Carl pushed him aside and headed for the bar.

`That sounded like a serious threat, Carl,` I said looking back at the table where Edison had resumed his seat.

`I`m sure it is, Sam. Though, let`s see if he can enforce it when I begin making my films.`

`Do you know Mr Edison, sir?` asked the barman as he pulled our beers. `What a great man, bringing us moving pictures an` all.`

`Let`s say our paths have crossed, young man,` replied Carl with a cynical smile.

Undaunted the barman continued. `He says he`s gonna make a film using the palisades in the near future. I guess he`s over here from his studio in West Orange to check it out.`

We took our drinks to a distant table, away from the Edison group.

`Do you want to tell me what that was all about, Carl? That overbearing character was actually trying to intimidate you.`

`Sam, it`s all about trying to ensure he has the monopoly on the film business. I`ll give him that he has done some great things. You can`t take that away from him. But to progress, to meet the voracious appetite of the public for moving pictures, you`ve got to allow a little leeway on some of the patents he has filed. Frankly, many are outdated, but he still demands his pound of flesh. There are new ideas coming from film makers all the time. But he is holding on to the basic principles by which all films are shot with the camera, and projected onto a screen. He holds most of the patents that apply to moving picture production, and he won`t ease any of his restrictions. If you want to make a movie, you have to obtain Edison`s permission and pay a handsome fee. Well, enough, I say. I shall go elsewhere for my equipment and use thirty five millimetre film stock with four perforations each frame.`

`Is Edison`s studio in New Jersey?`.

`Hmm, about twenty miles west of here. He set it up years ago to produce short film sequences for his Kinetoscope. Have you seen these contraptions?`

`Yes, we`ve got several Kinetoscope parlours in Brighton. I think they`re a passing phase: turning a handle and watching a short film through eye slots can`t last. People, nowadays, want to sit in a seat and watch a moving picture on a big screen.`

`You`re right, and I believe Edison knows it too.`

Just then there was a scrapping of chairs and the Edison party started towards the door. Once again, the tall man gave Carl a thunderous look.

We toured the town, stopping to watch someone direct the shooting of several outside scenes while hordes of noisy onlookers took in the action. I thought, it is a good thing there`s no sound, it would be the devil of a job to keep any spectators quiet.

`It`s quite a dynamic spot, don`t you think, Sam?` remarked Carl. Seemingly intoxicated by the general air of purpose Fort Lee was generating.

`I can`t wait to get started. I reckon we could produce my film on those bluffs overlooking the town.`

`You already know what you`re going to make first?`

`It`s already planned, my boy. At least, in my mind. It`s the story of *Hiawatha*, Longfellow`s poem.`

Carl took special notice of the open fields on the side roads off Main Street as we strolled back to the tavern. Taking a table Carl called over the young barman.

`What`s your name, son?`

`Clive, sir.`

`OK, Clive two more beers. And while you at it can you tell me who might own those plots of land near John Street?`

`By the smithy?`

`That`s right.`

`They could belong to either Mr Bailey or Mr Steinmetz. They both have stores here on Main Street.`

When Carl paid for the beers, there was an extra coin for the barman.

Later, we walked over to the two stores. Steinmetz was away on business, and Bailey was also absent, but would be back later in the day.

`Do you mind, Sam, if we wait until he returns? I would like to make him an offer. I can just see my studio there now with the banner, "Independent Moving Pictures Company".

He grinned. `It has a nice ring to it, don`t you think?`

Mr Bailey did not return until well after seven o`clock. We had wandered Main Street and the adjacent Lemoine Avenue leading into Coytesville, but kept coming back to the plot Carl thought would be ideal for his studio.

`I hear you have been waiting to see me, gentlemen,` boomed the voice of the generously proportioned Mr Bailey. `If it`s a private matter, perhaps we should use my office.`

We followed him through a door to the rear of the shop.

`Take a seat, please. Now tell me, how can I help you?`

Carl smiled. `I wish to propose something to you.`

It was dark by the time they had come to an agreement. When concluded, Carl Laemmle was now the owner of a tract of land for his new film studio.

`Well, sir, it`s been a pleasure doing business with you. Are you now returning to New York City? If you are you`ll have to hurry to catch the last ferry If you wish, I`ll run you down to the terminal in my buggy?`

As he was locking up, Mr Bailey said over his shoulder. `The stable is just round the back.`

We followed him up a passageway between the buildings.

The first I was aware of anyone was when a fist slammed into my cheekbone. It was quickly followed by a rain of blows to my head and body. I pitched forward to the ground. Slowly losing consciousness, I dimly perceived Carl being thrown down and kicked unmercifully by heavy boots, until someone called. `That`s enough, Luke`.

CHAPTER SIXTEEN

I awoke with a start.

I was lying in a bed. But whose bed? I went to pull back the bedclothes, and a searing pain knived through my chest. I fell back gasping.

I lay there for a few minutes staring at the ceiling. The memories of the beating came back to me with a rush.

`Are you awake?` came a muffled voice.

I eased my head sideways to see Carl lying on a nearby bed. His distorted words had been uttered through puffed lips. I looked closer. One eye was closed, there was a large gash on his forehead, and one side of his face was swollen.

He saw my bewilderment

`You don`t look so good either,` he mumbled.

`What happened?` I croaked. `I must have passed out.`

`Apparently, three ruffians jumped us. Not Mr Bailey, just you and me. He thinks it was an attempted robbery. More likely Edison`s heavies teaching me a lesson. They thought we were together, so you got a share of the beating.`

`I`ve got pains in my chest,` I wheezed. `Something`s not right.`

`Bailey called a doctor, who thinks you have a couple of broken ribs from being kicked. Same as me.`

`Where are we, do you know?`

`Bailey has put us in one of his spare bedrooms,` replied Carl. `We were unconscious, so he had to get help to carry us here. We`ve been in this room all night.`

The next morning, after checking us over, the local doctor declared there was nothing more he could do. We would be uncomfortable for a couple of weeks. Other than strapping up our chests, with the admonition that we should try not to exert ourselves, nature should be allowed to take its course.

We climbed gingerly into the buggy and Mr Bailey drove us to the ferry terminal.

On board, as we eased ourselves onto an unforgiving bench, I could not discern if the stares of the other passengers were of sympathy, or they were labelling us as roustabouts who had got a taste of their own medicine.

Eszter was concerned. She fussed over me, and not only ensured I did little, but when Carl called by, gave him a very vocal piece of her mind. He was both amused and contrite.

`You have a champion fighting your cause, Sam.`

I was a little embarrassed. `She`s been very kind to me, Carl.`

`I can see that. Anyway other than painful ribs and an array of bruises, are you all right?`

`Yes, what about you?`

`Much the same, I guess. So, have you fixed the date of your return to England?`

`Eszter has done that for me. I gave her the money and she reserved me a third class cabin on the *Carmania* this coming Friday.`

At first we shook hands. But he was more demonstrative than I, for he clasped me to him and patted me on the back.

`Listen, Sam, I mean it. If you ever want a job in the American movie business, come and see me.`

Eszter and Peter came down to the dock to see me off. I had said goodbye to all the others the previous evening. It was surprising the bond of affection that had grown between us in a just a few short weeks. Eszter had tears in her eyes...and so did I. She kissed me, and Peter did as well. I wasn`t used to being kissed by another man, but seemingly they do it from where he comes from.

`When you come back, come straight to see me, do you understand?` declared Eszter forthrightly.

One last wave, then I was lost to them in the milling crowd boarding the ship.

I dropped my case in the cabin, and went back up on deck. I moved slowly and carefully. No one could see the strapping around my body, but there was no mistaking from the bruising on my face that I had been in some sort of incident. I stood there a long time, watching the Manhattan skyline slowly dwindle, wondering if I would ever see it again.

CHAPTER SEVENTEEN

I had been away almost five weeks, but it seemed an age.

Mrs Earl greeted me warmly, but I could not help comparing her with Eszter. Like me, she suffered from ingrained British reserve. We find it hard to display our emotions. Whereas, Eszter, and the others I had met in and around Eldridge Street, made no secret of their feelings.

I sat at the dining table and looked at the empty seat opposite. It had been a bad mistake confiding in Mr Gunn. Only by good fortune had he been exposed. I would never make that error of judgement again.

`Here we are, Mr Lockhart, your favourite soup, oxtail.`

I had never mentioned in all the time I had been her lodger that I detested oxtail soup. Perhaps, I should have exhibited some Lower East Side candour. Still, the sleeping arrangements were more to my liking. All the while I had been in America, there had been people sleeping alongside me.

After a long day travelling by train from Liverpool to Brighton, tiredness suddenly engulfed me. I thanked Mrs Earl for the meal, and made my way stiffly up to my room.

`Well, the traveller returns!`

Geoffrey Summer greeted me with a smile, and a warm handshake.

`Coffee, Sam?`

`Please. So, Geoffrey, anything happen while I`ve been away?`

`Quite a lot, Sam...quite a lot. Our friend Urban`s been busy. He finally moved from Warwick and set up on his own. He is now the Charles Urban Trading Company. He has also taken on a fellow called George Rogers, who speaks French, German and Russian. With him on board, he aims to expand our pan-European sales.`

`What about George? Is he happy with the new arrangement?`

`Haven`t seen a lot of him lately. Charles seems to be monopolising him, proposing this or that scheme to occupy his mind.`

`How do you mean?`

`Well, we haven`t produced a film for the past three weeks.`

That was worrying. We needed to maintain output to ensure our survival. If George were not producing at least one a fortnight we could be in trouble.

`Do you know where he is?`

`I believe he is working at the house in Southwick he had built recently.`

`Do you know the address?`

He saw the concern on my face.

`Sam, I think it`s in Roman Crescent. But I don`t know the number.`

I hailed a passing hansom by the main gate, and we drove westwards at a good pace. No more than three miles from St Ann`s Well Gardens, George had built a house on a good size plot in Southwick village. He had frequently told me of the builder`s progress, and it`s design of a balcony to the front, with the whole topped off by a tower which allowed a three hundred and sixty degree view of the sea and surrounding countryside. I should not have much trouble locating it.

A hansom cab was pulling away from what was obviously George`s new dwelling when I arrived, and he was still standing at the door.

`Sam! What a pleasant surprise! I got your letter...well done. So we`ve got a new distributor. Come in...come in.`

We moved into a spacious hall, and he directed me to a room clearly used as a study.

`You`ve just missed Charles...Charles Urban. He stayed overnight. We had things to discuss.`

At that moment Laura, George`s wife, put her head round the door. Saw me and came up to kiss my cheek. I winced as she came close and nudged my chest.

`Sam, how nice to see you. Did you have a good trip? Though, on closer inspection you look as though you`ve been in the wars. Did something happen?`

I gave them an abridged version of all that had taken place. When I mentioned the visit to Fort Lee with Carl Laemmle, and the beating we had suffered Laura was most perturbed.

`I always thought America was full of ruffians, and that confirms it. What a horrible place.`

I grinned.

`Laura, the people are really quite friendly, hard-working and very, very helpful. It was only that one incident that marred the trip. And the effects of the attack will soon wear off.`

She sniffed. `Well, I have my own thoughts about them.`

George said. `I`m glad you`ve come, Sam. I`ve got a surprise for you.`

I glanced across at Laura, and saw her face darken in irritation.

`Come with me. I want to show you something.`

We went along a passage to an outside door which led to the rear garden. He threw it open, stepped to one side, and said proudly.

`Look at that!`

A brick building was under construction. The walls were in place, and half the roof had been tiled.

`What`s that? Stabling and a carriage store?`

He stared at me intently. `No, my young friend, it a laboratory. When completed, I shall use it to produce films in glorious colour. What about that?`

I stood there dumbfounded. Laura came up behind us.

`Another one of Urban`s ideas. And George has fallen for it, hook, line and sinker.`

He turned to his wife. `I haven`t put any money into the project, have I?` When it`s a success, we`ll reap the rewards.`

`Listen to him, Sam. If it`s any way half successful, it won`t be you, my darling, who will gain anything. You can bet your life Charles Urban will cream any reward. that`s going!`

`Well, he`s paid for building the laboratory.`

`Did you read what you signed? I`ll bet you didn`t. You`re too trusting.`

I listened to the exchanges with a great deal of foreboding.

`If you are going to  spend time developing a colour system, George, what about our film production company? You can`t do everything.`

Laura retorted. `That`s exactly what I told him, Sam. Do you know what he said? "You and Sam can run it just as well as me". With due respect, Sam,` she looked in my direction, `I don`t think either of us are up to it.`

`But it would only be for a few months, six at the outside,` George declared. `We`ve already got hold of the process from Edward Turner and

Frederick Lee. Charles has acquired their patent. It needs modification, but I`m sure I can make it work.`

Laura walked away.

`How does it work, George?` I asked.

Excitement came into his voice.

`The Lee and Turner system works on the additive principle, employing a rotating wheel with red, green and blue sectors positioned on a camera, and a three-lens projector with similar rotating filter wheel. It`s complex, but I can simplify it and get it to work.`

`So it doesn`t work at the moment?`

`Well, no. They were unable to turn their system into reality, they didn`t have the finances. They turned to Charles Urban, who, instead of investing in their project, bought the idea and hardware from them. At the moment, it requires a projection speed of forty-eight frames per second, combined with precise registration of three separate images from lenses positioned in parallel. So far, the result has been an unwatchable blur.`

`And you`re going to change all that?`

`Absolutely.`

Just before I left I had a discreet word with Laura.

She arrived when I was in conversation with our cameraman.

`I think Geoffrey ought to stay, Laura. We are all in this together.`

She nodded and pulled up a chair.

`The crucial point to consider is this,` I said, scanning their faces. `Are we three able to provide good commercial moving pictures without George?`

`What are you saying, Sam?` queried Geoffrey. `Is George no longer involved? Is he ill or something?`

`Worse, Geoffrey,` answered Laura. `He`s been persuaded by Charles bloody Urban, to give time to a project that, if it works, which I doubt, will make Urban money. I`m sure poor George won`t see anything for his efforts.`

`But how can we carry on without him?` asked Geoffrey.

`As I said, that`s the real question. He said he would be no more than six months working on this scheme of Urban`s.`

`What exactly is the idea of it?` Geoffrey questioned.

Laura explained before I could answer him.

`It`s a system whereby the moving pictures we produce will appear in colour.`

`Colour? That`s remarkable.`

`Except, Geoffrey,` declared Laura, `the system doesn`t work. Urban took the project from its two failed inventors. Now he hopes George can perfect what they never could.`

`Oh...`

We agreed that we would meet at the pump house in a week`s time, and each of us would submit three ideas for films. Although I had suggested earlier we consider one reel motion pictures lasting fifteen minutes, for the moment we were forced to restrict ourselves to tried and tested one minute productions.

I wrote to the American Mutoscope And Biograph Company, officially cancelling the distribution agreement; sent the contract to George Kleine in Chicago; and penned notes to Eszter and Carl Laemmle thanking them for their hospitality and kindnesses.

Then I settled down with our accountant to assess where GAS Films stood financially. It was not a heartening résumé. There were funds in the account, but there were also outstanding demands that had yet to be met. I shuffled the bills into two piles: those which had to be paid immediately, and those we could deal with in due course. The company was solvent, just, providing our debtors paid by the allotted time. I was not surprised to learn the Charles Urban Trading Company was a major culprit. There were a number of invoices still unpaid from the last quarter.

With the financial stability of the company much on my mind, it was difficult to come up with any sound, creative ideas. When we met seven days later, I had little to offer: Geoffrey had the outline of an idea. Fortunately, Laura saved the day with three excellent suggestions.

One was a dream of the principal actress, she saw herself in the part, of assuming the role of Aladdin, Bluebeard, Cinderella, and Dick Whittington, and telling of their exploits. She even had a title for the film, *Dorothy's Dream*. Another, which she had also named, *Don't Fool With The Paraffin*, was a mishap with the kitchen stove, which ultimately explodes, and the cook appears as a ghost. The third of her proposals was a remake of *The Sick Kitten*.

`I`ve always like the pathos in that picture,` she explained. `And I think we could make it even more appealing.`

Geoffrey`s submission was that we make an amusing, reality film of Miss Florence, an American music hall artiste, completing a walk from London to Brighton on a globe two feet in diameter. He suggested the title, *The Girl On The Ball.*

My modest contribution was a short picture of two little boys watching an incident, and one being called upon to testify tearfully, but courageously, to what he had seen. The prosaic title I gave to it was, *The Young Witness.*

In fact, we immediately adopted Geoffrey`s suggestion. Although, neither Laura or I could see merit in filming it. Nevertheless, it was a start in the right direction. Geoffrey quickly organised where he would like to position several cameras along the route, and had a Brougham rigged for him to film the walk from its roof.

Although other cinematograph operators were anxious to get a "living picture" of the young woman, no one had thought to film much of her journey.

Geoffrey had been enterprising, and it paid off. On her arrival at the Aquarium in Brighton, gallant police inspector Bridle lifted her off her globe and carried the young lady to our Brougham, whence she was driven to her hotel. More film footage was obtained, and Geoffrey even captured pictures of the seven pairs of boots she had worn out on the fifty mile walk.

It was a remarkable coup. The film was shown in numerous picture parlours and theatres across the country, as well as in the United States – courtesy of The Kleine Optical Company.

CHAPTER EIGHTEEN

Buoyed by our surprising success, Laura, Geoffrey and I set to with a will, planning and setting in motion the rest of the proposals.

After several meetings in the pump room, some weeks later Geoffrey and I went to the house in Southwick. When we arrived a carriage was standing in the driveway. I rang the bell and Laura opened the door.

`Come in. We`ll go elsewhere. George is entertaining Charles Urban in the sitting room.`

We followed her through the garden room which led into an orangery. A maid brought coffee and we sat in rattan chairs among the plants. There was the pleasing sound of flowing water from a shallow, ground-based fountain.

`I have been giving *Dorothy's Dream* a lot of thought, Laura,` I began, glancing at Geoffrey, `and although I said we should concentrate on what we know best, namely one minute films, to give it justice, *Dorothy's Dream*, needs to be much longer. We can do it if we plan each sequence carefully and adhere to a precise shooting schedule.`

She smiled. `Do you know, I`ve been thinking much the same thing. I was going to suggest I play the lead, but I want to be involved in the scene setting, and give some input to the continuity, so would you agree to my sister, Eva, playing the part of Dorothy?`

It was a good suggestion, and I was about to say so, when George and Charles Urban walked into the orangery.

`I was saying to George, that moving picture of the woman walking the ball was a splendid piece of cinematography, up to his best work. But he then told me you three had produced it.`

I did not like his patronising tone.

`As George is preoccupied,` I said staring up at Urban, `someone has to carry on the business.`

`Yes,` he turned to George. `I was going to talk to you about that. As my trading company is GAS Films` sales agent, what gives Sam the right to sell the film?`

Before George could respond, I said. `You were not around. I contacted your office, and they told me you were in Paris. It was a newsworthy item, and we couldn`t wait for you to come back.`

`I was tieing up a deal with a company called Eclipse. Anyway, that`s not the point, is it George? Your employees should have waited for me to return.`

`Excuse me, Charles, as a principal shareholder in GAS Films,` said Laura furiously, `in George`s absence I make the necessary decisions. I certainly don`t have to ask you for permission.`

`If you read the contract, my dear, you will find you do. Not only have I invested money in GAS Films, I am legally entitled to demand observance of the distribution agreement. I overlooked the deal struck with Kleine Optical, but I still want my fee even if you have gone directly to an American service company.`

`Now wait a minute,` I said angrily. `You couldn`t organise anything. You asked George to send me. You effectively renounced your right when you passed back responsibility for securing our own American agent.`

`As I said, read the contract, my friend,` said Urban softly.

Throughout the heated exchanges, George had not uttered a word. Laura turned towards him.

`George, tell this "gentleman" that he may be our sales agent, but that does not give him the right to dictate how we conduct our business`

`Err...he can to some extent, Laura. He can tell us what will be popular and what won`t.`

`Don`t shilly-shally, George,` announced Laura, rising from her chair. `Tell him he can`t. We decide for ourselves!`

Urban looked at George. Then, uncertain of what he might say, declared.

`I do not want to be the one to bring discord into the household. I am leaving. George, I shall call again when tempers have cooled.`

With that Urban moved into the hall, while we processed after him. He picked up his hat and cane, and went out the front door. Climbing into the waiting carriage, he tapped the roof to prompt the driver. As it pulled into the roadway, he nodded stiffly in our direction.

George wandered back to his "laboratory" in the garden.

`I don't know,` said Laura. `I can't get through to him when he has a project he's working on. And this time he is totally absorbed in what he is doing.`

She glanced at Geoffrey and I.

`Right. We shall carry on as we agreed. Ignore Urban. We shall make what we please, and we shall stick to the plan.`

Dorothy's Dream eventually became an eight minute feature film. It was an immediate success. We not only achieved substantial coverage in Britain, the Kleine Optical Company was delighted with the production. What is more, the company pursued the proposal of renting the film to exhibitors, and it was shown widely not only in the Midwest but also on the east coast.

The Charles Urban Trading Company also engineered a worthwhile uptake of *Dorothy's Dream* in Europe. As a consequence, previous outbursts were forgotten, and the working partnership restored. Personally, I found it hard to get on with Urban; but George regarded him highly. For the sake of harmony I accepted the situation. I was civil and cooperative, but deep down I could not dispel my feelings of mistrust.

George became more and more of a recluse. He rarely left the confines of his workshop. Whenever I wanted to discuss business affairs, get him to sign cheques or documents, I had to go to the laboratory, away from the house.

On one occasion when I visited Roman Crescent, Laura drew me aside.

`I'm worried, Sam. He has taken to eating his meals out there now. Stay to lunch, and bring him with you when you come over.`

The few items I had for his attention were quickly dealt with.

`How's the project coming along?` I enquired.

`Do you know, Sam, I'm almost there. What is more, I've made an important discovery.`

He rubbed his hands together with glee.

`Let me explain.`

I had not realised how sceptical I had become. The idea that film makers could actually show a moving picture in colour was too fanciful for words. I genuinely thought the whole project was doomed to failure, and George was wasting precious time. He had a far better appreciation of constructing a film than Laura, Geoffrey or I. He knew instinctively when to create reverse shooting between actors; when to instill emotion; and how to maximise the drama in a scene. *Dorothy's Dream* would have been much improved if he had devised camera positions and done the editing. But no one could deflect him from pursuing *The Dream*. Again I cursed Charles Urban for taking George away from what he did best.

`Until now,` he explained, `I had taken for granted the three colour process created by Turner and Lee was the only approach. But, guess what,` he laughed out loud. `They were wrong. Because I've done it with two. Let me show you.`

We walked over to a side bench on which sat a curious apparatus. It reminded me of the time I visited the pump house and saw my first projector.

`In my system,` said George, `the camera resembles the ordinary cinematographic camera except it runs at twice the speed, at thirty-two images per second instead of sixteen, and it is fitted with a rotating colour filter in addition to the ordinary shutter.

`I'm using panchromatic film, and exposures are made alternately through the red gelatine and the green gelatine. The positive is printed from the negative in the usual way...and that's about it...simple. Do you want to see the result?`

`Panchromatic film, you say? How do you make the film sensitive to red as well as blue and green?`

He grinned.

`I dip ordinary negative film in a bath of sensitising dye.`

He had obviously installed electricity in the laboratory, for he went through an elaborate performance of igniting carbon rods and spinning the electric motors that turned the fans.

`I have had to revise the gearing when cranking the handle to increase the shutter speed. OK, now pull down that blind, Sam?`

The apparatus rumbled into motion, and after a brief grainy film beginning, suddenly coloured images appeared on the screen. I was enthralled. The film ran for less than thirty seconds, but it was enough to witness what he had achieved.

`That is remarkable, George.`

`There is still some way to go, Sam. I want to remove the halo effect caused by colour distortion around the images, and I'm still getting some flicker. But, in principle, it works I think,` he added modestly.

`Has Laura seen this?` I asked.

`No, she thinks I am a loony and a crackpot.`

`Well, if you can iron out the wrinkles, you`re on to a winner. The only drawback I can see is the investment exhibitors would face in buying new projectors. Would they be expensive?`

`Charles is working that one out. I have no idea.`

`I see. Let`s talk over its future as you see it over lunch.`

He allowed himself to be drawn into the dining room for the meal.

George said little at the table. At soon as he had finished he scuttled back to his laboratory. After lunch Laura and I reviewed our schedule for the forthcoming picture, *Don't Fool With The Paraffin*.

`I think you should take the lead, Laura. It calls for a more dramatic portrayal than Eva could give to the part. I`ve had a word with the technical people, and we shall have no problems with the superimposition to suggest ghosts. Geoffrey is OK with the mix of wide, establishing shots and medium close-ups.`

`Well, if you believe I should take the lead, I`ll speak to Eva. She won`t mind. So when do we start?`

`Wednesday. They`ll have finished the scenery by then.`

I left after confirming we would meet at the pump house in two days time.

CHAPTER NINETEEN

We were in the second week of filming, and about to complete the last few scenes when Charles Urban came into the pump house. He stood well back from the camera and lights as Laura`s ghost goes to her final resting place.

`That`s it everybody,` called Geoffrey. `Everyone here at eight o`clock tomorrow for the close ups.`

I was turning off the arc lights, and Laura, dressed in the diaphanous robes of her ethereal being, was talking to Geoffrey when Urban strode onto the set.

`What`s this epic called then, Laura?` he enquired in his supercilious tone.

She glanced in his direction, and for a moment I thought she was going to say something biting. But she murmured. `*Don't Fool With The Paraffin.*`

`An odd title. Not very catchy. Sounds like a public health warning.`

She turned to him, and I walked quickly in their direction.

`So what would the great impresario suggest?` she sneered.

He was quiet for a moment. `What about, *Mary Jane's Mishap?*`

`Actually, I quite like that,` I said as I neared them. `It is more descriptive and at the same time, more appealing to moviegoers.`

Laura stared at me quizzically. The obvious thought in her mind, had he gone over to the enemy?

`Any time, Sam...any time.`

`So what brings you here Charles?` I enquired.

`Just checking on my investment, you might say. After all, as your sales agent, I like to keep abreast of what`s going on, what I shall be selling.`

`Actually, you`ve saved me a telephone call. I wanted to have a word with you.`

`Oh, what about?`

`You are our agent, you represent our interests, right?`

He nodded. His eyes narrowing as he wondered where this was leading.

`According to the small print in the contract we have signed, we can use no other agency, unless you default on service?`

`You know that to be true,` Urban said. `That's why you appointed Kleine Optical. Mind you, I still get a cut of their margin.`

`So why doesn't it work both ways?` I said innocently.

`I don't understand.`

`I think you do, Charles. Why is it GAS Films cannot appoint another company to represent its production, yet the Charles Urban Trading Company can work for another film maker?`

`What are you saying, Sam?` asked Laura.

`Ask him why he is now selling Williamson's films as well as ours. Ask him where his real allegiance lies? It's certainly not with us. I'll tell you what I think, shall I?`

I had unconsciously raised my voice, and suddenly all those on the set stopped what they were doing and stared in our direction.

`Mr Charles Urban wants to use George for his colour project, but realises if he does, the film making side of the company could wither and die. So he takes on the distribution of James Williamson's productions as a safeguard when GAS Films dries up. Deny it!` I pointed a finger at him. `Go on, deny it.`

Urban's face was a furious red mask. `So what. That doesn't mean I'm not doing a good job for you. Just spreading my interests.`

`What gets me, Urban, is not that you have taken on Williamson, but you did not have the decency to tell us! I call that feathering your nest at someone else's expense.`

He whirled away. `I'm not going to stand here and listen to all this! I'm going to see George. I'll let him know what I think of your slanderous remarks!`

The door slammed behind him.

`OK everybody, the show is over,` called Geoffrey. `Let's get back to work.`

`Who is Williamson, Sam?` asked Laura in a quiet voice.

`James Williamson was our local pharmacist. He branched out selling film materials and processing chemicals. Then he moved premises and started making his own films. He is one of those rare people in this business...an honest gentleman. We know him well. It was he who told me about his arrangement with the Charles Urban Trading Company.`

`Can Urban take on another film maker?`

`I went through the contract to check what George had signed. I`m afraid, Laura, the way it`s worded, our sole agent can do anything he likes.`

Laura, Geoffrey and I spent many hours editing the film, *Mary Jane's Mishap*.

The running time was eventually close to four minutes, and we were delighted with the result. It differed little from our original concept, with Laura Bayley portraying a housemaid who starts a fire in the kitchen stove with paraffin. It causes an explosion that sends her up the chimney, and her scattered remains fall to the ground. It could be thought macabre, but Laura played it with such style that it was both moving and laughable. Later, Mary Jane's ghost rises from the grave to find her paraffin can. Once found, she retired happily to her final resting place.

Laura had charmingly combined all the emotions: humour, pathos and drama. We knew we had a winner on our hands.

We moved on to shoot three one minute features, *The Sick Kitten*, a remake of our film *The Little Doctors*, made some years earlier. This was followed by *The Little Witness* and *The Baby and the Ape* , which received more acclaim in the United States than in Britain, where it was renamed, *The Baby, the Monkey and the Milk Bottle*.

CHAPTER TWENTY

We devoted every spare minute to filming.

When Laura arrived at the studio, my first thought was that we had worked her too hard. She was listless, and subdued. I looked more closely. Her face was drawn, eyes red-rimmed.

`Is something wrong, Laura?`

`There could well be, Sam...there could well be.`

I glanced at Geoffrey.

`I think you'd better tell us what it is.`

She chewed at her lip. Then it came out in a rush.

`George is selling the lease on St Ann's Well Gardens.`

`What!` exclaimed Geoffrey. `But he can't...I mean it's really working well. We're making terrific films and the processing unit is making money. Lots of people rely on us.`

I stared hard at Laura. `It's Urban, isn't it? He's put the idea into George's head.`

She sniffed. `Yes. I think Urban wants to get his own back, and on you in particular, Sam. You're the thorn in his side. He doesn't want you to distract George from this colour thing he's working on. The only way he can stop my husband from being side-tracked, thinking about making films instead of perfecting this process, is to cancel out all notion of film-making. And getting rid of all this,` she opened her arms to embrace us and the building, `would be the easiest way to achieve it.`

`Doesn't George see what he's doing, Laura?` cried Geoffrey. `Giving this up now will mean his hard work, our endeavours, will all count for nothing. We'll have wasted our time.`

`When are you returning to Southwick, Laura?` I asked.

`Well, there doesn't seem any point staying, does there?` she replied unhappily. `I just cannot get through to him. He's like someone in a trance.`

`Would you mind if I came with you? To try and talk him out of the idea.`

`You can try, Sam. If he'll listen to anyone he'll listen to you.`

The hansom cab drew up outside the house just as a carriage eased through the gates. I helped Laura alight and we walked towards the front door where George was standing.

`Hello, Sam, come to make me change my mind?`

I could see by the set of his features that it would be a futile attempt. More so, because I had glimpsed Urban's smile of satisfaction from the carriage in which he was accompanied by another gentleman.

`Well, I have to tell you you're too late. The deed is done. St Ann's Well Gardens is now the leasehold property of a Mr A H Tee, who was leaving with Charles when you arrived.`

Laura strode past him into the house.

`In which case I shan't stay long, George.`

I too, strode past and took a chair in the drawing room. He followed, a little uncertainly.

`So, let me understand what you have done,` I said, as Laura entered the room. `You have sold the lease to the Gardens. But what else? Have you also sold off all the equipment, title to the films, and the people you employ?`

He stared at me.

`Mr Tee has acquired only the lease to the Gardens, and his intention is that they shall remain open to the public.`

`Right,` I glanced at Laura. `What about the films? Who has those? Do you?`

`Err...no, Charles has bought them.`

`Including the ones we have just made?`

`Yes.`

`So what do you intend to do with the staff? Will you continue to employ them?`

`No, leastways, not the film people. The gardening team will simply transfer to the new owner,` declared George.

`Let me get this straight. As from this moment we no longer work for GAS Films, because the company has been dissolved. Is that right?`

`Not exactly,` said George, wringing his hands. `GAS Films will continue, but we shall only take on people when we make colour pictures.`

I was getting angry. Unthinkingly he had made six people redundant, with no provision for their future. Cast out, no doubt, at Urban`s command. This seemed so alien to the George Smith for whom I had long had high regard.

`In which case, there is nothing more to be said,` I exclaimed, rising from the chair. I nodded to Laura and left, slamming the front door behind me.

CHAPTER TWENTY - ONE

James Williamson offered me a job.

I had been on my way to Mrs Earl's when a hansom cab came to halt beside me.

`Sam! Sam! Come over here!`

I walked slowly to the open window.

`Hello James. What can I do for you?`

`Get in.`

I knew that in addition to his pharmacy, he had set up a studio in Cambridge Grove, not far from St Ann's Well Gardens. He had named the business, "The Williamson Kinematographic Company". James and his family occupied the house, Rose Cottage, adjacent to the glasshouse film studio, and he had built another smaller building, which he identified to everyone as his "photographic atelier".

A few minutes later we were seated in his drawing room, while his wife made afternoon tea. She brought it in on a tray, and left James to pour.

As he passed the tea cup, he said. `Sad business, Sam. Word is that George has sold the Gardens and walked away from the film company. It seems everyone is out of a job. Is it true?`

`I'm afraid it is, James.`

`And you...what are you going to do?`

`Do you know, I haven't really thought about it. I might go to France. Georges Méliès has always said we could work well together. In truth, I've been more worried about the others.`

`Look, Sam, I won't beat about the bush, come and work for me. With your talents we could go far. What do you say?`

`That's generous of you, James, but, you have a contract with Charles Urban to distribute your films.`

`So what?`

`It`s too complicated to pick over the bones of our relationship. I`ll just say Charles and I don`t share the same views on what is honourable in this business. If he is doing a good job for you, great. Personally, I couldn`t work with the man. Though you could do me a favour.`

`What`s that?

`You could employ Geoffrey Summer, the cameraman. He was one of GAS Films` biggest assets.`

I had not realised Geoffrey was married. When he came round to my lodgings, he was effusively grateful for recommending him to James Williamson.

`I was getting desperate, Sam. I didn`t know which way to turn. Now I`ll be able to look after my family properly.`

He grabbed my hand again.

`If I can ever help you, Sam, you`ll only have to say the word.`

`Geoffrey, listen, I was only to willing to advise James to take you on for one very good reason. You`re a damned, fine cameraman. It wasn`t out of kindness, it was the right thing to do, and I expect you to live up to the abilities you undoubtedly have.`

I clapped him on the back, and sent him on his way.

For the first time I gave serious thought to my own predicament. If I remained in Brighton I would be lucky to hold on to my rented room at Mrs Earl`s. But where would I go? Film-making was a precarious occupation, companies carried few employees. As with actors, they resorted to hiring additional staff only when a project required extra numbers. I could go back to gardening I suppose. At least it would keep me fed and clothed. But the thought was brief and readily dismissed. I had been too long exposed to the world of creating and producing films. I could no longer return to that sedate, more ordered way of life dictated by the seasons.

I needed the excitement, the sense of achievement, to suffer those moments when hopes were blighted, when grand ideas turned to dust. However, it was at such times you learned the pitfalls. You picked yourself up, plunged into another epic...and tried to avoid making the same mistakes. No...I had to continue in the profession. It was three o`clock in the morning before I finally came to a decision.

The following day was Sunday, and after breakfast I asked Mrs Earl if her husband were not using his pony and trap after church, could I borrow it for a few hours.

Just before midday the trap climbed the short rise and dropped down into the town of Newhaven. With a slight tug of the rein the pony veered left onto the Lewes Road towards Piddinghoe. My mother always cooked a hearty meal on Sundays, and I usually visit home every three or four weeks to enjoy their company, eat well, and relax. Even though I had been a fortnight earlier, I was still sure of a welcome as well as a good slice of beef. I never went empty-handed. On this occasion, I had procured two rabbits for a stew that I knew was one of my father's favourite meals.

When the door opened I enjoyed the warm reception of a motherly embrace and a firm, paternal handshake. I was poured a glass of beer, and served a full plate at the dining table. It was a convivial atmosphere; and when we had washed up and cleared away the dishes we sat once more at the table watching the boats making their way up and down the River Ouse.

`So, Sam, what prompted your visit today? We didn`t expect you for another week or two,` remarked my father.

It was then I told them of the situation with the film company, and that I was now out of a job.

`What have you got in mind, son?` he enquired.

`You know you can always come here until you find your feet,` said mother.

I took a deep breath. `I`m going to America. For a while, at least. When I was there last year a film maker said he could employ someone like me. I want to find out if he meant it.`

On the way back, the lasting impression I had of the visit were the silent tears shed by my mother.

The ship was the *S.S. Adriatic* sailing from Southampton. This time I paid twenty pounds and had a second class cabin to myself. An uneventful journey, for which I was grateful. I am not a good sailor, and even these large ships have little resistance to strong winds and heaving seas.

Seven days later, when the Statue of Liberty and the promontory of Manhattan came into view, I was nervous. Perhaps, my reception would not be as welcoming as I had imagined. A year has passed: faces were forgotten; things change; people move on. My mood swung between hope and uncertainty.

Where should I go first? Logically, I should find a rooming house. I would have a base, which would dispel any notion that when calling on friends I was seeking a bed. I hailed an electrobat and told the driver to drop me on the south side of *Washington Square* Park. I recalled from my previous visit that whilst to the north it opened onto Fifth Avenue, the opposite side had a less genteel quality. In fact, when I told the driver my destination, he replied. `Are you sure? That`s Tramps` Retreat.`

I had not been aware of the numbers of homeless people circulating the Park until I alighted. Fortunately, we came to a halt beneath a sign advertising The Judson Hotel. I entered the lobby and spoke with a large, no-nonsense female behind the desk, who booked me in for five nights.

It was cheap, and I soon realised why. A bed, chair, miniscule chest of drawers and a mirror comprised its amenities. A stained, threadbare carpet covered much of the floor, which did little to raise the chill air of discomfort. I quickly came to the decision I would not remain long in these surroundings.

I imagined Henry James was not enamoured of the neighbourhood either, for he had written the short story, *Washington Square*, in a rooming house not unlike the one in which I now found myself.

Surprisingly, I slept rather well. The next morning I found a restaurant serving breakfast on West Fourth Street, just off the Square. As I sat at a table eating fruit and oatmeal, broiled ham and poached eggs on toast, I smiled at the thought of the bowl of porridge served unfailingly every day by Mrs Earl. Over coffee, I also considered how I might best approach Carl Laemmle.

It would be better if he learned of my presence from someone other than myself. If then he did not wish to meet me, neither of us would be embarrassed. I would look for a job with another film maker in Fort Lee. The last act before leaving GAS Films had been to acquire copies of the motion pictures made with Laura and Geoffrey. They featured my name prominently in the credits as producer and director. They might be useful when trying to impress people of my worth.

It was late morning when I made my way across town to the Lower East Side. I walked the streets, noting the characters I had come to recognise. The barrows piled high with fish, fresh produce and dry goods; the cries of the vendors piercing the general hubbub. People of all ages, and all nationalities, mingling and jostling one another amid the shops, stalls, cafés, saloons, dance halls, and cheap lodging houses. And it was all happening against a backdrop of soaring tenements, the cast-iron zig-zag of fire escapes scarring their facades. So different from the easy-going, less frenetic pace of Brighton and Hove.

As I headed along Broome Street leaving behind Little Italy, so the accent changed from a soft, Latin intonation to the more guttural tones of Northern Europe. When I turned into Eldridge Street, suddenly an arm was thrust into mine.

`I knew you would be back,` said Alice, smiling up into my face. She was swinging a basket of provisions in her other hand.

`How are you, Alice? Still working in the hat shop?`

`Of course. I was doing some shopping for mama, before going to work. Are you coming to see us?`

`Well, yes. Just to say hello before I move on.`

She looked at me in that curious way I had noticed about her last time. `Where to?`

I found myself struggling for an answer.

`Err, probably up at Fort Lee, where the film studios are.`

She nodded in a way that suggested she saw through my reply.

`Right...with Uncle Carl?`

`Not necessarily.`

By now we had halted outside the apartment block. To break the silence, I said. `Here, let me carry that upstairs.` Then a thought struck me. `Come on.`

In a nearby store I filled the basket. Climbing the stairs to the apartment, Alice remarked, `Mama is going to be pleased. She has been waiting months for a letter from you. Every day she checks the mail.`

I was embarrassed. I had written on my return to England, promising to write regularly. But we had been so busy. In truth, it was a feeble excuse, one I could not glibly convey to Eszter. My face flushed with self-reproach.

`Mama! Mama! Guess who I found outside?`

Eszter's voice came from the kitchen area. `The rent collector, he`s giving us our money back! The Rabbi is handing out food! No, I know, a porter from the fish market is ...` She came into the passage wiping her hands on a cloth, and stopped mid-sentence.

`Sam!` she cried, and rushed to hug me. `I knew you`d come back!`

She never questioned why I had not written.

We sat in the kitchen talking long after Alice had gone off to work in Clinton Street. It was an easy, comfortable chat. She told me that Peter now worked in the Fulton Fish Market, and Steven and Thomas were employed at the East River piers. As a consequence, they had moved out and the three of them were living together in a rooming house in Peck Slip, near Brooklyn Bridge.

`So, what have you been doing with yourself?` she asked.

I recounted all that had happened at GAS Films during the past year, although I omitted the fact I was no longer working for the company.

`Have you come to check on the distribution company you are using? Or is there another reason?` she enquired shrewdly.

`No...`I hesitated. `Well, yes. The company I am...was working for has closed down. I`m really in New York because Carl Laemmle once said if I were ever interested he might have a job for me.`

She patted my arm. `There`s no need to be coy about it, Sam. You`re looking for a job. Around here people are doing so all the time. When one job closes you look for another. It`s a fact of life. So, how can I help you? Do you want me to speak to Carl? He`ll be over here on Saturday. We`re all going to the synagogue on Sheriff Street, near Hamilton Fish Park.`

I looked at her blankly. `What`s a fish park?`

`Sorry, Hamilton Fish was a man`s name.. He was in the government and I believe a New York senator thirty years ago. They commemorated the park in his honour. Anyway, as I was saying, Carl will be with the Bernsteins, on Saturday. That could be your chance to speak to him.`

Eszter studied my face. `But you don`t want to do that, do you?`

`Well no. You see, I don`t want to embarrass him or myself if there isn`t a position with his company.`

She nodded. `So you would like him to learn of your arrival beforehand, and to be aware you are seeking employment.`

`Hmm.`

She sat there for a moment. `OK, I have an idea. Are you using this company in Chicago?`

`Yes, they are still renting out our films. I don`t think my old boss, George Smith, has notified them we are no longer in production.`

`Then this is what I`ll do. I`ll go round to the Bernsteins, to check on the arrangements for the evening meal on Saturday. During the course of the conversation, I`ll mention that Sam Lockhart is here, in New York, and is going to Chicago to see a film distribution company about a job with them. What`s the company`s name?`

`The Kleine Optical Company. I usually deal with Mr George Kleine.`

`Right, so this Mr Kleine wants to discuss a job with him. I`ll make sure she tells Carl, and if he`s interested he`ll tell you to forget the Kleine people and come and work for him. If he doesn`t,` her shoulders flexed upwards, `you`ll know where you stand.`

Thursday evening I met with Peter, Steve and Thomas in a bar by the East River. After a few beers we found an Italian restaurant where we spent the rest of the evening and late into the night, celebrating their good fortune. I left them, much the worse for wear, by the Bridge, hailing a cab to take me back to the Judson. The result, I slept late the next morning and staggered into a restaurant on Fifth Avenue for lunch.

I had been invited to an evening meal by Eszter. When I knocked on the door at six thirty, it was instantly thrown open, and bodies crowded into the passageway to greet me. Another bountiful evening: this time my stomach complained, not of the excess of alcohol, but the overwhelming amount of food. I was told to try everything. I have never encountered the full force of Jewish mothers before. There were at least three at the table, and I soon succumbed to their commands. For the first time I witnessed this innate ability they possess to hold everyone in their thrall.

It was a balmy evening on Saturday, The sun was setting, the crowds and street sellers had melted away. For once, there was a disturbing silence about the Lower East Side. For many, the calm before the post holy day merriment. I walked the six or seven blocks to the Bernstein`s apartment, wondering with every step, where my future might take me when I met with Carl Laemmle.

Isadore Bernstein, Carl`s brother-in-law welcomed me in.

`Sam! It`s good to see you again. Come in...come in.`

I shook hands with relatives and friends of the Bernsteins. Eszter and her husband came over to me, and when I kissed her cheek, she whispered. `I think the word's been passed on, but I can't be sure.`

At the table I sat next to Isadore, who welcomed me as "their special guest from England". I spoke with an elderly woman next to me, also a member of the Bernstein family who lived in an apartment across the road.

As the meal progressed, she told me of her life in Moldova, a country within the Pale of Settlement to which Jews were confined. It seemed they were even forbidden to live in the main city, Chisinau, and were beaten if they ever attempted to go there.

She and her husband had lived from hand to mouth like peasants, scratching a meagre existence. Eventually, they had escaped to the shores of the Black Sea, crossed the expanse of water to Istanbul, and walked for more than three months to Italy, where they joined an emigrant ship to America. Her eyes lowered when she told of the loss of two of her children on the journey.

It was a moving story. Simply told, the tragedy of their pilgrimage to freedom was all the more telling. I squeezed her hand. I could see the memories, and the anguish mirrored in her eyes. Then she gave a sad smile.

`What do you do for a living , Mr Lockhart?`

A hand gripped my shoulder. `He works for me, Rachel. Don't you, Sam?`

On Monday morning I took the train on the Sixth Avenue Elevated Rail to Fifty Ninth Street, the south side of Central Park, and walked the six blocks to West End Avenue. Carl's wife, Recha, opened the apartment door.

She showed me into the sitting room, and returned to the kitchen, saying as she went.

`Carl won't be a minute, he has just slipped out for something. I'll make some coffee`

I sat on an over-stuffed chair and admired the décor. It was less cluttered, much simpler in style than the over-ornate furnishings, the many ornaments and paintings, and the knick-knacks covering every flat surface that one still finds back home. We were only adapting slowly to more modern concepts, and had yet to leave aside the influence of the Victorian era.

From a side window I caught a glimpse of the sun glinting on the surface of the North River. This was the sort of accommodation I would aim for if I stayed in New York. I was still intrigued by Carl`s remark at the family gathering, for all he said afterwards, was, "come over my place on West End Avenue first thing Monday morning".

Carl swept into the room, followed by Recha carrying a tray.

`That was a good evening at the Bernsteins, don`t you think?` remarked Carl, sprawling on the couch. Recha set down the tray on a coffee table and sat next to him.

`I saw you chatting to Rachel,` she said, pouring from a cafetiere. `An amazing woman.`

`It was a great party, and she certainly is a remarkable woman,` I agreed. `She was telling me how she and her family came to the States. What a story. I must admit I felt choked by the time she had finished.`

Recha passed me a cup, and the sugar bowl.

`So, young Sam, I was told you were going to Chicago to see George Kleine about a job. What has brought that about?`

I recounted the events, and the change of fortune GAS Films had suffered now George Smith had sold out and was totally absorbed in producing a colour system.

`Do you know Charles Urban, Carl?` I enquired.

`I`ve heard the name bandied around, but I`ve never come across the guy. But that`s by the by. What are we going to do about you?` He stared long and hard. Then grinned. `Perhaps, I was a little hasty last night, saying you worked for me when I hadn`t asked you. So, what`s it to be? Will you work for me, Sam?`

`I`d love to, Carl.`

`What about Mr Kleine in Chicago?`

`I`ll write to him.`

He looked at me knowingly, then said, `Fine. When can you start?`

`How about now?`

`I was hoping you`d say that, because today I want to go up to Fort Lee, and you can come with me. Don`t worry, we won`t get beaten up, but I want to show you something.`

Once again we took the ferry boat to Edgestone.

`We could have taken the trolley,` Carl said over his shoulder as we disembarked. `But Isadore has organised a buggy for us.`

We climbed aboard, the driver gave a flick of the rein, and the horse started trotting up the road to Fort Lee.

`You remember that piece of land I bought, Sam?`

`I remember that evening all too well, Carl.`

`Hmm...Anyway, I eventually got the money together to start the distribution business, and I'm now working on the studio. I haven't got that far, but it's gradually taking shape.`

We turned onto Main Street, and I noticed that more buildings had sprung up, and many more people were walking the roadway. Some waved to Carl, who returned the gesture. As we neared the centre of town, the driver turned up a side road and brought the buggy to a standstill.

`OK...this is it. What do you think?`

I had not appreciated that the field we had inspected over a year ago was so large. The area had been enclosed by a post and rail fence, and in the middle of the plot stood a solitary, but substantial wooden hut. To one side were the footings for another good-sized structure, with workmen toiling to lay a concrete base. Prominent on the roadside verge was a large painted sign, which declared:

`Property of THE INDEPENDENT MOVING PICTURES COMPANY`

`Why independent?`

`You haven't heard of the latest developments over here?`

`No.`

`Edison has started taking the minnows like us to court. He has cowered the big boys, companies like Essanay, Selig, Lubin, and others, with lawsuits. Now he thinks he can use the courts to bring us into line. Well, not me, no way. Hence the name, Independent Moving Pictures. There are still two companies fighting him in the courts, because do you know what he charges to make use his patents on equipment and film? A half cent for every foot of film. On a one reeler that's fifty dollars!`

`Which are the two companies?`

`Your old partner, Biograph, and your new partner, Kalem.`

I must have looked bewildered.

He laughed. `It stands for George Kleine, Samuel Long, and Frank J. Marion. The company was named after their initials K, L, and M. Like me, they are setting up in Fort Lee. George Kleine also believes there should be greater freedom in the film making business. Studios should be allowed to turn out what they like. Leastways, he did. Now I`m not so sure. There are some operators, Sam, producing very questionable material. Not family entertainment, if you see what I mean. I`m told he is now thinking a brake on producers might be a good idea after all, if it removes the less welcome side of the industry.`

`Where do you stand on that?`

`Using moving pictures to parade suggestive material? I`m strongly against it. But kerbing the efforts of the majority to control the few is no way to solve the problem. It will just drive those studios producing prurient material underground. You won`t eradicate it, because there are people who derive pleasure from that sort of thing. Moving pictures is yet another medium by which they can exploit those with that turn of mind.`

We opened the five bar gate, and walked along a cinder track to the hut. Déjà vu, I thought as we entered the building. It was not unlike the gardeners` hut at St Ann`s Well. Sitting at a long table, with site plans and numerous drawings spread across its surface was a man about my age.

`Walt, this is Sam Lockhart. He has just joined Independent Moving Pictures. Sam this is Walter Johnson, the site foreman. Everything shaping up, Walt?`

`Yes, we`re on schedule, Mr Laemmle. We should have the shell up in eight weeks time, then the cladding and brickwork should take another three to four weeks. After that, we can start the glazing. So, given the right weather, the studio should be finished in about three months.`

`Good. I want to start planning our first film now, Sam. The outline is finished. I want you to work out the scenes, the dialogue exchanges, the text we show on the screen, and the location shoots. We should do the location scenes before the weather closes in for the year. We can do the close ups and the interiors in the studio when it`s finished.`

I was startled by the speed the task was thrown at me. But that`s what I should have expected of the man.

`Fine...what film are we actually talking about, Carl?`

`The one I've always wanted to make. You know, *Hiawatha*.`

We went to the bar in Main Street. The same barman served us.

`Hello, Mr Laemmle, what can I get you?`

`Two beers, please, Clive.`

`I'll bring them over to your table, sir.`

When they came, I took a deep draught, wiped the froth from my mouth, and said.

`OK, so where do you want me to work. Here, or in the city?`

`Not here. Anyway, not yet. I've got an option on some premises on Eleventh Avenue and West Fifty Third Street, not far from my apartment. We could use it as a studio if you wanted, but set up an office there. I'll leave you and Isadore...you remember Isadore, my brother-in-law. Well, the two of you can organise the furniture, telephones and so on. Come by first thing tomorrow, and I'll give you the keys. By the way, where are you staying at the moment?`

`*Washington Square*, in a small hotel there.`

He grinned. `Not the Judson?`

`Well, yes.`

`I stayed there for a while after vacating the crummy apartment I shared with a friend. You know the cab drivers are paid to drop you off there. I couldn't take more than a week. Perhaps you ought to get a room nearer to the office, before you catch something.`

`It's not that bad,` I replied defensively.

`It's not that good either, Sam.`

There was movement behind me, and Carl looked up.

`Hello, George, how are you? You know this fellow, don't you.`

I turned in my chair. It was George Kleine. The last person I wanted to see.

`Mr Lockhart! How are you, sir? Say, those recent films you sent us, *Dorothy's Dream*, *Mary Jane's Mishap*, and the one we changed the title, *The Baby, The Monkey and The Milk Bottle*, have been sure fire winners. Have you seen them, Carl? Keep them coming, sir, keep them coming.`

`Actually, George, Sam has left GAS Films in England, and now works for Independent Moving Pictures.`

My little ruse was about to fall apart. I looked across the table to see how Carl would react.

`Damnation! I would have offered him a job with Kalem. He would have been just the man for us.`

I swivelled round in my chair and stared at him.

Carl had this infectious grin, which he employed now. `Too late, George, too late.`

We stood up and shook hands with Kleine, before he wandered away to join another table.

`Do you know, Sam, when my sister told me you were in town, she also mentioned  you were going to see Kleine about a job. I thought you had planted the idea so I would jump at offering you one instead. Guess I was wrong.`

Under the table I crossed my fingers.

We were still sitting there when George Kleine and his companions pushed back their chairs and headed for the door. As he passed by our table, Kleine leaned over and said in a low voice.

`Don`t forget, if you find him difficult to work with.` He grinned at Carl. `Come round to Kalem. We`re looking at a site on Palisades Avenue, and are going to build a brand new studio.`

`Sam will be fully occupied working at our new studio, which is not a pipedream, it`s almost finished,` said Carl through gritted teeth.

While Carl met with his lawyer in Fort Lee, I returned to the hut and chatted with Walter Johnson, who showed me the drawings of the proposed studio. Afterwards he took me to see the steel construction they were erecting.

On the ferry going downstream, Carl asked. `What do you think of Walt, the site foreman?`

`He knows what he`s about. And I found he tells it straight, as he sees it. No bullshit.`

`Yer, that my opinion. He`ll have the studio up and running for the inside shots on time, I reckon. By the way, Sam, I should tell you, I`ve already appointed a director for *Hiawatha*. He was called in before I learned you were free.`

`I understand, Carl. But why do you want me to set the scenes and the angles, as well as the schedule if you've already got a director. That's his job, surely?`

`It is, but there's something I want you to take into account. Firstly, the guy I've chosen is also playing the lead. His name is William Ranous, and he wants to develop his career behind the camera as well as in front of it. The thing is he's a rookie, still new to the directing game. So I would like you to make it work, and come in on budget.`

I nodded. `So he's directing, but I'm making sure the film is produced, is that right?`

`That's about the size of it, Sam. I want to know it's in a safe pair of hands.`

The rooms on Eleventh Avenue and Fifty Third Street overlooked a park, and beyond that the North River waterfront. When I walked through the door, Isadore Bernstein was there to greet me.

`Great rooms, aren't they, Sam?` He rubbed his hands together. `At long last we're ready to make some films. The distribution side is OK, but this is where we can make the money.`

I looked around. `There's certainly plenty of space. But, tell me Isadore, what's that smell?`

`The smell? Oh, that's the gasworks up the road. Don't worry you'll get used to it.` He added. `That's why we got this place cheap.`

In the afternoon Isadore and I toured the shops buying furniture; arranged for the telephones to be connected; and purchased all the many items needed to get the offices up and running. When Carl arrived the next day, he came with a man who painted the company name of the door. Now it was official.

`Isadore's got his office, and I suggest you set yourself up in there, Sam,` said Carl, pointing to a room on the other side. `It has plenty of light and a good view of the river. When I want I can use this area, which will be a general office cum studio for close-up filming.`

As the head of the company, surely you want the best room, Carl?`

`It's not necessary, Sam. I don't need an office, just an occasional chair.`

He called Isadore over.

`Let's outline everyone's contribution here, so there's no confusion. The set-up, as I see it, is this. Isadore runs the company on a day-to-day basis. His responsibilities are to keep things afloat. The finances, administration, and the general well-being of Independent Moving Pictures. `

He turned to me. `You, Sam, will work on the productions we are going to make. I've been giving this a lot of thought. With your experience, there will be times you direct a moving picture, but I see your principal role as making sure films actually happen. Film directors may have the flair, the temperament to get the best out of a scene, but most often they haven't got a clue what it takes to make a moving picture. The mechanics of bringing everything together. The choice of subject, script, the best actors for the roles, locations, publicity, getting the picture houses interested. You are ideally suited to do that, Sam. You'll look after production. `

Intriguing, until now we had not actually discussed my role in the company. Nor, for that matter, had a salary been mentioned.

`Also, Sam, we are just starting up our film business, and I want you to help me develop it. Simple as that. So at times you could be acting as a producer and also seeking out new ideas for moving pictures. All the time, Isadore will be keeping a close eye on the finances, making damned sure we make a profit.

`In the meantime I shall be fending off the lawsuits that could be winging our way, selling our company's output to key people in the distribution chain, right down to the exhibitors who show the actual films, OK?`

I stepped forward and shook his hand. `That's a clear job description. There's only one area we haven't touched upon. `

He raised an eyebrow.

`Autonomy. I am not going to run to you every minute for a decision. But I will give you weekly reports on the actions I have taken. Finally, when it comes to it, we all three decide on the people the company takes on. Agreed?`

`Agreed. `

CHAPTER TWENTY - TWO

William Ranous appeared to be in his late forties, early fifties. Too old, I thought, to be playing the part of a young brave. Especially when Gladys Hullette, who was playing Minnehaha, was only a teenager.

He came into the offices in Manhattan and I talked him through the scenes; the filming sequence, timing, the establishing shots, angled and reverse dialogue shots, and told him we would do the exterior scenes first. I mentioned I was going up to the Palisades to look at possible locations.

At first sight this rocky outcrop which borders the western bank of the Hudson River appeared an ideal backdrop. But I spent almost a week looking for suitable sites with little success. For the next few days I read and re-read Longfellow`s *Song of Hiawatha*, and pored over numerous references to the supposed locations in the epic poem.

All the so-called experts identified an area within the Western Great Lakes. Was this a clue to why Carl was so enamoured of the subject? His first experience of Americans and their way of life had been working in Oshkosh. As a result of the poem, the term `Hiawatha` was used quite freely in the region, from town names to a telephone company.

I took a train bound for Chicago, and another to Minneapolis. I hired a hansom cab at the station and drove ten miles south to Minnehaha Falls.

Four days later I was back in New York.

`Where have you been, Sam? I thought you`d gone back to England.`

I explained about my search for a worthwhile location in the Palisades, that it had come to nothing. Taking a deep breath, I said casually. `So I went to where Longfellow decreed it all happened...Minnesota.`

`Are you saying you want to take a film crew, actors, costumes, and all the equipment over a thousand miles just to film some hill and river scenes? Are you mad? We`d lose our shirts on the film! You just can`t tear off halfway across the country because the scenery is better.`

He was looking at me intently. I could tell what he was thinking. What have I done, employing this crazy Englishman? He will lose all the money I`m sinking into this picture.

`You want this project to be as authentic as possible, right? Because many people almost believe that what happened to *Hiawatha* is true. They feel an affinity for the Indian brave, like we do back home with King Arthur and His Round Table, or the Loch Ness Monster. We want to think they`re real, even if they aren`t. If I were making a picture about either King Arthur or the Monster, I`d film it where people believe they once existed. What you would do in this case is to publicise the fact that *Hiawatha* was actually filmed in the happy, hunting grounds of the poem. You mark my words, Carl, it will double the number of moviegoers who go to see it.`

He stopped pacing the office, and stared out the window for some minutes.

`What you mean is advance publicity, right? Tell them this is where it all happened, a sort of homage to the poet?`

I nodded. `That`s what I had in mind.`

`And we won`t lose any money?`

`Not if we do it as I suggest. If we drum up the publicity, we`ll make a handsome profit.`

`OK...` I waited for the judgement. `Let`s do it.` He shouted, `Let`s do it!`

I was William Renous` shadow on location. I had worked out every sequence, every word of silent dialogue, every movement and gesture. In many ways I was surprised how quickly William picked up my discreet advice, and made it his own. The only time he relinquished his role as director was when he was acting a scene. Then I stepped forward and gave more obvious guidance.

After a week on the outskirts of Minneapolis - we stayed in the village of Longfellow, and filmed against the backdrop of the Minnehaha Falls, and around Lake Nokomis. Then we headed back east, and did the close-up exterior shots in the Palisades

I was anxious to see the results; and even more perturbed when Carl declared he would sit in and view what we had taken before I had had a chance to vet the material. A section of the general room had been curtained off, and a projector installed. William Ranous also joined us. I could detect he was equally concerned about his dual role in the production.

When the cans of film arrived, I threaded the first through the machine. Checking the electrical supply, I turned off the lights and switched on the carbon rods. Then I turned the cranking handle to feed the film through the gate.

We viewed all the unedited material: the scenes along the shores of `Gitcheegoomie`; of *Hiawatha*'s childhood adventures; plighting his troth to the beautiful Minnehaha; the slaying of the evil magician Pearl-Feather; and finally, the location shots of *Hiawatha* approaching the village in his birch canoe, where Minnehaha joyously welcomes him. When the projector clattered to a standstill, I switched everything off, opened the blinds, and looked at Carl.

A slow grin, his trademark, spread across his face. `You were right my boy. An excellent move to film the exteriors in the right place. Terrific material. When the interiors and close-ups are done, we'll have a winner on our hands.`

He swung round and pumped William's hand.

`A first-class job, my friend.`

I don't know what made me say it. Perhaps, I was buoyed by Carl's enthusiasm.

`Walter Johnson is going to be another month finishing the studio at Fort Lee, so why don't we shoot the close-ups and the rest of the interiors, here, in these rooms? If we get all the filming completed, the picture could be edited and copies out to exhibitors before Christmas. Even if Walter comes in on schedule, we still wouldn't be able to circulate *Hiawatha* until the new year. This way we hit the holiday period when everyone wants to go to the movies.`

Hiawatha, the fifteen minute film produced by Independent Moving Pictures, was released on the twenty fifth of October.

I worked all the hours there were. We had transformed the IMP offices into a vast studio. During the day I was William's *doppelganger*. Standing at his elbow, whispering suggestions, filling in when he was playing his part under the arc lights.

At night, when the film went off for processing, I spent my time doing a rough cut of the material we had taken thus far. Carl was a frequent visitor, never offering advice, just taking note of all that was happening. There were occasions when he would sit with me at the editing machine. He never said much, not that I could hold a conversation. I was concentrating on the interplay of the long scenes, close-ups, and text inserts.

Eventually, it all came together, and we issued a press call to the magazines and newspapers inviting their critics to a private viewing. Both the invitation and handout emphasised the point I had made at the beginning, that the motion picture was filmed in Longfellow's chosen setting. A feature that would give it meaning and sincerity.

The event took me back to that moment in the Brighton Aquarium, when all our hopes rested on the projector working, and that the production would be well-received. We wanted *Hiawatha* reported as the movie everyone should see. At this point in IMP's infancy, we needed people to flock to the movie parlours, theatres, and nickelodeans in their thousands.

Carl gave the introductory speech to a full auditorium. He then called upon me, the man behind the production, to talk about the locations, the actors, and the future of our studio. Nearing the end of the presentation, I nodded to the projectionist. The lights dimmed, and the screen was filled with the title, *Hiawatha*, An Independent Moving Pictures Production.

The next morning, at Carl's apartment, we read the early editions of the newspapers. The first I picked up damned it with faint praise. The review concluded with, `*Hiawatha lost credibility early on when it became obvious that all the "Indians" were heavily-made up Caucasians.*`

I reached for the next: this was not much better. The last line read. *"Nor were the costumes, which were apparently designed to show off the heroine's feminine pulchritude, entirely authentic."* Although both mentioned how the film maker had stayed true to the poet's chosen location, giving the film a measure of integrity.

Fortunately, the reviews Carl read were far more positive. But I would have welcomed a resounding declaration of praise from the press instead of the half-hearted acknowledgement. As a consequence, I was still undecided if we had produced a winner, or whether, for all our efforts, the one-reel version of Henry Wadsworth Longfellow's narrative poem *Hiawatha* was destined to sink into early oblivion.

For several days after the press film show and the appearance of their reviews, I moped around, doing little work. Did I still have a job, I wondered? Was this attempt at being a film maker in America about to blow up in my face?

I arrived at the Eleventh Avenue and Fifty Third Street premises on the Friday morning, to find Carl sitting at my desk. This is it, I thought, getting fired always takes place on a Friday.

`Sam, my boy, come and sit down.`

I went to sit the other side of the desk.

`No, no. This is your chair.`

He rose, and we swopped places.

`So...what do you think?`

`Well, I guess I gave it my best shot....`

`You certainly did, my friend!` The famous grin appeared. `Have you seen the distribution figures?`

`No...no I haven`t.`

`We can`t produce copies fast enough. Orders are pouring in. We`ve already sold *Hiawatha* into thirty two states! What about that!`

CHAPTER TWENTY - THREE

Carl and I rushed up to Fort Lee soon after he received the phone call.

The steel frame of the studio, the cladding and glass side panels were on the site, ready to be erected. Now many of the spars and struts had been damaged, and few of the glass sheets had been left intact.

`Who did this, Walt?` cried Carl surveying the damage.

`Your guess is as good as mine, Mr Laemmle. The people working for Edison? It is hard to say. Fortunately, I keep my eye on the site, and even late at night sometimes check all is well. I came over last night before going to bed, and must have disturbed them. I've had a structural engineer make an assessment, and it's not as bad as I first feared. We can replace parts of the frame and get more glass, but I estimate we'll be delayed a week to ten days. What I will do, with your permission, is make damned sure it doesn't happen again.`

`Do what you think is necessary, Walt,` declared Carl, breathing heavily. Then he looked rather sheepish. `I have to admit it could have been my fault.`

Unabashed, Walter Johnson said. `Yes, you have been baiting them recently.`

`Sorry, who are they? Edison's crowd?` I asked.

Walter turned to me. `Haven't you seen the headlines, Sam?`

`No, I haven't had time to read anything. What's happened?`

`Your boss has been very vocal about not playing ball with Thomas Edison. I quote, *"I will not kowtow to the likes of those who would impose such restrictions on myself and other independent film makers".*`

He strode off towards the metal skeleton of the future IMP workplace.

`Carl, if it affects the business, perhaps I should know.`

`You obviously haven't read the latest edition of Moving Picture World.`

`You know I haven't.`

He pulled a copy of the magazine from his overcoat pocket.

`Pages eight and nine is what Walt was referring to. It has also been quoted in the New York Times, the Tribune and the Wall Street Journal. Here, read it while we get some lunch.`

We sat at a table in the saloon we regularly visit when in Fort Lee. Carl ordered a light meal for both of us and two beers, setting one down in front of me while I turned to the relevant pages. The headline caught my immediate attention.

"LAEMMLE SAYS GET LOST EDISON"

I read the article, spread across two pages with a mixture of disbelief, incredulity and concern. In fact I read it twice. The opening sentences were enough to provoke open warfare. Bending our metal structure was mild retaliation. There would be more to come: in and out of the courts.

"I don't believe in a dictatorship, not in politics, and certainly not in business. Particularly, the film business. It is stultifying: constraining new ideas, new practices, and all the potential innovations that would take this industry forward. One such man is seeking to dictate to us. He may have come up with a few inventions. He may even have set film makers on the path to a new form of mass entertainment. For that he should be applauded, and given rightful acknowledgement. But in showing us the way, he is deliberately building barriers to stop us, the independent film companies, moving on to the next generation of movie making.

That man is Thomas Edison. That man has to be stopped. I, for one, will not be intimidated by his threats, by his strong-arm tactics. I shall continue to make films like Hiawatha, and if equipment and film stock suppliers in this country are too timid to stand up to a tyrant, I shall buy my needs abroad. There are many European companies which would be only too pleased to supply my company."

It went on in this vein for two whole pages. Within the body of the article was a picture of Carl, smiling benignly upon the reader.

`Have you heard from Edison's solicitors yet?` I enquired. `If you haven't, expect a letter or even a personal visit with a writ any day now.`

I handed the magazine back to him. We sat in silence for a while, until Carl said. `Do you know why I gave that interview? Why I wanted it to appear in the trade journal?`

I shook my head as I munched through a miserable lunch.

`I'll tell you. Edison's aim is to stifle the little guys like me. He wants to dominate the industry. At first, when he explained his ideal of ending fly-by-night film makers offering prurient material, I went along with the notion that tighter controls through patent rights enforcement could be effective. But I soon changed my mind. He has gone too far, and has got to be stopped. What brought it to a head is the fact that now he is trying to gather together all the big moving picture companies. He wants to pool their various patents, which means that if they act in concert, we could be out of business.`

`So have you had any writs for lawsuits from Edison, or are they still to come?`

`A few,` he remarked.

`Come on, how many?` I asked, taking a swig from my glass.

`Err...a hundred and six.`

I could not help choking on the beer.

On the ferry downriver I asked to look again at the copy of Moving Picture World. Flicking through it, I realised I should make a point of reading the magazine. Although a lot of the material was trade gossip, there were one or two nuggets of interest among its pages. One item, in particular caught my eye.

"An 8-minute British short film *A visit to the Seaside (aka A visit to the Seaside at Brighton Beach, England)*, directed by George Albert Smith, is the *first* commercially-produced film in natural color using the revolutionary *Kinemacolor* process, invented by Smith himself."

CHAPTER TWENTY - FOUR

I secured a cabin all to myself, which gave me the luxury to review the situation hanging over the Independent Moving Pictures Company. I strolled the decks, sat in the lounge, ate my meals in the company of others at the table; but much of the time I sought seclusion.

It had worked out well. *Hiawatha* was making its foreign début; but because it would not create the same level of interest among European filmgoers as it had in the United States, I had opted to represent IMP instead of Carl Laemmle.

I also wanted to keep the promise to my parents – that I would be back within the year. I had actually been away eighteen months. Time had passed all too quickly. The other reason was to seek out George Smith, my erstwhile employer, and congratulate him on perfecting the colour system. I was quite keen to see it in operation. Having told Carl what George had been working on, he was equally enthusiastic, and wanted me to find out if IMP could introduce the process in America.

I had worried about the pending court cases Edison was bringing against the company, and wracked my brain to find a way from under the mountain of writs. My initial disappointment had gradually changed to one of anger that Edison-like projectors should be subject to patent infringement. Logically, there was no other way to convey images on a roll of flexible nitrate film. Everyone had to use a light source which shone through a lens with the series of continuous pictures passing between. That such a system was unlawful if monies were not paid for right of usage was nonsensical. Carl had been correct in standing up to such oppressive tactics. As soon as I was back I would join him in the fight, and encourage other independent film makers to do the same.

By the time the steamship docked in Southampton I had the glimmerings of a solution. As I saw it, we needed to gather more voices in the dispute, and as William Dickson of the Biograph Company had pointed out, the most influential ally would be the great mass of filmgoers. There were now ten thousand movie theatres in the United States, and it was hard to keep up with their demands. Mobilising the support of their patrons would be a strong argument in our favour.

The first step would be to tell the public they could well be deprived of films which excited the imagination and the emotions. Edison was still producing short films and reality moving pictures, whilst we were aware that people were now seeking fuller length productions, portraying tales with an intriguing beginning and a satisfying end.

I stayed overnight in a hotel, and the next day caught a train to Fareham. From there, the London and South Western Railway conveyed me as far as Portmouth. Another train, of yet another railway company, conveyed me along the south coast to Brighton.

On a whim, when I hailed a hansom in the forecourt, I gave the address of Mrs Earl`s lodging house.

`Good Lord, Mr Lockhart! Harry, it`s Mr Lockhart!` she shouted to her husband. `Have you come back? Come in...come in, don`t stand on the doorstep. Come into the parlour. Harry, light the fire, it`s Mr Lockhart.`

Her dutiful husband gave me a nod and a smile, and ushered me into the front parlour. In all the years I had lived in the house, I had never once seen the inside of the room. It had always been kept locked; used only for special occasions. I was honoured.

`So, what are you doing in England, dearie? Are you here to stay? I can put you in your old room if you are.`

`That`s very kind, Mrs Earl, but I`m only in England for a short time, I`m afraid. I have to return to New York. But if the room is vacant, could I rent it for a week?`

`Course you can. Stay as long as you like. Are you going to see Mr Smith over in Southwick? I read in the Evening Argus he`s invented colour films or some such. What a clever man. I suppose you`ll be visiting all your old friends, too.`

`Yes, though first of all I shall be visiting my parents in Newhaven. Saying that,` I turned to Mr Earl. `Can I possibly rent your trap, sir, for a few hours tomorrow?`

`Course you can, can`t he Harry?`

`How am I going to get to work then?` he replied soberly.

`Mr Lockhart will drop you off and pick you up later in the day when you finish, won`t you Mr Lockhart?`

It was soon organised, although I was not sure her husband was entirely happy with the arrangement.

`Now dear, what about some supper?`

I was ushered into the dining room, and took my usual seat. Mrs Earl put her head round the door.

`I`m afraid we haven`t got any soup to start, so will you be all right with bangers and mash?`

`That would be wonderful.`

After depositing Mr Earl at the Council Offices in Brighton, I continued onto Saltdean and Newhaven, before turning northwards and following the course of the River Ouse to Piddinghoe.

Tying the horse to a convenient tree I smoothed my hair, brushed the dust from my coat, and knocked on the door. I could hear movement, and suddenly the door jerked open and my mother stood there. Her mouth dropped, and she burst into tears. I swept her into my arms and held her tightly. I could feel her body jerking with the heavy sobs. We remained on the doorstep, motionless, until at last she wiped away the tears on her apron and pulled me into the house.

Having cycled up from the docks, my father was eating his lunch, He jumped to his feet, and the three of us held onto each other.

`Sit down, son, have something to eat,` he said in a voice thick with emotion.

I was served a plate of stew, and the memories of my childhood flooded back. I have never enjoyed the stews my mother made. She added all sorts of vegetables to chunks of rabbit and boiled the ingredients in a stockpot, together with copious amounts of pearl barley. I hated the small bones that lodged in your teeth and in the crevices of your mouth; and the taste of pearl barley was quite unpalatable. But that day I emptied my plate.

My father had to leave shortly afterwards, and I said I would stay until he returned later in the day. I helped mother with the dishes, and chatted about my experiences in America. She hung onto my every word as I described the country, the people and the work I was doing. She made afternoon tea, and asked me the question I was reluctant to answer.

`Are you home to stay now, Sam?`

`No, mother, not yet. There is still so much to be done. But, besides writing regularly, I will be back as often as possible to see you and dad.`

She nodded, resigned to the notion I had become a distant son.

`I asked because your father has not been so well lately. He may have to give up work if his health does not improve. Not that I want to worry you, but please write more often, and I'll do the same.`

`What, is he ill with something? Is he finding the work difficult?`

`Sam,` she replied with a sad smile, `neither of us is getting any younger. He is sixty, and the years are beginning to tell.`

As she said that, she brushed a strand of hair from her forehead. For the first time I noticed it was streaked with grey.

I had but a brief moment with my father before I had to return to Brighton to collect Mr Earl.

The next day I took the train to London and called upon IMP`s distributor, the Albion Cinema Supply Company, in Wardour Street. They looked after our British sales. Our continental distribution was handled by a sister company called, Albion Exclusives Limited. This organisation, based around the corner in Old Compton Street, distributed Éclair Films in this country, and they undertook a reciprocal role for us in France and Germany.

With our discussions at an end, they arranged for me to be interviewed by the cultural editor of the Times newspaper. With time to spare, I decided to call upon Charles Urban. I had learned his company had moved to Wardour Street, and was told, with some amusement, that he was now to be found in "Urbanora House".

At the reception desk a young man enquired after my business.

`Just mention my name. He'll either decide he does not want to see me, or he will welcome me as an old acquaintance,` I responded.

Apparently he was prepared to see me, and I waited the predictable ten minutes before he appeared at the top of the stairs.

`Sam Lockhart, well I'll be damned! Come up to my office.`

I shook hands with him when I reached the landing.

`So, how are you? How`s my old country?`

`Entertaining, Charles, and just a little unpredictable.`

He indicated a chair, then took his seat behind a large, ornate desk.

`What brings you to London, Sam?`

`Primarily, discussions with our agents, and to promote our latest film *Hiawatha*. There are also some personal matters I need to attend to.`

`That`s right, I`d forgotten. You work for Carl Laemmle, don`t you? The guy who is sparring with Thomas Edison. I doubt he`ll win. Edison`s got the film business sown up over there. You`ll find it hard, as an independent, to get the better of him.`

`Perhaps. We`ll have to see. Tell me, I saw a reference to George in the trade press over there about perfecting the colour process. Is that right? Has he solved how to introduce colour effectively?`

`We`ve made some breakthroughs, and we shall be showing what we have produced in London in the near future. George is just making the final adjustments.`

`Right...sounds interesting. When will it be available in America?`

He smiled. `Can`t say at the moment, Sam. But it will only be a matter of months. Then we shall be speaking with the big studios.`

That was a snub, but I expected it. `Well, I won`t take up any more of your time, Charles.`

I rose from the chair and leaned across the desk to shake hands.

`By the way, are you going to see George?` he asked casually.

Yes, among others in Brighton and Hove.`

`I might see you there. Goodbye, Sam.`

A cool dismissal. There was no love lost between us; and that would stand in the way of Carl getting hold of George`s colour process.

The hansom cab stopped outside the house in Roman Crescent.

I had telephoned earlier from Brighton, and it had been answered by Laura. Her voice had a distinctive quality, if only we had sound with our moving pictures, I thought.

`Sam! How wonderful. Where are you?`

I mentioned I was staying at my old lodging house, but at that moment

I was at the Grand Hotel attending a meeting. In fact, I was having a drink with James Williamson and Esme Collings, film making friends of yesteryear.

`When are you coming to see us?`

`I was wondering if it were possible to call this afternoon?`

There was a hesitation. `That might be a little difficult. Are you free tomorrow?`

`Unfortunately, I`m not, Laura. I have to go to London, and the following day I take a train to Southampton and board the ship for the United States.`

It was not strictly true. I was not leaving for another two days. But her pause had provoked a query in my mind, and I wanted to probe a little further. Her response assumed a more positive note. `Then today it shall be. Is three o`clock all right?`

She answered the door and stepped forward to give me a hug.

`It`s wonderful to see you, Sam.`

She took my arm and led me into the sitting room.

`I`ll call George. He is looking forward to seeing you.`

Laura disappeared, and I heard her telling a maid to arrange afternoon tea. There was silence, just the gentle ticking of the clock. I crossed my legs and sank back into the armchair, enjoying the warmth of the fire. Some minutes passed before I caught the sound of excited conversation, Strident, almost argumentative, voices raised in conflict.

They got louder, until the door opened and George appeared, looking his usual, detached self. However, over his shoulder I glimpsed the rubicund features of Charles Urban. I was not surprised. It answered that feeling I had had when Laura attempted to put off my visit to another day.

`Sam, my dear fellow, you are a joy to behold,` he cried, and embraced me vigorously. `Come, tell me of your exploits. I`m dying to hear.`

I caught sight of Laura. Her eyebrows twitched in apology.

`Well, I shall leave you, George,` declared Urban. `There is, after all, nothing more to be said on the matter. Good day to you all.`

He nodded curtly in my direction, wheeled round and strode into the hall. A moment later the front door slammed behind him.

`Sit down, Sam.`

George and Laura sat side by side on a settee. At that moment the maid brought in the tray; and as she poured out the tea and served us, a semblance of normality slowly reasserted itself.

`I've heard you are doing remarkable things with your colour process, George,` I remarked, taking the sandwich which was proffered.

His eyes took on a faraway look, as though he was immersing himself in a dream, not privy to the likes of others.

`It's coming on, Sam, it's coming on. But, we are not quite there. Charles, of course, doesn't want to wait until it's perfected. He wants to broadcast it to the heavens now. He has arranged this demonstration in London, and frankly, we are not quite ready for it.`

I nodded. That accorded with Urban's attitude.

George continued. `We've still got haloing around the moving figures, and the only way I can see to overcome the problem is to run the film at sixty frames a second. As we both know, that's an impossible task when you're hand cranking. I produced this film, *A visit to the Seaside*, more as a novelty, a first attempt. But we need to carry on experimenting.`

I looked more closely at my old employer. He had aged in eighteen months. His skin was sallow; his eyes deep-sunk; he was a little more bowed. All the characteristics of time spent indoors, working all the waking hours.

`How long will it take to get it absolutely right?`

Not my question, but Laura's.

George had been staring into the flames of the fire. He turned towards me.

`Possibly, six months, another year at the most. Anyway, enough about me, tell us all that you've been up to, Sam.`

I spent the next half hour recounting my adventures. Skipping over some of the problems: the beating we had suffered on my first visit to Fort Lee; the attack on the metal-framed studio; and the lawsuits we were now facing.

`I haven't seen this film of yours, *Hiawatha*, but I hear it is attracting huge audiences,` commented Laura. `It won't come down to Brighton for another couple of weeks, but we'll go and see it when it does, won't we George?`

However, George was already lost to us in his own world.

I rose to leave. Thanking Laura for receiving me at such short notice.

`Goodbye, George.`

His head swivelled round. `Oh, you're off, are you? Come and see us again.`

I leaned forward and shook his hand. `Look after yourself, old friend.`

Laura walked with me to the end of the drive, where a hansom had arrived to pick me up.

As I kissed her cheek, she said. `George and Charles were having the most fearful row when I went to tell him of your arrival. That fellow is too much. He was telling George that on no account was the process to be offered to you. He has much bigger plans for when it is launched in America. What is more, Urban wants to take the process which George has invented, and sell it now as a complete package to theatre and cinema owners.`

`But George is adamant it's not quite ready.`

`Urban's response to that is it will be by the time it's in production.`

I shook my head. `As you say, Laura, that man really is too much.`

I stepped into the horse-drawn cab and we were off. But suddenly a thought struck me, and I called to the driver to halt. I walked back.

`Tell me, Laura, is the process registered in George's name?`

`I asked the same question, Sam. George assured me it is.`

`Good...as a friend I would strongly suggest that he patents the colour system in the States,` I said thoughtfully. `Better still I'll come back into the house and have a word with you both.`

I turned to the driver. `Could you wait for me for half an hour?`

`As long as you're paying the waiting time, Guv'nor.`

Three quarters of an hour later I had all the drawings, photographs and a copy of the patent registration document.

`If you accept that I am trustworthy, George, I shall register the *Kinemacolor* process in my name. Our lawyers in America will prepare and send two letters to you. One will confirm that I am holding the patent in your name. The other will be for you to sign as authorisation to end the arrangement, whenever, you feel the need to do so. That way you have protection against me taking advantage of all your work.`

`Urban is more than likely to do that,` added Laura acerbically. `You never know what the fellow is up to.`

The next two days passed quickly. I had another meeting with our distribution agents in London, at which we formally signed a three year contract. Thereafter, I returned to make my farewells in Brighton and Piddinghoe.

I promised my mother that I would not leave it so long next time, and would definitely be back within the next twelve months. I caught up with Geoffrey, and complimented him on his camera work. He still favoured plus-fours and those wide caps that flopped around his head. He excitedly told me of the birth of his second son, and shyly mentioned that he had called him Sam in my honour. The last evening meal was taken at Mrs Earl`s, who requested I sent some photographs of America to her.

Early the following morning her husband, Harry, gave me a lift to the railway station, where we woodenly shook hands. I watched him turn the trap, and as the pony trotted out the forecourt, he called over his shoulder. `Don`t forget the photographs for Mildred, will you?`

In all the years I had lodged with them I never knew her name was Mildred.

CHAPTER TWENTY - FIVE

Eight days later we docked in New York Harbour. An odd feeling...it was as though I had come home.

A cab took me to the Judson, where I collected my belongings, paid the bill and went off in search of other accommodation. Until the future appeared reasonably stable, it seemed sensible not to lease an apartment but take a room in a more comfortable hotel. In my journeys around Manhattan I had noticed the Algonquin on West Forty Fourth Street. I checked in there, initially for a week. Its location was also closer to the IMP offices by DeWitt Clinton Park.

The porter explained, as doubtless he had many times to visitors and guests. 'The Algonquin Indians had their campsites on the land now occupied by the hotel, sir. Hence the name.' He leaned towards me. 'You know what I think?'

I shook my head.

'I think it was the Iroquois. The Algonquin tribes were much further north, towards the Canadian border.'

'Right...'

It was a pleasant room, with its own separate bathroom. No running down the corridor at the sound of a bolt being drawn.

I arrived at the offices the same time as Carl Laemmle.

'So, how did it go? Good trip? Did you sort out our distributors?'

I pulled the contract from the briefcase, and pushed it across the desk to him. He slumped down in a chair and quickly skimmed through it.

'It's what we prepared, Carl. The important bit is on the last page...their signatures of agreement to take fifty, one reelers a year for the next three years...and at a higher purchase price.'

He continued to read the entire document, before passing it back.

`At least we can send our films over there.`

I sensed something.

`What are you not telling me?` I asked.

He leaned on his side of the desk. `How long were you away?`

`Twenty six days...why?`

`You remember there was talk before you left of Edison forming some sort of consortium? You know, with the big studios that can afford to pay his licence fees. Well he`s done it. Edison, Vitagraph, Essanay, Selig, Lubin, Kalem, American Star, and American Pathé have all pooled their patents and are now known as The Motion Picture Patents Company. What is more, I reckon Biograph will shortly be joining them. They have even ensnared your friend, George Kleine, and, would you believe, the biggest supplier of raw film stock, Eastman Kodak. This will almost certainly curtail films coming in from abroad, and could hit us hard, Sam. We`ve really got a fight on our hands.`

I stared at him, trying to take in what he was saying.

`As Edison sees it, this is how it will work. The consortium, or as they call themselves, the Motion Picture Patent Company, colloquially referred to as the Trust, will pool its patents on the technology of cameras and projectors. With the threat of patent infringement lying over them, the smaller studios will have to submit to the Trust`s licensing agreements. If they get away with it the Trust will even dictate who screens their films and where.

`Another "gotcha" is Eastman Kodak. With its patent on raw film stock, it has agreed to sell only to trust members. All in all, they believe they now have a stranglehold on all us independents. Isadore is with our lawyers this morning, seeing if it`s legal.`

`Surely, it would be difficult to impose all their rules and regulations?` I mumbled. `There are a number of film makers like us. They can`t keep their eye on everyone, can they?`

`Sam, the patents owned by the MPPC permit them to use federal law enforcement officials to execute their licensing agreements, to prevent so-called unauthorised use of their cameras, film, projectors, and other equipment. I haven`t told you of the other organisation the Trust has formed. It`s called the General Film Company, run by a fellow called Luke Mitchell. Ostensibly, it monitors distribution. In reality, I`ve heard it makes use of hired thugs to disrupt unlicensed shoots, and is not adverse to breaking equipment and destroying film.`

Just then, the door opened and Isadore walked in, his face a picture of dejection.

`Carl, they say we can`t do anything about it. You can try fighting it in the courts, but they believe our chances are slim to non-existent. We`ve got a mountain of writs already issued against us. They are saying, "do you want to continue and receive more"?`

Carl Laemmle glanced at me.

`What do you think, Sam?`

`It`s a tough one, Carl. At first sight, we should give up film making all together, and join those working in Fulton Street Market. But let`s think about it. We`re still making money from *Hiawatha*, aren`t we, Isadore?`

`Yes, there`s cash in the bank.`

`Enough to keep us going for a while?`

`I`d say about six months.`

`And we`ve agreed a new contract with our European distributors, Isadore, which gives us a higher percentage, and should keep us afloat even longer,` added Carl.

`You`re forgetting we have all those court cases pending. How are we going to pay for those?`

`Well, this is the way I see the situation,` I remarked thoughtfully. `We`ve got to ensure we can finance at least thirty films. Good, money-making productions. We should also retain enough to pay our lawyers, and to keep us fed and clothed. Don`t concern yourself with meeting the lawsuits. Any one of them would probably bankrupt us.`

`Err, it`s now over two hundred, Sam,` said Carl in a low voice.

I could not help frowning at him in disbelief.

`They just keep arriving.` he mumbled.

`Well, that confirms it. We can`t go out of business. We have to keep going to pay the legal costs that just seem to mount up.`

I suddenly grinned at the two of them.

`Look, we actually can beat them at their own game. Didn`t you tell me that Edison still relies on reality pictures? You know, A view from the

Empire State building, or sailing up the Hudson River. Short films, interesting perhaps, but the Trust members don`t make films that tug at the heartstrings, or make people laugh.

`Moviegoers have moved on. Now they want good stories, love, romance, suspense, winning through against the odds. A bit like us. So that`s what we`ll give them. We`ll be innovative, we`ll make longer, multi-reel feature films, and let the ten thousand theatre owners decide what they want to show their audiences. This is make or break time.`

I didn`t realise that they were both hanging on my words, until I stopped, and suddenly there was silence.

`Bravo, Sam,` cried Isadore. `You`re damned right, boy.`

Carl was more sanguine. He just nodded his head and grinned broadly.

Between compiling the list of films to meet our overseas obligations, and calculating how we could do back-to-back productions using the same actors with only minor adjustments to the sets, I visited our lawyers. They prepared the necessary documents listing me as the patent owner of Kinemacolor, George`s colour process, and the letters allowing its registration to revert to him.

However, they soon uncovered a problem.

`It is this, Mr Lockhart,` declared the lawyer, polishing his spectacles. `George Albert Smith may have the patent registered in his name in the UK, but here, in the United States, someone called Charles Urban registered the process long ago. In its present form, therefore, you will be prohibited from being recognised as the patentee.`

`Right, I`ll improve on the earlier submission and ask you to re-present it.`

More writs came in the mail; but each delivery only increased our determination to fight the constraints the Trust was seeking to impose upon us. Isadore seemed to be permanently anchored at our lawyer`s office; and on the rare occasions we met in the offices, a miasma, a pervasive air of gloom, hung over him like a cloud.

One early morning I met up with Carl at his apartment before taking the ferry upriver. That afternoon, Carl was meeting other film makers opposed to the Motion Picture Patents Company. If they could band together, the independents could also close ranks, and rail with a louder voice against the actions of the MPPC.

`You would be surprised, Sam, at what some of these guys have suffered,` Carl declared angrily. `They`ve had equipment stolen, broken, openly confiscated by louts wielding baseball bats. Their sets have been destroyed, in a number of cases burnt down. Even some of their production people have been beaten. They are not just attacking us through the courts, they are threatening us physically, and the law enforcement agents are doing nothing about it. Well, I for one am not going to let Edison and his mob run roughshod over me. I`m going to fight back...an eye for an eye...`

`Carl, don`t do anything hasty. Defending yourself is one thing, hitting back puts you on their level. Use a little subtlety. Let`s get some cameras hidden around the sets and in the studios, and, if possible, take pictures of them actually doing damage. Get as much visual evidence as we can, then show the public what the Motion Pictures Patents Company is really about. Not protecting people`s morals, but trying to monopolise the film industry by strong-arm tactics. I`ve heard there`s a film magazine being launched soon, I believe the title is Motion Picture Story. Get in touch with the editor, or whoever runs it, and bring him in on what you`re doing. It would make interesting reading, and strengthen your case when you could get moviegoers on your side.`

He gave that characteristic grin. `That`s smart, Sam. I`ll bring that up at the meeting.`

Walter Johnson had done a good job. He went up further in my estimation when he told me of the attempted break-in.

`They must have come through the wire fence over there in that corner.` He pointed in the direction of some distant trees. They didn`t get further than fifty feet from the building when the dogs went for them. I think they made it back to the other side of the wire, but not without some personal damage.`

He pulled pieces of torn clothing from his pocket. On some there was evidence of blood.

`I`m going to increase the number of dogs and handlers at night, just in case they come back, Sam. Do you think Carl will agree?`

`Without hesitation, Walter. Go ahead and do it. By the way,` I added, `you might find they will come back during the day. I have spoken with Carl, and he agrees it would be worthwhile always having someone with a camera ready to photograph any break-ins. I'd like to catch whoever it is red-handed. So for a few nights let's dispense with the dogs and their handlers.`

`A good idea, Sam. Leave it to me. By the way, when do you think you'll be finished with my services? Only, I need to start my next project soon.`

`I would say in two weeks time. I'll be shipping all that we need up here. Cameras, a few projectors, set materials, and of course the actors. Tell me, do you know any carpenters and painters in Fort Lee?`

`If you wish I can organise a work force, say five or six people, and have them here when you arrive.`

`That's exactly what I'm looking for. Great, thanks Walter.`

We shook hands and I started back for the city. On the ferry I was preoccupied by two thoughts. I could never get used to calling him, "Walt". To me, he would always be "Walter". What was this preoccupation with abbreviated names? The second was more rational. Walter Johnson was a first class man to have on your side. Why don't we appoint him the Fort Lee studio manager?

`I agree,` said Carl. `What do you say, Isadore?`

`Fine by me.`

`OK, I'll raise it with Walter when we take all the props, raw materials and equipment up there.`

`I'll follow a few days later with the actors,` added Carl `Have you got the set directions, cue cards, and the dialogue exchanges ready, Sam?`

`They are being typed as we speak, Carl. I'm using an agency on Fifty Second Street. They'll be ready for collection tomorrow.`

`Fine. How many films are we shooting in this batch?`

`Four. I'm allowing two to two and a half days for each movie, though some will probably take less. Then we break for three days, return to Fort Lee and do the next four, and so on. I've budgeted twelve hundred dollars for each one reel. This covers the cost of set pieces, film, developing, editing, and the equipment needed for the production, as well as ten dollars a day for the actors. That's what you said we were paying them, Carl. That still stands, I presume?`

`Sure. That's more than they get for theatre work. They'll be quite happy with that. By the way, Sam, have you had any ideas yet for a three or four reel picture?`

`Actually, I have, Carl. Though it's all up here at the moment.` I tapped my head.

`He nodded. `So…give us a clue to what it's about then.`

`I'd rather leave it until I have worked out the format.`

`OK, just the subject matter.`

I was not sure how he would react. It was a daring topic, perhaps a little too risqué for an earnest, synagogue-attendee holding forthright views on morality and ethics.

`Well?`

`As I say,` I muttered, `it's still in the early stages. Nothing concrete.`

I glanced at Isadore, then back to Carl.

`It's about white slave trafficking. The working title is, *While New York Sleeps*. Thousands of young women disappear each year. In a way it's a pseudo-documentary. A criminal organisation abducts poor immigrant women, forcing them into prostitution. The arch-villain is a seemingly respectable businessman who handles the money while his underlings do the dirty work. When a young woman is drugged and kidnapped, her sister teams up with her policeman boyfriend to rescue her.`

I could see the dismay on Carl's face. He took a deep breath.

`No. We are *not* going to make that, Sam. It is a deplorable subject. I know it goes on, but who are we to attempt to make money out of such practices. Think of something else.`

And that was it. The idea was destined for the trash can.

CHAPTER TWENTY - SIX

We had been at Fort Lee for two days when Walter came over to me. I was supervising the build-up of the sets. The first production, with the working title, '*The Forest Ranger's Daughter*', was a ten minute standard which I expected to complete in a day and a half. That is if the players Carl had hired were accustomed to film work, and were passably good actors.

The backdrop for the next moving picture was on the reverse side of the staging; and we could move smoothly on to the next single reel epic.

`Everything all right, Sam?` he queried. I had left it to Walter to bring in the carpenters and painters from the township.

`They're doing a good job, Walter.`

Since we had arrived, with everything packed on four big wagons, there had been little opportunity for a discussion. Unloading, storing, briefing the construction teams, checking the equipment, preparing the stage floor and turn-around order of the schedule, had all taken priority.

He was walking away when I called him back.

`Walter, do you have a moment? You live in Fort Lee don't you?`

`Not exactly, I've got a place just outside Edgewater. It's was once my parents' house. When they passed on my wife and I took it over. Why?`

`You mentioned that you were heading off on another contract as soon as you finished here. What's that? Another construction job?`

`Yes, of a kind, over in Scranton, about eighty miles away. Which means I'll have stay there until the job finished.`

`Ideally, you'd prefer working closer to home?`

`Naturally...but you have to go where the work is. I guess my wife is used to that by now.`

`Tell me, Walter what does your wife call you?`

`How d'you mean?`

`Is it "Walt", or "Walter"?`

`Isabel says my name is Walter, and she would never call me anything else.`

I smiled to myself.

`Sounds a sensible lady. Tell me, Walter, if I said cancel the contract in Scranton, stay here at Fort Lee and run the IMP Studio, what would you say? We'd pay you the going rate, and, of course, you wouldn't have to pay for a rooming house or travel. The bonus would be you wouldn't have to leave your family.`

There were two actors. Carl said a third was delayed, but he would definitely be here tomorrow. I got to know them over dinner, and learned that the leading lady, a young blonde, was actually married to the director, Harry Solter. Her name was Florence Lawrence, and she had first appeared in a film made by the Edison Manufacturing Company. She had a refreshingly, honest personality which came over as the evening wore on.

`I got the part of Daniel Boone's daughter in *Pioneer Days in America* because I knew how to ride a horse,` she said laughingly. `After that I went to work for the Vitagraph Company in Brooklyn. My introduction to films was as Moya, an Irish peasant girl in a one-reel version of Dion Boucicault's *The Shaughraun*. In all I've done eleven pictures for Vitagraph. That's where I met Harry,` she explained, laying a hand on his arm.

`When Harry moved to the Biograph Company, it wasn't long before he told D. W. Griffiths about this woman he knew who would be ideal for a part in *The Girl and the Outlaw*. Ever since then I've worked for Biograph.`

It was then I put a name to a face. I had seen several of their moving pictures in which she had featured. She still had much to learn, but the essentials were there, and she was decidedly attractive.

`So, what do you think?` asked Carl, when the couple had left the table.

`Good choice, Carl. But she's not with us yet, officially I mean, is she? How did you manage to entice her to star in this batch of films? She could get fired by Biograph.`

`I told her that the films we were making were all destined for Europe. There was no chance of anyone from Biograph seeing them.`

`And that was it?`

`Well if they are not working or directing a moving picture, they don't earn anything, other than a nominal retainer fee. They've got to eat, and as you know, I offered each of them ten dollars a day.`

I nodded. `OK, so Harry takes over as director tomorrow, and presumably they'll run through the scenes before shooting. I'll be in the studio finalising the staging of *The Brave Policeman*. It will be a split reel production, on the same spool as *The Forest Ranger's Daughter*. I'll come by the set in the afternoon, just to check we're on schedule.`

It was a simple plot. *The Forest Ranger's Daughter* decides upon the man she wants as a husband and ensures he is caught with her in a situation which her father regards as highly compromising. As a consequence, a minister is hurriedly brought in to officiate at their marriage. Ten minutes of lighthearted comedy: ideally suited to British, French and German tastes.

Over the next nine days we completed *The Forest Ranger's Daughter*, *The Brave Policeman*, *Her Generous Way* - a wife innocently inspires suspicion by giving away money she had received to buy a hat; and *Lest We Forget* – a little rich girl helps a little poor girl make her Christmas memorable.

On the tenth day we were all back in New York City.

We said our farewells at the ferry terminal, and Carl and I took an electrobat to Eleventh and Fifty Third Street. As we weaved our way through the traffic, he said. `That was a good session, Sam. By the way, I've booked Florence and Harry for another four films after the next tranche. Is that OK with you?`

`Fine, but we need a couple of male leads for the next series. Got any suggestions?`

`Leave that to me. I'll sort it out,` Carl declared. `I've got some people in mind.`

He tapped on the roof. `Driver, can we go via Fifty Ninth Street, please?`

He smiled at my puzzled frown.

`There are occasions when I have to look at the place I slept in that first night I arrived in New York. Forgive me, this is one of those times.`

We turned into Fifty Ninth Street, heading towards the distant Central Park.

Carl banged again.

`Driver, stop just for a moment.`

We had come to a halt outside a rundown block of apartments. There was a depressing shabbiness about the area. Although the Lower East Side was perhaps similar in character, it had a vivacity, a carefree spirit of hope. That had long drained from this mean street.

Carl sat there staring up at the building.

`We were just seventeen, my friend, Leo Hirschfeld and I. We were taken to the boarding house of one of our travelling companions. Just like you were, Sam. It was there, on the corner of 59th Street and Third Avenue, where I spent my first night on this new continent.` He nodded slowly, almost to himself. `You know, I often make this pilgrimage. It keeps my feet on the ground.

`It was an unsettling time for a naïve kid from Laupheim, from the backwoods of southern Germany. I used to delight in travelling on the elevated railway that runs down the middle of Third Avenue. I'd never seen anything like that before. We'd get off the EL train at Houston Street, exactly ten stops, visit family friends, and go to the nearby synagogue.`

He took a deep breath. `So much has changed in my life, Sam. I really do count my blessings.`

After the clear air of Fort Lee, the fumes from the gasworks seemed even more pungent when we walked up the stairs to our offices.

`Ah...you're back,` said Isadore in welcome. `All's well I trust. Talking about trust, we've received ten more writs from Edison's people. And I'm told by our lawyer the first has to be answered in court two weeks next Tuesday.`

`Shan't be here, Isadore,` declared Carl airily. `You'll have to represent IMP.`

`But your name is on the summons.`

`So is `Independent Moving Pictures`. You work for and are a shareholder in IMP, so, as I say, you can represent us. Anyway, you know more about what's going on. You spend enough time and money with that lawyer of ours.`

He looked uncertain. `I'm not sure I would be the best man to answer for our actions. Moreover, the early lawsuits were for activities before I joined the company.`

`Actually, he is right, Carl. I think you should be there. If we can muster a stout defence against the opening salvo, we might well be able to hold our own against all the others. By the way, Isadore, what`s the total at the moment.`

`Close to two hundred and fifty, Sam.`

`If I can get through the next batch of films on time, do you mind if I join you, Carl? At least, then there would be two of us they can shoot at.`

I worked solidly for the next three days, and went up to Fort Lee jaded but content with the four films we were about to shoot. The first two I particularly liked. One was called, *The Coquette's Suitors* – a beautiful woman has numerous suitors who lavish presents upon her; but when one presents her with a ring, he becomes the man of her choice. Florence was playing the lead, and an actor called King Baggot was performing alongside her with Owen Moore, another unknown stage actor.

The same cast was in *The Governor's Pardon*. An honest man trades places with a convict, so he can visit his dying wife. But he is killed on his way back to the prison. A melodramatic offering, with a heartfelt tug at the emotions. We got both pictures in the can quickly and efficiently. Harry Solter had got the best out of all three actors.

We had just started filming *The Awakening of Bess* when there was a concentrated barrage of blows rendered by baseball bats against the glass sidewalls. They splintered, fractured and gave way under the assault, glass flying everywhere. A dozen, burly men broke through into the studio, and pushed us roughly to one side while they calmly and deliberately began breaking up our equipment, lighting, and exposing the film stock.

Walter appeared with three or four men ready to do battle. But I shouted at him not to interfere. Heavily outnumbered they would only have suffered a severe beating. In ten minutes it was over, the sets and equipment were totally wrecked. I moved towards the stage area and stood beneath an overhead light. The ringleader came over to me and pushed me heavily in the chest.

`See what we do, Mr fucking Lockhart, if you tangle with us. We`ll break you in the courts, and we`ll break you physically!`

He pushed me harder this time, his voice full of menace.

`And you will be first on my list!`

I provoked him further.

`Don`t you realise that you will go away for a long stretch when they

151

bring you to trial? Mr Edison won`t save you then. He won`t want to know you. He`ll drop you like a hot potato.`

I knew what his response would be; and was ready for the blow when it landed. The full force of the swinging baseball bat was partially deflected by leaning away and taking it on my upraised arms. But I was still sent sprawling.

I rolled away to avoid further damage.

`Let`s get out of here, Luke! We`ve done what was intended!`

The leader stood over me for a moment, before kicking me hard. As he walked through the broken glass wall he turned, lofted the bat in my direction and shouted. `Don`t forget, Lockhart, you`re a marked man!`

Florence was led away in tears, the two male actors were also shocked by the incident.

`You didn`t tell us this might happen, Sam,` Solter commented with feeling. `We could all have been injured in that rough-house. Who were they?`

`Don`t you know, Harry? They work for the General Film Company, an undeclared offshoot of The Motion Picture Patents Company.`

Walter helped me to the pharmacy across Main Street, and called the local doctor.

`Been in the wars again, Mr Lockhart? I wouldn`t make too much of a habit of it if I were you,` he murmured as he treated my cuts and bruises.

There was nothing more we could do.

It would take time to rectify the damage and resolve the situation with the insurance companies. Suddenly, it all hinged on the outcome of the lawsuits. If the many decisions went against us, the insurers could claim we were operating illegally and the policies were void, regardless of the fact that a deliberate attack had been made upon us.

Walter was determined to get the studio up and running as soon as possible, and when I spoke to Carl on the telephone he gave the immediate go-ahead to repair the building.

`We can`t sit back and wait for the insurance to pay up, Sam. If they ever do. We`ve got to repair the damage and carry on.`

`What about all the equipment? To replace that would really drain our resources,` I said with a heavy heart.

`Don`t worry about that for the moment. I`ll sort that out. Your job is to convince Harry and the actors to soldier on.`

`But how? There`s nothing left, Carl.`

`Sam, speak to Harry first, offer them more money if you have to. Then get him to have a word with Florence, King and Owen. I`ll telephone you back within the hour.`

With that the line went dead.

`Yes, they`ll stay on. I`ve agreed to pay them each an extra two dollars a day inconvenience money. I`ve had a word with Harry, and we`ll do the exteriors for the two remaining films, which will take a couple of days, but what happens after that?`

`Sam, I`ve been speaking with Mark Dintenfass. He runs the Champion Studios over on Fifth Street in Coytesville. He is quite willing for you to use his studio. If you can rig the sets we`re back in business.`

After the outside scenes shot on the heights of the Palisades, we transferred to Champion Films. The sets had been rebuilt and filming of *The Broken Oath*, which was about a girl who saves her sweetheart from the dealings of a deceitful gang that he has fallen in with, went off without a hitch. At the end of the week I called everyone together, thanked them for their efforts and declared we would soon be filming again in the IMP studio. Naturally, there would be a slight delay because of the repairs, but I would be in touch with the date when we would recommence.

I did not mention that during the interim Independent Moving Pictures was facing a legal battle that would make or break the company.

CHAPTER TWENTY - SEVEN

The one piece of news that briefly brightened the gloom was the jail sentence handed down to Luke Mitchell. He was sent down for three years hard labour which he would serve in the Blackwell Island Penitentiary, located in the middle of the East River.

He was the leader of the mob that destroyed our film set up at Fort Lee. Although we had witnesses to the onslaught, the most telling evidence were the photographs of Mitchell threatening and knocking me to the ground. Having a cameraman on standby had served us well. Although they clearly portrayed his thugs meting out damage to our equipment, they could not be readily identified. However, the image of Luke Mitchell was clear. I had moved to a well-lit area and goaded him into striking out at me.

The police had no hesitation in arresting him; and once the photographs were shown at the trial, his defence evaporated.

Having given evidence in the case, I remained in court for the sentencing. When Mitchell was led away he saw me sitting in the public area. He halted, stared hard in my direction, wagged a finger in my direction and mouthed, "The first on my list!"

But I had bigger worries to think about. The all-important court hearing, the confrontation we were about to face, would be make-or-break for IMP. We had to win to survive.

CHAPTER TWENTY - EIGHT

Both sides dispensed with the need for a jury, opting instead for a bench trial.

The Trust's lawyers believed their case was watertight, that the ruling would be found in their favour, setting a precedent for the remainder of the lawsuits. We were more concerned with limiting costs.

That morning, before attending court, I checked the current number of summons served on us.

`The grand total to date, Sam,` declared Isadore, as he ran his figure over the list, `is two hundred and eighty nine. And the damages MPPC, the Trust, is now seeking amounts to over a quarter of a million dollars. So, *mazel tov, boychick*, you'll need it.`

We had received a stack of mail and numerous telephone calls from well-wishers. All the independents were following the outcome, for the verdict would have repercussions for us all.

The case was being heard at the Red Hook Courthouse in Brooklyn; and the issue before us, by way of a test case, was the supposed illegal use of the Latham Loop. Some years earlier, engineers at a company owned by Woodville Latham, had come up with the invention of a loop system which isolated the filmstrip from vibration and tension, allowing movies to be projected a greater number of times.

Latham's patent was eventually sold to the Biograph Company. Selecting this particular issue stemmed from an action taken by Edison, himself, against Biograph, before they were united in membership of the Trust. Thomas Edison had questioned the validity of the patent, and lost when a federal court had upheld Biograph's rights. So the Trust felt supremely confident in their claim against us.

In fact, of the pool of sixteen motion picture patents held by the Trust, Carl had discovered that ten were considered of minor importance. The key patents pertained to film, cameras, three to projectors and more significantly, the Latham Loop.

Carl, our lawyer Lewis Milestone, and I pushed open the double doors to the courtroom. It was a high-ceilinged, uninviting room, with the judge`s forbidding dais rising before us. On the left-hand side were the tiered jury`s benches, which would remain vacant during the trial. Pushing through the low swing gate, we entered the well of the court and took the available table. The Trust`s lawyers, four of them, as well as a representative of the litigant, were seated on the opposite side.

The public seats began to fill. I recognised and nodded to a number of fellow film makers, seated among journalists working for leading newspapers. The rest were seemingly occupied by people off the street, giving half an ear to the proceedings.

The court reporter entered through a side door and took her place beside the Stenotype machine: three ushers took up positions around the room. One, standing by a side door, called in a loud voice, `All rise`; and the robed figure of the judge mounted the steps, ready to determine the outcome of the lawsuit. After many months of being the recipient of writs proclaiming legal action, for IMP the moment had arrived.

Another usher, with an even louder voice, declared `Case number eight, nine, one, four, brought by The Motion Picture Patents Company against the Independent Moving Pictures Company, for infringement of patent number seven, zero, seven, nine, three, four, first awarded to Mr Woodville Latham on August the twenty sixth, 1902, and subsequently transferred to the American Mutoscope and Biograph Company on February the fifth 1908, with allowed title currently awarded to the Motion Picture Patents Company.`

Lewis Milestone whispered. `That`s good, we`ve got Judge Learned Hand. He`s a fair-minded, no-nonsense arbiter.`

`Is that a title, or is "Learned" his real name?` I asked in a low voice.

Milestone grinned. `Actually, his full name is Billings Learned Hand. His family always assign surnames as their children`s forenames.`

The judge frowned at our whispered conversation. `When you`re quite ready Mr Milestone.`

Lewis Milestone bowed his head. `Your Honour.`

'Right, well before we proceed, I understand both parties have chosen for this case to be heard as a bench trial. Does either party now wish to change that decision?`

He stared over his glasses at both tables. Nothing was said, and in this instance our silences were taken for the status quo to remain.

`Very well, let's get on with it. Mr Levett, I understand you are representing the plaintiff. Would you, or one of your colleagues, care to submit the cause and nature of this action against the defendant?`

A thin, ascetic-looking man rose from the opposing table. He stared hard in our direction for a moment, before commencing his opening statement.

`Your Honour, you may well be conversant with aspects of the motion picture industry, and noted that the pace of change that has occurred during the past ten years has been quite remarkable. My client is actually a group of companies that have come together to represent all that is good and morally decent within this industry. It has done so to protect moviegoers against the prurient, the obscene and less-welcome aspects that could, unless regulated, infiltrate the production of motion pictures. I would point out that already close on a hundred thousand people attend movie parlours and theatres each night to be entertained; and this number is increasing rapidly. Safeguards have to be introduced and carefully monitored.

`The Motion Picture Patents Company, which if Your Honour will allow, I shall refer to as the MPPC, the company's acronym, earnestly believes standards have to be maintained. This is a dynamic medium, one that could easily attract the worst kind of film maker. It is in this belief that the MPPC, working collectively, as a body in trust, should uphold all that is honourable by managing what is offered to movie parlours and theatres. It is, in fact, for this reason that the MPPC is identified by all within the industry as the Trust.

`It has no wish to suppress talent, merely to ensure film makers and exhibitors hold true to this country's moral code.`

Levett stopped briefly for a sip of water. Carl leaned towards me.

`This is a new approach, the upholders of public morals. Is that what their thugs were doing?`

`Your Honour,` continued their counsellor, `because this industry is in its infancy, still finding its way, the methods open to the MPPC are perforce, somewhat rudimentary. My client recognises that the only way to subscribe to a common cause, is literally that...to subscribe. To pay a fee for the right to the materials and methods used in the production of motion pictures. Enforceable because Trust members hold the requisite patents.

`By making a subscription, film makers are bound by the conventions of the Motion Picture Patents Company. In effect, Your Honour, it allows the Trust to become a regulatory body.

`The charges are not exorbitant, yet predictably, there are those who would evade subscribing to this well-intentioned cause. They may even be contemplating the production of motion pictures that fly in the face of what my client is desperate to eliminate. I am satisfied, Your Honour, that the path the Trust is pursuing is the only way we can safeguard the probity of the motion picture industry, and the moral welfare of the increasing numbers who flock to see what is being portrayed on screens across this country. It is when the Trust is confronted by those who deliberately flout requests to subscribe to common ideals, that we are forced to take the action that has brought us here today.`

This time he turned fully in our direction, and pointed at us with an outstretched finger.

`These gentlemen represent all that runs counter to maintaining the integrity of the motion picture industry. That is why we are taking them to task for the blatant  infringement  of  my client`s patent. It is done in the certain hope that they will be forced to observe the sensible and honourable conditions the MPPC feel justified in imposing on behalf of this nation`s viewing public.`

Even if inaccurate, it was still a powerful opening statement. I knew the press would make capital of it. Tomorrow`s headlines would blare out such phrases as, `The MPPC, champion of the film industry`s morals`.

I glanced at our lawyer, and thought, well, you get what you pay for, and perhaps we have not paid enough. I had met another of his colleagues when I dealt with the patent registration of George`s colour process. He had done the job quickly and competently. However, this fellow had failed to impress me when we first met on the steps of the courthouse.

I studied him as he shuffled papers before rising slowly to his feet. He was not much taller than Carl, who was only five foot three. His hair was slicked back from his forehead, and although he wore a pencil moustache, Mr Milestone appeared to be fresh from law school. In fact, at a second glance, fresh from high school. He wore glasses, probably more to give a semblance of maturity; but he could not disguise the slight tic under his left eye.

When he stuttered his opening words, I stared down at the floor thinking this could not get any worse. We were going to lose this and all subsequent lawsuits by a country mile. Under lowered eyebrows I saw Levett at the next table openly smirking.

`Do you want to begin again, Mr Milestone?` the judge enquired.

`Perhaps, I should, Your Honour. I was searching for notes that were not immediately at hand.`

`Well, if you now have them available, would you care to submit your opening statement on behalf of the defendant. I`m sure those present are as anxious as I to hear what you have to say.`

The slight put-down was not unkindly, and the brief titter of amusement from the public area was not scornful. Nevertheless, I wondered how Milestone would react.

`Mr Levett puts forward a very cogent argument. So much so, one cannot fault the idealism that resonates throughout his submission. Every word was a tribute to his client, the Motion Picture Patents Company, which, it would appear, is committed to defending the moral welfare of all American moviegoers. A profound ideal...a lofty ideal...one that all of us can only admire.

`In effect, he is taking this country`s motto, "In God we trust", and adding another dimension. "In the Trust we trust". The moral high ground adopted by his client should be applauded by every one of us...if it were true.

`I will demonstrate to this court that the Motion Picture Patents Company, which we are told everyone trusts, is nothing more than a cartel bent on securing total control of the American film industry. Not, I should point out, for any wish to elevate the morals of this nation to the highest level, but for financial gain. It is bringing about these lawsuits to cower earnest, well-intentioned film makers, and draw them under its thumb. Greed is the motivating force here, Your Honour. Nothing more.`

He, too, stopped to raise a glass of water to his lips. But, I had the impression not to quench a thirst, but to allow his last comment to sink into our thoughts.

I waited for his next salvo. Suddenly, I was enjoying the moment. Mr Milestone seemed to know what he was about.

`Why do I say that greed is their motivating force? Simply this.`

He picked up a sheet of paper, the one he declared earlier was not to hand.

`Mr Levett has stated that the aim of the Trust is to bring to moviegoers entertaining motion pictures that safeguard the morals of this nation; and my client, the Independent Moving Pictures Company, should be made to contribute through the Trust's demanding fee system to the imposition of such an ideal. *Ipso facto*, it stands that all the members of the Trust are principled, conscientious organisations which adhere rigidly to their own lofty code.

`So, Your Honour, I find myself questioning why Mr Levett paints such a commendable picture of Trust members, when in practice, they openly flout these high-minded principles when making their own motion pictures.`

He appeared to study the sheet of paper.

`One only has to recall such films as `*What Happened On Twenty Third Street*, made by the Edison Film Company, `*Beauty Unadorned*` from the Vitagraph Studios, `*Drunkeness*` by Pathé Films, and Biograph's `*From Show Girl to Burlesque Queen*`, and of course, `*Peeping Tom in the Dressing Room*`, to realise that for all Mr Levett's praise of his clients in the guise of the Trust is, when it comes down to it, just empty words.

`I will demonstrate, Your Honour, that the patent right with which the Trust is beating my client about the head, is an archaic, stifling brake on the earnest intentions of the Independent Moving Pictures Company, and other like-minded film makers. If allowed to continue, it will lead to the stagnation and ruin of an industry that could soon be making a valuable contribution to this country's economy.`

When Lewis Milestone sat down, I gazed upon him in a completely different light.

CHAPTER TWENTY - NINE

The Trust's counsel, undeterred by Lewis Milestone's stinging attack on their client's virtues, began assembling a powerful case against Carl and IMP. They painted him as an opportunist, an uncaring exploiter of other people's endeavours, who ignored all the proper business conventions to fulfill his own ends.

If I did not know the man, he would have appeared an ogre, a tyrant, certainly one not to be trusted. They called witnesses, even people personally associated with Carl in the past, and drew from them the picture of a man ruthless in his ambition, ready in a instant to ride rough-shod over those who might stand in his way, and significantly, to show contempt for any rule, statute or ordinance that protected other people's property.

They started with several individuals, whom Carl had known in his early days when owner of his first nickelodeon. They declared stoutly, he cared little for his staff, exhibitors or patrons. He had taken films destined for others, sabotaged rival nickelodeons, and short-changed those who would frequent his premises. Even when questioned by Lewis Milestone, they were undeterred in their recounting of Carl's checkered history.

During the lunch break, when the three of us occupied a table at a nearby diner, it was clear Carl had been hurt by the stories told of his former activities.

`They are simply not true, Lewis, I want you to know that. They are twisting events to suit the MPPC version of me as a businessman.`

`I can tell that, Carl,` declared the lawyer. `They have been well schooled in what to say, how to interpret their recollections, how to portray you as an unsavoury character.`

He paused.

`This afternoon, it's likely to get worse. Their tactics are to portray you, IMP, and by association, all the other independent film makers, as grasping, money-grabbing chisellers. Business men who have little thought for the well-being of others or for the industry you serve. It`s not going to be pretty, and it`s going to be painful to hear yourself denigrated and not able to fight back. Do you want to stay away from the court? I can get hold of you if I need you to testify.`

Carl thought about it for a moment. `I`ll hang on for a while, I guess. But thanks, Lewis, I might just do that.`

They moved on to his role as a film distributor.

This time one of Levett`s colleagues took up the dissection of the film distribution company, Laemmle Film Service. I knew that originally the idea had sprung from Carl's need to secure good quality films for his own theatres. He quickly realised that he could not afford to buy each film he wanted to show if he had to change the programme several times a week. Film exchanges solved the problem initally; but it became increasingly obvious that it was a hit-and-miss system. Films were not delivered on time, occasionally did not arrive at all, or would be withdrawn by a film exchange if another theatre owner offered a higher price. To overcome the problem he created his own service company, renting films out to exhibitors.

He was so successful that Laemmle Film Service soon opened offices in six major cities across the country. In less than two years, Laemmle became one of the major film distributors in America.

However, this rapid expansion invited a number of detractors: most often rivals who, by their own inadequacies, had suffered loss of business at his hand. Now, a number of his erstwhile competitors had been chosen by the opposing counsel to hammer nails in his commercial coffin.

The first to take the stand was the former owner of a film rental organisation in Indianapolis. After he had declared his name, previous occupation and location, the counsellor for the Trust moved swiftly through the preliminaries to get to the heart of his testimony.

`Am I right in thinking, Mr Ryan, that until two years ago you had a thriving film rental business in the city?`

`I did, sir. Until that man there,` he pointed at Carl, `set up in opposition, just two blocks away.`

The judge, sensing an air of belligerence, intervened.

`Counsellor, advise your witness not to use extravagant gestures in my courtroom. If any identification is to be made it will be by word of mouth only. Is that understood?`

`Yes, Your Honour. Mr Ryan just answer the questions. Please refrain from gesticulating. Now would you say that your relationship with Laemmle Film Service was one of friendly rivalry?`

`No, it certainly was not.`

`Was there at least a cordial understanding between the two companies?`

`No.`

`Mr Ryan, could you please explain the reason why?`

`Within a day of opening, Mr Laemmle and his newly appointed manager strode into my premises and declared they wanted to see me. Of course, one must always be ready to face competition, it's a fact of commercial life. Although, I must admit, I was put out that they had deliberately set up on my doorstep. Then to walk in and demand I see them that instance made it an even harder pill to swallow.`

`Did you meet with them, Mr Ryan?`

`Despite everything, I felt obliged to be sociable, sir. I told my secretary to invite them into my office.`

`What happened then?`

`I couldn't believe my ears. Laemmle told me, straight off the bat, that his film service was going to take over my customers. He would offer the latest releases to exhibitors at cut-price rental, and keep doing so until he had all the nickelodeans and parlours I served sown up tighter than a drum. It soon became clear that, if necessary, he would run his business at a loss to close me down.`

`Did you fight back to hold on to your customers?`

Ryan was getting angry. You could tell from his reddening complexion that he was finding it difficult to control himself. I wondered if the counsellor was not deliberately baiting him, encouraging an outburst.

`Of course I damned well did! No one threatens me like that!`

`What happened, Mr Ryan? Were prices cut?`

`Of course they were! How could I compete otherwise? Moreover, the blasted man spent hundreds of dollars advertising his blasted film service. He told my customers he was offering a "square deal". If they ordered a film at an agreed price, he would ensure they received it. His advertisements even told the public that where they saw the "Laemmle Sign" outside a theatre, it was their guarantee the film advertised would be on the programme. The damned man bought his way in.`

`Do I understand from what you have experienced, Mr Ryan, that this was not what anyone would regard as an ethical way to do business?`

`It most certainly was not!`

`In your attempt to save your company did you meet with Laemmle Film Services?`

`I went round to see the manager about some form of equable arrangement. He would have none of it. I was rough-handled, and thrown out. They wouldn`t answer my letters or telephone calls, and when I engaged the manager in the street, his hired bodyguards struck me down, sir. Eventually, I went out of business because of that man,` he shouted, standing and pointing agitatedly in Carl`s direction.

`Thank you, Mr Ryan. Thank you...that will be all,` declared the opposition`s counsel.

`Before the witness steps down, do you have any questions for him, Mr Milestone?`

`Not at this stage, Your Honour.`

There was hurried whispering between Carl and Lewis Milestone. When I glanced across, Carl`s face was scarlet with fury.

`In which case, gentlemen, we shall finish now, and resume at nine o`clock tomorrow morning.`

Outside, Carl`s temper spilled over. Fortunately, not in the earshot of the Trust`s legal team.

`Why the hell didn`t you tear that man`s evidence to pieces. It was a catalogue of lies. A gross distortion, Lewis, and you left the impression with the judge that I was an unscrupulous rogue and a bully.`

`Listen to me, Carl. Tomorrow, they are going to trot out more like Mr Ryan, and they will all be telling similar tales of woe. Let them bore the judge with same story, over and over again. When they`ve finished I`ll set about demolishing their whole, tedious submission in one go. Much more to the judge`s liking, believe me.`

`Hmm, well I`m certainly appearing as the ogre of this piece.`

`You`re meant to, Carl. They are trying to establish the fact that you are a ruthless, egotistical businessman. You have no morals in your dealings with others, you take all you can get. That`s why you ignored this so-called law of patent infringement. You, on behalf of the Independent Moving Pictures Company, took the Latham Loop without respecting ownership rights, and for that you should pay the penalty.`

`OK, Lewis, we`ll play it your way. But I`m not going to sit there and be vilified. If you want me tomorrow, I`ll be in the offices at Eleventh and Fifty Third Street.`

As Lewis Milestone predicted, the counsel for the Trust trotted out aggrieved film distributors, and even a couple of unhappy theatre owners, from Memphis, Omaha, Portland, Salt Lake City and Minneapolis. Places where the Laemmle Film Service had opened rental centres.

Each time, when asked if he wanted to question the witnesses, Lewis declined, but requested possible recall, to re-examine their testimonies if it became necessary. They had been well rehearsed, too much so. You could see several of those sitting in the witness box mouthing their answers almost before the questions were posed. There was a sameness about the responses that may have influenced judgement by their sheer weight. To my mind, Lewis had been right to hold off until the last witness occupied the stand.

`Your turn, Mr Milestone, if you want to take it.`

`Thank you, Your Honour, yes I have a few questions for Mr Bilton.`

I glanced at the witness list. Joseph Bilton had a film distribution company in Salt Lake City.

`Perhaps you could help me out here, Mr Bilton,` said Lewis casually. `You were quite adamant in your testimony that when Laemmle Film Service arrived in Salt Lake City, Mr Carl Laemmle came in person and declared`, Lewis Milestone hesitated and turned to his notes, `here it is, sir, and I quote, "he said there was only room for one film rental company in the area, and it was not going to be yours", end quote. Yet, as far as I`m aware, you are still in business, are you not?`

`I am, no thanks to Laemmle`s scheming ways.`

`So, am I right in thinking that you matched his every move to capture the trade in the area, and have succeeded in repelling his advances to your customers?`

`Yes, but not without losing money.`

`So, Mr Bilton, are you claiming that your company made a financial loss because of the Laemmle Film Service tactics?`

`We certainly did. I had to let a lot of my people go because of them.`

`Mr Bilton, think carefully before you answer this...it's important. If I were to draw any conclusions from your company's recent tax returns to the State of Utah, what would I find?`

Lewis rummaged through a file and drew out an official-looking raft of papers.

`Now wait a minute, those are confidential...`

Lewis Milestone cut across him.

`Answer the question, Mr Bilton. What would I find?`

All four counsellors from the opposite table were on their feet. Levett shouted, `Objection, Your Honour. An outrageous question. Our witness has no obligation to reveal his company's finances.`

`Your Honour, everyone heard the question. It's quite straightforward. I simply asked what I would find, not the amount of the losses you said you sustained.`

Lewis continued to stare at the witness, weighing the document in his hand.

`Overruled. You don't have to state figures, Mr Bilton, just answer the question,` responded the judge, waving down the advocates across the well.

Suddenly, the witness was flustered.

`I'm waiting, Mr Bilton. Or are you reconsidering your earlier statement about your profit and loss?`

Lewis began to rifle through the document in his hand.

`Well, I...err...may have thought , at first, we lost money. Perhaps I was confused by some of the figures. I now recall it was not as bad as I had feared.`

`Meaning what, Mr Bilton? That you actually made a profit?`

`Err...yes, I believe we did. I would have to confirm that with our accountant.`

`Is there any room for doubt, sir?`

`Err...no.`

Lewis put the document on the table.

`So, Your Honour, we have established that Mr Bilton's company did not suffer irreparable harm because of the arrival of Laemmle Film Service. He faced a downturn in trade, because he was no longer the sole rental agency in the area.

`But let us move on. Mr Bilton, you stated in your earlier testimony that your employees faced threats, abuse and physical attack. Can we examine the precise nature of these incidents, which from what the opposing counsel would have us believe, happened to every company that has testified...and in exactly the same manner.

`Please could you repeat what you told the court this morning when asked,` Lewis turned to his notes, "were you or your members of staff ever threatened or physically abused by people from Laemmle Film Service"?`

The tension showing on Bilton's face visibly eased. He was on safer ground.

`On the first occasion, we were confronted by Mr Laemmle and two of his henchmen when they came to our premises within days of having opened. They demanded to see me, and would not leave the building until I appeared. At that point, Mr Laemmle declared there was only room for one film distribution centre, and that his company would survive, for he would do whatever it took to see me out of business. He would drop prices until we were bankrupted, he would advertise special offers to exhibitors, and would tell moviegoers that his sign outside a picture house would be their guarantee that the film shown on the programme would be the one displayed on the screen.`

`When did the physical abuse take place?`

`Carl Laemmle came back a second time and asked to speak to me again. I requested them to leave, and opened the door for them to pass through. They resisted and hit at me and my three assistants.`

`That is how it happened, is it? Remember, Mr Bilton, you are still on oath.`

`It is.`

`Would it interest you to know, sir, that the other distributors, who allege that people representing Laemmle Film Service physically assaulted them, all gave remarkably similar responses. An amazing coincidence, don't you agree?`

`I wouldn`t know.`

`Just to acquaint you with what they said, let me read you a few of their replies to the same question posed by the Trust`s counsel. "When the Laemmle people came a second time there was a fracas when I showed them the exit, and we were knocked to the ground". The next, "four of my employees were there to ensure they did not stay, and asked then to leave immediately. There was a scuffle when shown the door, and we were battered and bruised". Yet another, "when the Lammle Film Service people came to make trouble on the next occasion, they were politely shown out. They resisted and we were injured in an unprovoked attack".

`Unfortunately, Mr Bilton, whoever coached you all failed to change the script sufficiently. You, yourself, said, "Carl Laemmle came back a second time and asked to speak to me again. I requested them to leave, and opened the door for them to pass through. They resisted and hit me and my three assistants".

`That was your testimony given under oath. Now, allow me to refresh your memory of what really happened on the occasion Carl Laemmle`s vicious mob came to your building in Salt Lake City. To help, here is a photograph taken by a reporter from the Intermountain Catholic, a newspaper serving Salt Lake City. May I pass this photograph to the witness, please, Your Honour?` The usher can also pass a copy of the photograph to the bench and another copy to the Trust`s counsel.`

Judge Learned Hand nodded, and the copies were duly circulated.

`Now, Mr Bilton, would you kindly describe the scene depicted in the photograph?`

The witness glanced quickly in the other counsel`s direction.

`Err...it shows two men running.`

`Go on, Mr Bilton. Can you explain why they are running?`

`Not clearly. There are other men behind them.`

`Let us finish this charade, Mr Bilton. Your Honour, the photograph clearly shows Mr Laemmle and his local manager fleeing Mr Bilton`s premises. What is all too apparent is the mob chasing them, note with heavy sticks, and would you believe, hot on their heels is Mr Bilton himself, who displays no sign of injury. The dark stain on the Laemmle manager`s shirt, by the way, is blood caused by a hefty blow from one of those sticks. I find, Mr Bilton that your testimony lacks credibility, as do the cultivated testimonies from all the previous witnesses. I have it on good authority that at no time did Mr Laemmle ever visit a competitor's premises with more than one additional person in attendance.`

`Your Honour, we only have the counsellor's word for that,` declared Levett, rising to his feet at the next table.

`That is not the case, Your Honour. I have the attorney-authorised statements from previous employees of several of the distribution companies. They affirm that Mr Laemmle, accompanied by only one other, visited their employers' buildings with the declared intention of holding an amicable discussion. These are their own words when present at the time.`

The judge glanced at the clock on the wall.

`Any more questions for this or any of the previous witnesses, Mr Milestone?`

`No, Your Honour.`

`Then this case is adjourned until nine o'clock tomorrow morning.`

The gavel was tapped once lightly, the usher called `All rise`: the day's proceedings were over.

The next morning I met our counsellor on the courthouse steps.

`Good morning, Lewis, I wonder what they will throw at us today?`

`Well, according to the pre-trial discovery, that's an exchange of key elements each side will raise during the trial, there were a few scanty notes on the Jewish influx into the film industry. But I can't see them bringing that into play, a racial thing, it's too delicate an issue.`

When we took our seats at the table, this time we were first into the courtroom. The counsellors for the Trust were cutting it fine when three of them trooped in a minute to nine.

`All rise.` And so began the fourth day of the trial.

Immediately the preliminaries were dispatched, Levett, his tall, angular figure rising to a round-shouldered stoop, looked even more predatory. In fact, when his head swivelled in our direction, the picture of a vulture eyeing its next meal was vividly realistic. I gave an involuntary shiver. He was circling for the kill.

Lewis had grasped their tactics early on. Denigrate Carl, fix him in the judge's opinion as a hustler who exploits people's weaknesses and ruthlessly takes advantage of them by every possible means. Then bring forward his unwarranted use of the patented Latham Loop, and a court decision to stop this rogue in his tracks, make an example of him before all other independent film makers, would be the predictable outcome.

Thus far, Lewis had sabotaged their plan, even making them appear wrong-footed. Now, Levett was about to make us pay for daring to put up such a stout defence.

'Your Honour, in my opening statement I declared The Motion Picture Patents Company was acting as a guardian of all that was decent and right. We stand by that contention. In joining together, the ten members of the MPPC also stand for fair play in this industry. They have banded together to ensure that the quickening pace of the motion picture industry does not run away with itself. Restrained growth allied to innovation are the watchwords of this organisation we refer to as the Trust.

'It would be detrimental in the long term to this medium, with its vast potential, if there were not a measure of self control employed: to temper the mavericks who would take this form of family entertainment and prostitute it for their own selfish ends. And believe me, it is happening. That is why, in Chicago, they have established the nation's first censorship board, to protect its population against the evil influence of obscene and immoral representations.

'In New York, we have just introduced a similar body, although, as yet, it is not effective. Fortunately, the Trust is effective. It stands for and upholds the same ideals. Because there are those, circling like sharks, who would take this industry into dark corners, to bring to the screen motion pictures lacking in taste, lacking in entertainment, lacking in morality. Sensation-mongers that, given half a chance, would titillate, horrify, outrage the decent folk of this country.

'I number the Independent Moving Pictures Company among such organisations. That's why we are here today, to minimise their wanton disregard of all things we respect and hold dear. There is a growing, ravening army of film makers, led by Carl Laemmle, who have come into this country to take over the direction and purpose of the American film industry.'

Levett paused, took his customary theatrical sip of water, and continued.

'The Trust is not anti-immigrant. The Trust is not opposed to films that are artistic, demonstrate new methods, new ideas. But it is concerned it could be railroaded by immigrants that hold to different values to our own.

`As I said, I do not want to portray any notion that we are anti-semitic...far from it. Siegmund Lubin, a Polish Jew who owns the Lubin Manufacturing Company, is one of out staunchest members, as is William Selig of the Selig Polyscope Company. Mr Lubin expresses grave concerns that many, fresh to our shores like himself, are massing with the sole intention of cornering the production of motion pictures in this country. And they are led by Mr Carl Laemmle. To avoid the Trust being termed racist or prejudiced, Your Honour, I would like to call to the stand, Mr Siegmund Lubin.`

Siegmund Lubin was duly sworn in.

It was evident from the brief note in the pre-trial discovery, the MPPC was going to mount a full-blown attack on many of Carl`s associates. Levett was going to make use of the ploy "stop foreigners taking over our inventions in our own country". A notable tactic, that was grist for the newspaper mill, and would make sensational headlines. A persuasive argument in favour of applying the law against patent infringement.

`Mr Lubin, may I ask you, is Lubin your family name?`

`No, it is not. I was born Siegmund Lubszynski in Breslau, Silesia, on the German border.`

I studied Mr Lubin.

He was a mild-mannered, deliberate gentleman in his sixties. `What is it, do you think, that attracts so many Eastern Europeans to the film industry?`

`I believe, sir, because it offers two important elements. You don`t need vast sums of money, and secondly, the market demand will continue to grow and grow. Most of the people I know with backgrounds similar to mine, have saved their money and bought into the parlours, theatres, nickelodeans. As I said, it`s a short step to making your own films.`

`How do you see the industry developing in the next ten years, Mr Lubin?`

Lewis was on his feet.

`Objection, Your Honour, this is crystal ball gazing. What has this to do with the matter in hand?`

Justice Hands nodded, and asked. `What has this to do with the lawsuit before us, Mr Levett?`

`Your Honour, I wanted to determine what a respected figure like Mr Lubin might see as the merits and likely shortcomings the future may hold.`

`I do not agree with speculation, sir. Rephrase your question.`

`Mr Lubin, what investments and safeguards will your organisation, the Lubin Manufacturing Company, put in place for the near future?`

I had to admire their counsellor, he was certainly quick on his feet.

`If immigrant film makers, were to gain a powerful foothold in this film business, I would opt out of the industry and return to being an ophthalmologist. Why? Because I could foresee their involvement as being the death of the strong, cultural influence motion pictures can provide, and which the Trust, in its earnest application of patent rights, stands as a measure of censorship against the wayward direction many of my compatriots could take us.`

Beautifully phrased, no doubt by the hand of the opposing counsel. But the delivery was well-judged, and had clearly made a strong impression.

`Is that why you became a member of the Motion Picture Patents Company, Mr Lubin?`

`Not entirely, no. At first, I thought I was being pressurised into joining because the MPPC had a virtual monopoly by reason of the raft of patents it holds. No one could ignore them if they wanted to be in the film making business. It was later, I recognised the Trust for what it is ...a bulwark against those who would tear down the edifice we have built purely out of self-interest.`

`Thank you, Mr Lubin. I have no further questions, Your Honour.`

He did not need to, the witness had said enough.

Judge Hand glanced in our direction.

`Mr Milestone?`

Lewis got to his feet. The intense look on his face mirrored the processes going on in his mind.

`Mr Lubin, let me get something clear in my mind. Are you saying beware those immigrants who come from Eastern Europe, they will exploit the film business? I am at a loss to appreciate the precise interpretation of the problems you foresee.`

`I thought I had made my meaning clear, sir. Mr Laemmle and his cohorts, will band together to change the complexion of the American film industry for the worse.`

`In using the term `cohorts`, you are referring to whom?`

`If you want me to name them, I shall. Louis Mayer, Marcus Loew, Adolph Zuckor, Harry Cohn, Jesse Lasky, all four of the Warner brothers, Sam Goldfish, William Fox. And they are headed, as I stated earlier, by Carl Laemmle. All are motivated by arrogance and greed.`

`A powerful indictment, Mr Lubin. For you to declare such stinging words with authority, you obviously have first-hand knowledge of their preparedness to act in concert to exploit the motion picture sector. The manner in which they will go about undermining the fabric of the industry; and how they will employ the monies they reap before abandoning this arena for something equally rewarding. Do you, Mr Lubin?`

`A foolish question, young man. Of course I don`t know what`s actually going on in their minds.`

`Then tell me, sir, what prompts your outspoken allegation. Where is your proof?`

Lubin stared at Lewis for a moment, then replied in a low voice. `Because I am from that aprt of the world,  I know how they operate.`

There was a lengthening silence in the courtroom as the words sank in.

Finally, Lewis said. `Do you know how I am thinking, Mr Lubin?`

`Don`t be foolish, how could I possibly know what a *goy*`s  thoughts might be?`

`But you should, Mr Lubin. According to your dictum, you know exactly how we think. Do you know what I was first named? Lev Milstein! Like many immigrants, my parents were overwhelmed to be received by this nation. This goes for those in the film industry. Most certainly, it applies to those who fled the oppressive regimes in Eastern Europe. They were naturalised at the first opportunity, and raised their children to be first and foremost, good American citizens. All of them are more than eager to have the chance to repay, in some small way, their debt of gratitude. Don`t talk to me about exploitation. We, your family included, have been the ones exploited. And it is for that reason we would never repay the people of this nation for their kindness, by going against all that they hold dear. Just remember that.`

I would never thought to hear applause in a courtroom. It was prolonged, accompanied by bursts of cheering. The judge did nothing to quell the noise, until it slowly petered out.

When he sat down, I put my arm round his shoulder. I could see tears in his eyes. The closing remarks by Lubin had struck deep: what Lewis had said had been more a personal declaration rather than an oration on our behalf. But it did not matter.

Carl joined us for lunch, and during the conversation I asked Lewis how Milstein became Milestone.

`When my family came through the immigration process at Ellis Island, we entered as Milstein, but a harassed official registered us as `Milestone`. It was easier for him. My father thought, at the time, that being given a new name when entering a new country was all part of the process.`

He shrugged and grinned at Carl. `How on earth did you manage to get away with "Laemmle"?`

`It was so difficult for the immigration officer, I wrote it down for him.`

In the afternoon Lewis made the case for the defence. It was a simply structured submission, involving just two witnesses —a rabbi and an academic. When the first took the witness stand, Lewis opened with the essential preliminaries.

`For the record, Dr Margolis, would you please state your full name and your current responsibilities?`

`Of course. My name is Gabriel Wolf Margolis. I am Chief Rabbi of the United Hebrew Community of New York. I have held a similar post in Boston, and am life president of the Assembly of the Orthodox Rabbis of America and Canada.`

`Dr Margolis, I requested your presence here today to establish the true character of a man who, in this lawsuit, has been thoroughly vilified. The plaintiff's counsel has painted him an ogre, a tyrant, and a bully. Someone who will mete out physical assault, whose morals will lead the burgeoning motion picture industry into disrepute. That man is Mr Carl Laemmle.`

The Chief Rabbi had been gazing at Lewis intently during his opening remarks, and when the name `Carl Laemmle` was stated, he burst out laughing. Lewis had to proffer a handkerchief to stem the tears.

`Unfortunately, Dr Margolis, it is not so amusing where Mr Laemmle is concerned. The opposing counsel has attempted to cast him in such a light.

Could you tell me of your association with this man?`

The Chief Rabbi looked across at Carl Laemmle sitting next to me.

`Carl, my friend, I always told you people would envy your success, and delight in your misfortune. Still, I know you are a man who can rise above the bitterness of *schadenfreude*, an all too common trait in this day and age.`

Fascinating. It was as though there were only two people in the courtroom, and they were having a conversation with each other.

Carl looked solemnly across at the witness stand. `I am here, Gabriel, having been charged for a supposed infringement of a patent on an item of machinery used in cameras and projectors. An essential feature used universally in the film world.`

`I see, well I`d better tell this young man what I know you to be. I shall report exactly what I have seen you do, Carl, both in business and socially. I shall not portray you in an over-generous light, because I am aware that you can be a hard-nosed when it comes to business. You`ve taken risks, some I certainly would not have entertained. Frankly, I`ve not been happy about some of the deals you have told me about. How you`ve engineered them in your favour. But, I suppose that is the way business is conducted. I would say this about you, Carl. There has never been anything in your commercial life which I would consider underhand, malicious, or harmful to others. Overall, I think you are tough but fair. In the secular world, this must be right, I guess.

`Where you stand socially? That`s all too easy. I have never come across anyone who cares for others as much as you. I know you help out in the synagogue, more importantly perhaps, you are ready to rescue, finance and set up others less fortunate than yourself. Personally, I think you go too far. Sometimes people need to flounder, to bring about their own salvation.

`Anyway, I would just say this. Carl Laemmle has a high sense of moral duty, which embraces his work and private life. Now what questions do you want to ask me, young man?`

Lewis grinned. `I don`t think I want to ask you anything after all, Dr Margolis. Although, the opposing counsel may have a question or two, Your Honour.`

`Mr Levett?`

`No questions, Your Honour.`

`In which case we`ll move on. Do you want to call your next witness,

Mr Milestone?`

`Yes, Your Honour, Professor Lowell.`

While the gentleman was escorted to the stand, I leaned towards Lewis.

`Why didn`t their counsel ask any questions?`

`They had more to lose than gain, Sam. Levett judged the situation correctly. Whatever the Rabbi said would never have been unfavourable, nor would any question be answered with a simple yes or no.` He grinned. `You saw the man, the way he responded to me. Can you imagine the knots Levett would have tied himself in?`

With that he rose from his chair and addressed the witness.

`For the benefit of the court, Dr Lowell, would you please state your full name, and your responsibilities?`

`Certainly, I am Abbott Lawrence Lowell, President of Harvard University, and President of the American Political Science Association.`

`Thank you, sir. This witness has been brought into this court today because, in addition to the lawsuit before us, the counsel for the plaintiff has seen fit not only to denigrate my client and his methods of trade, but also to impugn the business activities of his fellow brethren, his Jewish compatriots in the motion picture industry. Doubts have been raised about their future aims. If they were to expand their influence in this sector would it diminish the very standards by which we live. The Motion Picture Patents Company believe they would.

`I want to dispel that argument. Although it is what some regard as a side issue, it could still be relevant to the outcome of this trial. As the counsel for the MPPC Company is only too aware.

`Besides being a noted academic, and the president of a highly-regarded seat of learning, Dr Lowell has long pursued the thorny question of cultural integration. This court will recall we encountered the subject earlier. In fact, much was made of it. Today, I want to examine the same question from a more logical, more measured standpoint.

`Dr Lowell, would you please indentify the problems of racial absorption into the current American culture?`

`With pleasure, sir. Firstly, we have accepted the principle, at central government level, that for this country to achieve its full potential, economically, politically and socially, it has to expand its population. Not at the rate of normal organic growth, but by encouraging immigration. We take all races, all nationalities, providing they meet certain basic requirements. The problems arise when, either because of language, religious persuasion, family connections, or work opportunities, immigrant groups gather together. When such groups reach a critical mass, it is then they can be perceived as a threat to others. It is almost tribal in the way the threat is viewed. Will it spread and dominate my interests? Will it change my cultural habits? Will there be aggressive acts against me and my people?

`From relatively early on in my professional career I studied the role of racial and ethnic integration in American society. For example, when there was an influx of Irish emigrants in the last century I wrote, "*What we need is not to dominate the Irish, but to absorb them. We want them to become rich, send their sons to our colleges, share our prosperity and our sentiments. We do not want to feel that they are among us, yet not part of us*". I strongly believe that only a homogeneous society can advance and safeguard the achievements of American democracy.`

`Tell me, Dr Lowell, how could that ideal be achieved?` asked Lewis.

`The answer, sir, is assimilation, and controlling immigrant numbers.`

`I now want to ask you about the fears some people have of the impact the Jewish community is likely to have on our society,` Lewis put to the academic. `For various political reasons, they are coming into the United States in substantial numbers, and developing a strong presence here. In your capacity as an authority on immigration and assimilation, is this likely to be a problem in the near future?`

`An interesting question, sir. I would answer it this way. Only for those who fear competition. And by that I am not referring just to business, I am including other demands such as a safe environment, welfare, housing, and medical care. But life is competitive; we want the best we can afford, the most we can obtain; the security and comfort we can provide for our families and ourselves. You cannot avoid having to compete with others for your wants.

`You have to accept that as this country grows in wealth and prosperity, it is as a direct result of the increasing numbers of people making their contribution. In a recent census, the figures show the United States has a population of ninety two million. Fourteen million were immigrants, fifteen per cent of the total. It won`t ease until we have a population of two hundred and fifty million souls in this country.`

Dr Lovell gazed round the courtroom.

`So I would suggest two things. Accept the fact we are, and will be for some years, a multi-cultural society. Accept the fact, that we shall have neighbours, in business and in our domestic lives, who have foreign roots. We shall all, in the future, be working alongside or sharing apartment blocks with Asians, Africans, Eastern Europeans, all speaking a multitude of languages. But the longer they are here, the more they will identify with this country. We need them, and future generations will reap the benefits of their presence, and their industry...so make the most of it.`

`Thank you, Dr Lovell. I now want to ask you a specific question, relating to the film industry. You may not be aware, but this business sector is divided by the major studios on one hand, and the independent film makers on the other. This latter group comprises individuals mainly of foreign origin. At the moment, the efforts of the independents are being heavily subjected to control by the majors. Part of that control, it is submitted, is to stop this cultural group taking a greater interest in this expanding medium. I would ask you, what have the majors to fear?`

`I can only answer this question based on my knowledge of racial integration domestically and commercially. I have always appreciated that this country stands for the individual. If he, or she, has the wit and perseverance to achieve their goal, let him or her have a go. I should imagine these people to whom you refer are all naturalised American citizens. Thus, they enjoy the same rights as anyone else. So, the short answer to your question...is fear itself.`

`Thank you, Dr Lovell, no more questions.`

Judge Learned Hand leaned forward. `Mr Levett, have you any questions for this witness?`

`I have, Your Honour. Dr Lovell, is it true you are an honorary vice-president of the Immigration Restriction League?`

`It is, sir.`

`Surely, that flies in the face of all the court has heard you tell about tolerance, assimilation, and the supposed benefits of racial integration, if you are openly campaigning to keep people away from these shores?`

Dr Lovell nodded. `A common misconception, sir. Let me explain the purpose of this body. Its aim is to be more selective in whom we allow into this country. We have a base population of close to a hundred million. Until now our immigration programme has been inclined to leniency in those arriving in America, and it is no secret that ne`er-do-wells and criminals, have attempted to take refuge here. The Immigration Restriction League is trying to weed out those who are unwelcome, by tightening the enforcement on arrival and promoting literacy tests. We continue to invite *bona fide* immigrants, but they must have a measure of the language in order to communicate, and we must be assured they have no criminal record.`

`Thank you ,Your Honour, no further questions.`

`If that`s the case, we shall adjourn this hearing until nine o`clock tomorrow morning, when we shall hear closing statements.`

`All rise.`

And that was it, the day`s session was at a close.

When the three of us were walking to a nearby bar, I asked Lewis what we had actually achieved by putting the two witnesses on the stand.

`I guess it`s not so obvious if you are rarely in a courtroom, Sam. Perhaps, it would be easier if we looked at the way the MPPC counsel laid out their strategy. They believed that, in this particular lawsuit, they had an open and shut case. A win, win situation. So their thinking, at the outset was, let`s pile on the pressure. Let`s paint Carl Laemmle as an upstart, a bully, a rogue without conscience, just like the rest of his fellow independent film makers. It will make our lives easier when we hit IMP with all the other patent infringements. We can sink this guy without trace.`

He pushed open the bar door and Carl and I followed him inside.

We took our beers to a table.

`As I was saying...that was their strategy. What little I gleaned from the pre-trial discovery, the need to tell opposing counsel of your submission, gave me an inkling of what they were about, and I marshalled our defence accordingly. It started to unravel for them when they went too far by introducing Siegmund Lubin. Today, I wanted to give Carl a moral boost by inviting the Chief Rabbi to testify. By the way, I got a bit worried when he indicated he wasn`t going to pull any punches, but in the end he did a superb job.`

Carl interrupted. `What about Dr Lovell? I couldn`t get the hang of what he was talking about at first. How on earth did you manage to get him into that courtroom, Lewis?`

`He is one of my father`s closest friends, and I went to Harvard.`

`Well I thought he did a tremendous job. He certainly put Levett in order,` Carl remarked.

`So his role was to stabilise the ship, was it?` I queried. `The other counsel had taken us off down the racist track, and Lovell put everything back on an even keel, using a naval metaphor.`

`That`s right. So all in all, I think we have blunted their attack on you, Carl, and tomorrow we shall finally get to the meat of the case.`

CHAPTER THIRTY

Mr Levett stood waiting to make his closing submission.

The usher by the door was having difficulty with someone wishing to enter. After a heated exchange in low voices, a person was grudgingly allowed in. It was the Chief Rabbi.

`Come in, Dr Margolis, we are just about to commence,` commented the judge, a hint of a smile on his lips.

`Thank you, Your Honour,` responded the rabbi, and slipped into a seat at the rear.

`No, no, sir. If you have come especially to watch our little drama play out, you should at least have a more favourable seat. Come, sit near the front, there are several vacant chairs.`

Embarrassed by Judge Hand`s cordiality, Rabbi Margolis shuffled down the aisle and quickly seated himself.

`Right, Mr Levett, I shall be pleased to hear what you have to say.`

`Thank you, Your Honour.`

Before uttering a word, he turned to stare fixedly in our direction.

`The Motion Picture Patent Company brought this case before the court, Your Honour, because it is their firm belief that the rule of law be upheld. The MPPC hold, by right, a number of patents relating to devices for taking moving pictures, and the production and projection of films. The members of the MPPC are not out to stifle or prevent others using equipment or the processes controlled by patent law. But there are obligations. Those who seek to use our registered systems must first meet certain criteria before the Trust affords them a licence. Naturally, this comes at a cost, not onerous, just enough to cover administration and to ensure the MPPC`s policies are observed.`

I glanced at Lewis, and raised my eyebrows.

The customary sip of water, and Levett continued.

`The administration also includes employing companies such as ours

181

to undertake the rigorous application of the law when we identify an infringement of patent rights. Thus far, Your Honour, we have issued to the Independent Moving Picture Company two hundred and eighty nine notices of patent violation. Instances when Mr Laemmle`s company has blatantly transgressed those rights. It has done so with impunity, without seeking permission, without regard to the consequences, and importantly, without caring for the standards which the Trust upholds on behalf of all filmgoers.

Today, we are considering just one such infringement...the illegal use of the Latham Loop. The patent for this system lies firmly in the hands of the Trust. Yet the Independent Moving Picture Company totally ignores the rule of law. It is my contention, Your Honour, that justice should now prevail. Mr Laemmle`s company is setting a dangerous precedent in attempting to flout the hard-earned efforts of patentees. If someone like him, and indeed his compatriots from other lands, can come into this country and walk all over its laws and conventions, it will be a sad day for the legitimacy of the American legal system.`

Lewis leaned towards me and whispered. `Pretty slick, eh? Notice how often the words "law" and "justice" cropped up. A hint to the judge, no doubt.`

Lewis got to his feet and walked to the front of the table. Carl had opted out of today`s proceedings.

`Your Honour, I believe we have firmly established the true character and sound business ethics of Mr Carl Laemmle, and therefore the manner in which the Independent Moving Picture Company goes about it trade. Despite the efforts of the MPPC`s counsel to portray him in a different light.

In fact, I would go as far as declaring that as the case has progressed, the defendant has been shown to exhibit the American spirit of initiative, enterprise and hard work. The same goes for his associates cited by the witness, Mr Siegmund Lubin.

As I do not see the need to re-establish Mr Laemmle`s standing I shall focus on the key issue of this lawsuit, the use of the Latham Loop. Three characteristics stand out in this system. Firstly, the invention followed an international path in its development.

Taking place not only in America, but in several countries at the same time. The inventors adjusting and improving on each other's work.

`Secondly, it was a typical nineteenth century concept, in that it was a smart combination of many existing technologies. And, thirdly, cinema itself is a major innovation, which has been quickly and universally adopted throughout the western world. Quicker, I would submit, than the acceptance of the steam engine, the railroad or the steamship.

`Thus, while we argue over the right to use a basic piece of equipment, we have to recognise that we are debating ownership of something that is now dated, has been continually modified, that little can be identified of the original process. No one can keep fully abreast with what is happening, ideas blossom almost daily. As my learned friend, Mr Lovett, emphasised on the opening day of this hearing, and I quote, "the pace of change that has occurred over the past ten years has been remarkable."

He paused, and slowly surveyed the court.

"As a consequence, this outdated patent is no longer relevant or enforceable. I, therefore, submit, Your Honour, that the case against my client is nugatory, of little merit. The use of the Latham Loop by Independent Moving Pictures, owned by Mr Carl Laemmle, does not constitute an infringement. The company is merely making use of a much altered system that is now commonplace. One that will continue to evolve as cameras and projectors themselves, improve. Your Honour, we cannot let what were once innovative ideas, that laid the foundation of this industry, constrain its future.`

To my mind it was a brilliant closing speech, and judging by the faces of the opposing counsel, they thought so too.

`Thank you, Mr Milestone.  I shall now deliberate on all that has been submitted to this court, and we shall convene one week from today in this courtroom, when I shall announce my decision. This hearing is now closed.`

CHAPTER THIRTY - ONE

As Judge Learned Hand had so determined, the following week we assembled at the courthouse in Brooklyn.

Carl had not joined us. He had not given a reason, but taken the Pennsylvania Special to Chicago. On this occasion a room had been reserved for him at the La Salle Hotel, and if necessary, I could contact him there.

The two counsels and clients took their seats at the respective tables. On this occasion Lewis Milestone and I had been joined by Isadore Bernstein.

When we had arrived, the public seats behind the barrier were already full. I noticed a fair sprinkling of independent film makers, but the majority of the places were taken by the press; and not just the New York newspapers, but journalists from across the country, and news service reporters including Reuters. The case had gained notoriety.

At ten o'clock the ushers took their stations. One called, `All rise` as the judge swept into the courtroom. The same official stepped forward.

`Please be aware, the presiding justice, Judge Learned Hand, is present. This court is now in session.`

`Good morning everyone. I do not intend to keep you long, but before I declare the verdict, I want to review several aspects of both parties` submissions. I was aware, from the pre-trial discovery, that the Motion Picture Patents Company was seeking to highlight the likely consequences if the patent for the Latham Loop was not found in their favour. Equally, if the MPPC were triumphant, Independent Moving Pictures and other independent film making companies would have been greatly disadvantaged in subsequent lawsuits concerning patents held by the MPPC.

`My view is that the grandstanding behaviour of the counsel for the MPPC was irrelevant to their cause. The counsel for the defence had to spend time refuting the many allegations made against his client. All to no avail. I am an experienced judge, able to see through the posturing, the rhetoric and the personal slurs that were thrown at the defendant. This was a bench court. We had no need of the histrionics designed largely to influence juries.

`Mr Milestone also entered the flim-flam arena. The penultimate day`s witnesses were entertaining, but hardly the stuff from which verdicts are drawn. In any case, by then, I had already come to my own conclusions about the defendant.

`So what have I made of all this? I`ll tell you. Here then, is my decision...`

Carl phoned me from the La Salle that evening. Immediately after the decision, I had sent a cable to the La Salle hotel declaring, "JUSTICE HAS TRIUMPHED!" The wire that hurried back read, "APPEAL IMMEDIATELY!"

`Carl we won! The judge found for us!`

`Well, I`ll be damned! That`s great news! When I get back on Monday we`ll celebrate in style. Thanks for letting me know.`

The line went dead. I felt suddenly deflated. Somehow, I had expected him to want a blow-by-blow account of how the judge had decided in IMP`s favour.

As good as his word, Carl reserved a table at Mouquins Restaurant on Sixth Avenue. Lewis Milestone and I were invited to join Carl, his wife Recha and the Bernsteins.

`I read and re-read all about the judgement on the train home,` said Carl. `Amazing, and it`s all down to you, Lewis, for having the foresight to bring in those witnesses.`

`The judge said they didn`t count for anything in his summation, Carl,` he responded.

`I know human nature, my boy, and that counted. Believe me. What I don`t understand, from what I read in the *Chicago Tribune*, the judge held that the patent claim did not cover cameras, because it had been anticipated by Armat and Jenkins and others. But what about projectors? You can`t have one without the other.`

`Actually Carl,` I explained, `Although it wasn`t mentioned in the lawsuit, Judge Hand volunteered his opinion that the patent would be equally invalid when applied to projectors.`

`Well, that`s a relief. Now let`s enjoy our victory. Remember this is only one of two hundred and eighty nine. But who`s counting?`

As the evening wore on, Carl, who was sitting next to me, said in a low voice. `You haven`t asked me what I was doing in Chicago, Sam. Weren`t you a little bit curious?`

`Of course. But you`ll tell me when you want to.`

He grinned in his enigmatic way. `I went there to check whether Independent Moving Pictures should relocate to the "windy city".`

CHAPTER THIRTY - TWO

Carl joined me for the first day`s shooting at Fort Lee.

While the lawsuit was being heard, Walter Johnson had worked wonders repairing the studio. Fortunately, the insurance company had accepted liability, and though we had not yet been recompensed for the damage, on the strength of their acknowledgement, Carl had bought new cameras, lighting and all our many other needs. Film stock had been hard to come by, but letters home to James Williamson had resulted in the delivery of more than we immediately required.

Isadore had also been busy contacting Harry Solter and his wife, Florence Lawrence, and been in touch with King Baggot and Owen Moore. The result, with the lawsuit out the way, we now resumed filming. This time, Walter had arranged round-the-clock security by unsmiling guards and equally, unfriendly dogs. There could have been immediate reprisals following the judgement in our favour.

On the ferry upriver Carl explained his thoughts on establishing the company elsewhere, away from the clutches of Edison`s Trust.

`I reckon we are in the calm before the storm, Sam. As I said the other night, we still have a whole raft of lawsuits pending. If they take us to court, they could still wipe us out. Now, if we set up operations a thousand miles away, they would be less likely to come after us. Then we could focus more on the American market.`

I nodded. `So is IMP moving to Chicago?`

He stared out the ferryboat window. A sudden squall of rain spattered the glass.

`No...I don`t think so. It`s changed since I was there. It seems meaner, certainly larger, and from what I`ve heard, not a nice place to live.`

`How do you mean?`

`I met with a number of film makers. I even talked with William Selig.

By the way, he is opting out of the Trust, he felt he was pressurised into joining. He had some interesting comments to make, as did Gilbert 'Broncho Billy' Anderson and George Spoor, of Essanay Studios. I knew them when I was setting up my nickelodeans...used to buy films from them.'

Carl looked out the window, before eventually picking up the conversation.

'Do you know what they all said? Well not so much said...inferred. It was no longer safe to operate there. There are gangs moving in on businesses extorting money. Even when I was there the police arrested over two hundred known Italian gangsters in a raid in Little Italy. What with the Trust here, and hoodlums there, I'm not sure which is the worse of the two evils. I wouldn't want my family growing up in that sort of environment. What was interesting, George Spoor mentioned he was going to look at sites in California. Selig said the same. I wonder if it's worth a visit?'

We completed four films in eight days. The pre-planning worked well. The scenery was adjusted to accommodate two films at a time, and Walter had employed men from the town accustomed to changing scenery with the minimum of delay. By the end of the week we had the films in the can ready for editing back in the city.

Two days after we returned to New York, I came out the lift and almost stumbled over a character in a trench coat, wearing a blue fedora with a purple feather in the hatband. I stopped short. I could not see his face, for he was crouching in a resting position against the IMP office door.

He got up slowly. 'Mr Lockhart?'

I nodded.

'I'm Robert King. I write for Motion Picture Story magazine. You may have seen the piece we carried about your victory over the Trust?'

I nodded again.

'The thing is, Mr Lockhart, our readers would be really interested in the motion pictures you're making up at Fort Lee right now, and I wondered if you would like to give me details. Someone mentioned you had Florence Lawrence working for you. Is it true the 'Biograph Girl' is acting in your films?'

'You'd better come into the office, Mr King.'

He removed his hat and coat while I made the coffee.

`Nice place you`ve got here.`

`Not bad, if you ignore the smell.`

`That`s a quaint accent, Mr Lockhart. Are you English?`

`Hmm. I come from a town fifty miles south of London. Place called Brighton.`

When I handed him his coffee, he took a pad and pencil from a pocket, and said. `Do you mind if I ask you a few questions?`

`Depends what they are, Mr King.`

`Look, my readers are interested in what Florence Lawrence is doing. I`m not enquiring into your business dealings. They don`t want to know much about your run-in with Edison`s Trust, we leave all that to Moving Picture World, which covers the trade angle. All I`d like to put in our magazine is what she is up to at the moment. She`s not doing anything for Biograph, not anyway before next month as far as I can gather. So, can you confirm she`s working for you?`

This was a tricky one. If I told him Florence was featuring in a number of films, even though destined for overseas markets, how would that affect her standing with Biograph, now a major player in the Trust? Or even King Baggot and Owen Moore. It could rebound on IMP if we were seen to be poaching the Trust`s actors as well as taking advantage of their patents. The judge had found in our favour, but the verdict had yet to be upheld by the US Circuit Court. No way was I going to rock that boat. There and then, I made a decision to involve him in a scheme I had in mind.

`This is off the record, Mr King. I can confirm that Miss Lawrence has been in some of our motion pictures, but they are destined for foreign markets. The problem is, it would not do her a whole lot of good if people got to know about it at the moment. So let me put an idea to you. Supposing you report nothing for a month or so, then I promise I`ll give you the biggest scoop of your career. What do you say?`

`What are you saying, Sam? We give her a contract for a year, and give her salary of a hundred dollars a week! Are you nuts? No one pays an actor a fixed salary, it`s on a day-by-day basis. When they work, they get paid.`

`What you`ve got to remember, Carl, is that this magazine could seriously rock the boat if they print anything about Florence working for us. Just because the people in the Trust pay them peanuts, and never give them a billing, doesn`t mean we have to do the same.

`When we all started out, the people who acted in motion pictures never received any credit for their work because the films were too short. Now we are producing one-reelers, we have time to put their names up there on the screen. I had not appreciated the public have such a high regard for certain actors and actresses. We could make that work for us. Getting the newspapers and magazines, like Motion Picture Story and Photoplay, to write about and show photographs of the people who work for us could have a knock-on benefit. The public like Florence. If we suddenly proclaimed her to be the "IMP Girl", and made a publicity stunt out of it, it would reflect well on our studio.`

I give Carl his due. He quickly saw the merit in what I was saying. He stroked his chin. `What do you say, Issy?`

`I think Sam`s right. Get her to sign a contract. We can afford it. Then come out in the open and tell the world she is working for us.`

`You should know that I promised the story first to this fellow at Motion Picture Story .`

`Fine, I know Eugene Brewster, who runs the magazine. I`ll have a discreet word with him.`

`Is that the guy who ran for Attorney General some years ago?` queried Isadore.

`That`s the one. Fancies himself as a film director as well. OK, Sam, if we go with this idea, what have you got in mind?`

`This may sound a little bizarre, but stay with me. We sign her up, then put out the word to the newspapers that Florence Lawrence has gone missing. Obviously, we can`t declare the incident ourselves, we get Harry Solter, her husband to do it. Something like she`s disappeared, and he fears for her life. After a while, you, Carl, come out with the statement that you`ve found her and she was so grateful, she signed for IMP. The magazine gets the story first, and the newspapers afterwards. The idea needs a little refining, but that`s the gist of it.`

Carl`s eyebrows twitched. `You want her for a role in that film of yours, what was it called? . . *While New York Sleeps*`?

I laughed. `No, she`s too demure for that sort of film. It wouldn`t work.`

Florence eventually agreed to sign for the Independent Moving Pictures Company, not for the money, but more because we promised to feature her name at the beginning of the film. Harry had been keen for her to take the contract, and also approved the publicity stunt we were planning.

Carl had a meeting with Eugene Valentine Brewster. He did not tell me if he had mentioned the hoax we were about to play, all he said was, `Brewster is keen to do a piece on Florence and IMP when I give him the nod.`

The plan we eventually devised was to tie in with the release of the film, *The Broken Oath*, in which she appears with King Baggot. A story was wired to all the newspapers of Florence Lawrence`s sudden and dramatic disappearance. It was sent anonymously as breaking news.

Within days of it making the front pages, journalists began building upon the rumour, devising their own interpretations. For the next few weeks Americans followed the bizarre hysteria in the newspapers as reports of foul play were splashed across their pages. One account actually had Florence run down by a New York City streetcar in an attempt to escape her captors.

It was then a whole page advertisement appeared in the magazine, Motion Picture Story, and a number of small ads in newspapers proclaiming `We Nail A Lie`, with Carl Laemmle of Independent Moving Pictures quashing the rumour.

He declared that he had found Florence Lawrence alive and well, in her gratitude she had signed for IMP, and would be making a personal appearance at the premier of the film, *The Broken Oath*, in St Louis.

Brewster`s movie magazine did a lengthy article on Florence, and ended the piece with the question, "was this all a publicity stunt?" But it did not matter. I had not realised it at the time, but we had caught a tiger by the tale.

Suddenly, driven by the need to know, the public was elevating the actress to new heights. From lowly stage roles in the theatre, Florence was suddenly a film star, soon be appearing in a "ground-breaking new picture", The Broken Bath, the magazine declared. In their excitement they had mis-spelt the film title.

Nevertheless, it worked. When she arrived for the film's premiere at the Grand Opera House in St Louis, she and the leading man, King Baggot, were mobbed by the crowds.

From that day on Florence had her name and face plastered over *Billboards* and hoardings wherever *The Broken Oath* played. In a very short space of time she came to enjoy a degree of popular fame reserved, hitherto, for the likes of American presidents. Her salary matched her meteoric rise: it soon rose to a thousand dollars a week.

The compensating factor was any film in which she appeared was hailed immediately by her fans as a success, which meant we made money, and theatre owners had a ready sell-out on their hands.

CHAPTER THIRTY - THREE

Carl was away on another of his "fact-finding missions".

On this occasion he had gone down to Florida looking at possible studio locations, while I worked at the studio producing the next batch of films. They were all one-reelers, and I reckoned to begin the final editing in eight or nine days time.

When at the studio I stay at a rooming house in north Edgewater. However that evening I had a meeting in the city, and would not be back before filming commenced the next morning. As a consequence, Walter and I stayed behind after the day's shooting to work out the sequence of the scenes, how the scenery would be deployed, and the arrangements for the exterior shoot.

We worked on until dusk. Then I quickly gathered up my carry case and jumped into Walter's trap. At a fast trot, he drove me to the terminal to catch the last ferry downriver.

The remaining passengers were boarding, and the departure signal, two blasts of the ship's horn, echoed across the inlet. Walter urged his pony onwards, steering the trap along the quayside as two of the crew began manhandling the heavy gangplank.

Walter stood up and shouted. `Hold on...one more to come!`

Suddenly, out the gloom, a large, heavy wagon thundered past and hit us a glancing blow. At that angle the collision lifted the trap, pony, Walter and I into the air. We hurtled off the quay, rolling, tumbling, then plummeting into the dark, cold depths of the North River.

I felt a jarring impact...then nothing more.

CHAPTER THIRTY - FOUR

I could hear voices, but they were distant and wavering. This was a dream: at least, I was telling myself it was...except there were no images, just faint sounds. It did not matter, I was warm, contented, but my tongue was stuck to the roof of my mouth. It felt bloated, difficult to move against the harsh dryness.

The rasping cough, I realised, had issued from my lips. Forced open by the rising need to expel air, draw in a breath, to cough again. To fill my lungs with a surging intake, then flutteringly, I opened my eyes.

Blinking at the brightness, I quickly squeezed them shut. This was not a dream. I not only had a raging thirst, my body was wracked with pain. I gasped at the intensity of it invading my right side. I was hampered by dead weights on my leg and arm. Someone seemed to be pressing down on them.

When I peered through half-closed eyelids, the sounds I could hear were coming from two vague figures standing close. Their shapes gradually coalescing into white-coated strangers.

`Where am I?` I asked in an unrecognisable voice. Then in the same dry-mouthed, quavering tone, added. `Water...water please.`

One of them disappeared from my field of vision. The next moment I felt a hand lift my head and press a glass to my parched lips.

I emptied it, then drank another full tumbler. Then I was sick, and all my hard-earned efforts to take on liquid were wasted. They silently mopped up and left the room. Laying back on the pillow , my mind tried to grasp why I was lying in this bed. Glancing down, the burdensome weights I had felt on my arm and leg were the plaster in which they were encased.

Why was that? I was frowning, puzzled by what all this meant when the door burst open and Carl Laemmle, his wife Recha, and Isadore appeared in the room.

`He`s awake...thank God,` exclaimed Carl, and rushed to the bedside to peer intently into my face.

Even in discomfort I could not help saying, `Who are you?`

His features sagged. `He doesn`t know me! He`s lost his memory. What are we going to do?`

I grinned at him uncomfortably. `Don`t worry, no one could forget you, Carl.`

With that he leaned over and kissed my cheek. When he drew back unshed tears glistened in his eyes.

`Will someone tell me where I am?` I croaked. `And what I`m doing here?`

Recha said in a low voice. `Do you not remember anything about the accident, Sam?`

I looked round to where she was standing, on the other side of the bed. Slowly it all came back to me.

`We were chasing after the ferryboat. Walter stood up in the trap, and yelled for them to wait. There was an almighty crash and we seemed to lift off the ground. What happened after that is a complete blank.`

Carl glanced at his wife. `Sailors on the ferry reported that a large wagon suddenly appeared at speed, and careered into you. It pitched the occupants, the trap and pony into the water. You were rescued by several of the crew from the ferryboat who jumped in and hauled you ashore. You were in a pretty bad way, so the ferryboat took you across the river and sailors carried you on a board to here, St Luke`s Hospital. Luckily, it`s on Morningside Heights, directly opposite the terminal.`

Isadore completed the account. `You`ve broke your right leg and arm, and several ribs. But you were fortunate. . .`

`What do you mean? How`s Walter? Is he badly hurt?`

Recha looked sharply at Isadore.

Carl stared at the floor. `We weren`t going to mention it straight away. I`m sorry, Sam, Walter didn`t make it.`

`My God,` I whispered, almost to myself. `His poor wife. I must go to her, break the news. Help me out of this bed.`

`Sam, she knows,` said Recha quietly. `You`ve been in a coma for four days. We didn`t know even if you would pull through. Carl and I have spent much of the time between the hospital and with Isabel and the children. Her parents have come over from Pittsburgh and are comforting her now.`

I slumped back onto the pillow. Walter had had so much to live for: so much to give. To be cut down like that when the future, for him and his family, looked so promising was cruel and monstrously unfair. It should have been me, without ties or responsibilities.

A figure in a white coat came briskly into the room.

`I rather think my patient should be resting now he`s back with us. We don`t want to tire him, do we?`

`Okay, doc, we were just about to leave anyway,` remarked Carl, edging towards the door. He turned to me.

`Sam, we`re going to have a bite to eat. But we`ll call back for a short while after lunch, before we head home.`

The door shut behind them. The doctor took my pulse, and nodding his thoughts, wrote something on a chart at the foot of the bed. He smiled, `Everything is coming back to normal.` And exited the room with the same flourish as he appeared.

I lay there feeling desperately sad and dispirited at the tragic loss of Walter Johnson. How could things ever return to normal?

I was in hospital for another week before they discharged me in a wheelchair.

Carl had arranged a carriage, and I had been driven to his place on West End Avenue. Recha met me at the lift, and wheeled me into the apartment.

`The room`s all ready for you, Sam.`

She looked at me closely. `You`ve lost weight.`

She tutted and fussed. `Never mind, we`ll soon have you back on your feet. Now the doctor told us you have to rest, so you just take it easy. There are some books on the table in your room. Sit by the window, and I`ll get you some lunch.`

I sat there and skimmed through the books. Nothing really to my taste, but it did not matter, I did not feel like reading. There was too much on my mind.

The next day I had a visitor. Detective James Brampton from the New York Police Department. Recha showed him into my room, and left the door ajar, seemingly to overhear my version of the incident.

`Sit down, detective. Then I won`t have to strain my neck looking up at you.`

I pointed to a chair.

`Thank you, sir. I've been asked by the Department in Edgewater to report what you recall of the incident at the ferry terminal twelve days ago. Are you up to talking about it, Mr Lockhart?`

The memories of what occurred had come back to me in a haphazard fashion. Little things sparked off aspects of that fateful night. Each time I relived the event another piece of the jigsaw fell into place; and I relived it frequently. The problem was the recurring nightmare as all the elements came together. Each night, Walter was standing precariously in the trap shouting to the distant ferry. The thunderous noise of the wagon drawn by two enormous horses growing louder and louder.

Then we were flying over the water. The crashing noise of the trap, the pony screaming, Walter, beside me, screaming. I was screaming too when I woke up. Perspiration running off me, the bedclothes awry on the floor.

On the first occasion, Recha and Carl had rushed to my side, fearful that I was suffering pain. The pattern set in. It began to happen every night: some nights worse than others.

I recounted every detail to Detective Brampton. How we had worked on, then rushed to the quayside in Edgewater. It was dusk, little visibility, as the pony trotted through the township. Nearing the terminal all the signs were of the ferry cast off. The trap accelerated, and it was then the crash occurred.

`Did you hit the other vehicle, sir, or did it hit you?`

I drew a deep breath, and exhaled slowly.

`It hit us, Detective.`

He made a note in a pocket book.

`I had to ask, Mr Lockhart, just to make doubly sure. The sailors on the ferry were convinced it hit you. But the light was fading, and I needed your corroboration.`

He stared out the window for a moment.

`What do you remember of what happened then?`

`Only a sensation of flying. Nothing more.`

But I did. At that moment, the picture came back of plunging into the ice-cold water, being kicked repeatedly by the drowning horse as it was dragged down by the trap. I had no memory of Walter. Though I had been told he was tangled up in the harness when it was recovered.

`Tell me, Mr Lockhart, in your opinion, was it an accident, or was it a deliberate act by others?`

I sat there thinking about that moment. It would have taken a cool nerve and steady hands to steer a wagon at speed and deliver a glancing blow without getting caught up in a collision. But the critical question was, if it were accidental why did it not stop?

Detective Brampton must have read my thoughts.

`I have to tell you, the vehicle did not stop to see what it caused. Unless the driver was scared of the consequences, we have to assume it was done with intent. I have spoken with the deceased`s widow, Mrs Johnson. She told me of the troubles at your studio in Fort Lee, and the safety precautions her husband had put in place. It seems to me someone was out to do you harm, Mr Lockhart.`

I nodded, but said nothing.

He looked at me shrewdly, as if guessing the heavy hand of the Trust might be behind it. But there was no proof, they had not found the vehicle.

Ten minutes later he thanked me for my time, snapped shut the pocket book on his knee, and took his leave. Recha saw him out, then came into the room, her hands placed squarely on her hips.

`I heard what was said, Sam. It`s what I suspected, though Carl never acknowledged you might all be in danger. You wait until he comes home.`

Nothing is more daunting, more intimidating, than a Jewish mother when she is riled.

Carl wheeled me all the way to the offices by DeWitt Park.

After a week of kind but firm ministrations by his wife I had to get out the apartment. Anyway, Recha needed a rest. Coping with me all the time, and catering for the many visitors who called to check on my recovery. Eszter and her many relatives, people from IMP and other film makers called by. Florence Lawrence and her husband, Harry Solter came to see me. By the time Carl offered to push the wheelchair down West End to Eleventh Avenue, I could see she had had enough.

The door opened as we arrived, and Isadore came out to greet me.

`You`re looking a thousand times better than the last time I saw you,

Sam.`

`All due to Recha and Carl,` I declared. `Recha's been marvellous. I wouldn't have been able to cope without her.`

I glanced at Carl. `But after today, I'm moving back to the Algonquin.`

He started to say something, but I cut across him.

`No buts. It's time I fended for myself. I can get around...well almost. The hotel can serve me meals in my room, and if I use an electrobat to fetch and carry me, I'll have no problems at all.`

There was a long silence. Isadore glanced at Carl, then made a remark, which I realised was the prelude to a much broader discussion.

`Are we going to continue filming at Fort Lee, Carl?`

`Well...as you both know, I have been looking at possible locations. Until now they have been half-hearted, because the studio at Fort Lee was working so well.`

His gaze switched from Isadore to me and back.

`We won the first legal battle with The Motion Picture Patents Company, but we haven't won the war. If they want to pursue their cause, there are still two hundred and eighty eight lawsuits pending. It has been weighing on my mind...`

`And mine too,` added Isadore.

Carl nodded in acceptance. `And what with this latest incident,` he eyed me up and down, `it's probably time to pull out, before the Trust gets its teeth into another case against us. What are your feelings, Sam?`

I had been aware of Carl's thoughts of setting up a studio in another town, far enough away to deter the MPPC from taking action against us – physically or litigiously. Somehow, I had never believed it would happen. Now I could see the determination on both their faces.

`If it were the Trust, or rather its agents, that caused the accident at the ferry terminal, I can't believe that they were intent on killing us. Rather it was done to shake us up. Even over-react, perhaps, as we're doing at this moment. Walter's death may even put a stop to it all. Lawsuits, thuggery, loss of equipment. Personally, I'd like to wait and see. I've a feeling their efforts to quieten us, take us to court, will peter out now someone has died.`

`Are you saying you wouldn't come if the company decided to move elsewhere?` asked Carl intently.

`What I'm saying, Carl, is that we shouldn't get hustled out of Fort Lee because of what has happened. Take a measured view to where IMP might go. Give it a little time. As I say, The Trust, or more properly, their Film Services Company, may no longer have the stomach for bullying tactics. Or for Edison to keep up his legal battle with the independents. Wait and see... that's my opinion.`

`Hmm,` responded Carl, `You could be right, I suppose. But I'm not going to abandon the idea.`

It was difficult, even when the hotel staff were so considerate. They served my meals and ran occasional shopping trips for me. But I was glad I had moved out of Carl and Recha's apartment. Not only because it lifted the drudgery of nursing a patient and entertaining his visitors, it gave them back the tranquility of an ordered home life.

An electrobat cab collected me each morning, and ran me back to the Agonquin in the evening. At work I concentrated on editing the films and planning the next batch of movies we would be shooting. Walter had appointed an assistant when he took on the job of studio manager, a promising young man called Derek Bryant. He came to Eleventh and Fifty Third Street a couple of times a week, and gradually the next tranche of one-reelers took shape.

However, I was well aware that Carl was brooding over possible relocation: even though nothing had been heard of the Trust or its intentions.

I arrived at the offices one morning, a fortnight after the conversation concerning a possible move, to find a meeting taking place in Isadore's room. I knew he was not present. He had gone up to Fort Lee with Harry Solter.

Carl heard my wheelchair bumping through the main door and came out to greet me. `Sam, come in here a moment. Come and meet some people.`

He took hold of the handles and pushed me into the room.

`Hello, Sam, how you doing?` enquired Pat Powers of Powers Picture Company.

`Improving by the day, Pat.`

I was intrigued. Also present were Mark Dintenfass of Champion Films, Charles Baumann and Adam Kessel of the New York Motion Picture

Company, and David Horsley, the Nestor Film Company. Sitting around the table were the biggest independent film makers in the country.

Carl pushed me close to where they were sitting, and said. `You are the first to know, Sam...we are signing a contract to merge our studios. It will be a bulwark against whatever the MPPC is likely to throw at us. For the moment, we shall carry on as normal. However, the intention will be that in time we shall become one organisation called the Universal Motion Picture Manufacturing Company.`

Carl grinned at me. `We shall look for bigger offices in New York City. How about that, Sam?`

No further comment about relocation. I was pleased about that, but uncertain about the pooling of resources...and people.

CHAPTER THIRTY - FIVE

We all attended Walter`s funeral. The Laemmles, the Bernsteins, and myself.

A carriage met us at the terminal, and Carl and Isadore helped me up the steps. I sank back into the seat, and set my crutches to one side. The two horses trotted through Edgewater, then turned onto Bergen Boulevard heading north.

The church, as I gazed at it over a high stone wall, looked a forbidding edifice. The steeple jutting skywards, was out of harmony with the main building, which looked as though it had been erected against its will.

As we drew into the forecourt I could see gothic-style windows, complemented by a gothic-style main door. When we came to a halt, they helped me down. A laborious effort for Carl and Isadore, but they managed to point me in the right direction, and I swung myself through the door and headed for a rear pew. I waved the others forward, and settled at the end closest to the wall. It would be a welcome support when we had to stand.

The church began to fill, and I recognised many who worked at the studio. Other film makers too, had come to pay their respects. A group of mourners appeared and made their way to the first two rows. I realised they were members of Walter`s and Isabel`s family.

The coffin was borne up the nave by six young men, all with grim faces and downcast eyes. As they rested it on the trestle, I heard a loud sob.

The priest conducted the service with more than the detached regard often accorded the dead. Walter must have been a regular churchgoer, and I wondered if this was the first time Jews outnumbered the usual congregation in a catholic church.

Hymns were sung, there were several eulogies, and then the coffin led a procession into the cemetery for the interment. I let everyone else leave, then pushed myself up the wall and groped for my crutches.

`Don`t rush,` called a voice. `I told the priest we would follow in a moment. Here, let me help you.`

A young woman in a heavy veil held out my crutches. I thanked her and we walked slowly towards the adjacent cemetery. We moved to the graveside in silence. Except perhaps for the occasional grunt on my part, as I swung my right leg forward. She was obviously family and at moments like this words were irrelevant.

I stood at the back of the crowd gathered around the green-baized scar in the ground. She touched my arm reassuringly, then edged closer to the priest. The short commemoration was completed with sod tossed onto the coffin as it was lowered to its final resting place.

Caterers had been employed at the IMP studio, and carriages ferried guests to the building. I was last to arrive and joined the line being welcomed by family members. As everyone muttered their condolences, I inched forward, until the young lady, who had helped me in the church, came forward, took my arm and steered me round the milling throng to a table.

`Sit there, Sam. I`ll come back in a minute with something to drink and eat.`

I sat there, my plastered leg outstretched, my right arm resting on a crutch, and wondered who she might be. At the table were others from the studio.

`Isabel is holding up. What a shock it must have been for her,` said one of the scene shifters. `How are you managing, Sam? When are you coming back?`

`Some weeks yet, Tom, I`m afraid,` I replied. `By the way, can you point out Isabel to me? We`ve never met.`

He stared at me strangely, and was about to say something, when the veiled, young lady materialised by my side. `Here we are, Sam. I hope this is all right.`

She placed a glass of wine and a plate of food in front of me.

`Thank you...err.`

`Isabel,` she replied, and disappeared into the crowd.

Three weeks later Isadore accompanied me to Fort Lee. Derek Bryant had managed to hold everything together surprisingly well. His twice-weekly visits to the city, when we had gone over the storylines, scenes, dialogue inserts and timings, had been implemented almost to the letter. The films came back to the offices, and required only nominal editing before being processed and copied.

Nevertheless, I was itching to get back to the studio and oversee the next batch. Florence and her husband Harry Solter had gone on an extended vacation in Europe. I did not find out until they returned that Florence Lawrence had signed for the Siegmund Lubin Company for two thousand dollars a week.

Fortunately, by then we had a new leading woman. Mary Pickford, like Florence, was Canadian. She was married to Owen Moore, who had suggested her as a possible actress.

Carl had asked Thomas Ince to direct the films which again, would be all one-reelers. Their working titles were, *The First Misunderstanding*, *The Dream*, *Maid or Man*, and *The Mirror*.

The filming, scene shifting, exterior shots of all four films went well, almost without a hitch. Mary was an excellent choice, and worked well alongside Owen. The four films were finished in seven days, and with a half day to spare I decided to call upon Walter's widow, to pay my respects.

I hitched a lift on a buggy, and was dropped outside the house, a wooden-framed building with a large porch standing back from the dirt road. By now I was walking with a stick, and as I made my way up the path I noticed the grass needed cutting and the flower beds weeded.

The door opened before I got there.

`Sam, how nice of you to call,` exclaimed Isabel, wiping her hands on an apron. `Come in, please.`

I limped into the family room, and headed for an upright chair, collapsing onto it.

`I'm sorry I haven't been able to call sooner, but I've not travelled far from the rooming house until recently.`

`I know, Carl has been giving me regular updates of your progress. Can I get you some tea, a glass of lemonade...?`

`Lemonade would be fine, thank you.`

I heard her in the kitchen, the clink of glasses and liquid being poured. Then a door opened, and she called. `Girls, we have a visitor. Come and say hello.`

A few moments later, Isabel came into the room carrying a tray. Two small faces peered round her skirts.

`This is Mr Lockhart,` she said. `Mr Lockhart, meet Emily and Joanna.`

They came forward hesitantly. I set their ages at around two and four. Serious eyes examined me closely. Both had the dark auburn hair of their mother, and the same green eyes.

`Hello, Emily and Joanna. Now which is Emily?`

`I am,` declared the elder of the two. `Emily Margaret Johnson, and I`m nearly five. How old are you?`

`Shush, Emily. You must not ask grown-ups their age, it`s not polite.`

I grinned. `I`m twenty eight. How old are you, Joanna?`

Emily said primly. `She`s only two, so she won`t really understand, will you Joanna?`

The little one slowly shook her head.

`Sam,` said Isabel. `I`ll put the glass on this side table, beside you.`

The girls went through to the kitchen, and I could hear their voices between the gulps of lemonade and the biscuits they were eating.

`Not too many cookies, girls,` called their mother. `We`ll be eating in a few hours. Sorry, Sam.`

`Not at all, I`m interrupting your day. I just called by to see if you needed anything.`

She smiled wistfully. `Not really. The neighbours have been very kind. They`re going to tidy up the yard and do shopping for me. I thought the girls would be hit hardest, but they are adjusting better than I am.`

She sat on the edge of her seat, twisting her fingers. Shadows under her eyes told of the anguish she suffered when alone.

`Are you sure there`s nothing you need or want for the girls?` I asked tentatively. But I think I already knew the answer.

`Thanks, Sam. My parents come over now and then and do little jobs for me, and they take Emily and Joanna out as well, which helps occupy their thoughts. It`s just,` she looked down at her hands in her lap. `It`s just the emptiness I feel inside.`

Back in New York City I worked on the films. They were good...really good. Mary Pickford had star potential. Carl was missing again; and this time, so was Isadore. There were several young people working in the offices, which helped when I needed anything. Over the next week I arranged the titling through a local studio, and organised the copies of the films for circulation. Having nominated the release dates, I started sketching out ideas for a whole raft of films to be made over the coming months. Simple storylines, minimum numbers of actors, reusable scenery. All the ingredients for one reel motion pictures.

Sitting there overlooking the park and the river, my mind turned to the theme of the film I had long wanted to make: the one about white slave traffic in New York. No one acknowledged that it actually happened. But in past months I had seen a growing number of references to it in the newspapers. Not features that appeared on the front pages, but snippets tucked away in the back pages. It was a subject I knew I could really get my teeth into. Moreover, there was a growing sameness about the one-reelers I was producing. OK, the stories varied, as did the actors; but I felt we were getting a little stale. We needed something to pep up the interest.

Then it came to me. Why not create a series around Mary Pickford. She could get into all sorts of scrapes, and the films would depict how she ingeniously escapes from them. Each episode would be one reel. At the end of each film she would be caught up in some form of danger: at the beginning of the next, it would show how she extricates herself, only to be plunged into the next setback. It could be called, The Mishaps Of Mary, or something similar. I became quite excited by the idea, and worked on several plots and how the sequence of the action would work in each ten minute film.

Thomas Ince was a capable, though not outstanding, director. I wondered where Carl had found him. I knew he had started out as an actor, and done some film work for Biograph, but there the trail went dead.

I phoned a journalist friend at Moving Picture World, the trade magazine. He told me Ince came from a long line of not widely-known actors, but, in his words "he has the presence and enough ability to back up his bombast".

Interesting remark, I thought. One thing that did intrigue me was the way Ince observed my every move: going through the various schedules I prepared; noting how I timed the scenes, chose the players in the films; and how I pulled each production together. I did not mind, for a director should work closely with the producer.

Everything had been completed by the time Carl and Isadore reappeared. The screenplays, locations and scenery for the next two series were done; the actors commissioned; and Derek, at the studio, was standing by ready to implement my instructions.

`Good, I`m glad you`re here. Now we can discuss the next lot of films,` I said, a trifle acerbically. I had had no idea where they had gone, or when they would be coming back.

`Sure...sure, Sam. When does it suit you? This afternoon?` he responded with that characteristic, disarming grin. On this occasion I was feeling slightly nettled, and turned away to minimise its effect.

I caught the raised eyebrows in Isadore`s direction.

We sat round the conference table, and I presented my proposals. They agreed, but their usual insight was missing. The sought no detailed explanations, no queries on costs from Isadore, none of the expected reactions to the plots, no changes requested.

`Right, I`ll action these tomorrow,` I said. Then added, `Are you sure they`re OK? Aren`t you concerned there is a sameness about them? That we need new, fresher ideas?`

`They`re fine, Sam...for the moment,` Carl declared in an unconcerned tone.

`What`s that supposed to mean?`

I was getting irritated by their attitude. They were indifferent to all that I had put before them. There was no enthusiasm, no support forthcoming.

`If you`ve got something to say, then say it,` I continued angrily. `Let`s clear the air here. Something`s up, and I want to know what it is!`

Carl grinned. This time it spread across his features and spilled over to Isadore, who burst out laughing, and rubbed his hands together.

`Sam, you`ll gonna like this. Issy and I have been on a buying trip. And guess what...we`ve bought a site for a studio in California! Far away from the Trust, far away from the infighting, the constant need to look over our shoulders. Far enough away not to be threatened, even killed. What`s more, the weather for filming is perfect. Sunshine and bright skies almost the year round. It couldn`t be better. What do you say to that, Sam?`

I stared at him open-mouthed. Moving to the other side of America was daunting. I would be even further away from England, which I still regarded as home. Moreover, I was happy here, on the east coast. I had developed friendships, put down roots, well, temporary ones. Apart from the concerns for personal safety, it was a pleasant place to work

Isadore noted my uncertainty.

`I don`t think he`s particularly keen on the idea, Carl.`

`Is that right, Sam? You`d rather stay here in the city and work at Fort Lee? Even after what you`ve been through? The next time you might not be so lucky, my friend. You may end up like Walt.`

A stark comment. One that jolted. I felt his loss deeply. Even so, did I want to travel away from everything here?

`I can`t see your problem, Sam,` remarked Isadore. `You live in a hotel. You seem to spend most of your life working...either in the studio or here, editing, writing, producing. Out there, in California, you`d have a much better opportunity to relax once in a while. To enjoy life for a change.`

`When you say you`ve bought a site, Carl, does that mean you`ve got it for Independent Moving Pictures, or is it on behalf of this new outfit, the Universal Film Manufacturing Company?`

`Good point, Carl,` murmured Isadore. `Who is it really for?`

`As I see it,` Carl declared, `it`s an IMP asset. If Universal doesn`t go along with the idea, then we`ll keep it for ourselves. This Universal thing has no structure at the moment, only the intention to work together.`

This seemed like the moment to raise a personal issue.

`OK, so this new organisation takes off. Fine, but then where do I stand, Carl? Do I start looking around?`

`What are you talking about? We need you! You didn`t think you were expendable did you?` He stared at me intently. `You did, didn`t you? Then perish the thought, my young friend. We are all in this together!`

`Cards on the table, Carl. As Isadore hinted, I`m not so sure I want to go to California.`

I could tell by the tightening of his lips he was getting exasperated. He was brooding over my reaction to what he thought was the perfect solution.

`Sam, think it over carefully. If you don`t want to come that`s your business. Now, something is biting you. So what have you got to tell us?`

I told them what I thought about a sameness creeping into the one-reelers we were making. That we should either do something radically different, or hire a couple of screenwriters to give a freshness to our work. I then presented the idea I had of making the most of Mary Pickford by featuring her in a one-reeler serial. I expanded on my thoughts and showed them some visuals I had worked up. I could see Isadore was excited by the proposal; but after rocking back in his chair and looking up at the ceiling for a moment, Carl let the chair crash forward.

`No, Sam, I don`t think it`s a good idea, at all. But, if you wish, get some writers in.`

With that he stood up abruptly and stalked from the room.

We worked steadily through the summer. In August, the US Circuit Court ratified Judge Learned Hand`s decision, and the newspapers even carried the comment he had made earlier, that the unfettered use of the Latham Loop would also apply to projectors.

My bones had mended, and I now walked unaided, though I still felt pain if I stood for too long. Nothing more had been mentioned about California. I was aware that Carl was increasingly involved in meetings with the members of the Universal Film Manufacturing Company. Isadore Bernstein was also finding problems with membership of the Motion Picture Distributing Company, to which the individual film makers in Universal now subscribed.

Whenever the opportunity arose when working at the Fort Lee studio, I called upon Isabel Johnson. I would arrive with a few candy bars for the girls, and offer to do, or arrange to be done, minor house repairs. At first, Isabel was reluctant to take advantage of a semi-invalid, but having shed my crutches, then the walking stick, there were a number of chores that I was able to undertake. In fact, occasionally, I found myself buying manuals and reference books on household jobs for amateurs.

Summer moved into Autumn. Carl and Recha would occasionally invite me to supper on a Saturday evening after they had celebrated *Havdalah*, marking the end of Shabat, the Jewish Sabbath.

`How is the Universal project coming together, Carl?` I enquired on one evening.

He passed the tureen of potatoes.

`After a lot of wrangling we have finally agreed that Charles Baumann becomes president. You know Charles, don`t you?`

I nodded.

`Pat Powers is vice-president, and I`m the treasurer.`

`Why they made you treasurer I don`t know. You haven`t got a clue where money is concerned,` exclaimed Recha.

Carl grinned. `It`s only set up as a protective organisation, as a sort of pool of interests.` He glanced at me. `Its members will continue to release their pictures as they do at present. By the way, when we move to California, I`ve asked Thomas Ince to manage the studio and direct for us out there.`

He stared hard at me. `The studio in Fort Lee will remain open for some time, and I`d like you to continue to run it, Sam. But eventually it will close when all the filming is transferred to California. Is that OK with you?`

`Thank you, Carl, of course it is.`

He leaned over the table and shook my hand.

`I was going to ask you something, Carl. In a few weeks time we shall be thinking about closing the studio for the winter months. Would it be all right if I took a break when we do. I want to visit my parents back in England.`

Before he could say anything, Recha declared. `Of course you must, Sam. It`s important you see them. You should go more often.`

I told Isabel of my plans. `I`ve booked a passage back to England in December, to spend Christmas with my parents.`

`That will be nice, Sam. We are going to Pittsburgh to stay with mine, and in the New Year we are spending time with Walter`s family. They like to see their grandchildren.`

I was mending a dripping faucet. I had bought the washers and was trying to remember what the man in the store had told me. I had bought the tools and wrenches he recommended, but it was no easy task.

`Before you turn the water off, Sam, I`ll just fill the kettle for some coffee.`

Of course, turn off the water first. The storeman`s initial injunction.

`Perhaps, I`ll do it after we`ve had coffee,`

We sat at the kitchen table. Emily came in from playing in the yard.

`Mom, it`s cold. I told Joanna not to stay out there, but she won`t listen to me. You tell her. Hello, Sam.` She came over and kissed my cheek. Her cold nose briefly pressed against my face: then it was gone. I felt quietly elated. She had never done that before.

`Sam was telling me that he is going to England, Emily.`

`Are you going by train?`

`Not to New England, dear. England across the sea. It`s thousands of miles away.`

`Oh.` She went quiet. Tears appeared in her eyes. `Does that mean we shall never see you again?`

Isabel picked her up. `Of course not, darling. He is only going for Christmas...not forever.`

She looked at me over her mother`s shoulder.

`Is it true, Sam? You`ll be coming back?`

`Yes, Emily, I`ll be coming back.`

She squirmed down. `I must go and tell Joanna that Sam is coming back.`

Isabel smiled at me across the table. `When do you return , Sam?`

`I haven`t booked my return passage yet. Probably mid-January.`

CHAPTER THIRTY - SIX

The train clanked and puffed to a halt in Brighton station. Then expelled a great gush of steam, as though it were its last breath, before hissing gently at rest alongside the platform.

Nothing had changed, as the hansom cab trotted along the seafront towards Hove. But then why should it, I had only been away eighteen months. I had written to my parents, and enjoyed their replies. I had also penned a note to Mrs Earl, and she had quickly responded, saying my old room would be available for as long as I wanted.

When the cab stopped outside the boarding house, I was struck by the fresh coat of paint on the front door and windows. It was a light blue: all right for some dwellings, but it seemed out of character on this early Victorian building.

The front door opened and Mrs Earl sallied forth down the path. She had grown a little rounder since my last visit. But she was her welcoming, effusive self, grinning broadly and calling over her shoulder. 'Harry, he`s here! Come and take his case!`

Tea and Madeira cake quickly appeared, which we took in the front parlour. This was, indeed, an occasion.

`I told my friends you were coming,` she gushed, as she poured tea into one of her best cups. `I mentioned that you were a famous film producer in America, and we even saw your name in a credit recently when Harry and I went to see a film. Didn`t we, Harry?`

He nodded, munching stoically through his slice of Madeira.

I rested after my journey, and fell fast asleep, only waking when there was a knock at the door.

`Mr Lockhart, dinner in ten minutes.`

`Thank you, Mrs Earl.`

Predictably, it was soup and boiled mutton. I had forgotten that was always served on a Wednesday. I sat in the usual chair, looking across to the seat once occupied by Mr Gunn. My fellow lodger, who had listened intently to my unthinking comments about the projector Alfred Darling and I had constructed. Then had had the audacity to make off with it, and sell the machine to a willing buyer in Holmfirth.

Much had happened since then. I was aware, too, of the little changes that had taken place in my absence, However, I was not prepared for the comment from my erstwhile landlady that she noticed differences in me.

`You have filled out a little, Mr Lockhart, and I can`t get used to your American accent. But I suppose it`s to be expected. If you live among them you begin to talk like them,` she said artlessly.

That pulled me up short. In the United States, everyone immediately picked me out as an Englishman. Perhaps, I had become someone in between. Not exactly American, not easily recognised as English. I tried to listen to myself. In my room later, I read the newspaper aloud in, hopefully, a very English voice.

The next day a hansom cab took me to Roman Crescent in Southwick.

Laura, George`s wife answered the door .

`Sam!` she cried, and flung her arms round my neck. `This is the most wonderful surprise! Come in...come in. George will be delighted to see you.`

She shut the door quickly, rushed past me and out to the "laboratory". She came skipping back, closely followed by her husband. Laura had not altered, but George was a little more shrunken; and his wiry hair, invariably in disarray, was much closer to grey than the dark brown of the past. His moustache reflected the same off-white tones.

`Sam! Sam! It`s so good to see you! He sat down in an easy chair, and resting his elbows on his knees, said. `Come on, tell me what you`ve been up to.`

We sat there for almost an hour while I recounted events in America. I omitted the attack in Edgewater, and any references to the possible move to California. But there was plenty to relate, and when I had finished, Laura jumped up and exclaimed. `What a rotten hostess I am! Sam, would you like some coffee?`

While she was in the kitchen, George gave me the latest news on the

Kinemacolor project.

`We had this big event at Urbanora house , in London, and although there were still quite a number of faults with the process, at least it demonstrated that the two-colour system could work reasonably well. There was a lot of excitement about the idea of colour pictures, that they were the future. Charles gave those attending a glowing presentation of what it would soon mean to motion pictures. The reality, however, is that we still need to do a lot of work on it to come halfway close to the desired result. I know for a fact, Friese-Greene encountered a similar problem with motion fringing when he patented his Biocolour system.`

Laura carried in a tray, and handed me a cup of coffee.

`That bloody Urban,` she muttered, passing the sugar.

George carried on with the story. `Charles got over-excited. He opened fresh premises in Wardour Street, called the building, *Kinemacolor* House, and started his usual selling routine. The trouble is we still can`t overcome the fringing problem, and interior shots are out because the light source. Even carbon arc is not sufficiently strong to get a clean image through the filters. That`s why the films we have produced have all be outdoors, documentaries and travelogues. I think I told you, we have to run the camera and project the film at thirty two frames a second. Would you believe,` he gave a wry smile, `We use electric motors to maintain the correct speed.`

`What George hasn`t told you, Sam, is that Charles Urban is taking all the glory, leaving George out in the cold when he has done all the work!`

George shrugged. `Well, he is the salesman. I suppose if everyone thinks he invented it, they may be more likely to buy.`

`Well, it may be a significant step forward, natural colour films, but who is going to pay for the specialised equipment theatres will need?` Laura remarked.

When I eventually left, I could sense the air of despondency hanging over the house in Roman Crescent.

I spent a week in London. Visits had been arranged with our agents, and I also went shopping, buying presents for Isabel, Emily and Joanna. The stores agreed to dispatch them, and assured me they would arrive well before

Christmas. I then selected gifts for Laura and George, Geoffrey and his family, and my mother and father.

I stayed in a comfortable hotel on The Strand, and one evening saw a production of Franz Lehár's operetta *The Count of Luxembourg*, and on another occasion, H. G. Pelissier's, *The Follies*.

Back in Brighton, I decided to call upon Geoffrey, whom I thought was working for James Williamson's company at their studios in Hove. But when I arrived at Cambridge Grove, the name board outside proclaimed it to be, `The Natural Colour Kinematograph Company'. When I entered the building, it was to find Charles Urban in full flow lecturing a team of five people – one of whom was Geoffrey Summer.

`Well, well.` Urban turned in my direction. `I heard you were back, but didn't realise we'd be honoured with a visit from the eminent film producer.`

He smiled at the group of people. `For those of you who don't know, this is Mr Samuel Lockhart, late of this parish, now a leading light in my own country. He works for the Independent Moving Pictures Company, and if you've read the papers you may have come across a news item concerning their victory in a recent patent infringement lawsuit. What are you doing over here, Sam? Hiding from the wrath of Thomas Edison?`

`How did you guess, Charles,` I replied lightheartedly.

In my heart I felt like punching him in the mouth.

`So, for what reason do we owe the pleasure of your company?`

`I didn't realise that James was no longer here,` I replied.

`Hmm...gave up film making, sold up, and has gone fully into the distribution and equipment side of the business. When he moved to London I bought the premises. This is where we produce our *Kinemacolor* films.`

`I see. Well I won't keep you, Charles. I'll be off then.`

Geoffrey stepped forward. `I'll show you a way out to The Drive, Sam. You'll be able to hail a hansom from there.`

We walked out the gates and turned left towards the main road.

`It's good to see you, Sam. What about a drink later?`

We arranged to meet at the Rock Inn in Brighton that evening. It was within walking distance of where Geoffrey now lived.

When I arrived he was seated at a side table, a pint of beer before him. He made his way over to the bar and bought the same for me.

`Cheers,` I said.

He lifted his glass and tilted it in my direction..

`So, how is the family? Thriving?`

`About to be a father for the third time,` he declared proudly.

`Congratulations. What have you got at the moment? Remind me.`

`Two sons. We`re hoping for a daughter this time round.`

For an instant my mind turned to Emily and Joanna...and Isabel.

I shook my mind to clear a disturbing thought.

`So the American film business is doing you proud, by the sound of it,` Geoffrey remarked. `I get the impression Charles Urban is a trifle jealous.`

`He has little reason to be,` I said. `It`s rewarding, but it`s also tough.`

`How do you mean?`

As we sat there, over our beers, I told him all that had happened over the past three years. The highs, the lows, the excitement, the war being waged against us; and finally, the attack on Walter and me that resulted in his death.

`My God, Sam. It`s no place to bring up a family,` said Geoffrey in a tremulous voice.

`Apparently, it would be according to Carl Laemmle, if we all moved to California. He has just bought land there, and plans to erect a studio.`

`That sounds inviting.`

`Yes, it does. The only trouble is...I don`t want to go.`

`Really? I`d go there like a shot. What an opportunity!`

`Do you mean that? You and your family would move all that way?`

`Without any hesitation. Anything, to get away from Charles Urban.`

`Hmm...If the move takes place, I`ll recommend you come and join us.`

`I`d appreciate that, Sam. You got me my job with James Williamson, remember.`

My mother had prepared everything.

The cottage was festooned with coloured paper chains; a Christmas tree stood by the sideboard; and there were large, knitted stockings hanging by the fireplace. I had removed my hat and a long scarf wound tightly round my neck. Overnight, the temperature had dropped sharply, the wind had risen, making the carriage journey from Hove a miserable venture. I was still shivering in front of the large, open fire when my father walked into the room.

`Sam, good to see you, boy.`

He dropped the logs in the hearth, and shook my hand. Not for him the manly hug and backslapping I experienced in America, he was made of sterner stuff. But then the British have never been good with emotions. My mother smiled enigmatically at my reaction to the greeting. As a Frenchwoman she was given to hugs, kisses and tears; but after all these years, she had come to recognise that we did things differently this side of the Channel. Although, I took after the Gallic side of the family, I had grown to temper whatever show of emotion I might have felt with my father.

`Hello, dad, you`re looking well. Still working hard down at Newhaven?`

`They keep me busy, son.` He changed the subject. `What would you like to drink? Beer, wine, something hot?`

`A cup of tea would be welcome.`

My mother said, `I`ll get it. You two sit down.`

While she was out the room I loaded the stockings, which were more like sacks, with presents.

`I hope you haven`t been too generous, Sam. We don`t need much nowadays.`

`No dad, not overly so. Just a few things you might like.`

`Why are you talking in that funny accent? I suppose you`ve got into their ways. Never could understand foreigners.`

`You understood mother quick enough.`

He grinned. `That was different.`

Three mugs of tea arrived on a tray.

We sat around the fire. When my mother prompted me to tell her about the things I was doing, I recounted the best bits of the past year. She intrigued me by saying. `I went into Brighton with Mrs Goodchild, next door. We did some shopping, then went to see some films together. I`m sure your name appeared, but it was gone before I could be sure. I told Mrs Goodchild, but I don`t think she believed me. That young lady, Florence Lawrence, pretty little thing, do you know her?`

`Hmm...and her husband, Harry Solter. They used to work for us, and we paid handsomely for the privilege.`

`What does a motion picture actress earn then?` asked my father. `She only works for ten minutes at a time.`

I smiled. `There's more to it than the amount of time you see her on the screen, dad. She is no longer with us, but when she was we paid her a thousand dollars a week. Her husband, who directed the films, earned two hundred dollars a week.`

`A thousand dollars a week. What's that in English money?`

`About two hundred and twenty pounds.`

`Two hundred and twenty pounds! No one's worth that amount for prancing in front of a camera! It's unbelievable!`

`It's related to what audiences will pay, dad. When you have a leading lady like her, so popular people queue to see her in a film, and pay a good ticket price, then you pay those sums of money.`

`Shouldn't be allowed. Makes a mockery of those who work hard for a living wage.`

He was still grumbling when we went to bed that night. It would have been unwise to mention that the Lubin Company was paying Florence twice what we had paid her.

I slept in the small back room, which was as cold as the carriage that had brought me earlier in the day.

Christmas Day dawned. A bright, cold awakening. During the night I had added my overcoat to the bedclothes - but I still shivered. Frost covered the window, inside as well as out. I could hear the sounds of the cottage stirring. The fire being lit, pans scrapping on the kitchen stove. I was reluctant to move now that I had generated some degree of warmth, but I ought to offer to do my share.

I dressed quickly, shaved hurriedly in the bathroom, and donned my jacket to preserve body heat.

My mother greeted me with a kiss on the cheek, adding. `I'll soon have breakfast ready. Go and sit by the fire.`

`No, let me help. I'll set the table.`

As it was special we ate in the dining room. I carried the plates, cups and cutlery through, and set them upon the circular table.

`We'll have eggs, bacon and sausages, and I know you used to like fried bread, so I'll do some of that as well.`

`That would be nice.`

My mother was trying to please. I did not have the heart to tell her I would have preferred just rolls and coffee, or perhaps a croissant. More again of my French undertones.

She looked up into my face. `You don`t want that, do you?`

`Not really. I don`t eat much first thing, perhaps a roll if you have one?`

`Your father likes a cooked breakfast, but that`s what I`m having. What if I warm some croissants and rolls in the oven, and make some strong coffee?`

I kissed her loudly on both cheeks.

She had such intuition. She even made the observation. `Tell me, Sam, why are you limping?`

Later in the day, after we had opened the presents, enjoyed a full lunch, and my father had fallen asleep on the sofa, she asked me again. This time I told her of the more hazardous aspects of my recent past. She said little while I told the tale, though her eyes were expressive, showing first concern, then anguish at my exploits: even to the point of getting angry that I should expose myself to such dangers. Eventually, she exclaimed.

`Really, Sam, you are so uncaring. You caused the death of that poor man, and left a widow and two little children to fend for themselves. You should be ashamed of yourself.`

`No I didn`t. He was aware of all that was involved as well as me.`

`Perhaps, but he had more to lose, and you should have taken that into account. So what is this Mr Laemmle and you going to do about it?`

She calmed down, but I slowly realised that she was apprehensive for my safety. Her anxiety for the fate of Isabel, Walter`s widow, and the children, was also a means by which she could express unease. But it got me thinking.

Christmas Day, Boxing Day passed. My parents entertained some of the neighbours, and we were invited to the homes of several of their friends.

When it came time for me to leave, as usual, I found it difficult. My mother and father were not getting any younger, and there were marked signs of their advancing age. Something I could not ignore.

Predictably, my father shook my hand, and in his bluff manner said keep in touch. My mother clung to me for a moment, smiled and wiped away a tear. Then I was gone. The carriage taking me down to Newhaven, then along the coast road to Mrs Earl`s, where I would spend one more night.

CHAPTER THIRTY - SEVEN

A month is a lifetime in the film industry.

When I walked in the offices on Monday morning, Isadore pounced. He quickly shepherded me into his room and shut the door.

`Am I glad to see you back. It`s been mayhem here.`

`Why? What`s happened?`

`The film distribution service I`m running for the independents is haemorrhaging members so fast, it will soon be just IMP! And the arguments, the shouting and screaming that`s been taking place in these offices has been unbelievable!`

`Arguments and shouting? Who has been shouting?`

`The five of them involved in this Universal deal. It was supposed to have been an umbrella grouping, safety in numbers, harder to be picked off. Yet the so-called hierarchy has been close to tearing each other to pieces! And guess who the main culprit has been? . .Carl! He wants the Universal Manufacturing Company to be more than just a safety net. What`s more, he wants to run it. He doesn`t want to be treasurer any more, he wants to be president.`

`That figures.   As Recha once said to me, he hasn`t got a clue about money.`

`But if he upsets the others too much there won`t be a Universal,` declared Isadore despondently.

`I`ll take a bet with you, Issy. When the dust settles, Carl will be president, and the others will have accepted him as their leader.`

`Do you think so? Am I looking forward to  moving to California.`

Over the next few months I spent most of my time at Fort Lee.

I rearranged the studio, providing easier access from the scenery store to the shooting stage; revised the lighting system, putting in banks of carbon arc units; and installed a processing laboratory so that we could view the film more quickly, and if necessary, retake shots.

One other addition to the buildings on the site were stables for two horses and a couple of buggies. Now we longer had to rely on taking the trolley or hiring someone to take us to and from the ferry terminal.

I stayed at the rooming house in north Edgestone, not far from Isabel and the children. I would visit them once, occasionally twice a week to help out. It was a Thursday when I knocked at their door, and it was opened by Isabel, dressed soberly in black. She saw the disconcerted look on my face.

`Hello, Sam. I was just going up to the cemetery.` Her head dropped. `It`s the anniversary of Walter`s death.`

I took the three of them to the Madonna Cemetery in one of the buggies: standing back while they paid their respects at the graveside. Nothing was said on either journey, or at the house. I left soon after walking Isabel, Emily and Joanna to the front door.

Later that day, I caught the ferryboat to the city, and sat in my room at the Algonquin Hotel. I was in a sombre mood, and did not stir from it until Sunday morning, when I went to the IMP offices to make a start on ideas for a forthcoming series.

I was surprised to see Carl, and the board members of Universal, having a meeting with William Swanson of the Rex Motion Picture Company.

`Come and meet the new addition to our Universal Film Manufacturing Company, Sam. In fact, you will be the first to learn that from today, it will be more than an insurance against the Trust, we have taken the decision that eventually we`ll become one single film company, with me as President.`

When they had finally gone, having agreed the announcement to be issued to the press, Carl walked into my room.

`What a day...what a day. So...that`s it. Agreement at last. A new beginning, Sam. It`ll take time, of course. For the moment, we shall continue with our individual commitments, but eventually we`ll move the studios to California. I`ll sell the lot on Gower Street and Sunset Boulevard, and put the funds into the pot to buy a bigger site. Isadore can organise the purchase. I know he is as keen as I am.`

He looked at me quizzically.

`What about you, Sam? Still set on staying here, on the east coast?`

It was a week before I went visiting.

I knocked tentatively on the door, which was quickly wrenched open by Isabel.

`Hello, Sam. Come in. Derek is here, telling me about the recent works over at the studio. It seems you've been making quite a few changes.`

I stood on the porch for a moment, irritated that Derek Bryant was there. No, it was not so much irritation…it was jealousy. A stupid emotion, one that caught me unawares; and I could not shake off the feeling.

`Hello, Derek.`

`Hello, Sam. I was in Edgewater, collecting a few things, and thought I would see how Isabel was doing.`

`Right. Well, I guess you'll be wanting to get back then.`

He glanced at Isabel. `Yes, I suppose I ought.`

He pushed back the chair, and started for the front door. `I'll see you, Isabel. Thanks for the coffee.`

`Derek, thanks for calling in to see me.` She stood on tiptoe and kissed his cheek

The door clicked shut behind him.

`That was a little sharp, Sam.`

`He doesn't have time to sit around and chat, Isabel. He has a job to do. I don't pay him to go house-calling.`

`Then what are you doing here? Aren't you supposed to be working?`

`If he put in the hours I do, I would be more lenient perhaps. But he doesn't.`

Her cheeks reddened suddenly.

`God, you're so pompous. Are all Englishmen like you? You're serious all the time. Why can't you be more light-hearted? I've never known anyone so, so intense!`

I stared at her for a moment. Then stalked out the house, not mindful of the door crashing shut behind me.

Who does she think she is?…telling me I'm miserable all the time. I smile, have a sense of humour. I laugh at jokes…if I think them funny. Suddenly, the vision of my father passed behind my eyes. His appearance was invariably dour and unbending. Was I made in his image?

I flicked the reins to encourage the horse into trot. He took no notice of my request. I flicked them again impatiently. I could swear he was ignoring me because of the mood I was in.

I applied myself to film making. The scenes were changed, the cameras whirred, Thomas Ince, the director ensured the actors went through their gamut of emotions. We finished the next tranche of films in the time allocated. Viewing the results provided by our processing unit, I was able to start editing on-site, saving me time back in the city. Except for a few retakes on some of the close-ups, we were home and dry.

Derek said little to me. I figured he was still smarting at my comments at Isabel's place. That is, until we were packing the buggies to take us to the terminal.

`Sam, I saw Isabel the other day. She mentioned you hadn't been by recently. Anything wrong?`

`Look, Derek, I was wrong to comment on your visit to her house when I saw you there. I know you work hard, and do all you can for the company. It was an unfair remark, I apologise.`

`That's all right, Sam. By the way, I'm seeing her over the weekend, can I tell her anything?`

There it was again. The stifling feeling that spread through my chest. This time it was bigger.

`Err...no Derek. There's no need.`

I had a miserable weekend. On Monday and Tuesday I worked in the offices, and Wednesday caught the midday ferry to Edgewater. As the boat neared the terminal, I caught sight of the buggy that was meeting me. I also saw a woman standing by the landing stage. It was Isabel.

When the ferry tied up, and I made my way ashore with the other passengers, she came hesitantly towards me.

`I telephoned your company. They told me you would be on this boat. I wanted a word with you, Sam.`

`Unless you are doing some shopping in town, shall I ask my driver to drop us off at your house?`

She nodded. Her teeth chewing at her bottom lip. I helped her into the buggy that had now made its way across to us.

`Driver, could you take us first to River Road, and wait for me there?`

We trotted along beside the river, neither saying a word.

`Can you stop here driver, I shan`t be long?` I called, and followed Isabel up the path to the front door. She led the way into the parlour, where she turned and looking up into my face, said in a low voice.

`This is very difficult for me, Sam. Firstly, I want to apologise for my rudeness when you were here last. It was wrong of me to say those things about you.` She gave a sad smile. `I know they are not true, but you must realise I was upset by your attitude to Derek.`

`I`ve already spoken to Derek,` I said tensely.

`I know, he told me. That`s why I wanted to convey my feelings to you.`

I humphed. `I don`t think you can.`

`What does that mean?`

`Nothing, Isabel. Let`s leave it well alone.`

She placed her hands on her hips, her chin came forward.

`Sam, you are not leaving this room until you tell me what you meant by leave it well alone!`

Listen, forget I said anything.`

`I warn you, Samuel Lockhart! Don`t leave here without an explanation. If you do, don`t ever bother to return!`

`There`s no point anyway. Goodbye Isabel.`

I went to walk past her. Suddenly, I was staggering across the room. She had slapped me hard on the cheek.

`Don`t you dare! You come to my home, become a good friend, become someone the girls enjoy seeing , become...become.`

She was shaking. I pulled her to me. Close to I could see the tears welling up in her eyes. Without thinking, I put my arms around her. It was then she broke into deep, wracking sobs.

We stayed locked together for some minutes. I remember softly kissing the top of her head. When we broke apart, her gaze turned to concern.

`God, look what I`ve done to your face,` she sniffed. `I must get some cold water and some towels.`

She glanced quickly at me. It was a curious mixture of uncertainty and embarrassment.

`Don`t go away,` was her parting instruction.

But I did: briefly. I went out, and keeping my face turned away, told the driver I would make my own way to the studio.

When Isabel returned with a bowl of water and fresh towels, she gently tended my cheek. However, even though some of the swelling had partially subsided, the angry weals prominently displayed the shape of a heavy hand.

`Oh, Sam, I`m so sorry. Just look what I`ve done.`

It hurt, but it was worth suffering the blow to have her bathe it with such tenderness.

`What will they say when they see it at the studio? What will they think?`

`I`ll tell them it was some jezebel in the city who accosted me. I wouldn't go with her, and she did this to me.`

She laughed at that. `Do you believe for one moment they`ll be taken in by such a fanciful story.`

`Or I could simply tell them the truth.`

She stared at me thoughtfully. `Which is?`

`I was supposed to have mended a dripping tap. But I couldn`t do it, and it was driving you nuts. So you called in a plumber. He couldn`t fix it, either. In you annoyance you lashed out at him, missed, and hit me instead.`

She laughed again, out loud. `You don`t know how close to the truth that is.`

I left about an hour later. I did not bother going to the studio, but headed for the rooming house a half mile away. I thought long and hard about Isabel. We were good friends again. No, perhaps more than good friends, close friends. While I was elated, at the same time I could not shake off this feeling of despondency. I would have wished to have been closer, more than just a friends The trouble was this was a young woman still mourning her dead husband. I felt very much the unwelcome intruder.

CHAPTER THIRTY - EIGHT

I was in the city for a discussion with Mary Pickford and Carl Laemmle.

I presumed he would invite Lewis Milestone to sit in. Invariably, he came to these meetings when contracts and money were being discussed. We had had several such get-togethers with Mary. Each time they finished with her asking for more money, and each time we ended up giving it to her.

We had arranged to meet in her suite at the McAlpin Hotel, on the corner of Broadway and Thirty Fourth Street. Just recently opened, it was said to be the largest in the world. Nothing was too good for Miss Pickford.

We had just completed a batch of five films, ending with the longer one-reel drama, *A Timely Repentance*. As we were meeting in mid-town Manhattan, I had decided to spend a few days in the city, and complete the editing at our offices overlooking DeWitt Park.

When I walked into the lobby, which was like entering Grand Central Station, I caught sight of Lewis by a stand of aspidistras.

`No Carl yet?` I enquired.

`Of course not. He`ll be ten minutes late. He is always ten minutes late,` said Lewis with a grin, `and he`ll blame the traffic.`

Ten minutes later Carl pushed his way through the revolving doors.

`Sorry, damned traffic.`

Going up in the elevator, Carl thanked Lewis for coming.

`I know these sorts of discussion are not in your remit, Lewis. But it helps keep such conversations on a realistic level. They don`t get carried away with their demands when I introduce you as our legal representative.`

`Actually, Carl, I enjoy them. It can get a bit stuffy dealing with the often dull routine of the law.`

`I know what I wanted to ask you, Lewis,` I said, as the doors opened at the twentieth floor.

We walked along the wide corridor searching for her room number.

`We still have, what was the figure, two hundred and something lawsuits pending.`

`Two hundred and eighty eight, to be exact,` reminded Carl.

`Do we just sit back and see what happens, or do we seek to get them cancelled?` I enquired.

`It`s really up to the Motion Picture Patents Company, Sam. They have declared an intention. They now have to seek the court`s time if they wish to pursue them.`

`I ask for two reasons, Lewis. I`ve been reading President Taft`s speeches as he goes around the country seeking re-election, and he seems keen on upholding Senator Sherman`s Anti-Trust Act. You probably know all about it, but it was news to me that such a government decree existed. I was thinking, doesn`t the MPPC`s *raison d`être* contravene the spirit of the Act?`

He looked at me shrewdly. `You may be on to something there, Sam. Let me look into it and get back to you.`

We came to a halt outside two zero three five, and Carl knocked on the door.

Owen Moore, Mary`s husband opened it and welcomed us in.

`What would you like to drink, gentlemen?` he enquired.

`I rather get down to business if you don`t mind, Owen,` Carl declared for both Lewis and myself. `I think we all know what this is about. So why don`t I start the ball rolling by saying, straight off the bay, we can`t go a penny more than an extra hundred dollars a week.`

They glanced quickly at each other. Then Mary`s eyes dropped to the ground and she murmured. `This time isn`t about money, Carl. It`s about the material you`ve been giving me.`

`Wait a minute, Mary, we brought in outside writers. They`ve turned out some good screenplays. You can`t complain about that.`

`Frankly, Carl, I preferred the stuff Sam used to write. Obviously, he`s too busy producing to create screenplays now, but what`s being dished up now is poor. And so is the directing. Thomas Ince was a good actor, but he doesn`t come over nearly as well as a director. I was always hoping Independent Moving Pictures would cast me in a serial. I would have loved to have done a serial.`

Carl glanced at me.

`OK, we`ll do a serial, and Sam can give some ideas to some new writers. We can`t say fairer than that.`

`I`m afraid it`s too late, Carl.`

Owen moved to stand by her chair.

`What do you mean by that?`

`I`ve signed for Harry Aiken's Majestic Film Company, and Owen is going to direct me.`

`You can`t do that! We`ve got a contract! Tell her, and him, Lewis.`

`The thing is, Carl, you can be sued if you don`t pay your actors what is stipulated in their contracts, but you, the company, would have a hard time holding them to the letter of the small print. Who`s to say that a disgruntled actor, or in this case, actress, won`t deliberately under-perform and ruin the picture. Her fans would blame the film maker for giving her such awful material to work with. They won`t stop idolising her. It`s just not worth it, Carl, let her go,` declared Lewis solemnly.

We were back at the offices. Carl, pacing up and down, listening intently to what Lewis had to say.

`After all the breaks we`ve given her. Not counting all that money, and you`re telling me to let her go?`

`Yes, move on from here, Carl. You won`t win this one.`

He stopped, spun on his heel, and collapsed onto a chair.

`OK. No more Mary Pickford.` He chuckled. `I wonder how long she`ll stay with Aiken. Who can we use as a replacement, Sam?`

`We can use Vivian Prescott for the time being. She`s a good actress.`

`Didn`t she work for Biograph. I seem to recall D W Griffith using her in a number of films. Is she pretty.`

`Yes, in a conventional sort of way, Carl. She`ll never have the impact of Florence or Mary, but she`ll do a competent job, and she`s available.`

CHAPTER THIRTY - NINE

It was exactly as I thought.

Vivian Prescott was a good actress. She quickly picked up on the style of the films we were making, hit all her cues, never walked into the scenery, and got on well with the crew. Her portrayal of the characters, though varied in age, temperament and period, was always precise and accurate. When one saw her performing and bonding with her immediate fellow actors, you could not have wished for better.

The trouble was, the camera did not respond to her. It was remote and unyielding. What I saw on the set and what came over on film were two different things. Vivian was attractive, vivacious and warm. Not one of these traits was apparent in her films. She did not possess the curls and the character of Mary Pickford, nor the expressive eyes and winsome beauty of Florence Lawrence. Both were loved by the camera. Something had to be done, and quickly.

I told Isabel of the problem, showing her photographs of Vivian in her various roles.

`She's very attractive, Sam. I don't understand your problem.`

`It's not easy to explain. Let me put it this way. If you saw a *Billboard* advertising a film starring Mary Pickford, and another starring Vivian Prescott, which one would you pay to see?`

`Mary Pickford.`

`OK, why?`

`I suppose because she's a good actress.`

`I can assure you, so is Vivian.`

`I think Mary appeals to my womanly instincts. I have more sympathy... no that's not the word, empathy, with what she is doing on the screen.`

I nodded thoughtfully. Mary Pickford was appealing to both men and women. Men wanted to embrace her, women empathised with her.

`What about Florence Lawrence?`

`The same, I guess.`

I took the unedited films back to the offices in the city. I had a difficult task before me. I needed a leading lady who would captivate audiences and have them flocking to movie theatres. I sat on the ferryboat as it steamed downriver, wracking my brain to come up with a name. Someone we might tempt from one of the other studios.

I strolled around the deck searching for an answer. King Baggot, our leading male actor, had glimpsed the rough cuts of this most recent batch, and had said little. But I could tell from his eyes that he, too, was concerned.

He had turned towards me in the half light, and raised an eyebrow. A simple gesture that told me something. I thought about that gesture. It could have worked well in a close-up on film. Then an idea gradually began to form. Was I approaching this the wrong way?

I slept on it in my room at the Algonquin. In the morning I had the answer.

Both Carl and Isadore were there when I walked in.

Carl called out. `So, how did it go? Were you happy with Vivian Prescott alongside King Baggot?`

`The answer is, we got what I expected. Have you got a moment? I want to discuss something.`

We gathered round the table in Isadore`s office.

`Two things, Vivian is not our star. She never will be. She makes a good foil for leading actors in a supporting role. And as long as the camera dwells more on others in a scene, she performs her part well.`

`No good, eh?` commented Carl. `So what is the second thing you mentioned?`

`We change the emphasis. Instead of a female lead we introduce a male lead.`

`I don`t get you,` remarked Isadore.

`I do,` snapped Carl, `but that`s not the way we do it.`

`So change the way we do it,` I replied.

`Any studio done it before?`

` A few have tried, but with no real flair. I don`t think they have been aware of the potential of a male star.`

`OK,` said Carl, `what have you got in mind? You`ve got something buzzing away up there`. He nodded, gazing at my head.

`What about,` I said slowly, `making King Baggot our leading man? I`ll tell you how we do it. In the next batch of films, we still put him alongside Vivian, but this time the camera is very much on him. We do lots of close-ups, and we portray him as a cross between a knight in shining armour and Casanova. We present him as a compassionate yet passionate man, with conquests, yes, but also with a determined spirit, prepared to defend all that`s right and just.`

`Go on,` murmured Carl, a light gleaming in his eye.

`We have a number of screenplays by the writers we brought in. I`ll select those that will give us the latitude to present him in the way I`ve described. In fact, I`ll brief them now on what we are looking for in the next two series.

`I`ll sketch out some advertising material for the newspapers, and place some articles in the fan magazines. Then we`ll plaster the *Billboard*s, hoarding and handbills with King Baggot`s face, and arrange a number of interviews for him. Although the films are silent, he has a deep, well-modulated voice which will appeal to interviewers. You made the star system work with Florence Lawrence, Carl. Let`s take it a stage further by creating the first male star.`

King Baggot went along with the proposal, and before we started on the next run of films, I took him aside for the cameraman to do a selection of still photographs. I had adjusted the screenplays, and spoken with the director, Otis Turner, on what I wanted to achieve. The emphasis would be on King. More close-ups, focus on his profile and move the supporting players into the background.

There was little more I could do, other than pace up and down and await the results. After a while I got the stableboy to drive me into Edgewater in the studio buggy to buy flowers and candy.

Isabel had decided I was too thin. As a result, she insisted I had at least two good meals each week, and a pattern had developed of dining with her and the girls on Tuesday and Friday evenings. At first it had been a Thursday, until she discovered I was not Jewish, I only worked with them.

`With a name like Samuel, I automatically thought you were of their persuasion,` she had said laughing. The evening was changed to Friday, and from River Road it was a short stroll to the terminal to catch the last ferry downriver for the weekend.

I knocked on the door, which was immediately opened by Isabel.

`Come in, Sam. Derek was just telling me an amusing story.`

She led the way into the kitchen, where Derek was lounging in a chair, completely at home drinking a cup of coffee.

`Hello, Sam. Have they finished the day`s shooting at the studio, already?`

`I turned to Isabel. `Look, I can`t stay to dinner. I`m sorry, There`s an urgent meeting I have to attend in the city.` I thrust the flowers in her hand. `And some candy for Emily and Joanna.`

I left the house and walked swiftly down the road cursing my luck. Of all things, to find my rival seated comfortably in Isabel`s house, no doubt entertaining her with amusing stories. Just when I was looking forward to relaxing, and enjoying a pleasant meal.

Aboard the ferryboat I stood outside on deck. Despite a fierce, chill wind, whipping up the water and rocking the steamer. Why on earth should I get rattled by another suitor? One must expect competition when paying court to a singularly, attractive young woman? Even if she has been recently widowed, inevitably there would be callers. Just because I knew the other man, it should not exclude him from the pursuit. But, I was not that gracious, I realised. I did not want to vie for her attention. I wanted to be the only one in her eyes.

There again, she may prefer a fellow such as Derek Bryant. How would I know? Moreover, how do you judge what might be a suitable interval of time before you make known your sentiments? Perhaps, Derek is not so concerned. He might not wait for the appropriate moment. He could be there, this very minute, declaring his intentions.

By the time the boat docked I was bitterly cold, shivering, and utterly dejected.

I stopped in a bar for a warming glass of bourbon. My body slowly returned to normal, and my erratic thoughts took a more critical bent.

I realised that Isabel was completely unaware of my feelings for her. There was no way she could have guessed. I was polite, friendly, we laughed together, ate together: but that was all. She could have no inkling of what I really felt.

So, at the risk of be rejected, I must tell her of my affection for her. It was the only way to overcome the torment. If she told me to leave, I would be desolated. As well as the object of my yearnings, she had also become a dear friend. That would end in an instant if she showed me the door.

The following morning I caught the first ferry upriver.

Walking up to Isabel`s house from the terminal, I rehearsed what I wanted to say. I knocked tentatively on the door.

`Just a minute!` came a familiar cry. `Emily open the door, would you?`

Damn...being Saturday she would not be at school.

`Hello, Sam. Thanks for the candy. Mom told us you had to leave, so I couldn`t say thank you last night.`

`Err...you are welcome, Emily.`

`And Joanna is here, somewhere. She can say thank you herself.`

`Right.`

`Do you want to come in? We are just going to eat breakfast.`

`Oh, well I won`t disturb you. I`ll see you on Tuesday.`

`OK, Sam, bye.`

She shut the door.

I stood there for a moment and then turned on my heel and walked down the path.

Suddenly, the door flew open.

`Sam! Where are you going?`

`To the studio.`

`Not before eating breakfast with us, you`re not!`

I slowly retraced my steps. `I don`t want to be in the way, I just called.. .the reason I called...was to say sorry for missing dinner last night.`

She looked up at me and smiled.

`Come and sit with us. I`ll make some stronger coffee.`

She took my arm, led me into the kitchen and pushed me into a chair.

`Now what would you like to eat?`

`Toast would be fine, thank you.`

`Are you sure? No wonder you`re losing weight if you just eat toast at breakfast.`

`Yes that will be fine, really.`

She shrugged and went over to the toaster, hovering, ready to turn over the slice of bread to do the other side. The girls quickly finished their bowls of porridge.

`Come on, Joanna,` said Emily, `I think Sam wants to talk to mom.`

Joanna stared at me. At the door, she stopped and turned her head towards me in puzzlement. Exasperated, Emily dragged her out the room.

Isabel put the toast on my plate, and passed the butter. She poured two cups of coffee, before sitting down.

`Do you, Sam?`

`Sorry?`

`Do you want to talk to me, as Emily suggested?`

`Well, err, yes and no. I`d like to, but now doesn`t seem the right time.`

`Surely, now is as good as any other?`

I could feel myself blushing. The more I became aware of it, the redder I became.

`My, my, I`ve never seen a grown man go that colour before. It must be serious. Will I be pleased or sad?`

`I think you might be sad.`

All that I had rehearsed deserted me. It was all going wrong, and there was no way of avoiding the situation.

`I`m waiting, Sam.`

`Look Isabel...I know you still miss Walter, and will for some time to come. You had a marriage that would be difficult to improve on. But, it`s nearly eighteen months, and I wondered...I wondered...`

This is it, She`ll either kick me out or laugh at what I`m going to say.

`I wondered if I might have just a tiny place in your affections. You hold an overwhelming hold on mine. Forgive me, if I`m speaking out of turn...I just had to tell you what you mean to me. Now if you want me to leave I`ll understand. I don`t want to upset or anger you. The thing is...`

I never did finish. Emily pushed open the door and walked in.

`Is Sam going to marry you then mom? Derek says he wants to.`

My face went even redder.

I did not get thrown out.

I had my hand held, and we talked and talked. Isabel said she had very strong leanings towards me, but it was a little too early to contemplate marriage. Would I mind accepting that there was something there, and might grow as her mourning lessened. Would I wait for her? She would know when the moment was right to give her heart to another.

I closed my hands over hers.

`If there`s the faintest of chances, I`ll gladly wait as long as it takes.`

I cannot remember all that we discussed. I was still in shock. There was hope. Emily came back several times and finally stood there staring at us.

`Well?`

`Well what, dear?`

`Is he going to marry you?`

`No.` Isabel smiled. `At least not yet.`

`But he might?`

`Yes, he might.`

`Good. Uncle Derek was right.`

She wandered out the room.

`Uncle Derek? He seems to know the family rather well, doesn`t he?`

`Are you jealous, Sam?`

I was silent for a moment.

`Well, yes I am. I`ve had sleepless nights because of him.`

Isabel laughed.

`What`s so funny?`

`You are! Didn`t you know he`s my cousin. I was a Bryant before I was married.`

Later that day I went over to the studio and collected the unedited material of three films so far completed. Rather than work on them at the studio, where they were noisily preparing for the coming week`s filming schedule, I wanted the seclusion of the offices in the city. At the weekend, with no one about, I could be on my own to discover if we had captured the essential King Baggot.

In the euphoria I was feeling, it was no hardship to work through Saturday night and most of Sunday morning. When I telephoned Carl at his home in West End Avenue, Recha answered my call.

`Sam, how nice to hear from you. I haven`t seen you for a while. Is everything all right?`

`Recha, it really couldn`t be better. Look, I`m sorry to disturb you on a Sunday, but is Carl free, I need a quick word with him.`

There was a brief silence.

`Sam, what can I do for you?`

`I just wanted to check if you were in the offices tomorrow morning? I`ve got a surprise for you.`

`Yes, and I`ve got a surprise for you. I`ll be there at eight thirty. OK?`

When I arrived the next day, Carl and Isadore were there, together with Lewis Milestone.

`Let me reveal my surprise first,` grinned Carl. `I think you`d better tell him, Lewis.`

We took our seats around the conference table while our lawyer adopted his "speaking with client" mode. He took spectacles from a case and placed them carefully in position. From a folder he removed several sheets of paper, and placed them before him. Then he steepled his hands, and in an authoritative tone, began.

`Sam, do you recall the comment you made when we were going up to Miss Pickford`s suite at the McAlpin Hotel?`

`What about your president`s support for the Sherman Anti-Trust Act?`

`That`s the one. Before we went into her suite, I said I would look into it. Well, I have, and it makes for interesting reading. I`ve also been taking legal advice from a number of different quarters, both academic and judicial. Initially, there was some uncertainty about whether the Motion Picture Patents Company was in breach of the Act.

`Those to whom I spoke all quoted John Sherman`s mission statement. Namely, "*to protect consumers by preventing arrangements designed, or which tend, to advance the cost of goods to the consumer*". They suggested that it was not affecting theatre-goers. Well, we could argue that the MPPC`s efforts, or as we know it euphemistically, the Trust, were restrictive, and materially affected theatre-goers by pushing up ticket prices.

`But what was more relevant, Senator George Hoar, a contributing author to the Act, stipulated, "*a person who merely by superior skill and intelligence got the whole business because nobody could do it as well as he, could was not a monopolist.. but was if it involved something like the use of means which made it impossible for* *other persons to engage in fair competition".`

`Lewis, I think you`re losing us a bit here. Tell us what it all means.`

`It means, Carl, that I have effectively, got all the learned legal minds to agree that the Trust must answer the allegation. In the near future, a federal court will hear the case, listed as "*United States versus The Motion Picture Patents Company*". To determine if there has been a serious contravention of the Anti-Trust Act. I can tell you now that judgement will be found against the company for its actions.`

I jumped up, so did Carl and Isadore, shouting and cheering until we were hoarse.

Then a brief moment of back-slapping Lewis, who, under the beating, remarked.

`It was Sam who put me onto it.`

`Let`s get something to celebrate properly.`

Champagne was acquired, and the next thirty minutes were spent talking of the ramifications.

`Have MPPC been notified of this, Lewis?` asked Carl.

`They`ll know by now, or at least, their lawyers will.`

`What will they do, do you think?`

`Try to delay the hearing for as long as possible. But all the newspapers and the trade magazines will carry the news, So I don`t imagine they will keep up the pressure on you to answer the remaining two hundred odd lawsuits.`

Isadore looked over at me. `No more beatings, Sam.`

`Good. I don`t think I could have taken many more.`

Then Isadore had a further thought.

`So if we don`t have to move, Carl, is California out the window?`

`No, we`re still going to move. The Universal members have agreed to setting up studios on the west coast. We`ll be moving there in the near future, once you`ve organised the sale of the lot on Gower Street and Sunset Boulevard, and purchased a new site, Issy.`

Carl looked over at me, but I avoided his gaze. With the something indefinable existing between Isabel and me, there was even less chance I could be persuaded to go with them.

Lewis left shortly after the third bottle had been emptied.

Carl was getting a little wooden about the face, and before he lost all interest in what was going on, I said. ``Well after all that excitement, do you want to hear my news?`

`Absolutely, Sam. tell us what you`ve got to say.`

I had set up the three edited films on the projector the previous day; and though they still lacked text boards and credits, they would convey all I wanted.

`It was our intention to publicise King Baggot as IMP`s leading male star, if we could prove he had what it takes. That means he had to appeal to both men and women. I said earlier, when I put the idea forward, that on the screen he had to come over as a chivalrous, passionate, yet compassionate individual. A devil-may–care type liked by both sexes.

`Well,` I paused briefly, `see what you think. The three films I am going to show you are, *Lady Audley's Secret*, *A Caveman Wooing*, and *The Peril*. There are a further two films in this batch, and they follow the same pattern. Tell me what you think.`

Half an hour later, Carl stood up and slapped me on the back

`Brilliant, Sam. A good call. He`s our man. So, tell me, what`s your plan to publicise King Baggot as Mr IMP?`

I handed them a document presenting my thoughts on how it should be tackled, together with the photographs taken at the studio. I had briefed a poster artist and he had done a first class job of Baggot staring, full face, out the poster; a subtle profile illustration; and standing in an embrace with Vivian Prescott.

`These comprise the format for each of the films, and would appear on theatre posters, hoardings, *Billboards* and handbills. I`d place advertisements in the fan magazines, and release articles giving facts about his lifestyle, how King likes to relax, and his future ambitions. Frothy stuff which the public will devour. The key phrase in all the headlines, "*King of the Movies*".`

I saw Carl`s face crease into that famous grin which signalled approval.

`I`d follow that up with, "*The Most Photographed man In The World*", and "*The Man Whose Face Is As Familiar As The Man In The Moon*". Fortunately, he has a good speaking voice, so we`ll take him on a series of appearances in theatres, and arrange interviews with the press. I would say in no time at all, King Baggot could be the most popular male lead in motion pictures.`

`How much do we need to spend?` asked Isadore.

`I`ve covered that on page fourteen,` I replied, handing them copies. `A modest outlay, but the returns will be truly significant, for King and IMP. There`s only one snag as far as I can see.`

`What the hell is that, Sam? ` asked Carl.

`King intends to marryRuth Considine later in the year.`

`Damnit, he can`t,` declared Carl. `He`ll lose all his women fans.`

`I have spoken to him,` I explained, `and he knows the score, So everything will be kept secret, even from his family.`

`Well, you just make sure it`s kept well under wraps.`

By the time we quit the offices that afternoon, the last of six bottles of champagne was empty. I remember little of how I got back to the Algonquin.

CHAPTER FORTY

Isadore was missing for over a month. When he eventually returned, Universal Film Manufacturing Company was the owner of the Taylor Estate, a two hundred and thirty acre ranch in the San Fernando Valley, on the north side of Hollywood Hills. He had paid one hundred and sixty five thousand dollars, which he declared was a bargain. To my mind, at over seven hundred dollars an acre for farmland, it was the Taylor Estate that had secured the bargain. Isadore had also sold the IMP site on Sunset Boulevard, opposite the Christie-Nestor studio run by the Horsley Brothers.

When I questioned him about the trip he told me it had taken five days to get there. Fortunately, he had travelled Pullman, and had enjoyed good food and a reasonable bed. But sitting there watching the never-ending countryside roll slowly past your window, was tedium in the extreme. When making the return journey he had opted to ride on the Atchison, Topeka and Santa Fe line to Chicago, A journey that took less time.

`It took less time because the train went faster,` declared Isadore. `It`s called the "Scott Special". Never again. It did the journey to Chicago in two days, but I was frightened for my life. At any moment I expected the train to leave the rails. In future, I`ll sit on the Los Angeles Limited and be bored, not scared to death.`

`Anyway, a successful trip. Well done, Issy,` Carl declared. `We`ll start making plans for our move, though I guess there`s no immediate urgency. Until we are all under one roof, the members will continue making films independently, and hopefully distributing them through Universal. But when it comes to it, Sam, when there`s no more IMP, when we are one big company, you`ll have one last chance to join us...or others will.` A pretty clear message.

CHAPTER FORTY - ONE

I had my first kiss.

Not exactly as I had imagined. Not much more than a peck on the cheek when I arrived that Tuesday evening. Still, it was memorable. I caught the softness of her skin and the brief scent of her breath: then it was gone.

`How is King Baggot standing up to all the adulation?` Isabel asked as she was serving the meal.

`Who is King Baggot, mom?`

`A movie actor, Emily.`

`What a funny name for an actor.`

I had had the same thought. Wondering, before we began our campaign, whether to change it to something more appealing. But most people accepted it without any undue comment. There had been a few pointed remarks in the press. Some had considered "King" a pretentious forename, chosen in an attempt to elevate himself beyond his station. Whatever that meant. He had been concerned. I said ignore them. If you answer the critics you will fuel the flames, then the topic will never go away.

`But my name is King.`

`I know, but I`m still telling you not to react. It is bound to come up in interviews. When it does I want you to laugh, confirm the setbacks at being christened with the name, and add, how do you think it went down at school.`

Actually, I knew his first name was William. His mother`s maiden name had been King, and this had been included as a token to the distaff side of his family.

It was soon evident the campaign had been successful. These publicity campaigns develop their own momentum. The general public delight in motion pictures, and are more than ready to idolise the leading actresses; and now, we discovered, leading actors as well.

I was reading the New York Times when my eye caught an article in the business section. I was taking breakfast in the rooming house in Edgewater, glancing through the newspaper before going to the studio.

It reported the purchase of the US rights to *Kinemacolor* by two American businessmen, Gilbert H. Aymar and James K. Bowen. What was intriguing, it gave the background to the sale and dissolution of the agreement between George Smith and Charles Urban. It appeared they had quarrelled bitterly over the terms of their partnership. Poor George, I thought grimly, after all the hours he had devoted to the system. He must have been furious at the way Urban had manipulated him.

At the studio we were halfway through the next series of King Baggot films. Nothing special in their content, except, of course, they were the vehicle for IMP`s leading man.

Between takes he strolled over to Derek and me.

`How`s it going, Sam?`

`Couldn`t be better, King. *Let No Man Put Asunder* is going down really well in the Mid-West, and we have massive orders for this next lot. What is more, we are getting increasing interest in your films in Europe. What do you think of that?`

`I guess that`s good news, isn`t it. Have you got a moment, Sam?`

He drew me away from the set to a quiet corner of the studio.

`Look, Sam, could you do me a big favour? Would you be my best man when Ruth and I get married later in the year?`

I was slightly taken aback. I would have thought he had numerous friends he could call upon. But then he put it into context.

`If our marriage is to be a secret, I can`t ask anyone who knows me. You`re the only guy I could turn to. Would you mind?`

I smiled ruefully. `I`d be delighted, King. When and where is it going to take place?`

`Here, in Fort Lee, on the first of December.`

`That`s a bit obvious, isn`t it?`

`No, I`ve booked the chapel for the Sunday night. Everyone will be away for the weekend.`

`Right...may I bring someone?`

`I`d love to come! How exciting. Wait `till I tell my friends, they`ll be really jealous I`m attending King Baggot`s wedding.`

`Ah...there`s a snag. You can`t tell anyone. You mustn`t breathe a word it`s taking place.`

`Why ever not?`

`It would ruin his image. The thing is he is supposed to be a bachelor. Then, when he dates leading actresses and celebrities, there`s the interest in possible romance. Women like the thought of couples getting together, but not when their idol is already married.`

`Oh, half the fun is telling friends about it. What a pity. I`ll have to say I was at a party with him.`

I did the editing on site. Working on the first film I soon realised the director on this occasion, William Robert Daly, had not included enough close-ups of Baggot. I quickly briefed him on what we were seeking, and a number of the scenes were retaken.

I was chatting to King between shots when a thought struck me.

`King, aren`t you getting just a little bored doing these one-reelers? Wouldn`t you prefer to star in something more demanding? Something you could get your acting teeth into?`

`Well, yes. Now you mention it, Sam, I would. But I thought this is what the studio wanted.`

`It is at the moment. But I`m hoping to change that outlook. We`ll speak about it again.`

I took the final versions into the city to show Carl and Isadore. At the end of the viewing, they were both complimentary on the merits of the five films, and the mood shots that cast our star in an appealing light. They would certainly beguile his many followers.

`A few things to cover while you`re here , Sam. First of all, Isadore is going out to California as studio manager, to get the new site under way. He is also taking Tom Ince with him to produce one or two films, to check out the mechanics of filming out there.`

`Are they going to be all external productions, or are you renting a studio?`

`Charlie Baumann, you know, the New York Picture Company, owns Bison Life Motion Pictures. He says we can make use of their studio. Apparently, it`s on Allesandro Street in Edendale, wherever that is. I`m told it`s an open tract of land and they use a barn on the site. Still, it`s only experimental. I want him to make two or three films while he is there. As I say, to see what the conditions are like. How are things going your end?`

This was as good a time as to tell him what I thought.

`As I see it, Carl, we are falling into the same trap we did with Mary Pickford. We`ve created a star in King Baggot, but his fans are wanting more that the fare we are dishing up. Have you read the fan magazines?`

`Haven`t had time lately, Sam. You Issy?`

Isadore shook his head.

With all that was happening with the Universal project, I had been banking on it. They read the trade journals and newspapers, but rarely bothered with moviegoer magazines, unless we had a feature published in them.

`Well, I`ll tell you. The public are clamouring for films with more intense, more emotional storylines than the ten minute lighthearted productions we`re giving them. I`m not saying dispense with the one-reelers, but let`s add some half hour, even hour long films to our repertoire to stretch our actors` abilities.

`Make demands on them to give of their best. Let`s give moviegoers out there some real acting. It cuts both ways: satisfy the public, satisfy your stars. After all, we don`t want to lose King Baggot for the same reason as Mary, do we?`

Carl was staring at me. I could read his mind. Oh, oh...what`s is this guy up to this time?

`What do you think, Issy?`

He always referred to his brother-in-law in the first instance. It gave him thinking time.

`Well, I guess he has a point, Carl. Inevitably, there comes a moment when people get bored given the same thing. For years, when I was young, we had ham and Steinbuscherkäse and Steppenkäse for breakfast. Now I can`t stand cheese. When the same thing is dished up day after day, it eventually palls. Sam, is right. We have to guard against that.`

`Are you saying the people who watch our films have had enough? They want something else? The sales figures don't show it that way.`

`What I'm saying, Carl, it's time to mix it up a little. Look, I've raised this issue before, you know what I think. This time you should listen to what the people who go to see our films are saying. It won't happen straight away. You're right, at the moment the figures do look good. Let's keep them that way. Stay in front of the others. Be the first to produce more dramatic films.`

He stroked his chin. It was then I knew he would give me the go-ahead. I had become accustomed to his ways.

`If we went ahead with your idea Sam, what have you got in mind?`

`I would like to see us produce an epic. An hour long, six reel story. Something that has all the ingredients of knights in armour, chivalry and romance.`

`You've got something in mind, haven't you?` said Carl shrewdly.

`Yes I have, The story of *Ivanhoe*.`

`OK, tell us what it's all about,` he declared resignedly.

`It's a book written by Walter Scott set in the twelfth century England. Returning from the Crusades in the Holy Land, *Ivanhoe* learns that King Richard the Lionheart is imprisoned in Austria. His pleas for the ransom to be paid falls on deaf ears, and he has to confront the would-be usurper to the throne, Prince John, and a fierce Norman warrior, Brian de Bois-Guilbert, while juggling with the affections of the beautiful maidens Rowena and Rebecca. It's heady stuff, just right for a major film.`

`And this would be a winner, you reckon?`

`Absolutely.`

`Listen, Sam, I'll make a deal with you. You come to California when we're up and running out there, and you can make this *Ivanhoe*. What do you say? I can't be fairer than that. Why don't you talk it over with Isabel?`

I blushed for the second time in my life.

`What do you mean, talk it over with Isabel?`

`Come off it, Sam,` grinned Isadore. `Everyone knows you are keen on her.`

`No they don't!`

`Sam, we all know you like the young lady, and you're biding your time. There's nothing wrong in that, and it's not hard to see why you don't want to move out west. So, go and have a chat with her. After all, she may like the idea of living there.`

We were seated at the dinner table on Firday night when I mentioned it.

`And then he said, have a chat with her, she may like the idea. What an infernal cheek, telling me we should talk about moving to California.`

`He`s right, Sam. We should.`

I had not mentioned I did not want to move even further away from my homeland. But as my feelings had grown for Isabel, I would have gone anywhere, just to be with her.

`But, you haven`t said yet if we have a future together. I don`t know where I stand with you, Isabel.`

She leaned forward, and for the second time she kissed me. This time it was on the lips, hesitant at first, then lingering, faintly demanding. I shall always remember that moment. When we parted I was breathless, my heart pounding furiously.

`Right...we should discuss the move.` My voice was suddenly hoarse.

Isabel said a little shyly. `In a way, Sam, it would be for the best if we moved from Fort Lee. Began a new life together in different surroundings, and I`m sure the girls would be happy to do so. When would it be?`

`Not for some months. Perhaps another year. Isabel, do I take it that we are betrothed?`

`Sam, just for the moment let you and I just accept that we have an understanding. It`s too early to declare our intentions. It might be seen by others as unbecoming. I wouldn`t want that. Do you mind?`

I kissed her this time.

`Of course not. It`s funny though that so many people assumed there was something between us. I wonder how?`

`Derek, my cousin, is a wonderful man, Sam, but he is also an uncontrollable gossip. I should imagine he was only too ready to hint at it among your film fraternity.`

CHAPTER FORTY - TWO

`What do you mean, you want to film *Ivanhoe* in England. Are you out of your mind?`

`Carl, you said the same to me when I took a crew to Minnesota to film *Hiawatha*, remember?`

`Look on the map, Sam! England is a hell of a lot further!`

`OK, tell me where there`s a full-size castle in the United States. Tell me where I can find people who know about heraldry, mediaeval chivalry, and fighting in the lists.`

`The what?`

`The lists...jousting tournaments,`

`It`s still going to cost too much money. It would be cheaper to build a dummy castle here than take everyone to a real one in England.`

`Nonsense...it would look what is was, painted board. If we`re going to produce a worthwhile film, let`s do it properly, for Christ`s sake.`

`Stop blaspheming. Who are the actors you want to use?`

`The two women, Rebecca and Lady Rowena, would be played by Leah Baird and Evelyn Hope. Walter Thomas would play Robin Hood. Wally Widdicombe, Sir Brian de Bois-Guilbert, and Walter Craven, Richard The Lionheart. And, of course, King Baggot would be Wilfred of *Ivanhoe.*`

He turned away and stared out the window.

After a few minutes he said, `OK, here`s the deal. Go ahead, make the motion picture where you like. But if you lose money on it, no more so-called epics. In the future we concentrate on one reel movies, and that`s it.`

`Hold on a second. What about if I make money, real money that is, what do I get out of it?`

`You get to keep your job.`

I laughed out loud. `Not enough, Carl. I want something special.`

`Like what?`

`I get to make the movie, *While New York Sleeps.*`

`No way.`

`Come on. If you`re so sure I won`t make a profit, what`s there to lose. And if I lose I`ll never mention the film again.`

`Promise?`

`Promise.`

We grinned at each other for different reasons, and shook hands.

`England! How on earth could I possibly go to England? There are the girls to consider...their schooling, their activities. Then there`s my job. No, it`s out of the question, Sam. I couldn`t possibly.`

That was her first reaction when I mentioned the idea. I did not say anything more during the Tuesday evening meal. I chatted to Emily and Joanna most of the time, allowing her time for the suggestion sink in.

At the front door, when I was leaving, Isabel asked casually. `If you are going to England, when would it be?`

`I would say in July, coming back in August. There is a lot of planning and preparation  to do before the trip.`

`Yes...yes, of course.`

On Friday there were further questions, albeit posed in an off-hand way.

`Where will you be staying when you`re in England?`

`Actually, we won`t, geographically speaking, be making the film in England.`

`Oh...I thought you said you were.`

`Well, I`ve now arranged for much of the film to be shot in Wales. Just across the border from England...at Chepstow Castle.`

`What, a real castle?`

`Hmm...why?`

`Oh, no reason.  I was just trying to place where you might be working.`

During the meal, the topic came up again.

`Will you be working all the time you`re in England, or should I say, Wales?`

`No, I would like to see some of the countryside, visit our agents in London, and also go to Brighton. While I`m there visit my parents.`

`So there`ll be lots of occasions when you won`t be working.`

`Yes, particularly after we`ve finished filming and the actors and crew go home.`

Isabel nodded, weighing up my replies.

The following Tuesday the questions got a little more personal.

`Sam, if I were to come, and I haven`t decided yet, you wouldn`t expect me to share your room, would you?`

I shook my head. `Of course not, Isabel. In fact, if the girls came all three of you could share a house wherever we went.`

`Would you take me to meet your parents?`

`Only if you brought along Emily and Joanna as well.`

A slow smile spread across her features.

`How would you introduce us?`

`I would say, mum, dad, I want you to meet Isabel, the young lady I hope to marry, and the bonus is Emily and Joanna, whom I would delight in adopting, if they agreed.`

`Really, would you say that?`

`Well, it`s true, isn`t it? I would look after and protect them as though they were my own.`

I was rewarded with another kiss.

`Sam, The girls and I would love to come, if you can put up with us.`

I commissioned the British writers, Frederick and Walter Melville, to prepare the screenplay. I knew them to be accomplished writers with a feel for mediaeval history. With the agreement of Herbert Brenon, the American director, I also engaged the Englishman, Leedham Bantock, to direct the scenes at Chepstow Castle. He had produced a number of historical films for his Zenith Film Company.

The costumes, horses, make-up artists, accommodation and transport were organised by our agents in London; and I contacted James Williamson, who had moved to the capital, to supply the lighting, cameras, projectors and film stock. All this took several months to organise, but eventually, in early July we sailed on the *SS Imperator* for Southampton.

Eight days later, when we had disembarked and cleared everything through Customs, I walked out the arrival sheds to find Geoffrey Summer standing beside a Leyland flatbed lorry and a fleet of petrol-driven automobiles.

I clasped him to me and patted him on the back.

`It`s good to see you , Geoffrey.`

`And you, Sam.`

As the others emerged I told them to climb into the motor cars while porters stowed their baggage on the lorry. When everyone was seated in the cars, the convoy made its way to the main station. The party was shepherded to a reserved carriage, and all their belongings stored in the luggage van at the rear of the train.

We changed trains at Didcot. I did a head count to ensure no one was lost and the luggage placed on the train destined for Bristol. Another lorry and caravan of motor cars met us at the railway station. We crossed the River Severn by the New Passage Ferry to Wales, and after a journey of almost five hours arrived at the Abbey Hotel, just north of Chepstow.

Everyone was weary, with the exception of Emily and Joanna, who had slept much of the journey. They were keen to see their surroundings, so I took them on a walk to the nearby Tintern Abbey ruins, and later we joined Isabel for an evening meal.

According to the locals, the warm, dry weather was scheduled to last for several days, and so we decided to film as many of the outside scenes as possible. The temperament of both the crew and actors soared under the bright blue skies, and everyone set to with a will.

A number of townspeople had been co-opted for the crowd scenes and help move the lighting and backdrops. Gradually the grounds in front of the castle assumed the image of life in the twelfth century, as people donned the clothing of the period, covered stalls were erected, pennants flew, and knights in armour astride destriers, paraded across the lawns.

Isabel and the girls were awestruck by the scene.

`It looks so authentic, Sam,` she cried. `With the castle in the background, it`s as though we`ve travelled back in time!`

We walked round the castle wall to where tents had been set up for make-up, dressing and resting couches; to store our many items of equipment; and importantly, a mobile kitchen and refectory to feed everyone.

`Back to the present,` Isabel murmured, as we watched those in period costume lining up for coffee and smoking cigarettes.

Geoffrey's skills had not deserted him.

He discussed camera angles, lighting and the content of each shoot with Harold Brenon and Leedhan Bantock, and suggested at one stage that they put the camera on rails to run alongside the action in the jousting tournament.

To a large extent my job was done once filming began. We had fixed the number of scenes to be filmed each day, ensured everybody was happy with his or her role, and the dialogue cards, describing the events taking place on the screen, were agreed.

After a few days of working to ensure everything was going smoothly, we were on schedule and in budget, I was able to devote time to Isabel and the girls. They enjoyed the filming of the various scenes, and it was a pity we could not have had sound when filming the lists, for everyone got into the mood of the event. The girls stood cheering on their heroes, clapping each of the combatants.

We used stuntmen when it came to the actual fighting. We could not risk the stars of the film being injured. Fortunately, we had acquired the services of professional horsemen, whose speciality was mediaeval jousting and hand-to-hand combat. They were dressed in full armour, and used the weapons of yesteryear with unrestrained vigour. Emily and Joanna winced, turning away when heavy blows were struck. It looked frighteningly authentic, and bruises must have been commonplace. But the spectacle made the film.

After a few days I could see that they were becoming restive, and wanted to do something different. I took a motor car and we went on a tour of the Welsh countryside, and crossing the ferry, visited a number of the towns and villages in south-west England.

`Aren't these the prettiest places you ever seen, mom?` said Emily wistfully. `Look at those sweet thatched cottages, the stone bridges and the ducks on the pond.`

When we returned the outside sets were being dismantled. After two weeks, during which we had been blessed with ideal weather, the crew was now preparing to move into the castle for the interior shots.

Geoffrey was in his element; and both directors applauded his technique and competence. He would often suggest a particular scene be taken again, not only to ensure he had it on film, but to recommend subtle but valuable adjustments to the actors` movements.

A month after capturing all we required in and around Chepstow Castle, everything was packed away, a lorry and cavalcade of motor cars appeared, and we set out for the next location, The London Film Company in Twickenham, on the outskirts of London.

There we were going to do the many close-ups, and interior, mood shots. We would also have the film processed, just to be sure we had captured all the scenes. Most of the time I stayed on site, because these sequences were critical to the screenplay. However, there were several occasions when I had an afternoon free, and then I took Isabel and the girls to witness car racing at nearby Brooklands.

Finally, when everything was in the can, we held a farewell party before the actors and crew departed for Southampton and took the ship back to the United States. At the party, I had a long conversation with Geoffrey Summer. We had discussed his working in America in the past. He had done an excellent job on the picture, and I wanted to sign him up before the directors returned, broadcast his abilities, and another film company snapped him up.

Although I had said in the past to Carl and Isadore we should all agree whom we employed, I broke the rule that day by inviting him to join the company. He readily accepted, and it was arranged that he and his family would settle their affairs in England, and come over in six months time.

We took up residence in a London hotel, and during the following week I showed Isabel, Emily and Joanna the many sights of the city before we caught a train to the south coast.

CHAPTER FORTY -THREE

I had written to them, but it was still a shock to be confronted by a son they had not seen for eighteen months with a ready made family. I had explained the circumstances; although I accept it must have been hard for them to come to terms with the quartet that materialised on their doorstep.

My father, behind my mother when the door opened, stood there open-mouthed. She was quicker to recover, to welcome us in. What gladdened my heart was the way she took Isabel`s hands in hers and kissed her on both cheeks. I suppose, being French, she was more accustomed to this sort of situation.

"Isabel, I`ve heard much about you. And you must be Emily and Joanna. Come in, come in.`

I had only written one brief letter of explanation.

My father was still standing there, exhibiting a half grin of uncertainty. He edged back as they moved into the tiny hallway and my mother led them into the sitting room.

The girls took it all in their stride. At their ages life happened around them: there was little curiosity about grown-up relationships. Isabel had been nervous about the visit. Not that she had said anything, but I could read the signs. Teeth intruding over a bottom lip, the frequent touching of an ear.

`John,` my mother said to my father, `put the kettle on, we`ll have some tea. Or would you prefer coffee, Isabel? I know Americans mostly drink that.`

`Tea would be fine, Mrs Lockhart,` she replied.

`Or would you prefer a glass of wine?` asked my father, at last finding his voice.

In the end we opted for wine. A good Sancerre, which obviously my mother had chosen. The girls had lemonade.

The afternoon gently passed.

My father showed the girls the pond in the garden. Explaining about the types of fish he had. I could see from the window their interest, and the enjoyment when allowed to feed his prize carp.

The three of them came indoors briefly, then went off again to explore the river bank across the road.

`My, they like your father, Sam,` said Isabel, slowly relaxing.

`I think he delights in their company,` said my mother.

Then Isabel asked the question I had not thought to mention before.

`An interesting accent you have, Mrs Lockhart. You`re not English?`

`Most certainly not!` my mother laughed. `I am French, my dear. I could not possibly be an English woman. They are so, how shall I say, so stiff, so inhibited. They rarely show their feelings. It is quite frustrating at times.`

They both laughed together. The mood eased even more.

``Why don`t you go and see how your father is coping, Sam?` said my mother.

When we returned an hour later, they were still sitting there, chatting away like old friends. I noticed the empty bottle, the slightly flushed faces.

`Now we must eat something,` announced my mother getting to her feet. `What do the girls like, Isabel?`

We were staying in the Ship Inn at Brighton.

At dinner that evening I noticed a subtle change in our relationship. It began with more lingering looks in my direction, and my arm was touched frequently when Isabel was making a point. The girls were tired after the long day, and towards the end of the meal, Isabel suggested she take them to their room. As she stood up, she put her hand on my shoulder and whispered.

`Why don`t you order another bottle of wine, Sam? I shan`t be long.`

I chose a good white burgundy, and poured it into our glasses.

She took a sip, and said reflectively. `I`ve had a wonderful day, Sam, and the girls were full of it. They really enjoyed themselves...thank you. I think your parents are great. Your father was a little uncertain at first, but being an Englishman, that`s to be expected. You are like him in lots of ways.`

`I`m like him? . .nonsense! We are poles apart.`

`You don`t see it, do you? You are probably both shy...not reserved, disinterested as I first thought. Your mother is marvellous. She knew my feelings, my concerns immediately.`

`How do you mean?`

`Never you mind. Let me say we understand each other. Thank God she is French!`

I know my eyebrows rose in puzzlement.

She took my hand. `I think you and I are going to get along famously. So, what's the programme tomorrow?`

I want to introduce you to the man, and the woman, who first got me interested in film making. I've mentioned them from time to time. His name is George, she is Laura. In many ways I owe him a lot. George sent me to America when we lost our distributor. I found a replacement and also Carl Laemmle. When George decided to close the business, that's when I left and came to the United States to work for Carl.`

When the bottle was empty, I stood, eased back her chair and escorted her from the dining room. The wine had done its work, and I was in a mellow mood as we walked up the flights of stairs. I was slightly behind Isabel, who this evening, was wearing a tight-fitting dress which emphasised her soft, shapely curves as she mounted each tread.

Perhaps, like me the wine had made her less steady. Several times she seemed to miss her step. On each occasion I put out my hands, feeling the warmth of her body as I set her upright.

We had almost reached the top step when she again started to topple sideways. I reached out and carried her to the hallway. I went to put her down, but something stopped me.

She was looking directly into my eyes.

`You can let me go now...or perhaps you don't want to,` she murmured

`I don't want to...now or ever.`

Then I kissed her. Not one of those offered as a polite greeting, or signals departure at the end of a shared moment; not even one of gratitude for a small gift or act of kindness. This was an intense, all-consuming kiss that came from deep within me. And it was reciprocated.

We stayed there holding on to each other. Time went by...and I kissed her again.

People were coming up the stairs.

We parted and walked slowly down the corridor hand in hand. I took her key and opened the door. Before I could turn to wish her goodnight, I was pulled into the room.

I had never experienced such abandoned, joyous love making. I had found comfort in the arms of others, and thought those moments were the heights of mutual excitement. They merely satisfied basic needs. That night with Isabel reached new peaks.

We made love, slept, made love, and held tight to each other. I awoke at first light, gathered my things and silently dressed. I tiptoed to the side of the bed and stared down at this woman who had completely captivated me. Then, pleasurably happy and contented, I slipped back to my room.

I was the last down at the breakfast table.

The three of them were happily tucking into their food. I was surprised that Isabel had such a full plate.

`This sea air gives me a wondrous appetite, Sam,` she grinned.

`Well, we shall only be here another two days. On Thursday we must pack and take the train to Southampton for our homeward journey.`

`Oh, must we, Sam?` said Emily and Joanna in unison.

`It's not that all good things must come to an end,` I remarked, catching Isabel's eye. `It's the beginning of a new adventure. You'll see. When you get home something will be fresh and exciting will be just round the corner.`

`Really, Sam?` they chorused.

`I'm sure of it!`

The hansom cab deposited us outside the house in Roman Crescent.

`Call back for us in an hour and a half's time, please driver,` I instructed.

As we walked up the drive one could see signs of neglect. The stucco walls needed attention, the paint on the window frames was peeling, and the flower beds were over-run with weeds.

Before I could ring the bell, Laura opened the door.

`Sam! It's wonderful to see you! And you must be Isabel!`

Once again a hastily scribbled letter has forewarned them I would not be alone.

George appeared from his laboratory, and was equally effusive in his welcome. Laura took Emily and Joanna under her wing, asking them if they would like to see the dresses she had worn when appearing in films. Isabel was also keen to see them, and the four of them trooped out the room. I heard the excited chatter and the girls` footsteps on the stairs.

`So what brings you to England, Sam?` George enquired.

`We`ve been making a film at Chepstow Castle in Wales. One of those mediaeval dramas, with knights in armour and jousting, and a side order of passion.`

`What`s it called?`

`*Ivanhoe.*`

Really? That`s ambitious. How long is it?`

`I `ll keep it to six reels after editing.`

`That`s a good hour, Sam. Will cinemagoers stay in their seats that long?`

`You sound like Carl Laemmle, George. My answer must be yes. After all music concerts are longer, and so are many plays and revues in theatres.`

`Yes, but sitting in the dark for that length of time is a bit demanding, surely?

I smiled. `We`ll see. So, how are things with you?`

His moustache, always wider than his face, was no shorter; but now it had a permanent droop and was almost white. In the light from the window, I realised it matched the colour of his hair.

He grimaced. `Not too good, Sam. Financially, Laura and I are on a tight budget. You may have heard I sold my British patent rights to Kinemacolor. Would you believe, I sold them to a woman who would not take no for an answer. She was a very presentable lady, with a strong Scottish accent called, Ada Aline Jones. To get rid of her I asked five thousand pounds. Do you know, she paid me in cash. I had to sign numerous documents declaring I had no further interest in the patent here. I didn`t mention our little arrangement regarding the American rights. Anyway, the upshot was it reverted to her. We`ve been living on the money ever since. God knows what will happen when that runs out.`

George was silent for a moment. I could hear the laughter and high pitched voices upstairs.

`The joke was some months later Charles Urban got married,` George continued. `Guess who to?`

`No idea.`

`Mrs Ada Aline Jones. You know he and I fell out. If I'd known...if I'd had an inkling, hell would have frozen over before I sold out to him.`

`Are you aware, George, that Urban has just sold the rights to *Kinemacolor* in the States? Two American businessmen, Gilbert H. Aymar and James K. Bowen, have bought them. Now, even if you have transferred british patent rights to him, via his new wife, I could still legitimately take Aymar and Bowen to court. No doubt, they would then sue Charles Urban for misrepresentation. Or, instead of going to court I could simply advise them that they have bought a turkey. What would you like me to do?`

`A turkey? What do you mean?`

`Sorry, George, it's an Americanism. It means a failure in the film and theatre business over there.`

`Sam, I'm fed up with the whole concept. I should never have got involved with Charles Urban or his bright-eyed notions. Look what it has cost me. Forget it, Sam. Let it all die a death.`

I nodded. `OK, no court action, but I might just tweak Urban's tail. By the way, I used Geoffrey Summer, our old cameraman on the film. As a result, he is coming to work in America.`

`Do you know that was a bad mistake closing down GAS Films, letting you and him go. What a fool I was to be suckered in by that smooth-talking bastard!`

There was a brooding silence.

`Tell me, How far has Friese Greene got on his colour system?` I asked.

`Did you know he has moved down here, to Brighton, to be near the centre of things. I believe he is using Alfred Darling to do some work for him. I've been told, on the grapevine, he is facing the same problem, colour fringing, as I did. I'm not sure the problem can be overcome, but I'll give him his due, he keeps on trying to perfect his system.`

From Brighton it is only seven miles to the small town of Ditchling.

I had telephoned from the hotel, and not only was he was at home, but would be delighted to see me. When the hansom cab drew into his drive at Gallops Homestead, Selwyn Francis Edge came out to welcome me, a big grin spread across his features.

`So, how did the filming go? Did you get all you wanted?`

`Yes, and we've also got some film of you trying to break your neck. I'll send it to you.`

I had met Selwyn Edge when we had spent time in his company at the Brooklands motor racing circuit, not far from the film studios at Twickenham. Geoffrey had also been smitten by the racing bug, and had spent some time filming the cars as they hurtled around the circular track.

Selwyn was a well-known racing driver. Born in Australia, he had come to England as a child, where his passion had developed. He now sold and raced De Dion-Bouton, Gladiator; Clemént-Panhard, Napier and AC motor cars.

After a pleasant exchange, sitting in a comfortable chair, a glass of whisky in my hand, I put to him the proposal I had in mind. I explained the various details, and after he had posed a number of questions, Selwyn declared he was perfectly happy to act on my behalf, and we shook hands on the arrangement.

As the hansom turned in the drive, he called. `Don't worry, Sam. I'll contact him tomorrow.`

In the late afternoon, the hansom dropped me off at number twenty, Middle Street in Brighton. The iron railings and ornate front door seemed an incongruous setting for a building devoted to cinematography.

William Friese Greene was an engaging character. We spent a pleasant hour discussing film making, and in particular, the principles of colour photography. Eventually, I steered the conversation round to George Albert Smith's predicament, and put the proposal to him. On the face of it, it was quite startling. But having experienced, first hand, the procedures, the lines of argument to adopt, and the righteousness of the cause, he was finally persuaded.

Accordingly, early the following morning I took the train to London to visit a firm of solicitors recommended by the Albion Cinema Supply Company, our distribution agents. Their offices were just round the corner from Wardour Street, in a mews building called Pulteney Chambers.

I was shown into the room of Mr Nieman, of French, Grey and Nieman, and over the next two hours, he prepared all the requisite documents for the formation of the company, Bioschemes UK, of which Friese Greene, Selwyn

Edge and I would be the principals. Arrangements were also made for a bank account to be opened with the London County and Westminster Bank.

The next day I took Isabel, Emily and Joanna to the Aquarium. Their first ever visit to such a place. All three were enchanted by the displays, and we took tea in the Conservatory.

It was hard to believe this was the scene of GAS Films` first triumph. When my sweaty hand had turned the projector handle and pitched us into the public`s imagination.

CHAPTER FORTY - FOUR

It was difficult to repeat the nights we shared together in England.

It would not have been right to stay over at Isabel`s place, and the rooming house I used in Edgewater would certainly not countenance such a libidinous act as sharing a bed together.

On several occasions when there was a reason for her to travel into New York City, Isabel stayed in my room at the Algonquin; but I wanted her to be by my side the whole time. Enjoyable though they were, I did not care for hurried, snatched moments. I had a constant need of her.

Emily, being the elder, noticed a difference in our attitude to one another.

We were all sitting on the couch looking at the photographs the girls had taken in England. Suddenly, there was one of Isabel and I kissing. It was taken on the promenade at Brighton when we thought the girls had walked down to the sea edge. I hastily pushed it into the pack.

`Why did you do that, Sam? It`s a nice picture of you and mom,` said Emily, spreading the photos out on the coffee table.

`Here it is. Don`t you think it`s a nice picture, Joanna?`

`Mmm...nice.`

`So now you`ve got to marry my mom, Sam. When I showed the picture to grand`ma, she said the same thing.`

Once more my face went red. I glanced at Isabel, and two round spots glowed on her cheeks told me she was equally embarrassed.

`Would you like me to marry your mother, Emily?`

`Of course. You two wake me up when you say goodnight on the porch.`

Now Isabel`s face was the same deep colour as mine..

`Would you, Joanna?`

`Would I what?`

`Like me to marry your mother?`

`Sure...then you could read me a story when I go to bed every night.

Mom`s not very good at it.`

`Would you, Isabel?`

Tears sprang to her eyes. She nodded dumbly. That was the moment she agreed to be my wife.

The wedding was going to be a small affair, taking place in a side chapel at the Holy Rosary Church on the outskirts of Edgewater. My parents were coming over, and I organised a room for them at the rooming house.

Neither Carl nor anyone from his Jewish family could be my best man, so I asked King Baggot to return the favour. In total, we booked the reception for thirty guests at the Ocean House. A hotel out on *Shippan* Point, up the coast near Stamford in Connecticut. I had also arranged a suite at the hotel for our honeymoon.

When the day dawned, I had not realised I would be so nervous. Fortunately, King was a steadying influence, as well as the Jack Daniels he had brought with him.

`Got your speech ready, Sam?`

I took a sheet of paper from a pocket, and stared at it, trying to decipher the many additions and deletions I had made.

`I think so. If my hand stays still long enough to read it.`

. I waited anxiously in the front pew with King, until the moment Isabel appeared. From that moment, I really do not recall what I did or said during the service. Though presumably, I must have done everything asked of me. It was not until the priest announced we were man and wife, did the ceremony come to life.

We kissed, and walked hand in hand with Emily and Joanna into the vestry to sign the certificate. Outside we were doused in confetti, photographs were taken, and everyone climbed into carriages for the short ride to the ferry terminal.

Standing on the quay, my mind snapped back to that moment several years earlier when Walter and I had been pitched into the water. In a way, I felt sad that I was taking advantage of his death. Isabel must have seen that hint of anguish on my face. She stared up intently, then leaned forward and kissed me.

I had arranged for a boat to collect the wedding party at Edgewater, ferry us across the river, where motor vehicles would take us by road to the hotel. However, instead of a ferryboat, the steamer, *Shippan,* used to carry New Yorkers up Long Island Sound to its long, sandy beaches, was tied up at the quay.

My new wife also had a quizzical look on her face. `Why is that coming here? It`s usually the other side of Manhattan Island.`

`One of my surprises,` grinned Carl, coming to stand at my shoulder. `I wanted you to arrive at the Point in style.`

There were even more surprises. A band struck up onboard, and the many work colleagues , business acquaintances, and all the friends I had made from the Lower East Side crowded the rails and cheered. Isabel and I were pushed up the gangplank to a ticker tape welcome of streamers and yet more confetti.

Carl had taken over the hotel. The reception was now for over two hundred people. I learned from Recha that Carl had hijacked my arrangements, and created an event which far outshone the more modest celebration we had intended.

It was overwhelming, and I felt quite emotional when I stood to say a few words. My eyes were moist for so many reasons. Intense pleasure, the fact that all the people I held dear were with us on this day of days...and just a little sadness.

I cast aside the sheet of paper. I could not have read it anyway. At times it caught in my throat as I spoke from the heart. Again, I could not remember all that I said, but it did not seem to matter. Many offered words of congratulation. Isabel gave me a silent, meaningful hug.

We had a remarkable week together. The memories will always stay with me.

However, there were times when I missed the girls.

On several occasions we came upon something unusual, and I looked for them to point it out. I do not think Isabel noticed, or if she did she did not comment. Towards the end of the week I was quite looking forward to seeing them.

When the hansom cab dropped us outside Isabel`s house, mine and her parents came out on the porch to greet us. Ahead of them, racing down the path, were Emily and Joanna. They were keen to tell us that they too had had a great time.

`Your mom and dad, Sam, and mom`s mom and dad,` recounted Emily, `have been taking us out to all sorts of places. We have even been inside the Statue of Liberty!`

I briefly recalled my visit to the monument all those years ago.

`And, we went to the top of the Woolworth Building, the tallest in the world,` she said breathlessly.

`I didn`t like it,` exclaimed Joanna. `It`s such a long way from the ground.`

A few days later my parents went off to Pittsburgh with Isabel`s, and the adjustment process of living with three females began. I have always risen early, and Emily and Joanna began joining me in the kitchen. Never having cooked for myself, it took a while to come to terms with the toaster, warming their hot milk on the stove, and boiling eggs that were runny. After a while I got the hang of it, and enjoyed their company around the breakfast table.

However, the day came when I had to return to the studio.

The immediate task was to finish editing *Ivanhoe* with Herbert Brenon, the main director. As the producer, I believed we had created a good, commercial motion picture; but you can never really gauge the reaction of the public.

I took the finished copy into the city and met Carl and Isadore at the Regent Theatre, located on a Hundred and Sixteenth Street and Seventh Avenue. The theatre had only been open a few months, and the façade was an exotic blend of styles - from Early Renaissance to Moorish Spanish. The interior was equally lavish. Frescoes, ornate mouldings and elaborate chandeliers took the moviegoer from the street into a fantasy palace totally at odds with the outside world.

The significant feature of the theatre was its seating capacity. It could hold around two thousand, and we had invited that number to preview the film. To tell us if we were on the right track, or had produced a bomber.

The film was over an hour long. Would it capture their interest? Would they regard the picture as good entertainment? What did they like best about *Ivanhoe*? What did they dislike about it? Would they tell friends they must see the film? These were the sort of questions the audience would be asked as they left the theatre.

Three hours later we learned the answer.

Every aspect of the motion picture was liked. The conflict, the jousting, the tender moments with the hero and heroines, the sheer spectacle, all got the highest possible ratings. Its reception was the go-ahead to set the publicity wheels in motion, and, via the Universal Film Manufacturing Company, numerous copies were dispatched to all the regional distributors.

CHAPTER FORTY - FIVE

We made a lot of money when *Ivanhoe* was released.

It also raised King Baggot's rating and his fees. But Carl was happy to pay. He was not so enthusiastic when it came to our understanding.

`There's no way out, Carl. You said categorically, in front of Isadore, that if the film were a success, I could make *While New York Sleeps*. And I'm calling in our agreement.`

With bad grace he finally acknowledged the compact between us.

It did not take long to put the project into motion. I had worked on the screenplay, the cast I thought would do a good job; and I had encouraged Derek at the studio to start building the sets. In a matter of weeks everything was ready.

The storyline was simple. I had seen it enacted when I was waiting for my Polish friends when I first arrived in the United States. It was about two young Swedish female immigrants approached by men soliciting for prostitutes under the guise of legitimate work offers.

The entire length of the film takes place over three days. The main scenes would be filmed around the Battery, after the women had been transported there from Ellis Island. In many respects, I envisaged it as a semi-documentary, a wake-up call to the authorities. Prompted by that brief conversation I had had with the old, Polish gentleman at the immigrant arrival point all those years ago.

The main narrative was the kidnapping of one of the sisters, and the other sister and her boyfriend rushing to rescue her. The pimp is killed, the prostitution ring is broken, and the leader, a well-known philanthropist, unmasked.

What I had never mentioned to Carl was the time I spent cultivating a sort of understanding with the pimps. There were one or two nasty moments. On one occasion I was bodily picked up and taken round the back of the

266

terminal building by four of their kind. At first, my English accent confused them. Then, when I explained I worked for a film company, and we were going to do a motion picture on immigrants taking their first steps on American soil, they noticeably preened themselves as budding stars. Regardless of the fact they were criminals taking advantage of unworldly newcomers, they vied for the chance to become minor film celebrities. It was an object lesson in vanity; appearing on the screen would glamorise them, give added status.

Thereafter, they would all readily chat to me whenever I was there. I got to learn first-hand how the operation worked. I was keen to portray it accurately, even to finding out what the girls felt about being ensnared into a life of prostitution. At the time, I walked a very fine line, and had not appreciated all its dangers.

I asked George Loane Tucker if he would direct the film, and now Geoffrey Summer had arrived, he was the main cameraman. It was a big production with a cast of thirty people, and I envisaged it as another six reel motion picture.

Fortunately the good weather held, and we managed to film all the key outside scenes. Even showing the pimps approaching would-be innocents and enticing them into their ways. By the beginning of October the close-ups and interior shoots were in the can, and I spent a great deal of time briefing the publicity team.

They viewed the preliminary material, to get the feel of the picture, and came up with a change to the working title. Instead of, *While New York Sleeps*, they suggested, *Traffic in Souls* . A more telling description, which we readily adopted.

The preview seemed to go well; and the premiere took place at the Mark Strand Theatre in the city. Now I was really anxious. This was not humorous film, nor a tale of derring-do, it was a sober commentary on a major social issue; and the faces of the audience as they left the theatre portrayed its seriousness. Perhaps, I had made a monumental mistake.

The newspaper reviews suggested so. Many of them wrote that the film attempts to sensationalise prostitution. A definite thumbs down. Carl did not comment. Even Isadore avoided the subject. I had spent fifty seven thousand dollars on a dud. It was a very quiet Christmas for Isabel, the girls and myself.

In the New Year things seemed to brighten. I learned we had received a positive batch of sales figures. At least we had covered our costs. I started on several one-reelers, and stayed clear of the offices in the city.

I was editing the film, *The Dawn of Netta*, when a motor car drew up outside the studio, and Carl and Isadore got out.

I walked out to greet them, and admire the car. A brand new Hudson Model 37 sedan.

`What do you think of that, my boy?` said Carl expansively. `And it`s thanks to you. Tell him, Isadore.`

`Sam, we`ve had another batch of receipts. *Traffic of Souls* has made two hundred and fifty thousand dollars!`

The film went on to gross half a million. However, by then my mind was on events elsewhere.

CHAPTER FORTY - SIX

I was in the London offices of our distribution agent, the Albion Cinema Supply Company, when Archduke Franz Ferdinand of Austria and his wife, Sophie, were shot dead in Sarajevo.

Suddenly, all the rhetoric and the posturing by the principal nations of Europe were turning to thoughts of aggression. Treaties had been signed; sides had been drawn; war seemed an inevitable outcome. It was the initial threat of conflict, and how it might hinder our film sales across the Atlantic, that I had come to Britain. But events had now overtaken me.

I went round to Albion Exclusives Limited in Old Compton Street, the company looking after our European sales. They confirmed there was little point in travelling to the Continent: the answer was now all too obvious.

With a heavy heart I made my way to Brighton and hired a hansom to take me to Ditchling. I spent a great part of the day in conversation with Selwyn Francis Edge. He advised me that Bioschemes UK, the company jointly owned by William Friese Greene, Edge and I, had managed to buy the "Biocolour" holding owned by Walter Harold Speer, of the Montpelier Electric Theatre in Brighton. Speer had intended to exploit Friese Greene's two-colour system in his picture house. As a consequence, we now held sole title to the colour process.

Later that day I arrived at Friese Greene's house in Middle Street, and gave him precise instructions. He was to liaise with Selwyn Edge and arrange a meeting with Mr Nieman of French, Grey and Nieman of Pulteney Chambers in London. I passed over a sum of money, advising that it came from Edge, and that it was to be used to brief counsel who would take the Natural Color Kinematograph Company to court for colour film patent infringement. Friese Greene had patented his Biocolour, using the same principles as Kinemacolor, almost a year earlier.

Charles Urban was in for a surprise.

When I arrived at Roman Crescent I hardly recognised him. George was even more stooped than when we last met, and his pallor was a concerning shade of grey. Laura came quickly to the door when she heard her husband's shout of surprise.

`It's Sam!`

`I can see that, let him in for goodness sake,` she said forthrightly.

We sat in the kitchen while Laura made tea.

`Do you want a sandwich, a piece of cake, or something more filling?`

`I've just had a good lunch, Laura, thank you.`

So, tell me,` said George. `What brings you back this time?`

`I wanted to gain a first-hand assessment of how our sales might be affected if there were a war. I think I've already got the answer.`

`Do you know, I was reading in the newspapers that all the young men in Britain are just itching to join the army,` commented Laura. `When I go to the shops, it's all people talk about, fighting for one's country. It's sheer madness. You're not here to enlist are you, Sam?`

`It crossed my mind, Laura. But they are only talking about unmarried men joining up if there's a war. And I'm well and truly married.`

She smiled. `How very true. Isabel was all right when you left, was she? She writes to me occasionally, you know.`

George cut across her. `Tell me, how did *Ivanhoe* do at the box office?`

I smiled. `All right. In fact it allowed me to make a film I've always wanted to produce. It's called *Traffic in Souls* . It should be released over here soon. Do you know, it cost fifty seven thousand dollars to make, ten or twelve thousand pounds, and it has already grossed close to a half a million dollars.`

`I miss film making,` he said wistfully. Then added. `Did you know Laura is a budding camerawoman, Sam?`

I glanced in her direction. A look of embarrassment crossed her face.

`I mean it. I'll show you some of her work. Come out to the laboratory.`

I stood to follow George out to his workshop.

`Take no notice of him, Sam. It's only what I've taken around Brighton,` she said. `I used that portable camera, you know, the Biokam, it uses seventeen and a half millimetre film.`

`Let me show you some of her work, Sam.`

It was surprisingly good. It had been edited well, and the fifty second film length neatly portrayed the brief narrative. They were mostly outdoor shots, but then with only a modest amount of lighting, she had captured some extremely filmic indoor scenes. I was impressed.

I had never really thought of the merits of small, hand-held cameras before. There were moments, perhaps when someone was moving and one wanted to film the event, when a portable camera could be worthwhile. Some of the jerkiness one might encounter could well identify with movement.

I stayed another half an hour, complimenting Laura on the realism she had brought to her films, then took a hansom back to the Ship Hotel where the porter arranged for me to send a cable to the IMP offices in New York City. The message was intended for Isabel, telling her I would soon be on my way home.

I had one more visit to make.

I journeyed to Willesden in London to see James Williamson. It was a happy reunion, and on James` recommendation, I bought an Ernemann Kino seventeen point five millimetre camera, and a novelty I just could not resist. A Houghton pocket-watch style camera called a Ticka. It took the same size film as the Kino, and shot twenty five still pictures. The lens was situated in the pull-up winder knob, and the watch-face was set at seven minutes past ten o'clock. This indicated the viewing angle, and made it possible to shoot pictures with the Ticka without using a viewfinder.

She was at the quayside in New York City when the ship docked at Pier 54, close to Thirteenth Street. There was no mistaking the look on her face when she said fiercely.

`I`ve missed you, Samuel Yardley Lockhart!`

Then she hugged me so tightly, I could hardly breathe.

CHAPTER FORTY - SEVEN

Although I had only been away three weeks, Isabel appeared rounder. She was putting on weight. Her movements less energetic, she seemed to tire more easily.

It took Recha to tell me the reason: albeit unintentionally.

I was with Carl when she walked into the offices on Eleventh and Fifty Fourth Street. We had been discussing the final film to be made at the Fort Lee studio, a one reeler entitled, *The Nurse*.

`Hi, Sam, good to see you,` she said, kissing Carl`s forehead. `How`s everything?`

`Fine, Recha. Your husband and I were just finishing.`

`I hope I wasn`t disturbing you. I want him to take me to lunch. I thought my timing should be about right.` then she added. `I`m glad you are coming to California, Sam. I know Isabel is. A new start, a new baby, eh?`

`What?`

It dawned on both of us at the same time.

She, embarrassed because it was obvious I was unaware Isabel was pregnant. Me, because the realisation suddenly dawned, the extra weight signified an extra person.

My jaw dropped. I just stared at her.

It was an awkward silence. I caught Carl`s look at his wife.

`Well, I`m damned!`

`I`m so sorry, Sam,` said Recha wretchedly. `I just thought you knew.`

Then I grinned at them. `You`re right, a new start, a new baby. Sorry Carl, I have to go.`

I remember little of the journey to Edgewater, though I do recall vividly running up the path and calling her name as I entered the front door.

`Isabel! Isabel! Where are you?`

She came down the stairs, a worried look on her face.

`Is something wrong, Sam?`

I picked her up from the bottom step and swung her in my arms.

`Nothing is wrong, my darling. Now, is there anything you want to tell me?`

I could not stop the huge smile as I looked into her face.

`You know, don`t you?`

`Only by chance. Recha let it slip.`

`Oh, Sam, I thought about telling you before you went off on your business trip. But I wanted to make quite sure.`

A thought struck me.

`Did you mention it to Laura Smith?`

`Yes, though only as a hope in my last letter.`

We had both agreed going to California would be a sensible move, and as the day approached, she became even more excited. We were packing all our belongings and arranging the furniture removal at the house. Equally, Derek Bryant, and I were organising the transfer of all the equipment to the west coast. We now had a buyer for the studio who was anxious to occupy the buildings.

Carl had told me that Isadore was working hard to get the studio in the San Fernando Valley up and running. Isadore had brought in William Horsley to help him prepare the site, as well as arranging use of their Nestor studios, on Gower and Sunset, for the interior scenes and close-ups of the films we would be making.

He also told me Thomas Ince had resigned and joined Bison Life Motion Pictures. From what he had heard, Thomas was devoting all his energies to directing cowboy movies.

It was when we were in the final stages of the transfer that I read two significant items of news in the trade magazine, The Moving Picture World.

On page one was a lengthy article about the Motion Picture Patents Company, headed up by Thomas Edison. A date had been fixed when the organisation would be called before a federal court to answer supposed violation of the Sherman Anti-Trust Act.

The other, tucked away in the back pages was a brief reference to a court case in England. It appeared William Friese Greene was calling the Natural

Color Kinematograph Company to answer a charge of patent infringement for its unauthorised use of the two-colour film process.

There was a direct quote by Charles Urban. "According to my barrister, Friese Greene is a deluded eccentric. He has not an iota of proof to uphold his claim, nor the means to cover my costs when I win."

I was uncertain at first. It seemed too great a distance

But eventually we bought a house on the beach at Santa Barbara. The girls were delighted, they could take the rear steps directly onto the sands. I found driving to and from the studio in my Oakland Model 38 not nearly as irksome as I had imagined. I had a small apartment close to the studio. So the routine became leaving Santa Barbara late on Sunday afternoon, to spend two nights at the apartment. Then I would come home after work on Tuesday evening, and have two nights at home with Isabel and the girls. I would drive to the studio on Thursday morning, and return Friday evening. In fact, the journey became my respite from the world, providing quality thinking time.

Santa Barbara was a small, peaceful township of around fifteen thousand people. What I had not appreciated were the number of film companies in the area. Most well-known was the American Film Manufacturing Company, which also had a studio in Chicago.

Isadore Bernstein was working round the clock getting what Carl called "Universal City" up and running. In the meantime I was putting together ideas for a film based on the story of *Damon And Pythias*. The classic Greek tale of a friendship that overcomes even death could well make an entertaining four reeler.

It was a legendary tale, which we had adapted to current times when we made *The Governor's Pardon*, just before being hauled into court to answer the charge about the Latham Loop.

I had come across the original story in a book I bought to read to the girls. Called "*Fifty Famous Stories Retold*" by James Baldwin. As the title suggested, it was a collection of stories for children published around the turn of the century.

I handed over the weekly output of one drama, one comedy and an occasional western to Derek Bryant, while I concentrated on the bigger production.

In my mind I had figured out the essential elements of the tale, and conceived how I could produce it. I had even cast the actors I would like to use and the locations. In fact, Carl's sprawling acres would be ideal to portray the landscape of ancient Sicily. All I had to do now was find a good screenwriter.

The solution to my problem came from an argument with a policeman.

In Los Angeles I had collected a doll's pram for Joanna's birthday and was coming home early to deliver her surprise. As I turned into Channel Drive I came to a halt at a barrier manned by half a dozen police officers.

`Is there a problem?` I asked.

`Nope,` said one.

`In that case, I need to get through. I live here.`

`Wish I did,` said another officer.

I got out the car. `If you say there isn't a problem, then kindly raise the barrier.` `Can't do that,` replied the first policeman.

`Would you kindly explain why?`

`They're filming.`

I was getting angry. `Who's in charge here?`

`Mr Dwan. He's the director.`

I walked towards a standing of trees bordering the sand dunes. There was an assembly of people with cameras, lighting, reflector boards, and cables running across the road to a nearby property.

`I want to speak to someone called Dwan,` I shouted.

A fellow, standing by one of the cameras looked up. `I'm Allan Dwan.`

`Would you kindly tell your tame policemen to let me through the barrier. I want to get to my house.`

By now I was quite incensed.

`I've never met police so damned indifferent. I've a good mind to complain to their chief. I'm appalled at their uncaring attitude.`

`That's because they're not real policemen, Mr. .err?`

`Lockhart.`

`Lockhart...Sam Lockhart of Universal?`

`Yes.`

He grinned. `Let me introduce myself. I'm Allan Dwan, This is an American Film Company motion picture. We put the barrier there because of the electricity cables. I`ll get the extras to shift them.`

In the end I drove over them slowly, parked the Oakland, and resumed talking to Allan Dwan.

`Ive just seen your movie, *The Country Chairman,*` I remarked. `What was it, five reels?

Dwan nodded. `Yes, it seemed to go down well.`

`But I noticed it was a Famous Players` production.`

`Yes, well these days I tend to do a lot of freelance work, directing or writing.`

`Did you write *The Country Chairman?*`

`Yes.` he turned his head, and looked skywards to check the light.

`Look, I won`t keep you. But have you got a moment later to discuss something? If you have, come over see me when you finish here.`

I gave him the address.

Later, after Joanna`s party friends had been collected by their parents, Allan Dwan arrived. After a short conversation, I acquired a new scriptwriter

CHAPTER FORTY - EIGHT

`What do you mean a thousand extras? Do you know what that will cost?`
Goddamit, Sam, you`re way over budget this time!`

`I`ve got this new screenwriter, Carl, and that`s the way he sees it.`

`Then get someone else who sees it less expensively!`

This was a familiar tirade. We both knew he would eventually give me the go-ahead. It was his style. If anything he was a bit too generous, and I was the one who would often rein him in.

He had been delighted with the screenplay, the choice of actors and that we would be making full use of the two hundred and thirty acre film lot Isasdore had bought for the location shots. His concept of "Universal City" was still a long way off.

`If you go with this, when will it be available for distribution?` asked Pat Powers, senior vice-president and treasurer of Universal Studios. He was a large, no-nonsense Irishman, who owned forty percent of the company`s stock.

`Later in the year, around October,` I responded.

`Tell me the story again.`

I glanced at Carl, who sat there imperturbably, while I explained the gist of the tale to Powers. There was no love lost between the two. It was often rumoured that Pat Powers would be more than ready to lead a revolt to oust Carl as president.

`Pythias has been caught plotting the assassination of King Dionysis of Syracuse. Before his execution, Dionysis grants Pythias leave to put his affairs in order providing Damon volunteers to stand in his place. If Pythias does not come back to face the executioner, Damon would have to sacrifice his life. But their brotherly love goes beyond self-interest. When Pythias does return in the allotted time, King Dionysis is impressed enough to have a change of heart.`

`I thought all the Greeks were in Florida,` remarked Powers. `Not in upstate New York.`

`It`s a different Syracuse, Pat,` said Carl evenly. `This one`s in Sicily around the fifth century BC. OK, Sam, go ahead, but keep it tight.`

I had read a report of the hearing in Moving Picture World, the trade magazine.

So when I opened the letter from Selwyn Edge at the studio, it was no great surprise.

Typically, he got straight to the point.

"Sam, we lost the case against Charles Urban. The court found in his favour.
William was bitterly disappointed, but somehow, I don`t think all is lost.
Let me know what you want to do.
Regards, Selwyn"

I sent him a cable: APPEAL IMMEDIATELY!!

There was another message that day. Isabel phoned me.

`Hello, Sam, how are things?`

`Fine, darling, I`ll be home tomorrow. Is there anything you want me to bring?`

My mind was solving the production snags of *Damon And Pythias.*

`I was hoping you might be able to come back today.`

`Really, is it urgent?`

`Depends how you look at it. My waters have just broken, and I think I should be going to hospital.`

I drove to Santa Barbara in record time. When I got to the house I found a neighbour had taken the girls under her wing, and Isabel was doing an inventory of the Frigidaire.

`There you are, Sam. Here`s what you need to buy, OK?`

I grabbed her case.

`Fine, fine! Let`s go.`

`I think I should water the flowers. You`ll never remember to do it.`

`No! Let`s go...now!`

Her face twisted in pain.

`Perhaps, I should...they are coming fairly regularly.`

I almost carried her down to the car, then drove as fast as I could to the cottage hospital. She moaned several times on the way, and I had visions of Isabel having the baby in the car. When we arrived, I rushed inside and grabbed a wheelchair. I helped her into it and pushed it up the ramp and through the doors, yelling.

`My wife's having a baby! My wife's having a baby!`

Two nurses appeared and chatted amiably to Isabel, who then turned to me and said. `Go home now, Sam, have a cup of tea. Come back this evening.`

I walked slowly to the car feeling drained and shaky. I leaned against it for several minutes before driving slowly home.

When I went back three hours later, Isabel had produced the most beautiful daughter to add to our collection. Her name was Sophia.

Suddenly the tension was released, and I simply burst into tears when I saw her in Isabel's arms.

By the end of September, when we finished filming, part of the Universal lot had been levelled for the stages, and grading was completed for a network of roads, including the mile-long "Laemmle Boulevard" linking the rear of the old farmstead to the front gate. Over five hundred people were now living on the property, seventy-five of them in tents along the hills that provided the studio's backdrop. Isadore Bernstein had taken advantage of this permanent population to obtain a ranking as a third-class city, with its own post office and voting precinct.

Otis Turner, the director, of *Damon And Pythias*, relied heavily on Allan Dwan. I must admit I too was impressed with his work, and thanked the day he had put a barrier across the road in Santa Barbara.

During the editing process Otis and I invited Allan to join us. Again, a worthwhile addition to the team. He made several valuable suggestions, including the idea of introducing shots of the Acropolis at the beginning to give it an immediate Greek flavour. Everyone was delighted with the result when the five reel motion picture was released in November.

Allan and I were on our own in the editing suite on one occasion, when he remarked.

`So, have the Italians from the city been in touch with you yet, Sam?`

I glanced up from the splicing machine. `Sorry, what Italians?`

He shrugged. `You know, the protectors, the insurance company.`

He must have seen the puzzlement on my face.

`Forget it, Sam. Perhaps they won`t bother you like they did us.`

A week later, when Carl came out from our new offices in New York City, I mentioned Allan`s remark over lunch.

`Take no heed, Sam,` said Carl, wiping his mouth with the napkin. `Issy did mention that some people had been to see him. But he ran them off the lot.`

`But who are these people? What are they selling? Allan Dwan mentioned some form of insurance.`

Isadore stared at Carl, then said in a low voice. `It`s a protection racket, Sam. A bunch of Italians demanding money. If we don`t pay, they say they`ll create problems for us. At least, that`s the idea. But with the numbers we`ve got on the lot, they would find it hard to carry out their threat.`

As the winter rainy season progressed, it became obvious we desperately needed bigger indoor staging than the Nestor studio on Gower and Sunset could provide. William Horsley set to, and began converting a building intended for use as a huge warehousing facility. It was still being hung with Aristo Arcs and Cooper-Hewitt lamps when the flood hit "Universal City".

On the last night in January, a tributary of the Los Angeles River, usually a languid stream which meandered through the lot, was transformed into a raging torrent. It burst its banks, undermining new buildings in its path as well as demolishing the original farm structures.

The devastation it caused compared with the battle scenes from the war now raging in Europe. I had seen photographs of the conflict to secure Ypres, just across the French border in Belgium. The despair on people`s faces, the shattered homes, the broken, ragged trees, the all-pervading sea of mud as the waters slowly receded. It was totally disheartening.

What I admired was the passion, the drive with which Isadore set about restoring the site. He called in hundreds of labourers to help repair the damage, estimated at a hundred and thirty thousand dollars.

``We`ll collect on the insurance later,` he declared. `Let`s show we can`t be beaten. We won`t put it back as it was, we`ll do it better.`

`What do you mean can`t be beaten? Was it was a deliberate act? Who the hell would do such a thing? `

The insurance claims inspection team was adamant. Someone had dammed the stream in the certain knowledge that the heavy rains would create a build-up of the waters and inundate the film lot.

`Then who the hell pays for all this?`

I was standing next to him, surveying the scene with three representatives of the insurance company.

`I think you ought to see where and why the tributary broke its banks, Mr Bernstein,` said one of the insurance people.

He led the way to the back lot where it bordered the now fast-flowing stream.

`It was difficult to determine if it were a man-made obstruction, until we pulled out about a dozen heavy, concrete posts,` explained the insurance assessor. `They were lying on the bed of the stream, and from the depressions and scuff marks in the bank the other side.` He pointed across the tributary to a patch of ground. `It was clear the posts had been unloaded from a vehicle, carried to the edge and dumped in one spot in this stream to create a dam. And a very effective one, too.`

The posts, eight or nine inches square, and six feet in length, had been stacked on the path alongside the stream They would have required a great deal of manpower to shift them, but once in place they constituted a formidable barrier.

`It looks, sir,` the assessor announced to Isadore, `As though someone wanted to harm you and your business.`

CHAPTER FORTY - NINE

Everything ground to a halt.

We stopped work on both the motion pictures and the serials. The final episodes of *The Master Key* would be delayed; and the next, a twenty two part serial, *The Broken Coin*, was rescheduled for later in the year. The phone exchange was jammed with irate calls from exhibitors.

A week after the flood Carl arrived from New York.

When we toured the film lot, I glimpsed his face. It was strained and uncomprehending. From president of a dynamic film business one minute, he was now in command of a two hundred and thirty acre field of waste and debris. It was one of those rare moments when Carl was lost for words.

Later in the day we were sitting in a room at the Nestor Studio on Gower and Sunset. The weather had closed in, matching the despondency. Carl had agreed that regardless of whether or not the insurance claim was met, we had to push ahead with rebuilding. It was our number one priority.

Meanwhile, Isadore was contacting the regional distributors explaining the situation, and would take advertisements in the trade magazines showing how Universal would overcome the setback.

I was talking about future projects, one in particular I thought would make an interesting production. It was about birth control with the working title, *Where Are My Children*. We were facing up to each other, about to plunge into our ritualised arguments about decency and the boundaries of what constituted good entertainment, when the door burst open.

One of the studio hands stood in the doorway, and started to say.` I couldn`t stop them Mr Laemmle, they...`

That`s as far as he got. Four men, hats low over their eyes, tumbled him roughly aside. Each one went to a corner of the room. A moment passed. Then a fifth man strolled casually into the room. Isadore made to rise, but was pushed back into his chair.

The fellow who entered last had a cigarette in his hand, and wore an expensive, mohair coat draped over his shoulders. He stood at the end of the long table, looking down its length at the three of us.

`Mr Laemmle, we warned your man of the likely consequences if he were not prepared to insure your company with us.`

He glanced at Isadore.

`I understand you have now suffered a major setback. If he had listened to my people, I'm sure this catastrophe could have been averted. As I see it, to put everything back together will now cost you more than if you had engaged us.`

He pulled back a chair, and sat down.

`As I see it, Mr Laemmle, there are very few options open to you. So, let me give you a piece of advice. The next time my lieutenant comes to see you about buying insurance, accept the terms he offers. I can assure you in the long run it will be much, much safer for your business and the continued health of your colleagues. Don't disappoint me. Others have tried...they no longer have the inclination to go against me.`

He rose from the chair.

`We shall now leave. Expect *il mio tenente* to call upon you shortly. Good afternoon, gentlemen.`

`Who was that?` I asked the fellow who tried to warn us.

`You don't know? That was Pietro Matranga. He and his brother, Antonio, run a Black Hand organisation around the Plaza area in Los Angeles. They pick their targets and shake them down for protection money. It seems Universal is on their list.`

`What the hell is the Black Hand?` shouted Carl. `It sounds like something out of a Sunday comic strip.`

`The Black Hand, Mr Laemmle, operates in almost every "Little Italy" from here to New York. Its members resort to extortion, arson and murder to persuade people to pay them. Take my advice, pay them. Not just your company but your family could be a target.`

`Dammit, we can't run a film business with those threats hanging over us! `Well, we're not going to pay, and that's that!`

Isadore said nothing. Carl's family was still in New York. Isadore's and mine were here in California.

`You are right, of course,` I said, stroking my chin. `But let`s not be too hasty. What I mean is, let`s examine what they could do, then what we could do to defend ourselves.`

`It`s clearcut as far as I`m concerned! When their man comes call the police!`

`And say what?` I countered. `Here is a man ostensibly selling insurance. Would they lock him up for that? If they did half the world`s travelling salesmen would be in jail. No, my immediate reaction is to play along with them, and search for a way out.`

`No!`

`I think you should listen to reason, Carl,` said Isadore in a low voice, speaking for the first time since the hoodlums and their boss had left. `You`ve seen with your own eyes what they did to the lot. If that happened again there will be no Universal Film Manufacturing Company. Sam`s idea makes sense. Especially, as you want to throw open our doors to the world in seven weeks time.`

`What`s this?` It was my turn to question what was going on.

`Carl has only just told me, Sam. He wants to have a grand opening of "Universal City" in March.`

I turned round to Carl. `Are you serious?`

`Yes. It can still be done. We`ll erect some buildings, the others our scenery people can fabricate to look like the real thing. I`m going to bring a trainload of people and dignitaries out here and show them what we are about to present to America.. .the biggest film making company in the world!`

`All the more reason to think carefully about this Matranga fellow,` said Isadore grimly.

I devoted every moment of the quality thinking time on the journeys between Santa Barbara and the Valley to the extortion question. It took three trips before the semblance of a plan emerged.

Carl Laemmle had stayed on, fretting over the work being carried out on the lot. It was like an ant`s nest of feverish activity. I do not know how Isadore and William Horsley managed to organise and oversee every element of the re-construction, particularly with Carl hovering over them, querying each decision.

One of the buildings that had been erected had a tower-like structure with a panoramic view of the whole site. The operation was now being masterminded from this eyrie, and that`s where I found the three of them when I came up the stairs.

`Sam, tell this man it can`t be done, will you?` declared Isadore, red in the face.

He saw my puzzled look.

`You wouldn`t believe it...he wants to simulate a flash flood on the opening day!`

I laughed. `That`s a good one, Carl.`

`I mean it, Sam,` he said with conviction. `We`ll want some events taking place. People won`t just want to look at buildings and sites where we shall have more buildings in the future. They`ll want to see some action, and I`m going to give it to them.`

Isadore drew in a deep breath to argue, but I cut across him before he could say anything.

`If I find a way, Carl, to stop these Matranga people, to remove the demands these Black Hand hoodlums are making, would you let me make *Where Are My Children?*`

`No!`

`OK, then I guess they will do their worst. There won`t even be an opening day. Or if there is, the Matrangas will make sure it`s a disaster.`

His eyes narrowed.

`Think of something else. I don`t like anything about your idea. It`s offensive and immoral.`

`No. That`s the deal.`

`There are times, Sam, when I should fire you. You always have to be difficult, want your own way.`

The deal was this. Firstly, Carl would stop interfering and take the next train back east. He was to ask no questions, just sit by the telephone in the new offices at 1600 Broadway and await my call.

Secondly, I wanted a budget of five thousand dollars; use of a cameraman; sets made; and access to a great deal of equipment. Then, if I got the right result, approval to make the six reeler on birth control and abortion. At the end of the discussion he simply said, "OK", and that was that. He left Los Angeles that evening.

Three days later one of Matranga`s lieutentants, a heavily-built fellow called Tony Buccola, showed up at the Universal lot. When his name was announced I told Isadore I would see him alone.

`We have been giving it a lot of thought, Mr Buccola, and we`ve decided to accept your offer. How much is your insurance policy going to cost us?`

He was a self-assured individual, dressed similarly to his employer in a mohair coat. The discordant note, when he sat down and crossed his legs, were the brown and white spectator shoes he was wearing.

`Tell me, Mr Lockhart, what does someone like Douglas Fairbanks earn a week?`

`I would guess around two thousand dollars.`

`What do you pay King Baggot?`

`Fifteen hundred.`

`Our service is worth those two actors` salaries, plus an administration fee of another thousand dollars. We`ll round it up and call it five thousand dollars. Payable each Friday morning, which I shall collect personally.`

As we were walking towards the door, I said casually. `Have you ever seen a film set, Mr Buccola?`

His eyes portrayed interest. `No...no, I haven`t.`

`Would you care to?`

`Sure.`

`Well, as you can see we have no stages in operation at the moment, though we are filming at a studio in the city. If you are going back to LA, I`m on my way there right now. If I come in your automobile, I can show you what we do. Someone can bring me back later. What do you say?`

He could not contain himself. `Great!`

When we arrived at the Nestor Studio, the scene they were shooting was in a bar room. It looked authentic, with bottles ranged on shelves, beer pumps and glasses, and extras occupying adjacent tables.

Tony Buccola and I stood to one side and while we waited for the director to call "action". I explained what would be happening.

`It`s a gangster movie. The hero is having a quiet drink, when a rival gang raids the place. He dives over the counter, picks up the bartender`s shotgun, and fires back at the three men who have come to kill him. It`s supposed to be a fifteen second sequence. But they told me on the phone they can`t get it right. Let`s see how they do this time.`

`And...action!` called the director.

When the hero rolled over the bar and picked up the shotgun, it took ages for him to raise it in a firing position. The trio with the guns sauntered over, grinned, pointed their guns, and said, `bang`.

`What is it with you, John? Can`t you do it any quicker than that?` cried the director. `You`d be full of bullets by the time your head appeared.`

`It`s this gun, Harry. It`s too unwieldy. I have to step back to raise it over the counter.`

He`s right,` murmured Buccola. `That`s why we shorten the barrels.`

It was an involuntary slip, which he didn`t seem to notice.

`So where do you cut them?` I asked.

We walked over and he took the shotgun from the hero`s hands.

"You should cut it about here.` he put a finger down the barrel.

I turned to a stagehand. `Here, get the barrel cut where this gentleman is indicating.`

Five minutes later he was back, and handed the gun to Buccola.

`Is that about right?` I enquired.

`I would say so.`

The hero took up his position on a bar stool, the director called "action", and the scene was enacted again.

At the supposed sound of gunshots the hero dived over the counter, picked up the shotgun, rose, caught the edge of the bar, which sent the gun flying from his hands.

`For Christ`s sake, John! What the hell are you doing now?` shouted the director. `Can anyone show him how to do it properly?`

`Do you want me to show him?` whispered Buccola.

`It might be a good idea,` I replied. `Otherwise we could be here all day.`

Tony Buccola went round the counter and took hold of the gun.

For the next ten minutes he demonstrated how to hold the shotgun, lodging it close to his hip and firing the weapon. He even gave several lessons how to roll over the bar, and come up shooting.

`Thanks for that,` I said appreciatively, when I walked him to his car.

`Any time, I enjoyed myself.`

`Do you mean that? If you were to act as an adviser that would be really helpful. Though, I guess, you would have to clear it with Mr Matranga. Perhaps, he might be interested in seeing what we do?`

`Yeah, he just might.`

We shook hands and he drove away.

I was hoping for a phone call, but it never came.

I was at the tower block on Friday when Tony Buccola came for his money.

I leaned in the car window and handed it over. He nodded and the driver started to pull away. Suddenly, the car stopped, then reversed. The window was wound down.

`By the way, Mr Lockhart, the boss would be very interested in seeing how you make a movie. Particularly, the one you showed me. When I told him, we both had a good laugh at your leading man`s antics.`

`Sure, when would he like to come?`

`Let us say Monday morning about eleven.`

Experience has taught me that pointing a camera at someone has a threefold effect. They are flattered by being the focus of attention; almost unknowingly, they reveal more about themselves than they would normally admit; and, in time, they come to ignore its intrusive presence. As I discovered when making *Traffic in Souls* : the pimps around the Battery were more than willing to reveal much about themselves and their criminal activities. No one is above such reactions. Not even a gang leader. Pietro Matranga fitted readily into the pattern.

They arrived punctually at eleven o`clock.

This time we had created a wholesale market scene: baskets of fruits and vegetables were stacked high in front of open-fronted warehouses; lorries being loaded and unloaded; an army of porters carrying the produce to and fro. Tellers were standing by, making note of the goods as the packages came into the building, and then out to waiting vehicles when purchases were made. In all, a scene of bustling liveliness.

`How about that, boss? A real fruit and veg market!` exclaimed Buccola, his eyes switching from one aspect to the next.

Matranga, brought up in the family produce business, was more analytical. He nodded. `Almost right, but you wouldn`t display the fruit with the vegetables like that. They would be separated .And you wouldn`t keep the soft fruit exposed to the sunlight. That guy pushing that trolley has stacked it all wrong.`

This was from a man running an extortion ring, employing a host of money men, enforcers, and probably lawyers, telling me how to organise a produce stand. I had him hooked. The next move was even more interesting.

Matranga went over to the trolley, removed the boxes, and restacked it.

He came back wiping his hands on a silk handkerchief.

`We are ready to roll, Mr Lockhart,` said the director.

`Right, Harry. give me a minute.` I turned to the two racketeers. `Gentlemen, we`ll just step back to give them room.`

`OK, action!`

A lorry rolled up and two men got out. They started unloading boxes of nuts and blueberries.

`Stop!` came the director`s voice. `That`s fine, we`ll print that. Next scene, everybody!`

`Where`s the lorry supposed to have come from?` asked Matranga in a low voice.

`From El Paso,` I replied.

He raised an eyebrow. `Seven hundred miles for some nuts?`

The camera moved in on the back of the closed-in vehicle. Someone adjusted the light reflectors.

`OK, action!`

One of the men climbed up and shifted a small stack, uncovering a half dozen bemused faces. He pulled away a few more boxes, and looked round at his companion at the tailboard. He nodded urgently. Whereupon, the six men in hiding rose, slipped off the lorry and ran into the warehouse.

`Stop! Let`s do that again, everyone!`

Matranga was transfixed. `They`re Chinese,` he said in a hoarse whisper.

`That`s right. Under the Chinese exclusion law, they are illegal immigrants.

They come into Mexico and make their way to Juárez, Chihuahua. From there they are smuggled across the border into El Paso, evading the Mounted Guards and Chinese Immigration Agents. Certain people help them make their way to California. That`s a sideline of the gang depicted in the film.`

Matranga glanced at Buccola.

`What else do they do?`

`The usual...prostitution, gambling, even extortion,` I replied with a smile.

Matranga smiled back.

He returned a few days later, and watched another couple of scenes. This time he was quite vocal about the errors the leading actor was making, particularly when a shake-down was being enacted. The victim, a small businessman, was advised to pay a weekly sum or have his windows smashed, or one of his vehicles damaged.

`The guy`s too soft,` Matranga growled.

`Stop!` I called. `Let`s make some changes here.`

I called the actor over. `Listen to this gentleman a moment.`

But even in the second, third and fourth take, it was obvious he was not forceful enough for Matranga`s liking.

`I wouldn`t employ him to open a door for me!` he hissed.

`John, come over here again!`

But even with more advice he still failed to instill the required menace in his actions.

`It`s in the body language and the words,` declared Matranga. `Even if it`s a silent film, tell him to threaten him verbally.`

After two more unsuitable takes, Matranga said, `Let me show him.`

When the threat was made it was frightening in its intensity and menace. It was so convincing the actor playing the businessman literally quailed under the onslaught.

`My God!` said the director, `that was terrific!`

Matranga shrugged, and smiled at me.

Harry, the director, turned to me. `This guy`s a natural. Let`s have him in the film.`

I glanced at Matranga, who looked pleased with himself.

`What do you say?`

He shrugged his approval.

He repeated his approach to "persuading clients" several more times during the session, and agreed to come back the following day.

We took a number of scenes featuring Peter Matranga, before he asked me about the content of the movie we were making. We sat down at a table and over coffee I outlined what we were doing.

`This is about a gangster who is into every kind of racket there is. He works for "Il Supremo" – that would be you - the big boss who masterminds the operation. The hero is in love with your daughter, who doesn`t know what you do for a living. When the girl tells you, her father, the hero wants to marry her, you object. She wants to know why, and you tell her that the young hero is a gangster, and not for her. The realisation leads to the big boss changing his ways. What do you think?`

`I`m not so sure about the ending,` murmured Matranga. `Why would he want to give it all up? He is rich, powerful, successful, why lose all that?`

`Because audiences love a prodigal son. Someone who reforms. Don`t forget, Peter, this is a film, even though it`s realistic. In fact, to add to the realism, I`d like to take some long shots, nothing that would identify them, of some of your people in action. Would you go along with that?`

`You won`t see their faces?`

`I`ll show you the film we take.`

OK...I`ll go along with that.`

That weekend, I collected the hand-held Ernemann Kino camera, and for good measure brought with me the Houghton pocket-watch camera from our house in Santa Barbara. I also had a lengthy conversation with Geoffrey Summer, our chief cameraman.

The acting bug had bitten Peter Matranga. As I expected he revelled in acting in a motion picture; and the more scenes he appeared in, the more he let slip how The Black Hand operated in Los Angeles. One significant item he unwittingly revealed was the open warfare between rival gangs.

When the prominent leader of another gang, Joseph Ardizzone, killed one of Matranga`s people, a war of attrition ensued. Whenever there was a killing, most often it was one of Ardizzone`s or Matranga`s lieutenants. It seemed the local underworld watched both groups with considerable interest. As a consequence, each leader took great pains to be regarded as the other's superior.

Another nugget of information to be stored away.

When the exterior shots were taken, we used a flatbed truck on which to mount the camera. Matranga was not in the scenes, although he stood close by watching the action with his brother, Tony.

They called on a number of enterprises, and each time, the owner or manager was given a threatening ultimatum. On one occasion, violence was added to the confrontation. In several encounters money changed hands.

I strolled over to the brothers, to find a fierce argument going on.

`Are you crazy, Pietro? This could be really damaging. What the hell do you think you are doing openly making demands with a camera running?`

`It's only background material, Mr Matranga,` I quickly explained. `Just to give a sense of reality to the film.`

Tony turned on his brother. `What the hell are you doing in a film for Christ's sake? Telling the world who and what you are. You'll pull yourself down, and me with you if anyone sees it.`

Peter became very angry. His face reddened, that menacing look came into his eyes. This is it, I thought. I am in trouble.

But he turned roundly on his brother.

`Listen, I am the head of this outfit, not you. I am performing in a make-believe motion picture. Nothing more. Nobody's face will appear on the screen except mine, and the audiences will love me, won't they, Sam?`

`When it all comes together you'll be widely recognised, Peter.`

Tony Matranga walked away shaking his head.

`Ignore him, Sam. He always thinks the worst.`

CHAPTER FIFTY

I spent a lot of time on the editing.

The scenes taken of Matranga's hoodlums threatening real businessmen were clearly identifiable. Moreover, when the film camera, lighting units and other equipment moved to the next take, we interviewed the principals of the companies using the hand-held Ernemann Kino camera operated by Geoffrey Summer. We made sure they enunciated their responses, and had an experienced lip-reader confirm what was said. Each interview was shown as a text piece, and all those threatened by the Matranga gang were willing to testify against them. Every time there was a shake-down, the lead camera took shots of Peter Matranga standing nearby. On one occasion he was filmed with his brother.

The interior scenes were highly revelatory. Especially when the gang leader himself demonstrated how he issued violent, unimaginable threats against his victims; and if they did not cooperate, how they would be carried out.

In all, it was a two reel production, a carefully orchestrated exposé of the extortion racket being conducted by the Matranga family. It was a bleak, telling indictment of the Black Hand, and all the many gangs using that label to identify their criminal practices. I was quite proud of it.

When Tony Buccola came to collect, I asked him to step out the car. I had something I wanted to see. I ushered him into a seat in an improvised viewing room, Behind us stood six hand-picked heavies from the construction team. I waved to the projectionist, and up came the title on the screen.

The Insurance Salesman.

Thirty minutes later, I pressed a copy of the film into his hand, and gave him a message.

'Tell Mr Matranga that he really would have made a good film actor. In the film he is entirely believable, as are you, and all your racketeers. Although the interviews with the businessmen you were shaking down cannot be heard, they have all been verified by a panel of lip-readers, and cannot be refuted.

`There are any number of copies now available for circulation if the slightest provocative act is made against Universal properties, members of its staff, or their families. They are lodged with a number of law offices in Los Angeles, and will go unfailingly to the Justice Department. I also say this. There is an extra special copy addressed to Mr Joseph Ardizzone, your arch-rival. He would receive it within one hour of any accident or mishap occurring. Now, get out of my sight!`

CHAPTER FIFTY - ONE

Carl watched the film.

Afterwards he sat there for some time without saying a word. Eventually, he spoke. `Do you know what this is? The death knell for the Matrangas. If this ever got out they would be found dead in an alley somewhere. This is dynamite, Sam, and it`s frightening.`

`Are you saying I shouldn`t have made it, Carl?`

`No...I`m just realising what a powerful medium we play with. Motion pictures can alter one`s perceptions...even one`s values. Until this moment, I had given little regard to how we so easily manipulate people`s thoughts. OK, I know we catch at their emotions. We can make them laugh, make them cry, that`s superficial. I mean, deep down, we could be accused of changing long-held beliefs, principles that have been dear to most people`s hearts. Are we right to do that?`

This was new. I had not appreciated that Carl Laemmle was wearing his conscience on his sleeve. Suddenly, I thought all the more of him.

`I go along with that, Carl. In this instance, this film about The Black Hand had to be made. It was not just getting them off our backs, it was also for the many already in the Matranga brothers` thrall. The only way we could stop them was to fight fire with fire. Hopefully, we won`t have to resort to it again.`

If I remember rightly, Sam,` said Carl in a low voice. `You did something similar when you made *Traffic of Souls*.`

`How did you know that?`

`Isabel mentioned some time ago that you spent a lot of time with the pimps at the Battery in New York, getting to know how they worked and the girls they used. You were even about to be dealt with, until they heard your English accent and the sob story you told them. You play a dangerous game, my friend.`

I shrugged. `Is this the prelude to you saying don`t make *Where Are My Children?*`

`No, we had an agreement, I won`t break that. What I am saying is tread carefully, be mindful of people`s sensitivities, and don`t make a pariah of the Universal Film Manufacturing Company in the headlong rush to preach your message.`

I nodded acceptance. A sermon from on high.

Over the next few months I spent a great deal of time reworking the screenplay. I also spoke at length with Lois Weber, a woman director now making a name for herself. I had the feeling she would deal compassionately with the subject.

I was leaving my makeshift office, on the way to meet Lois to discuss featuring Tyrone Power and Helen Riaume in the lead roles, when a young woman thrust a cable into my hand.

`It looks urgent, Mr Lockhart, otherwise I`d have left it in your secretary.`

It was from Selwyn Edge.

Did as requested. Took the case to the House of Lords, the highest authority in the land They ruled in WFG`s favour. Urban now declared bankrupt. Letter to follow. Selwyn Edge.

I honestly did not know whether to feel elated or sad. The only consolation was that the man who had reduced George Albert Smith to a shadow of his former self was now experiencing the same hardships.

The studio opening was looming ever closer. Isadore rarely seemed to go home. When I left the studio for my apartment in the evening, he would still be working; and when I got in at seven thirty the next morning, he would be there. The only giveaway was the different shirt and tie he wore each day.

I had to admit he was doing a terrific job. You could not tell the difference between the temporary shells of buildings and the many that had been properly constructed.

What was impressive was the three hundred foot long external staging. It was divided into segments, and a number of different films could all be shot at the same time. A dramatic motion picture on one set might be flanked by a cast of actors rehearsing a comedy on one side, and a construction crew erecting scenery on the other. Sunlight was the only illumination, and this was moderated by a series of overhead diffusion screens. When it became too cloudy for uniform results, a banner with the words "DON'T SHOOT" was run up a pole and all production ceased.

Beneath the staging were various traps and water-tight pits, while one corner housed a revolving turntable and another a rocking setup. It was state-of-the-art within the industry, and would elevate Universal's place in film making.

Predictably, Carl managed to get his way. One of the film directors, Henry McRae, was commissioned to create a flood scene in which sixty thousand gallons of water would pour from a reservoir, sweeping away a Western township.

In addition to showing actual films being made, there were numerous other attractions being hurriedly installed, for Carl had decided the studio lot should also be opened to the public. Stands were being hastily built to house spectators who would be presented with a rodeo show, a high-wire daredevil act, tumblers and marching bands.

We had invited Isabel's and my parents over to witness the grand opening.

It was Isabel's suggestion that, after the lengthy sea voyage, it would be best for mum and dad to break their journey by going to her parents' place in Pittsburgh for a few days, before the they took the train westwards.

We all stayed at the Hotel Alexandria in downtown Los Angeles, a dozen miles south of the studio. I did not want to get caught up in the "celebrations" taking place at the Beverley Hills. We were driven to the studio that Monday morning, and joined the crowd waiting for Carl and his cortege. Shortly afterwards, we witnessed a fleet of buses drive up through the hills, and come to a halt at the gates to Universal City, freshly painted, its white stucco gleaming in the California sunshine.

Carl was presented with a golden key to open the gates, a band struck up "The Star Spangled Banner". Pat Powers grudgingly ran the stars and stripes up the nearby flagpole. Laemmle then led his army of executives and guests through the gates, followed by a cheering crowd. They marched between two ranks of Universal stars until they reached another flagpole, where Bob Cochrane, another vice-president, raised a special "Universal City" flag. The band played "I Love You, California," and Laemmle, Cochrane, and Powers were showered with flowers.

To my mind it was totally over the top. But the many visitors to the "City" loved every minute. By early afternoon it was estimated that twenty thousand people had flocked to see filming in progress and enjoy the events.

One thing that briefly soured the moment was seeing Carl Laemmle talking earnestly to Thomas Edison. I sought out Isadore and asked him why he had been invited.

`He`s one of the founders of General Electric, the company which supplies Universal City. Carl asked him to dedicate the new, all electric stages we are building.`

`After all we have suffered from that man, and Carl wants to be friends?` I was angry. I could not so easily forget the past.

`We can afford to be. It hasn`t been confirmed yet, but the word is the Motion Picture Patents Company is about to be penalised for breaking the Sherman Anti-Trust Law. All those lawsuits against us have never been rescinded, you know. Even now we could still be taken to court. Once they declare the infringement, we`re home and dry.`

`Hmm. . I cannot forgive so easily.`

Isadore patted my arm, then added. `Edison drove down from the San Francisco World Fair with Henry Ford. They are late, would you believe their motor car broke down.`

That was not the only thing that broke down that day. Henry McRae's flood scene, intended to sweep away a Western township, was a little too forceful and instead swept towards the spectators. Fortunately, my family was safely in the tiered seats. I was standing down at the front as the flood reached the crowd. I picked up Carl`s diminutive figure and placed him on an automobile. However, a number of our guests had to be taken to the wardrobe department for a change of clothing. Fortunately, no one mentioned the January flood, at least not in print.

The other incident was a tragedy. Frank Stites, Universal's stunt pilot, took off in his plane, crashed, and was killed before thousands of horrified onlookers.

It was later in the day, I learned of the build-up to the Carl Laemmle journey and arrival in Los Angeles from Bob Cochrane a Universal vice-president and friend of Carl`s from way back.

Apparently, it started ten days before the official opening when a cavalcade proceeded to the train station in New York. Carl, Recha, Pat Powers and Cochrane had arrived at the terminal in a large, open-topped touring car, leading an entourage of honking horns and waving banners assembled by the studio press office. To see them off, many of the company's employees gathered on the platform at Grand Central Station.

One of the nation's first prominent movie reviewers, Kitty Kelly, was there to cover the event for the *Chicago Tribune*. *Billboard*, the *Western Newspaper Union*; and the *National Magazine* , *Leslie's Weekly*, *Motography*, and the *Motion Picture News* all had representatives on the train.

As well as the media, there were many notable distributors. Bob said they were impressed. A gala such as this was one way of demonstrating Universal's size and strength. Moreover, a reception line-up of Universal stars was on the platform to add something special to the farewell.

The Lake Shore Limited pulled out of Grand Central and headed for Chicago, where more "Universalites" joined the train ready to take them all to the west coast.

The "Universal Special" left Dearborn Street Station in Chicago on Sunday evening, stopped in Kansas City, and reached Denver by Tuesday. The local agent was at the station with a circus band and open limousines. For eight hours the party saw the sights of Denver, was greeted by Governor Carlson on the steps of the capitol, and lunched at the Savoy in the company of Buffalo Bill Cody.

Bob Cochrane told me by then he had had enough. But still the partying went on. The group left Denver's Santa Fe Station en route to the Grand Canyon, a side trip that took another day and a half. Isadore Bernstein met the train at San Bernardino, and brought along a bevy of "poppy girls" bearing gifts of flowers and fruit to declare everybody welcome.

It was on Saturday, seven days after leaving Grand Central, that the Special deposited them all in Los Angeles. Jaded and tired, they had been taken to the Beverley Hills Hotel.

What Bob added ruefully, when told of what was planned, Pat Powers, treasurer and senior vice-president, had been dismayed at the spectacle and horrified by the expense. As a result, with all the members of the board present for the studio's official opening, he called an extraordinary meeting to question Carl`s profligacy. This was scheduled to take place a few days time.

The day after the opening, Carl, Isadore and I were sitting around the boardroom table in the new administration block. We had been discussing the film *Damon And Pythias*, released some months earlier. According to the exhibitors` reactions, it was continuing to be a resounding success, confirming the audience research conducted in November.

Pat Powers had not liked it: though the receipts must have cheered him as company treasurer.

I had voiced the comment. `What does he want? I give him a money-making picture, and he`s still not satisfied.`

That had started Carl on his tirade.

`That goddamned Irishman is out to cause trouble,` he ranted. `Why we put up with his antics is beyond me. Now he has called a board meeting to censure me! Would you believe it? I want him out, Issy!`

There was a tap at the door and Bob Cochrane walked in.

`I could hear you shouting in the corridor, Carl. Who do you want out?`

`Pat, goddamned, Powers, that`s who. He`s a pain in the butt. How he managed to run a film company is beyond me.`

Bob took a chair opposite Carl. He leaned forward and in a voice that carried just across the table, said. `He is itching for a showdown, Carl. Be warned. He wants your job as president, and he is calling in his markers. He may try to oust you Thursday, though in my judgement he still hasn`t got more than forty five percent of the voting shares. But this is likely to be the prelude. Cast doubt on your abilities, then go for your throat at the next board meeting in New York in a month`s time.`

There was a strained silence.

I sat watching them as they mentally gauged the strength of the opposition.

I felt a flicker of concern. I was no favourite of Powers. If he gained the presidency I too would be out on my ear. Carl must have glimpsed my face.

`Time for cool heads, gentlemen,` he said. `Issy can you calculate the members` holdings and the share movement. We need to know the strengths of those likely to side with Powers.`

`I can start, Carl, but I`ll have to come back to New York to get all the information we need.`

`OK, come back with us at the end of the week. Sam, I think you had better come too. Maybe not straight away, but in a couple of weeks time, when we`ve got all the details together. We`re probably going to need your screwball way of thinking to get us out of this one.`

Bob Cochrane told me later that as predicted, the meeting on Thursday was a stand-off. Powers attempted to deride the opening as a monumental waste of money and time. It was ill-conceived, badly organised which led to errors, and ended in a catastrophe.

At the meeting Cochrane declared the opening day had received a massive vote of approval from the business people who attended, and if Powers had read the newspapers and the trade magazines, he would have been only too aware that Universal had received positive coverage and glowing reports on the opening. Yes, there had been one or two mishaps, but when you are working on such a huge scale, it is inevitable a few things will go adrift.

It was evident Powers was relying on the blunders to effect a condemnation of Carl Laemmle. When the majority of board members agreed with Bob Cochrane, and applauded all who had been involved in the event, Powers was beside himself in anger. Thwarted, the big Irishman would be an even more dangerous opponent the next time around.

I joined others on the platform to say farewell to Carl`s cavalcade. Just before boarding the train Carl took me to one side.

`Sam, I relying on you to provide a solution. As I said, I want that man out for good. Issy will come up with the numbers, but I`ve a feeling it will confirm the inevitable. Pat Powers could well control more than fifty percent of the voting shares. Not just the stock he holds personally, but the proxies of a number of shareholders. So, do what you have to do. Use whatever resources you think necessary.`

He grinned suddenly. `Got a film you`re desperate to make?`

I grinned at him. `How did you guess? I`ve been thinking, perhaps we should create one or two horror movies. We used an actor called Lon Chaney in *Traffic in Souls* . He`s good with make-up, and could make a really gruesome character. Look, Carl, I`ll do what I can. After all, it`s my neck on the line as well.`

I stayed on when the family went back to Santa Barbara.

I had explained the situation to Isabel, that if Carl were deposed I would be out of a job.

`So what. I`m sure lots of other studios would jump at the chance of employing you,` she declared. I hugged her for the vote of confidence.

`Maybe...but I don`t want it to come to that. I`ve got to help Carl. He`s relying on me.`

`Of course you must. What I mean is don`t worry if things don`t turn out as you would like. We would manage, and I`m right behind you.`

After a relaxing weekend, I was on my way back to Universal City. Passing through the township of Thousand Oaks, I idly thought of the phrase, "you can`t see the wood for the trees", or as they say in America, "the forest for the trees".

Something caught at my imagination. An idea began to crystallise.

The following day I went to see William Horsley. Having worked alongside Isadore, getting everything ready for the opening, I felt sure I could take him into my confidence.

His brother, David, when he decided to opt out as a shareholder in the Universal Film Manufacturing Company, had sold his title to Bill Swanson of Rex Films. David went off travelling round Europe. However, William continued to run the Nestor Studio on Gower and Sunset, as part shareholder cum Universal employee.

We chatted for an hour or so, and besides posing one or two questions, I asked him to undertake a few discreet tasks.

I also spent some hours in the administration block asking questions. Getting to appreciate the complexities of paying employees now we were one company, trying to identify a common thread in our payroll system. When the independent studios first came together to form Universal, each company had had its own way of dealing with their staff. In particular, the terms on which they were employed.

They varied from loosely-phrased letters inviting recipients to join, to verbal agreements. The latter was true in my case, and undoubtedly in many others. It was my contention that now we were one organisation, there should be a common contract for cameramen, lighting technicians, scenery constructors, film processors and those working in distribution; and another for the actors and actresses working for us. That afternoon I sent a lengthy letter to Lewis Milestone, our lawyer in New York. This comprised a series of questions and a number of requests. The answers to most would be a simple yes or no, and I asked him to wire his responses to save time.

Ten days later a parcel arrived. It contained the contracts vetted by Lewis Milestone. The meat of the document stipulated the working conditions, and notably, an increased pay structure for staff, and an uprated fee system for the players. A strong inducement to sign the contract which would bear the president's signature.

I then wired Carl, and told him I wanted a letter to confirm my appointment as Director of Personnel; and that this item be included on the agenda for the forthcoming board meeting, at which I would give a verbal report.

He was intrigued, and sent me a wire asking why I wanted to take on the role.

"To regularise the working agreements we have with our key staff and actors", was my reply. I also added. "A courier will bring all the contracts to New York next week. You have to sign every one of them and return them by the same courier".

If there were going to be any problems, there were two people I could rely on to encourage acceptance of the new work agreement. My cousin–in-law, Derek Bryant, now a studio manager at Universal; and our leading man, King Baggot.

Although I knew I would have their unquestioning support, I spent time explaining the reasoning and content of the contracts, and their implications. Both agreed to champion the documents if there were any uncertainties about signing among their respective colleagues.

It took longer than I had imagined for the signed contracts to be returned, and I commissioned Derek to courier them to New York for each one to receive Carl Laemmle's signature.

Predictably, when he came across the references to increased salaries and fees in the documents, he sent an indignant cable.

"What madcapped stunt is this? It will cost us thousands of dollars! Whatever you are up to, if it fails you're going to pay all these people out of your own pocket!"

I was running out of time. It would be another week before Derek was back. Then I had less than three days before catching the train to New York.

When Isabel kissed me goodbye that morning I held on to her tightly.

`I love you,` I said in a voice tight with emotion.

She pulled away slightly, and looked thoughtfully into my eyes.

`I love you, too. That`s all that matters. Don`t you realise that?`

`The trouble is...I may come back without a job.`

She came close.

`No you won`t,` she whispered. `I know you too well.`

William Horsley came to see me. He had been busy and had brought all the necessary papers. I arranged with the bank to pay the holding deposit from my own account, and gave him the go-ahead to have large display boards erected.

I took Geoffrey Summer over to Gower and Sunset and he took a number of still photographs. Back at the studio I sat with him while he processed the film and created the batch of ten by eight prints.

`Pity Charles Urban won that court case against Friese Greene,` he remarked as he clipped the photographs on a line to dry.

I grinned at him. `Actually, the decision has been reversed. It went to The House of Lords, and a Lord Justice Buckley overturned the previous judgement. Urban`s so called patent rights are invalid. I`ll tell you something else, Geoffrey, I personally hold the patent rights to George`s colour process over here.`

`Really? Mind you,` he added, `it was a pointless exercise. George spent too much time attempting to perfect a process that was flawed. You need twice the film length because it runs a twice the normal speed and special projectors. Then, if there`s any movement you get heavy fringing, and you can`t film interiors because the lighting isn`t strong enough. I know from sad experience when I was working for Urban at Williamson`s old studio. It`s a nine day wonder. An imperfect system, to which people are attracted because of the word,"colour".

The next day I boarded the Santa Fe train to Chicago.

I also had a drawing room on the Broadway Limited when I boarded it on Friday night for the next leg of the journey to New York. It would be a close run thing. The train was scheduled to arrive at Penn Station early on Monday morning, allowing just a few hours to run over the tactics with Carl and Isadore before the board meeting in the afternoon.

According to the wire from Bob Cochrane, Pat Powers had been soliciting support for a change of leadership, and had even spoken to him about weighing in the balance his friendship with Laemmle against Powers' more dynamic approach to improving the affairs and status of the company.

The meeting heralded a clash between two major forces – and there could only be one winner. Whoever lost could not easily retain a position on the board, and would be obliged to relinquish all his holdings and involvement in the organisation.

After a brief dinner I settled down to read through the material Isadore had also given Derek to bring back to California. This was the first chance I had had to learn of the allocation and movement of the share holdings since the company's inception three years ago.

The original members that came together to form Universal were Charles Baumann and Adam Kessel of The New York Motion Picture Company; Pat Powers of The Powers Motion Picture Company; Carl Laemmle of Independent Moving Pictures; Mark Dintenfass of Champion; David and William Horsley of The Nestor Film Company; and William Swanson of the Rex Film Company,

As New York Motion Pictures was the largest, Charles Baumann had been nominated president, Powers became vice-president, Bill Swanson, secretary and Carl, treasurer.

A few months later, Baumann declared he and Kessel were pulling out and demanded their share of the assets, which amounted to half a million dollars in stocks and bonds. The other members were furious, for in the original agreement each independent film studio agreed to surrender its assets to the parent company. Powers, it seemed, even tried to take over the New York Motion Picture Company.

Baumann's departure prompted Dintenfass of Champion to sell his stock, which he split between Laemmle and Swanson. This created antipathy between the two, for Carl regarded Swanson as erratic, barely able to pursue a sensible business strategy. Later, when David Horsley decided to go globetrotting, he too preferred to sell out to Swanson, whom he considered a gentle soul, less given to making onerous demands upon people.

When Horsley returned from his travels, he persuaded his brother, William, to sell his holding to him: thereupon, he promptly sold it on to Carl for a handsome profit. From what I deduced from Isadore`s notes, Carl paid one hundred and seventy nine thousand dollars, a good forty thousand above the market price.

Later, when Bill Swanson opted out, a major reorganisation took place. Although, at this juncture a number of the original film makers had dropped out, this had been compensated by other independent studios, such as American Éclair, Republic, Gem, Victor, Sterling, Joker and Itala, joining the consortium. Moreover, several investment and insurance companies had acquired parcels of voting shares, and had seats on the Universal management board. It was in Pat Powers` absence that a meeting of the newly-conceived board had voted in Carl as president. The Irishman`s felt aggrieved, and was determined to reverse that decision.

I was beginning to understand the complexities, movement, and the underlying tensions within the structure. Significantly, the reasons for the ambitious Mr Powers to believe he had been manipulated, and why he was now out to swing the board`s opinion in his favour.

I must have fallen asleep while still absorbing the implications in Isadore`s summary. I awoke with a start when the train jolted to a standstill. I glanced at my watch, it was almost three o`clock in the morning. I lay there for a while, but could not rest. Was there a problem with the train? Would I get there on time? I had to find out. I shrugged on my jacket and went to find the attendant.

He was at the end of the carriage with the door open, talking to another official, dressed in Pennsylvania Railroad livery, standing on the track below.

`Excuse me, can you tell me why we have stopped?`

`No problems with the train, sir,` said the car attendant. `We`re just held up for a while because of electrification at Paoli.`

The attendant on the track added. `There`s new signalling being installed. Lights instead of the old semaphore system. Shouldn`t take long.`

`Where are we now?` I asked.

`Just outside Exton, sir.`

He must have seen my quizzical expression.

`Exton, Pennsylvania,` he added. `Seven or eight miles from Paoli.`

`How far from New York?`

`About a hundred miles, sir.`

We still had not moved when I went along to the dining car for an early breakfast. Although, all I could manage was a cup of coffee. I was getting worried.

Again I caught the attention of the train attendant.

`I am seriously concerned. It is vital I get to New York as soon as possible. Just how much longer is this train going to be delayed?`

`At this moment, sir, I don`t rightly know. Someone has gone up the line to check when we shall be clear to run. But there are trains ahead of us, and others, going west, held up on the opposite side of the installation. It looks like they are using just one track, which will make it slow going for everyone.`

We were held up five hours.

When eventually we started moving, the train raced towards New York; but then there was the delay at Manhattan Transfer, just east of Newark in New Jersey, where they changed the steam engine for an electric unit to haul the train under the North River to Penn Station .

I ran to the cab rank and jumped in a Model T town car painted yellow. It was the first time I had seen such a garish-looking motor car. Then it was a mad dash up Eighth Avenue to the Universal offices at 1600 Broadway, one block up from Times Square.

I pushed through the swing doors and called to the receptionist. `Where`s the board meeting? Can you look after this suitcase?`

She had obviously been told I was expected.

`Down the corridor! The door facing you!`

I came to a halt in front of imposing double doors. Putting down the briefcase, I straightened my tie, smoothed my hair with both hands, and took several deep breaths, and turned the door handle.

They acknowledged my presence, but I could see that Carl was irked by my tardiness, even though I explained the circumstances.

`Well now that you are here, we can revert to item four on the agenda, which refers to your appointment as director of personnel,` declared Carl, sitting at the head of the table.

`I can see no reason, Mr President, why we need such an office, or indeed why the current employment arrangements cannot stand,` said Pat Powers forthrightly. `What concerns me more is that you have taken it upon yourself, Mr Lockhart, to offer substantial raises in salaries to all those behind the camera, and fat increases in fees to our players in front of camera. What you`ve done is put up our production costs at a stroke. It will cost us thousands more than we budgeted in this fiscal period. So where do you think the money is going to come from to pay everybody?`

There was little doubt the Irishman scented blood. I had been in the room five minutes and he was on the attack. He clearly wanted to have at Carl Laemmle`s cohorts and reduce them in the board`s eyes before moving in for the kill.

I nodded. `A reaction, Mr Powers, I wouldn`t have expected from one as conversant with the finances as yourself.`

He went to respond, but I quickly cut across him.

`Let me remind members of the board that from the outset, there was agreement between those who signed the founding document to surrender their assets to the parent organisation. Moreover, to create a fund of talent available to any of the member film studios within the consortium. As a result of this arrangement, it soon became logical for all the technicians and actors, as Mr Powers puts it, "those behind, and those in front of the camera" to be employed centrally.

`But then I discovered that, firstly, there was no consistent method of employment. Members may have been most able film makers, but in almost every single case staffing arrangements were either non-existent, or at best, haphazard. There was no one system in place for setting salary scales, agreeing work hours, specific duties.

`I compared what the member companies paid their people, and what the Universal administrative department had to contend with in doing the payrolls. It was a real eye-opener. Those "behind the camera", the technical staff doing the same job were paid wildly differing rates.`

I looked slowly around the table. I had their attention. Not even the

Irishman deigned to interrupt.

`It would be only a matter of time before people in the new company discovered what their counterparts were earning, and then the lid would come off. Gentlemen, we could well have had mutiny on our hands. So I set out to create a series of standard pay and work time rates for every activity we ask people to perform. Yes, Mr Powers is right, many will receive a bigger pay cheque, but it is graduated. The current top earners in each category will have a much lower increase, and conversely, the lower paid will enjoy a higher uplift in salary. It is the only way to work towards a standardised system.

`Overall, only a modest amount will be added to our wage bill. But, I stress, we need to bring about a single system of remuneration which the administrative department can cope with. Believe me, if we can do that we shall need less admin staff, and save ourselves money that way.`

Pat Powers was first to comment.

`What about the actors and actresses we're paying fees to. Where's the sense in paying them more than we need? That's daft. we'll look a soft touch to our competitors. They'll be laughing up their sleeves.`

`I don't think so. I'll tell you why. I work with those, as you put it, "in front of the camera" every day. I have been aware for some time that film companies like Fox, Paramount, Adolph Zukor and his Famous Players Studio, even Samuel Goldfish, who is looking to set up his own studio, are hungry to poach the players presently working for Universal.

`By giving more now, we are lessening the possibility of losing them, and at the same time avoiding protracted arguments and debates over the size of their fees. I have forestalled all that, and our forthcoming film schedule will continue uninterrupted.`

Powers humphed. There was a momentary silence, broken by a voice that came from down the table to my right.

`Mr President, I haven't met Mr Lockhart before, but what he has just told us makes a great deal of sense. We at MetLife have a clear policy on wage structures, working hours and conditions. I hadn't appreciated that the film industry has a much looser approach. So, I am delighted to hear that Universal is getting its house in order. I, for one, fully support Mr Lockhart's approach and the steps he is advocating.`

There was murmured assent around the table.

`So everyone we employ, technical staff and our acting personalities, will have contracts will they?` sneered Powers.

I opened my briefcase. `In here, gentlemen, are a number of contracts. I have the rest in a suitcase left with the receptionist. All have been legally drawn up and signed by cameramen, lighting technicians, scenery builders, laboratory and processing staff. I also have our copies of the individual contracts signed by our actors and actresses.`

I took out a number of them and passed them around the table for the board`s perusal. Then I sat back and waited.

There was a lengthy silence while they studied copies of the contracts.

I could feel the perspiration wet against the back of my shirt. I discreetly mopped my forehead

One by one they were passed back to me. Some had glanced briefly at their copy and noted the president`s signature. Others had read, re-read a page, checked a detail, and eventually arrived at the last page.

The MetLife man commented. `I think that contract represents an excellent first step in regularising the situation. More importantly, I believe our gratitude should be extended to Mr Lockhart in spotting the likely poaching of our players, and the areas of weakness in our employment system.`

`It shall be minuted as such, Mr Thoresby,` declared Carl, who nodded to his secretary sitting close by.

There were other matters listed on the agenda that were quickly dealt with.

The last item, "Any Other Business", prompted several members to make comment on minor issues. It was when the president was moving to close the meeting, that Powers made his move.

`Mr President, we have discussed the official opening of the studio in California both today, and at the hurriedly convened gathering of the board during the event. To my mind, the pomp and supposed glamour of the occasion masked people`s sight of what really happened. OK, mishaps can, and will happen when conducted on such a grand scale. But why did we do it on such a scale in the first place? It was outrageously expensive, we nearly drowned the audience, and someone was killed. Frankly, it was ill-conceived and badly planned. Is that the sort of reputation Universal wants to garner for itself?

`Let me put it into perspective. Universal is profligate with its funds. We are frittering away hard-earned income in order to pay public homage to our current president.`

Pat Powers glared defiantly at Carl Laemmle. He went on.

`At a time when the competition in the film industry is growing, every dollar we bring in should be destined to making decent, worthwhile films. It should not be diverted on junkets to entertain Mr Laemmle's friends. It should not be used to pay handsome salaries to any member of his family who fancies a job in our company. If, as one of his minions has now inadvertently pointed out, why hasn't he got to grips with the administration, the backbone of the company.`

At this point Powers rose to his feet to enforce his personal tirade on Carl, who sat stone-faced, isolated at the end of the table.

`Do you know what they call our president on both coasts?` ranted the Irishman. He stared into each of the board members' faces. `"Uncle Carl", he has so many of his family on the payroll.`

He thrust his finger in Issy's direction. `Isadore Bernstein, the arch-planner of the monumental botch-up at Universal City is his brother-in-law, for Christ's sake!`

The Irishman turned in my direction. `Here's another of his cronies, who seems to do what he likes in deciding the films we make. I've looked into his background. Do you know what he was before he left England? A gardener! The likes of which I employ to weed my rosebeds! What on earth is he doing sitting at this table? This is friendship and nepotism running wild. We must cut it out before Universal founders on a welter of aunts and uncles and itinerant jobbing gardeners!`

Carl Laemmle now rose to his feet. White-faced and furious, he said heavily.

`Do I assume Mr Powers that you are asking the board to limit what you are suggesting are my excesses?`

No, Mr President, I am asking for your resignation!`

Total silence. Powers slumped back in his chair.

Carl found his voice.

`Is it the wish of those sitting round this table that Mr Powers' proposal be put to the test? That a change of presidency be considered?'

`In the light of what Mr Powers has so blatantly declared,` said Thoresby of the Metropolitan Life Insurance Company. `We cannot let the matter go unanswered. It would appear his denouncement of you, Mr President, and of your associates in the company has gone too far. It has got to be resolved... one way or the other.`

There were hushed murmurs of agreement.

Powers rose again to his feet.

`My proposal, so that everyone is clear on the matter, is this. That Mr Carl Laemmle be relieved of the presidency of the Universal Film Manufacturing Company, and is replaced by Mr Patrick Anthony Powers. I would further propose that Mr James Thoresby of MetLife, being a board member not directly associated with the film industry, act as interim chairman while this motion is considered.`

It was evident he had been advised what to say, and how to table the motion.

`If that is the board`s wish?` said Thoresby.

Again murmurs of agreement.

Carl left his chair and sat next to me.

`I hope you`ve got something up your sleeve, Sam,` he whispered hoarsely. `We both need it now.`

Thoresby, from the chair now vacated by Carl, said. `Well, gentlemen, this is the manner the decision will be made. It will be determined by the stock holding of those supporting the candidates. What I shall do is ask each of you to call out your name, the amount of the voting stock you hold in Universal, and the name of whom you support for the presidency. I shall move clockwise around the table. Let us begin.`

All eyes turned to Roberts of American Éclair, sitting on Thoresby`s immediate left.

`Michael John Roberts, four percent...Powers.`

Thoresby wrote down the details, and also nodded to the secretary to do so.

`Next,` he called.

`Patrick Anthony Powers, forty percent, Powers.`

The declared holdings and the nominations moved around the table. When it was Carl`s turn, he said. `Carl Laemmle, thirty eight percent,

Laemmle.`

It was clear the vote would be a close run thing.

When it came finally for the interim chairman`s declaration, he said in a clear voice. `Gerald Thoresby, Met Life seven per cent Laemmle.`

But the vote had already been decided.

Powers, fifty two percent, Laemmle, forty eight percent.

Powers was now destined to be Universal`s next president.

Thoresby was about to declare the result officially, and offer the presidency to Pat Powers, when I said.

`Mr Chairman, a moment please. I am not sure every aspect in determining the presidency has been considered. `

`What do you mean by that, Mr Lockhart?`

`Well, sir, before Mr Powers is ratified as president, could he explain of what he would be president?`

`I still don`t follow , Mr Lockhart.`

Powers was getting exasperated. `Can we get on with it, Chairman? This fellow has no right to comment on the ways we board members conduct our business. This jobbing gardener, soon to be replaced, is out of his depth and out of order.`

He glanced in my direction. `Kindly remove yourself, sir.`

`I have regard for Mr Lockhart`s role in this company, Mr Powers,` said Thoresby, irritated by the Irishman`s behaviour. `As he has already proven, we could do well to listen to what he has to say.`

I continued. `Let me explain something. It was Mr Laemmle who alerted me to the widespread employment problem we were facing, and which has now been addressed. As he saw it, something had to be done, and quickly. To turn a well-known saying on its head, he realised "we could not see the trees for the forest". Universal City, with all its buildings, gigantic staging, special effects units was the "forest"; but we had completely ignored the "trees", the technicians, the actors, the very people that make the whole thing work.`

I took a sip of water.

`I did just as he asked. As I said earlier , we were sitting on a time bomb. In a stroke we could have had numerous squabbles, arguments which may had led to a walkout of the very people we rely on. The players could so easily have been seduced into moving elsewhere. Then what would Universal have had? Wonderful buildings and facilities…empty of the people that really mattered.

`That's why we went ahead and did what was vitally necessary for the good of Universal. There was no time to raise the problems at board level, to await a decision. Action was needed immediately. Mr Laemmle staked his own finances to keep everything afloat. He personally put his own signature to an agreement with everyone in the company that could materially affect its wellbeing. You saw the contracts for yourselves. There is no mention of Universal, no time for the proposal to be put before this board. He, unselfishly, committed himself to pay the staff and actors.`

I paused deliberately, letting what I had said sink in.

`Now we have an interesting situation. In effect, Mr Laemmle could, if he so wished, walk out of here as the ex-president, holding the working contracts of all the people that matter to Universal.

`You,` I looked around the table, `would quite literally have no one working for you. Yes, you could seek to employ other technical people, gather around you a new clutch of actors. In all probability, you could be back in business in two years` time. But how do you think the banks would react to that?

`I have long been aware that Mr Powers has no love of me. To him I'm merely, in his words, "a jobbing gardener", of little or no account. That's why I am about to start my own film company. I have even leased Universal's old studio, on Gower and Sunset in Los Angeles. It's called "Global Art Services". The fascia boards showing the name of the company are already being displayed.`

I opened my briefcase and passed round a series of photographs. I glimpsed Carl's bemused face.

`Of course, I shall soon be looking for technicians and actors. Now, if Mr Laemmle would like to join me with his ready coterie of people under contract to him, it would solve all my problems.`

Thoresby had been studying me intently.

`Are you saying, Mr Lockhart, that at a stroke Universal City could be depopulated, without a single member of its key personnel? without any actors? That it was merely a set of unrelated circumstances by which Mr Laemmle now finds he has control of the employees essential to the running and production of this company? That there is a film company set up ready to take them into its employ at Mr Laemmle`s say-so?`

`I guess it looks that way, Mr Chairman.`

`Hmm...as I see it, gentlemen,` said Thorsby heavily. `Universal is uncomfortably situated between a rock and a hard place. Remove all those essential to the business, and what have you got? No machinery will automatically produce your requirements, no system spews out film to reflect the art of comedy, drama, that for an hour suspends belief and delights an audience. This is an industry that relies on people`s talent and technical ability. Remove them, and you have nothing.

`I believe, in the circumstances, I must ask you to leave, Mr Powers, Mr Laemmle, and Mr Lockhart. We must discuss the matter without your presence.`

Twenty minutes later we were called back into the boardroom.

`We have deliberated on what could conceivably happen to the company if Mr Laemmle were to step down from the presidency,` declared Thoresby. `Clearly, if that occurred his position on the board would be untenable, and doubtless he would wish to resign from the company.

`That being so, he could hold Universal to ransom by a set of circumstances designed initially to protect the company, but now could conceivably become its sword of Damocles. I have put the situation to the board members, gentlemen, and they have weighed the matter most carefully.

`A fresh vote has been conducted, with your personal holdings taken into account. I must now inform you both that the board requests Mr Laemmle continue as president, for he has now been given the approval of those holding fifty three percent of the stock. I hope, Mr Laemmle, you will accept the role, and you Mr Powers, will accept the result.`

Powers turned on his heel and walked out, slamming the door behind him.

Thoresby had a chat with me afterwards. Or shall I say, he told me that he had strong suspicions I had manipulated the outcome. Not that he blamed me, far from it, he was quite content with the result. If I were on the management team, he and Met Life would be happy their interests were in good hands.

When all the board members had finally departed, Carl called me into his office.

`A neat trick, Sam. Pity I didn`t learn about it before the meeting. But what the heck, it worked thanks to your devious mind. I would never have thought of such a way to thwart Powers. When I get his share holding no one will do that to me again.`

He grinned hugely, and rubbed his hands together.

`You don`t really want to be director of personnel, do you?`

I shook my head.

`I didn`t think so, So what if you become Universal`s Group Production Director, with a seat on the board?`

`Only if I get a contract, Carl.`

CHAPTER FIFTY - TWO

Carl, Isadore and I agreed to celebrate with dinner at Mouquins Restaurant on Sixth Avenue.

I rested in my room at the Algonquin, and bathed and dressed in a leisurely fashion. There was an inner contentment. I had achieved what I had unconsciously been working towards. There could be no further upsets. Leastways, nothing as daunting as what I had been through in recent weeks. From now on any problems would be those one invariably faces when making films: and I could deal with those.

Downstairs at the reception desk I arranged for a wire to be sent to Derek Bryant at Universal City, then strolled casually through the hotel lobby. Outside, I was about to ask the doorman to call a cab, when an automobile drew sharply into the kerb.

Our attention was fixed on a rear door which opened slowly. No one emerged. In the gathering dusk nothing was visible in the vehicle's interior.

Suddenly, I was picked up and catapulted through the door to land sprawling across the back seat. I heaved myself up as the door was slammed shut, to see two heavily built men push the doorman to the ground.

For one heart-stopping moment the thought came that this was the work of the Matranga brothers. They would show little mercy to someone who had spoiled their plans, jeopardised their organisation. I was in serious trouble.

As the car accelerated away I noticed the dark outline of a man next to me. He was looking straight ahead, his profile outlined against the street lights. The figure seated next to the driver twisted round.

`Well, this is a surprise, though not a pleasant one,` I remarked. `What brings you to New York?`

`Business, my friend. Business I should have dealt with long ago,` Charles Urban declared flatly. `Let me introduce you to your fellow passenger. He is keen to make your acquaintance. Mr Henry Brock.`

I glanced at the fellow next to me. The name meant nothing to me. I had no inkling who he was.

Urban went on.

`For your information, Mr Brock is a theatre owner, with a chain of picture houses in the United States and Canada. More significantly, he heads up the *Kinemacolor* Company of America. And you, my friend, have created a major problem for him.`

I peered again at Brock`s profile in the fading light. His gaze was fixed, staring intently out the side window. He deigned to utter not a word or glance in my direction.

I turned back to Urban.

`Charles, you`ve been seeing too many motion pictures. Who in their right mind kidnaps someone in front of their hotel?`

`Who`s going to do anything about it?` he snarled. `The doorman? The manager? No, Sam, no one will do anything until much later, when you are reported missing. By then it will be too late. Or should I say, too late for you.`

This was the stuff of movies. I could hardly believe it was happening in real life. Yet here I was, in the rear seat of an automobile sitting next to a silent, forbidding character, being driven at speed up Sixth Avenue.

When we entered Central Park I started getting edgy. I felt for the door handle.

Urban must have read my thoughts.

``It won`t open from the inside, Sam. So don`t bother.`

A few minutes later we came to a halt. In the half-light I could see the outline of the Central Park boathouse, moonlight shimmering across the wide expanse of the lake. Suddenly, my door was wrenched open and I was pulled from the car by the two heavies. They had followed in a car now parked behind.

Holding my arms they frogmarched me up an outside stairway of the boathouse to the first floor, then along to a belvedere located at the end of the terrace. Twisting my head round I saw Urban, Brock and his chauffeur following along behind. I was pushed roughly onto one of the benches.

Urban came towards me. `You put Friese Greene up to it, didn`t you, you bloody jumped-up gardener! You paid for him to take me to court, you and that damned racing driver, Edge! Well, you`ve only yourself to blame.

If I can`t make any more films in *Kinemacolor* or release those I`ve already made, Mr Brock is going to lose out on his investment. And I can tell you, he doesn`t take kindly to that.`

The driver stepped out the shadows. It was then I became uncomfortably aware it was Luke Mitchell. The hoodlum whose thugs had smashed up our studio at Fort Lee. With my testimony and the photographs taken of his exploits, he had been sentenced to three years hard labour at the Blackwell Island Penitentiary. I remember all too clearly his threat as he was taken from the dock.

`Wait a minute, what do you want from me?` I asked, turning towards Brock.

Before he could answer, Mitchell stepped forward and poked me in the chest. `Your life, sucker, after what you did to me.`

Brock pushed him aside and said in a menacing tone.

`Mr Lockhart, you have nothing I want. Before this court case charade in England I was going to exhibit the *Kinemacolor* films made by Charles Urban. Thanks to your interference, you have put me to a great deal of trouble. I now have only a dozen or so films released by him before the British legal system stepped in. On top of the licence fees we have already paid him, producing films in *Kinemacolor* over here will now become an unwelcome expense. I cannot let that go unheeded, or the culprit, you Mr Lockhart, go unpunished.`

His henchmen jerked me upright, and started binding my wrists and ankles with heavy, unyielding ropes.

` When my men throw you off this terrace into the lake, Mr Lockhart, you could well survive...if you are lucky. Luke Mitchell here, will patrol the water`s edge, and not permit you ashore until you have reached the Bow Bridge. As I say...if you make it that far.`

I could tell from Mitchell`s eyes and the sneer on his face, I would never be allowed to make it. I was hefted onto the railing. My mind racing to come up with a possible solution. I was not a good swimmer.

`Tell me, Mr Brock, what makes you to think you can make films in *Kinemacolor* in America?`

`Mr Lockhart, as I have just patiently explained, thousands of dollars were paid for the licence to use Urban`s patent when the *Kinemacolor* Company of

America was set up.`

`I`m not sure he`s been entirely honest with you, Mr Brock. Did he tell you much about the patent?

`What are you talking about, Lockhart?` demanded Urban, stepping forward aggressively. `Is this another of your damned tricks? Throw him off! Now!`

I felt the tightness of their grip increase as the two men gathered strength to cast me over the railing into the lake`s murky waters.

`Wait a minute,` said Brock softly. `What do you know about Urban`s patent? What are you trying to say?` Brock was close, his face within inches of mine.

`It`s been a memorable year, has it not?` I said unsteadily in a voice I scarcely recognised as my own. `War in Europe, W.G.Grace retires, the formation of Universal City, and the expiration of Charles Urban`s patent on the colour film process in America.`

Brock frowned.

`Pull him down,` he commanded.

`No! Throw him in! `shouted Mitchell. `Let`s get rid of the bastard for once and for all!`

`Shut up, Mitchell. You`ll do as I say, or you may well find yourself swimming in the lake as well. Stand him down.`

I was jerked off the railing and dumped unceremoniously onto the terrace. I fell to my knees. The two men hauled me upright to face the *Kinemacolor* president.

`Mr Lockhart, you are only making it worse for yourself. You may have to swim even further if you continue to upset me,` Brock said softly.

It could not get much worse than this I thought.

`Not only has his patent expired, has he not told you someone else actually holds the patent of a very similar process?` I mumbled.

I broke my gaze with Brock, glancing past him at Urban. His face portrayed a mix of emotions, his eyes reflected uncertainty.

` No...I thought not,` I said.

Brock turned slowly to Charles Urban.

`Is he right? You don`t own the patent any more?`

`Of course not! The patent is registered in the name of The Natural

Kinematograph Company, which has licensed the *Kinemacolor* Company of America to make full use of it.`

`If that`s the case,` I said to Brock. `you should question why the Patents Office allowed the registration of a process if the original patent is still in force. Let me explain something, Mr Brock. William Friese Greene won the verdict in the English Courts on appeal. Do you know why? Because of the inaccurate wording of the *Kinemacolor* patent application in the first instance.`

I looked at Charles Urban, standing there, a hostage to the tale now unfolding.

`Charles` patent has expired, take my word for it. However, before it even ran out, a number of faults, inherent in the registration document in Britain,were corrected and my lawyers submitted a fresh application.Though similar, the new submission was sufficiently different to be accepted. In effect, I now own the patent in the United States.`

It was a bizarre scene. Six men, one bound with ropes, standing on a moonlit terrace overlooking a stretch of water. The prisoner, nonchalantly discussing legalities, the person responsible for Brock`s displeasure varying with each exchange.

There was a palpable change in the atmosphere

`Did you sell the original buyers, Aymar and Bowen, a pup, Urban?` queried Brock menacingly. `When I`ve got some really big investors about to back the project, could it be you don`t even own the *Kinemacolor* patent in this country.`

His full attention was now directed to Charles.

`Perhaps, it is you who should be swimming across the lake,` Brock mused.

`I think he`s in worse shape than I am, Mr Brock. He`d never make it,` I said, adding. `However, I think there is a way to settle the problem without anyone taking to the water.`

An hour later a relieved Charles Urban and I were deposited outside the Algonquin. Still tied up, Henry J Brock and I had discussed the matter, and come to an agreement. He would meet me the following day at our lawyers` offices.The colour film patent rights would be transferred to the *Kinemacolor* Company of America, and a cheque would be passed over for ten thousand dollars. Lewis Milestone would arrange all the details, and wire the money to George Albert Smiths` account at the Capital & Counties Bank in Brighton, England.

I eventually arrived at the Mouquin two hours late. Carl and Isadore were enjoying their after-dinner brandies.

`Where the hell have you been?` asked Carl.

`For a ride in the park,` I said blithely. Though I was still shaking from the experience.

`Very funny. Anyway, you`re too late, we`ve eaten.`

`I couldn`t eat anything at the moment. Though I`ll join you in a very large brandy.`

When a little calmer, I recounted the evening`s events. The hubbub of the diners around us in no way distracted their rapt attention. Carl and Isadore listened to every word in stunned silence.

Isadore was the first to react.

`Jeez...I would not have wanted to have been in your shoes.`

Carl was more deliberate in his comments.

`I know Henry Brock. I reckon he did that to scare the shit out of you. You crossed him. He wouldn`t exact a life for that, but he would have wanted to teach you a lesson. Looks like it worked.`

`I think when he found out Urban no longer held the patent, he genuinely thought about tossing him into the lake. What I can`t understand is how this fellow, Luke Mitchell, got involved.`

`Well, I know, said Carl, staring into his brandy.`A few years back the American *Kinemacolor* company joined the Trust, the Motion Picture Patents Company. They were the only film organisation to join after its original formation. When Mitchell was released, the General Film Company took him back on. Being an off-shoot of the Trust, Brock could well have come across him; and when it was discovered that you had blighted Kinemacolor`s development, it would have been an obvious step to engage his strong-arm services.`

`So you saved Urban`s bacon,` remaked Isadore. `Was he grateful?`

`Not one tiny bit.`

The conductor held open the door, and I climbed aboard. He showed me to my drawing room, where I threw down the cases and flopped onto the narrow couch. After Newark, when the train was connected to a steam locomotive, I made my way to the dining car.

With my evening meal I ordered a good claret. It was a time to be self-indulgent. When I poured the second glass, I sat back to contemplate all that had happened.

I took from my pocket the photographs passed around at the Universal board meeting. Those that featured the sign boards over the studio lot in Los Angeles. I would relinquish my deposit and remove the name boards, The site would no longer be needed.

I stared at them for a long time.

Over the high wire fence, the name of the company, "Global Art Services", was displayed brightly on a white background. The over-riding element of the name at the top of the board was, "GAS Films".

As they lay on the table, I began thinking of all that had happened in Brighton. The way Charles Urban had gradually sucked the vitality from George Smith, my early mentor. The man who had first sparked my interest, then my involvement in the film making business. That ten thousand dollars would be a welcome boost to his dwindling reserves.

We had met in Lewis Milestone`s office, and the transfer had been arranged quickly and efficiently. The cheque had been passed over, and Mr Henry J Brock had deposited the relevant documents in his briefcase.

As we shook hands I asked him. `Last night, would you really have pitched me into the lake and made me swim for my life?`

His face broke into a smile. `You will never know, Mr Lockhart…you will never know.`

`Well, your friend Mitchell would have done.`

`You need have no further fears about him, Mr Lockhart. He is well under control.`

He picked up his hat and headed for the door. It was half open when he swivelled his head towards me. `Here`s a piece of advice, sir, that has long stood me in good stead. "Always keep the element of uncertainty up your sleeve, and know the moment to introduce it."

CHAPTER FIFTY - THREE

She was there to meet me at the station when the train rolled in.

Isabel ran down the platform and jumped, literally jumped, into my arms. The cases dropped to the floor. We kissed, laughed, and kissed again.

Then she held my arm tightly while I tried to gather my things.

`I've only got the barest details. Derek telephoned me and read out your cable. However, he did tell me you've been made group production director, whatever that means.`

`It means, darling, I can decide what films we make, who stars in them, and what we should spend. Something I've been doing for years, only now it's official.`

Two days later we went back to Los Angeles to say goodbye to both sets of parents. They were going to Pittsburgh, where my mother and father would stay for a while before sailing home. Isabel went shopping in town, and I went up to the studio and had a long chat with Derek Bryant, giving him a blow-by-blow account of the board meeting.

I had decided to take a week away from Universal City: to recharge my batteries, to spend time with my wife and children. I wanted to go up to our inland retreat: to the ten acre plot of land on the gentle slopes of the Santa Ynez Valley, off the South Refugio Road.

A wire fence among tall hedges surrounded what I had come to regard as a haven: a hideaway from the rest of the world. Somewhere I could be alone with the four females who occupied my life. I had bought it so that the family could enjoy the fresh air of the surrounding verdant hills. Different again from our house on the sands of the Pacific coast.

There was also another reason.

A cabin had been erected on the land so we could sleep there. It provided our basic needs. Cooking was over an open fire, and water still had to be carried up from the stream. Though that was about to change.

When we arrived everyone set about their allotted tasks. Emily and Joanna went to fetch the water. Isabel packed the food cupboards. I checked the gas lamps, opened the shutters and windows to air the rooms, and swept the dust out the front door and off the porch. I had almost completed the piping and plumbing. My main task this week would be to install the pump so we could have running water in the cabin. In fact I had two pumps. The other powering water to a separate area of the plot. We had a leisurely lunch, and while Isabel fed Sophia, I walked across the slope to a clearing encirled by Black Oak, Rocky Mountain Maple, Dogwood, Buckeye and Locust trees.

Pat Powers and Charles Urban had both been right. At heart I would always be a jobbing gardener.

Hidden among the trees was a good-sized shed where I stored my tools. I unlocked the door and dropped onto a low wooden bench. As I sat there, the vision of St Ann`s Well Gardens came to mind. The morning allocation of jobs by Mr Masters: the wheelbarrow, his mark of seniority. My early days with the Brighton Parks and Gardens Department; growing plants, tending flower beds; cycling around the streets of Brighton and Hove.

I wheeled out the barrow filled with a spade, rake, and hoe. The same implements I had had when George Albert Smith first ordered made me dig a hole. I grinned to myself as I trundled it towards the flower beds.

Many of the plants were the same as those in England, and provided the same joy to the eye. It was my abiding passion to drink in the scent of the flowers; to kneel and clear away unwanted growth; to plant fresh, young seedlings; to feel the soil running through my fingers; simply to absorb the harmony and profusion of colour.

I had travelled a long way from my homeland; but I was content. I had my garden, but above all, I had what I most prized...my little bit of Heaven in the hills.

I could hear the faint sounds of their voices .

There was movement behind me and two arms stretched round my waist.

`A penny for them,` Isabel murmured.

`I`d need a lot more than that before telling you,` I sighed.

But when she pulled me round and looked deep into my eyes, she knew instinctively without having to pay for the privilege.

AUTHOR`S NOTE

Essentially a work of fiction, many of the people depicted in this novel were real characters; and most of the events in this book actually occured. Although, in one or two instances, the timeline and the locations may have been adjusted to suit the tale.

What the book does illustrate is the speed with which the making of motion pictures was conducted in its formative years. Everything was done at a frenetic pace. Although the first silent films lasted less than a minute, they would often complete each one in half a day; and because of their limited length, basic humour was the ideal emotion to portray.

However, as interest grew, so audiences wanted longer motion pictures with a stronger narrative. This also prompted marked improvements in the craft of film making, as well as in the mechanics of cameras, projectors, lighting, and advances in film stock.

Innovation was the watchword, and each marginal development was jealously guarded. This resulted in a constant flow of lawsuits through the courts as film companies found they had infringed, inadvertently or with intent, someone else`s registered creation.

Although film making was much in its infancy, pioneers of the art were beginning to flourish in a number of continental countries. However in the last years of the nineteenth and into the early twentieth century, it was Brighton, on England`s south coast, which played a major role in the development of the European motion picture industry.

The "*Brighton School*" of film makers - men such as George Albert Smith, James Williamson, and Esmé Collings - were making films as early as 1896. With others of the same pioneering spirit, they helped make this part of the country the most significant film making centre in Britain.

Smith, a stage hypnotist and showman, built one of the first film studios, and created numerous filming techniques, many of which are still in use today.

Collings, a successful Brighton photographer, shot some of the first ever films in Hove. As early as 1897 he had made nineteen moving pictures. Williamson, a pharmacist by profession, became one of the most inventive and accomplished film makers of his generation. Supporting their endeavours was Alfred Darling, a talented engineer, who created a successful business producing cameras and projection equipment for national and international film makers.

While it is true to say California was being explored as a possible location by film makers at the turn of the last century, many acknowledge that Fort Lee, New Jersey, was the earliest site of the American motion picture industry. Today, the township, which lies in the shadow of New York's George Washington Bridge, shows little evidence of its former glory. The buildings that once housed the sets for hundreds of films are long gone, even though many of the famous names that led the industry started their careers here.

Sam Goldfish, who changed his name and his studio to Goldwyn Pictures; Metro Films, Goldwyn's eventual partner; Fox Films, headed up by William Fox, who later teamed up with Darryl F. Zanuck to create Twentieth Century Fox; and, of course, Carl Laemmle of Independent Moving Pictures (IMP), who went on to found Universal Pictures.

Laemmle's Universal studio was the biggest in Fort Lee, and he erected a huge water tower on his lot, which survived until 1964. He did so to overcome the drop in water pressure on Mondays, which for the local townswomen was invariably "wash day".

In 1912, Fort Lee was the epicente of the cinematic universe. Icons from the silent era, such as Mary Pickford, Lionel Barrymore and Lillian Gish came up the North River by ferry to act out numerous one-reel fantasies.

Thomas Edison, the widely-acknowledged father of invention, was in retrospect, a brake on the American film industry. He held numerous patents, and charged substantial sums to those seeking to use his camera and projection systems. When the smaller film makers rebelled, he tightened his grip on the sector by forming the Motion Picture Patents Company (MPPC). A consortium of major producers who pooled their patents in an attempt to monopolise the burgeoning industry.

Laemmle led a fierce protest against the exorbitant costs, and refused to pay for licences. It is a known fact that the MPPC was not above resorting to physical violence and inflicting damage to equipment to bring the small, independent studios into line.

At one stage, Carl Laemmle faced almost three hundred patent infringement lawsuits against the Motion Picture Patents Company. He finally emerged victorious when the MPPC. was found to be operating counter to the Sherman Anti-Trust Act. Thereafter, it was disbanded.

When the Universal Film Manufacturing Company was formed by six independent film companies, they made for strange bedfellows. There was tension and lack of harmony between them. It is a wonder the amalgamation of very individual interests survived. Pat Powers was a major agitator, and vied with Laemmle for the presidency. He eventually lost out, his stake in the studio being transferred to Laemmle.

The Black Hand, a forerunner of the Mafia, was an Italian concept primarily engaged in extortion with extreme menace. The name derives from their method of contacting their prey. Most often they would send a letter describing what would happen to the luckless victim or next of kin if their demands were not met.

The dominant gang operating in Los Angeles around the turn of the last century, was run by Pietro and Antonio Matranga. When their arch-rival, Joseph "Iron Man" Ardizzone, returned from an enforced stay in Sicily in 1917, the long-standing vendetta resumed and not long afterwards both Matranga brothers were eliminated.

Charles Urban was a salesman of remarkable ability. He was also a ruthless businessman, who exploited every opportunity to advance his own interests. One cannot deny that many of his developments in the film industry assumed success by the very force of his personality.

George Smith's efforts to develop the *Kinemacolor* system were doomed technologically, even though Urban persevered with it and gained a following for the process. Britain could not sustain it with the advent of World War One; and the *Kinemacolor* Company of America failed to exploit the system which resulted in its demise in 1915. Urban eventually returned to live in England in the late 1920's, and moved to Brighton, where he repaired his fractured relationship with George Albert Smith.

Patrick Gooch

CPSIA information can be obtained at www.ICGtesting.com
Printed in the USA
LVOW09*1837071114

412566LV00002B/12/P